THE PRISONER

BY SARA ALLYN

Book layout by www.ebooklaunch.com

CHAPTER 1

Maria laid in bed staring up at the distressed ceiling of her studio apartment. She watched the stains and cracks in the plaster swirl, bulge and morph into the stones of an ancient cave created by an ancient tree buried deep in a mountain somewhere in a place she had never been. Maria sat up and cringed at the familiar smell of damp stone and unripe pears. Her alarm clock told her that it was four o'clock in the morning, that weirdly silent hour after all the late-night parties have ended and before even the earliest risers might deign to start the new day. She swung her feet over the edge of the bed, took a deep breath, then looked up. There, where her window should have been, was the Prisoner, that mysterious and impossible tree growing inside a cave made of stone, soil, and giant crystal boulders unlike anything she knew to exist outside her mind.

"What do you want this time?" Maria asked the tree.

"Go," it said.

"Go where?" Maria asked.

"Outside," it said.

"If I actually go this time, will you stop haunting my dreams?" Maria asked.

"No," it said.

"Ugh!" Maria said. "You can't keep doing this to me! I have an exam tomorrow, and..."

"Go!" the tree repeated, this time in a deafening roar that rocked Maria's brain.

Maria gripped the sides of her head and cursed at the tree.

"Ok, ok, I'm going!" she said as she got up off her bed.

Maria pushed her long wavy black hair behind her ears, pulled an old sweatshirt on over her flannel pajamas and headed for the door.

"Follow me," said the tree.

"Whatever," Maria mumbled as she opened the door to her apartment and went outside.

It always happened on a night like this, she thought, when even the still air seemed to hum with clandestine purpose and the stars beat down on her awareness like shrapnel from heaven.

Standing beneath her apartment window, Maria struggled to see in the dim light of the waxing moon. She scanned the dark wooded area behind the parking lot, then looked back up at her bedroom window two stories above her. The tree was gone from sight. It was only in her head now.

"Where are you taking me?" she asked aloud. She could only hope that her neighbors would not hear her. The last time they saw her standing outside in the middle of the night talking to herself, they had called campus security. Determined not to end up in an inpatient psychiatric ward like her mother, Maria had refused to tell them about her "dreams" or about the tree that lured her out into the woods at night. Instead, she had pretended to be only drunk and lost. It was not any of their business anyway.

"Follow the path," said the Prisoner.

"What path? There is no path!" Maria said.

"The path in your mind. Follow it," the Prisoner repeated.

Maria took a deep breath and unfocused her eyes. Yes, indeed, there was the path. It was clear in her mind. The tree had put it there.

"This is stupid," Maria muttered as she began to walk, both hands rubbing at her temples.

Maria walked and walked, until she could no longer see her apartment building, or the campus lights, or anything at all but darkness.

• • •

When Maria woke up again, she found herself back in bed, warm and comfortable. She nestled her face deeper into her pillow and sighed. It was over, she thought. Finally, the dream was over. Maybe that creepy old tree would leave her alone now. She tried to sit up but could not. She could barely lift her head. When she opened her eyes, she realized that she was not in her own bed, or even in her own apartment.

She was not in an apartment at all. Unable to move anything other than her neck, Maria scanned her surroundings, slowly rolling her head from one side to the other. The light was dim and eerily inconsistent. As Maria took in the interior of the room, she saw that she was not alone. There were dozens, maybe hundreds, of other beds with other people in them. All the beds appeared to be identical and enclosed within their own sectioned off area. Walking amongst the beds were men she assumed to be wearing costumes or weird hats of some kind. Maria tried to ask one of these men where she was and what was going on, but quickly found that her throat was too dry for speech. Exhausted, Maria rested her head back on her pillow and closed her eyes. "It's just another dream," she told herself.

The next time Maria woke up, one of the men she had seen earlier was standing at the side of her bed and holding up her head. He helped her drink water from a small cup and spoon fed her a flavorless gelatinous substance. As he did this, Maria puzzled over his youthful face, which seemed incongruous with his stolid eyes and stark white hair. Once the attendant was finished, he put away the empty cup and spoon and informed her that she had just deboarded a Pegasean space ship and was now in what was called the "Intake Hall." He advised her not to panic, then smiled and promised that everything else would be explained to her in due time. Maria stared at his lavender shirt, as he instructed her to stay within her designated area. Feeling sleepy and dizzy, she closed her eyes as the strange man encouraged her to try to move her arms and legs as much as possible.

There were no windows in the Intake Hall, no clocks or exit signs. With no means by which to monitor the passage of time, Maria had no idea how long she had been asleep. After what felt to her like a few hours, she was able to sit up, then stand up. Tentatively, she walked unsteadily around her bed. Once she could walk without having to lean on the bed, she ventured outside her assigned area. She tried to speak to the women in the areas around her, but they were too groggy to engage in any meaningful conversation. Believing that nothing good could possibly be going on, she looked for a door or other way out of this place. Unfortunately, every time she walked more than two hundred meters or so from her cubicle, an attendant would gently but firmly escort her back to her bed. The attendant would again tell her that she must be patient and that everything would be explained to her soon.

As Maria laid in bed, she considered possible explanations for her present situation. Perhaps, she thought, she had been kidnapped by a strange political or religious cult. She also considered the possibility that, after wandering from her apartment in the middle of the night one too many times, she had been committed to a mental hospital. Unfortunately, Maria was unable to think of any scenario in which waking up in a strange bed, in a strange place, with men wearing masks, could possibly be a good thing. She left her bed in search of an exit at every opportunity.

After Maria was returned to her bed for the fifth time, one of the attendants placed a heavy circular band around each of her wrists. The two cuffs were not attached to each other by any visible cord, but when she walked too far from her assigned space, they suddenly pulled her wrists together and locked. These restraints did not keep her from wandering, but they certainly dampened any hope she had of escape.

Maria had no idea how many hours, or possibly days, passed before one of the attendants finally came around to her bed to explain where she was and why. Maria glared at the strange looking man as he began his spiel.

"Thank you for being so patient," the attendant said with a smile. "I apologize for the restraints, but they are for your own protection. It is not safe to wander about out here."

"Look, I don't know who you are or what you think you are doing, but you need to let me go. There are people who will know I'm missing. And I need to go home and walk my dog and I have an exam in two days. If you don't let me out of here -," Maria said before the attendant raised a hand to stop her.

The attendant smiled, a bit wearily, then resumed what sounded to Maria like a well scripted and well-rehearsed briefing. He explained that he, and the other "attendants" were not going to hurt her. He claimed that they had taken her, along with the other women in the Intake Hall, from Earth to the very Earth-like planet of Olrona, and specifically to the mountain city of Pegasea. Maria would be quarantined for several weeks, during which time she would be evaluated and allowed to rest and recover from her long journey through space. Following quarantine, her keeper would take her home and she would live a comfortable and mostly care free life in Pegasea.

"What the fuck are you talking about?" Maria asked. "My *keeper?* What is a keeper?"

"Never mind that for now," said the attendant. "Please try to stay calm and trust us. You will live a long and peaceful life here. During your trip, we either halted or reversed your body's programmed aging using beneficial viruses native to this planet. You will look and feel as if you are between the ages of 25 to 35 for the next 325 to 350 years. You will not be required to do any manual labor or other work - unless you want to, of course. We will not perform experiments on you or subject you to any other such indignities. You will not be used as a slave, put on exhibit, or be expected to perform any lude acts."

Maria realized, with a dream like sense of déjà vu that the attendant was systematically going through this list as if he had personally seen every alien themed movie ever produced on Earth. He was assuring her that none of these horrible or distasteful things would happen to her here. The last thing he explained to Maria was how and where to go to the bathroom. When he was finally done speaking, Maria could only blink at him.

"I know you must have a lot of questions, but for now, rest assured that you are safe and that we will take care of you. An inventory clerk will be around shortly with food. We could not allow you to eat until your body re-acclimated to surface life and until most of the drugs passed through your system," he said.

Maria looked around to see how many of the other women were satisfied with the information they had been provided. More than half of the women in her immediate area appeared to be in a kind of daze, apparently still recovering from whatever they had all just been through. After the attendant left her and moved on, Maria continued to look around the Intake Hall until she found another mostly coherent woman with whom she was able to communicate.

"Hi," Maria said.

"Hi," the woman said back.

"I'm Maria," she said.

"I'm Helen," the woman said.

"So, what's going on?" Maria asked.

Helen shrugged.

"You don't know?" Maria asked.

"Didn't that elf over there explain everything to you?" Helen said, pointing her head in the direction of the flight attendant who had just spoken with Maria.

"Elf?" Maria said.

Helen smiled, "Well, what else should we call them? Aliens?"

Maria turned to look at the attendant again. To Maria, he did not look much like an elf. His ears were tall and elongated. They narrowed as they approached the top of his head but were not the sort of ears she pictured on an elf. Maria could not see his ears in their entirety because they were half hidden behind his hair, which was not just blond, but completely white. His face and hands were covered in a thin downy fur that reminded her of fuzz on a peach. There was something about him though, that did remind her a bit of the elves of Middle Earth. He was exceptionally tall and had narrow facial features. More than that, there was something almost regal about the way he carried himself, the smooth and graceful way he walked and moved. He was calm and confident, but always on high alert. Maria watched the other attendants and found that they were all this way.

"I guess I see what you mean," Maria said.

Helen only nodded as she scanned the Hall for the food service.

"I'm sooo hungry," she said.

"Me too, but what if they poison us?" asked Maria.

Helen pulled a face. "Why would they poison us?" she asked. "Whatever they are doing, they obviously went through a lot of trouble to bring us here alive. Why poison us now? That would be stupid."

"Ok, drug us, then," Maria said.

"Oh sweetie, I'm pretty sure that ship has sailed. We've all been high on somethin' since before they even put us on that - whatever it was. I suppose it must have been a space ship," Helen said.

"You seem remarkably calm about all this," Maria said.

"Well, like I said, I'm pretty sure we've all been drugged. Besides, what do I care? I had nothin' goin' for me before all this happened. And I don't hear any screaming or wailing coming from any back rooms. Maybe after the drugs wear off I'll start to panic. But right now, I don't know - I'm just glad not be at work," Helen said with a snort.

"You must have a horrible job," Maria said.

Helen hugged chest and turned away, her jaw clenched.

"I love their clothes," Maria said, trying to lighten the mood.

Helen turned back around and gave Maria a faint smile. "Yeah, I hope they give us clothes like theirs," she said. "They look so comfortable.".

Maria nodded in agreement, then said, "What is that thing they each have on their forearms? I always see them using it. They tap it, shake it, wave it over and in front of things - what is it?"

"I don't know, but I think it's a kinda all-in-one thing - like a cell phone, key fob, ID card, everything - all rolled into one."

"That makes sense," Maria said.

"Have you noticed how they seem to be color coded?" Helen asked.

"Color coded? No, they all look really white to me," Maria said.

Helen laughed, then said, "No, not their skin silly, their clothes! Most of them are wearing purple or green, but a few of them are wearing blue or red. Only the ones in purple or green ever talk to us. The blue ones go to the monitors on the wall and look like they're checking or recording something. The red ones just pace around the room as if they are guarding us."

"And the one that put these cuffs on me was wearing red," Maria added.

Helen looked down at Maria's wrists and said, "Yeah, I wanted to ask you about those, but I didn't want to be rude."

"I guess they don't like when we wander off," Maria said.

"Do they hurt?" Helen asked.

"No," Maria said. "But if I walk too far away from my area they snap together like strong magnets and I can't pull them apart until I get back in bed."

"Cool - can I see?" Helen asked.

Maria demonstrated for Helen how the cuffs worked.

"I bet the cops would love those," Helen said.

Maria shrugged, then frowned.

"I'm sure they are just trying to protect you," Helen said. "I mean, if we really are on a whole other planet, there must be all kinds of weird crazy shit out there. Maybe the air outside isn't even breathable."

"Yeah, maybe," Maria said. "But even if you're right, I don't think they have any intention of letting us go home."

"Yeah, probably not," Helen agreed.

Helen gingerly asked Maria if she had a family back home. Maria told her that her father had died when she was a teenager and that her mother had been in and out of mental hospitals since the time she was little.

"I don't have any brothers or sisters," Maria told her. "I guess you could say I have a boyfriend, but I don't know - it's complicated."

"I don't have any real family either," Helen said. "I wonder if everyone here is like that - you know, so they don't have to worry about people coming to look for us."

"If we really are on another planet, why would they have to worry about anyone coming to look for us?" Maria asked.

"Good point," Helen said with a frown.

"I wonder what they want with us," said Maria.

"I don't know," Helen said, "but they don't seem like psychos or anything. Then again, maybe they're just pretending to be nice for now so that we don't all stampede the door."

"What door?" Maria asked. "I can't find a door anywhere."

Helen turned as she looked around the Intake Hall before conceding that she could not see any doors either.

Maria and Helen then both looked around together, searching for a door. They only stopped when an inventory clerk with food finally reached their area of the Intake Hall. The clerk handed them each a thick lukewarm fluid in a large glass cup which smelled far better than it tasted. Maria and Helen were so hungry by that time that the taste was of little consequence. They both greedily consumed everything they were given. Both women began to feel sleepy after consuming the heavy warm liquid and soon fell asleep in their assigned beds.

For the next few days, Maria did very little besides sleep and pace around the Intake Hall. The attendants did not tell her when to sleep or when to wake up. At some point later on, the women were gathered into small groups and instructed on where they could shower and change clothes. Each was handed a set of plain, sandy colored clothes which resembled hospital scrubs, simple undergarments, thick socks and a loosely fitting sweater. The sweater was so soft that Maria could not help but rub the sleeve of it against her cheek. She thought to herself that if she ever did find her way out of this place, she might be tempted to take the sweater with her.

CHAPTER 2

After Maria and the other new arrivals were all showered and comfortably clothed in their new uniforms, the attendants placed a flexible and loosely fitting band around each woman's left wrist. Maria noticed that the strange symbols on her wrist band matched the ones on a small placard at the foot of her bed. The band itself reminded Maria of the kind amusement parks gave people after buying an admission ticket.

Shortly after receiving their identification bands, the attendants organized the women into small groups. Each group was taken in turn to separate rooms where they were guided through exercise routines to help them rebuild muscle they had lost during their journey from Earth. When Maria realized the full extent to which she had lost both mass and strength in all her limbs, she started to feel faint. What had happened to her? Could she really have been on a space ship? The reality of the situation suddenly came down on her like a heavy blow. Moments later, Maria fainted. The next thing she knew, she was back in her assigned bed. She opened her eyes and saw an attendant standing over her, looking concerned.

"You passed out," the attendant told her. "How do you feel?"

"Confused, overwhelmed, scared, take your pick," Maria said.

"That is all to be expected," the attendant said.

"Who are you?! What are you?" Maria barked.

"I suppose you could say we are aliens - but we try not to use that term," said the attendant.

"Aliens?" Maria asked.

"Yes, but we are not monstrous or insectile," the attendant said. "We have no intention of taking over Earth or ever even living there for that matter. I suppose it is fair to say that we kidnapped you. However, considering that Earth is..."

"And you expect me to believe all this?" Maria interrupted.

"Not right at this moment, no," the attendant conceded. "I understand that humans have a tendency to deny the reality of things which they are not emotionally prepared to accept."

"Are you serious?" Maria asked.

"Absolutely," he said, "but do please let me know if there is anything I can do to help you accept this new and strange reality."

"Show me the outside of this place then," Maria said.

"Would that help you believe?" he asked.

"I think so, yes," she said.

"Alright, come with me," said the attendant.

Maria felt the cold stone floor of the corridor through her thin slippers as she followed the attendant down a long dimly lit corridor hidden at the far wall of the Intake Hall. She nearly collided with the attendant when he stopped abruptly and opened a door into a room lit only by soft moonlight.

"Go ahead," said the attendant as he held the door open for Maria. "Go in and look up."

Maria looked at the attendant, then back down the corridor. Cautiously, she stepped into the room and looked up.

"Wow," she said. "Is that really the night sky? Or is it just some kind of projection?"

"It is real," he said.

"Well, that's cool and all, but there are plenty of glass ceilings on Earth," Maria said.

"It's not glass," he told her. "But that is not important. I did not bring you here to show you the ceiling. Look up at the stars."

Maria looked up again, then back down at the attendant.

"This doesn't help me," she said. "I could be somewhere on Earth right now."

The attendant gave her an incredulous look.

"You must not have been much of a star gazer on Earth," he said. "If you had been, you would clearly see that the arrangement of the stars above us now is nothing like the arrangement of stars you would see back on Earth."

At this, Maria looked up again and tried to find any of the several constellations of stars she might have been able to identify back on Earth. When she could not find any, she looked back at the attendant and said, "Ok, but how do I know you didn't just take me to the other side of my planet? Maybe we're in Australia or something."

"Clearly, astronomy is not your strongest subject," he remarked, not unkindly. "Maybe we should try something else."

"Ok, well, you must have some kind of animal or plant you could show me - something I would know couldn't possibly have come from Earth," Maria suggested.

"Indeed," he said. "And I would be one of them."

"How do I know you're not just a man wearing a mask?" Maria asked.

At this the attendant smiled patiently, before saying, "I would invite you to see for yourself, but I have regretted inviting human women to do that in the past. Your kind can get a bit aggressive when determined to prove something."

"Ok, so show me something else," Maria said.

The attendant looked up, then said "follow me."

Again, Maria followed the attendant as he led her into another room, that was larger and looked like a kitchen. The attendant opened a large cabinet which released a burst of frigid air. Maria looked inside and saw the carcass of an animal which she could not identify. It was round and furry, like a huge rabbit, but with thin muscular legs like a goat or giraffe. Maria leaned in closer, then cringed and stepped away.

"Does that help?" he asked.

"I guess," Maria said, feeling dizzy again.

"Then let's get you back into your space," said the attendant. "Too much stimulation is not good for you right now."

"Alright," she said dully and followed the attendant back to bed.

Overwhelmed and exhausted, Maria slept for what must have been a long time. When she awoke, her limbs ached and her head hurt. An attendant came by and gave her water and more of the gelatin like substance. For the next few days, Maria was put through more group exercise sessions. She talked with Helen whenever she had the energy, until the two women ran out of things to talk about.

After what felt like a few days, various different attendants took Maria aside and asked her a multitude of questions about her family, education, jobs, pets, and every intimate detail of her life. Several times, she was taken to a small room where different attendants interviewed her, asked her to fill out questionnaires, and subjected her to different kinds of tests. At one point, an attendant asked her to play a game on a tablet-style computer. At another time, she was handed a series of three dimensional puzzles to solve; then asked to "reset" the puzzles to their unsolved configurations. The strangest of these tests was one in which Maria was left in a room with a small box that appeared to be made of wood. The attendant told her that she must not touch the box. When Maria asked why, the attendant left the room without answering her. Of course, Maria touched the box as soon as he left. She also opened it and was annoyed to find nothing inside.

Under normal circumstances, Maria would have grown tired of these tests and evaluations. In the Intake Hall, they were a welcome distraction. She was actually disappointed when one of the attendants told her that the test she had just completed would be the last.

"What happens now?" she asked.

"Within a day or two, your keeper will come by to take you home," he said.

"Is anyone ever going to explain to me what the fuck a keeper is?" she asked.

"You will have to limit your use of profanity inside the city," the attendant warned. "Your keeper will explain to you what a keeper is. He will also orient you to the rules of the city and everything else you need to know."

Maria groaned.

"And what if I don't want to go home with this keeper?" she said.

"You will," said the attendant.

"I'm really starting to hate you people," she said.

"None of that now," he said. "Go back to your bed and try to get some rest."

Maria rolled her eyes, then walked to her bed and crawled under the blankets. When she felt herself starting to cry, she squeezed her eyelids tight and took several deep breaths. She tried to imagine that she was back home in her apartment, sleeping in on a Saturday, with her loyal dog curled up at her feet.

CHAPTER 3

In the office of the First Sociologist, Pullmoo contemplated what to do with Maria. Her office was near the Center Council Hearing Hall, was larger than most, and smelled like the blossoms of a citrus tree. Pullmoo's desk was constructed of a dark artificial wood that resisted any kind of wearing, a quality which Pullmoo personally found irksome. She preferred it when things shaped themselves in response to her repeated use, the way the arms of her natural wood chair had grown indentations where she rested her elbows repeatedly over the years. Across from her desk was a curvy and plush sofa. The sofa had been constructed no less than three hundred years ago and had since been reupholstered several times with the same soft sky-blue fabric. Pullmoo inherited the charming little piece of furniture from the former First Sociologist of Pegasea, who now sat on the Center Council. She stared at it now as she thought about the woman from Earth, whose life and fate were now in her hands.

The preliminary reports from the Intake Hall staff had described Maria as pleasant and agreeable, but with a tendency to wander. Her objective physical and mental health evaluations all came back normal or unremarkable. Personality testing showed that she was even tempered, generally secular minded, and had no propensity for violence, or worse, political activism. She was socially competent and mostly friendly but had a proclivity for social isolation. A more nuanced and thorough evaluation of Maria showed that the young woman had a mercurial psychology which allowed her to be highly adaptable, but also unpredictable. None of this concerned Pullmoo. What concerned and intrigued the First Sociologist was a small abnormality in Maria's brain which could not be characterized or even adequately described by the City's body biologists. All they could tell

Pullmoo was that the abnormality appears to create connections across areas of her brain which did not ordinarily connect. Odder still, these connections appeared to be transient.

Pullmoo sighed and leaned back in her chair. She then instructed her arm band to call Linoo, the Governess of District 2. She asked Linoo to come meet her in her office. When Linoo arrived, Pullmoo told her to take a seat and handed her a warm beverage which smelled like pineapples and freshly cut grass. The two Pegasean women, who were both colleagues and friends, first caught up on their everyday lives, and a few work-related matters, before Pullmoo got around to the issue of Maria. She told Linoo that, due to circumstances and events which remained nebulous at best, they had an extra human woman in the Intake Hall.

"What do you plan to do with her?" asked Linoo.

"I am not sure. I suppose I could have her trained and put her to work somewhere. Then if she bonds with one of the unmatched Pegasean men, well...," Pullmoo said and shrugged.

"And if she doesn't?" Linoo asked.

"Well, that is the problem," Pullmoo said. "If she doesn't become a companion to someone, I'm afraid she may become restless. Her evaluations warn us that she is not likely to bond sufficiently well with the other human women. I am told that she made a friend in the Intake Hall, but that she initiated the friendship primarily for the purpose of gaining information. She is intelligent, for a human, but that does not necessarily help her here."

"What are the other options?" Linoo asked.

"We could always euthanize her, but that would be wasteful. I would prefer to come up with another solution," Pullmoo said.

"And you think I might have one?" asked Linoo.

"There is nothing about Maria which is fundamentally incompatible with life in Pegasea. She just needs someone, or something, to keep her mind occupied - and to keep her from wandering too far or getting too restless. I predict that her curiosity and tenacity will prove very distracting to any man with whom she might be paired. Can you think of any man particularly in need of company and distraction?" Pullmoo asked and raised an eyebrow at Linoo.

"I do hope you are not suggesting we match her with Orook," Linoo said.

Pullmoo smiled.

Linoo forced a laugh.

"I can tell you that when I ran the long-term compatibility algorithm for the two of them, they scored very high," Pullmoo said.

"Well, I suppose he is going to need someone soon," Linoo said. "I have to break off my partnership with him before the summer season or else I will be sanctioned. On top of that, my other partners are starting to whine about how I spend more time with him than I do with them. One of them even threatened to file a complaint against me."

"The Second Biologist in District 3?" Pullmoo asked.

"Who else?" Linoo said, tossing up her hands.

Pullmoo suppressed a smile, then leaned back in her chair and said, "Oh, the burden of the beautiful! I should be so lucky. I almost have to ask for partners. You have them practically knocking down your door and fighting over you."

"You know that is not true. They all want desperately to partner with you. They are just all too afraid of you to ask," Linoo said.

Pullmoo smiled thinly, then shrugged.

"Let us return to the matter at hand, shall we? What do you think, my young apprentice? Should we try it?" Pullmoo asked.

"Match Maria with Orook?" Linoo asked.

Pullmoo nodded.

"No human woman deserves to be paired with Orook," Linoo said. "Then again, I suppose a lifetime with him is preferable to a lifetime of inventory work or death."

With her long thin fingers, Pullmoo traced the grain in the wooden arm of her chair as she thought.

"It is odd, isn't it?" she thought aloud. "How did she get on that ship? And once she was on it, why did the crew not recognize that she was not supposed to be there?"

Linoo shrugged.

"Well, in any case, I do not believe you are being fair to our First Engineer. He might not be the warmest of men, but he is not unkind,"

Pullmoo said. "More importantly, he is remarkably gifted in his field, and we cannot afford to lose him."

"Why would we lose him?" Linoo asked.

"Some men do just fine all on their own. Some find comfort in the company of other men. Orook is neither of these types of men. When you end your partnership with him, as the law will soon require, he will need someone to keep him company," Pullmoo explained.

"I suppose that is true," Linoo agreed.

"Whatever happened between you two?" Pullmoo asked. "Clearly, you are no longer so enchanted with him - else I assume you would have asked him to marry you by now."

Linoo bit her lower lip and looked away.

"Well?" Pullmoo prompted.

"I would rather not get into that right now," Linoo said.

"Oh, but you must," Pullmoo said. "It is important for me to know - now more than ever. Whatever the reason, you must know that I will neither condemn nor condone your change of heart," Pullmoo said.

Linoo closed her eyes and let out a long breath.

"When our first son was killed, I blamed him," Linoo said. "This was not rational of course. It was not his fault. But being in love is not quite rational either - so it is no surprise to me that something equally irrational put an end to it."

"That is ironic," Pullmoo said.

"Ironic?" Linoo asked.

"Yes. I do not imagine that you are quite so attached to each and every one of your 37 children - none of us possibly could be. The fact that you were attached to the child you had with Orook was because of your love for his father. It is ironic that that attachment would ultimately cause you to stop loving that same man," Pullmoo explained.

"I still love him - just not in the same way," Linoo said.

"Of course," Pullmoo said dismissively.

Linoo sighed.

"In any event," Pullmoo continued, "the man needs a distraction and I do believe that this Maria will prove to be quite distracting. All we need now is a way to make sure he ultimately agrees to host the young lady. He is not particularly fond of humans. I think he finds them…"

"Inferior?" Linoo suggested.

"He finds everyone inferior. No, it is something more than that, but I can't put my finger on it. In any case, he will need some subtle form of encouragement," Pullmoo said.

"I must say, Pullmoo, your concern for him is admirable. You know he loathes you," Linoo said.

"Oh, but this is what we do my dear. This is our job. We are Pegasea's top sociologists. We need to make sure our most critical staff remain emotionally stable so that they can continue to do their jobs."

"Of course, you are right," Linoo said. "We need to make sure that he agrees to take her as a companion. At the same time, we should also consider if there is anything we can do to facilitate her emotional attachment to him."

"Hmm, true. He is not exactly the most charming man, is he?" Pullmoo said.

"Not at first, no. In the beginning, she will simply need to blindly adore him, or at least feel indebted to him," Linoo advised.

"I do believe I have a plan which may work," Pullmoo said.

CHAPTER 4

O rook awoke early that morning, as he did every morning, and reviewed his electronic messages before he started getting dressed and ready for the day. The first message was from the First Biologist, politely asking him to stop requesting that his Second Biologists test and identify field samples of common mountain flora and fauna.

> *To First Engineer Orook,*
>
> *I do not know what you are attempting to find, my friend, but you are wasting our time. If you happen to obtain a truly unique sample, by all means, bring it to us. Until then, I must kindly and respectfully ask you to refrain from bringing us any additional samples.*

Orook frowned at the message. He began composing a reply, then changed his mind. It was no use. If he persisted any further in proving the existence of an as-of-yet undiscovered organism of immeasurable size and unknown taxonomy living inside and throughout the mountain, he would risk being sent to the Body Biology Center for an involuntary psychological evaluation.

The second message was from Pullmoo, the City's First Sociologist. Orook braced himself, then opened the message, which cheerfully informed him that he had been matched with a woman from Earth. The message must be a mistake, he thought. He had not submitted a request to be matched. While the First Sociologist did have a lot of power, Orook was fairly certain that she did not have the power to match a man against his will. The bottom of the message included a time, scheduled for that day, when he was expected to come meet the Earthling. This was followed by the question:

Will you be able to meet her during this scheduled time?
Please touch the word [Yes] or [Reschedule].

Orook had no interest in meeting the woman from Earth. Even if he had wanted to, he had a work conflict with the scheduled time. He continued to read through the rest of the message looking for a place where he could select "no." At the very bottom, in small print, there was a line which stated that if he believes he has received this message in error, has already been matched with a companion, or would otherwise like to decline this match and stop receiving messages, he should touch the word [decline]. Orook touched the word [decline] and moved on to the next message.

An hour later, Orook put on his coat and stepped out his front door. As he turned to walk down the street to the nearest subrail station, a serpentine growth along the path at his feet caught his eye. He bent down and touched the eerily smooth vine-like tendril. It was a shade of green so dark it was almost black and was coated in a thin layer of clear slime that felt like some sort of organic lubricant. Using his utility knife, Orook began to dig the growth out from the stone in which it was embedded. Once he could get his hand around the thing, he tugged on it, gently at first, then with more vigor. Suddenly, a strange static-like sensation came into his hand, then rapidly shot up his arm, into his neck, and then into his head. All of his senses suddenly felt fuzzy and dull, as if he had just fallen instantly asleep and into a dream. Orook had no idea how long he had been in that state of mental twilight before he was roughly tossed back into sharp reality. He dropped the vine and stood up, looked around, then back down at the road. The mysterious growth was gone. Only the indentation in the stone remained. Where had it gone? What was it? Orook considered calling the First Biologist, then thought better of it. He called Pullmoo instead.

"Why did you match me with one of the human women?" he asked without introduction.

"Good day, Orook," Pullmoo said. "I matched you because you need a companion. You will slowly lose your mind if you do not have someone to keep you company for the next 250 years or so."

Orook rubbed the strange lubricant between his thumb and index finger. He had not imagined it. Something had been there, crawling through the stone like a worm through soil.

"I do not need company. I will meet her, but only to humor you," he said.

"Do hurry, Orook," Pullmoo said.

"Why? What will happen to her if I refuse to accept her?" he asked.

"She will be dispatched," Pullmoo said.

"What? Why?" Orook asked, but Pullmoo had already ended the call.

Orook postponed his work meeting by a few hours, put on his heavy sapphire blue coat, and left for the Intake Hall. Once he arrived at the hall, he approached the attendant wearing the darkest shade of lavender, a Third Sociologist by the name of Dasook. Dasook was the active person in charge of the Intake Hall and the highest-ranking sociologist present in the hall at that time.

Orook introduced himself. Dasook made the first gesture of respect in recognition of Orook's status and authority. Orook acknowledged Dasook's gesture, then explained that he would like to meet a woman from Earth named "Maria."

"Of course," said the attendant. "I will take you to see her. However, I must say that I am a little surprised to see you. According to my most recent information, you declined the match."

"I did. Then I changed my mind. Is that alright with you or do I need speak with your superior?" Orook asked.

Dasook frowned.

"It is perfectly alright. I just hope you are not too late," he said as he hurriedly typed something into his armband and headed towards the main body of the Intake Hall.

As they were walking, the two men suddenly heard a woman scream. They both quickened their pace towards the source of the sound. When they arrived at the scene of conflict, they found a woman struggling violently against two attendants. Dasook approached the two men, told them to release the woman, then asked what was going on.

"She just freaked out all of a sudden, I don't know why," said one of the attendants.

"He's going to kill me!" Maria shouted, pointing at the other attendant.

"Shhh, quiet down. No one is going to hurt you," Dasook told Maria.

"Yeah right!" Maria said.

"I swear to you that we are not going to hurt you. Now you must quiet down. You are going to frighten the other women here," Dasook insisted.

Maria stared at Dasook intently as she tried to read the truth from his mind. While she was mostly convinced that he was not going to *hurt* her, she was not convinced that he did not intend to kill her quickly and painlessly.

"Your keeper has come to meet you," he told her.

Orook wanted to correct him. He was not her keeper *yet*.

After a few long, tense moments, Maria calmed down enough to allow Dasook to escort her to a private room located half-way down a corridor running perpendicular to the main body of the Intake Hall. He showed her to a chair and asked her to please wait while he spoke with her keeper.

Orook stood outside the room, arms crossed across his chest, as Dasook left the room and quietly closed the door behind him.

"Do you always inform the human women of their ultimate fate just before you euthanize them?" Orook asked.

Dasook shook his head.

"No, we most certainly do not," he said. "You should also know that we only very rarely have any cause to euthanize one of them. Up until today, the only reason we ever did so was if something happened during transport which rendered a woman too ill or too injured to live on in the city. This is the first and only time I have been given an order to euthanize a perfectly healthy woman. Your change of heart comes as a relief to me - and without much time to spare I might add."

"Please do not jump to conclusions," Orook cautioned. "I have not yet decided to be her keeper. I never requested to be matched. I only came here to meet her."

"I see," Dasook said with a sigh.

"Do the sociologists routinely - or ever - match a man without his request or even his consent?" Orook asked.

"Well, no," Dasook conceded. "However, this is a special case. This particular woman was never supposed to come to Pegasea. She boarded the ship on her own. The First Sociologist looked at her test results and ran the matching algorithms and decided to match her with you."

"How odd," Orook said, as he looked towards the room holding Maria with renewed curiosity.

"When you declined the match, I was ordered to euthanize her," Dasook continued. "Those two attendants she was struggling against are my assistants. I asked them to start preparing. The first step in the process is to remove her from the main hall. That is what they were doing when you arrived. If you do decide to keep her, you will need to reverse the order. I do not have the authority required to reverse an order from that high up."

"May I talk to the woman first - alone?" Orook asked.

"By all means," said Dasook.

The two men then walked back to the private room where Maria was waiting. Dasook unlocked the door and held it open for Orook. Maria stared at the two men with wide frightened eyes. She flinched at the sound of the door clanging shut. The man standing before her now was clearly not one of the attendants, and he did not look particularly friendly. She held the edge of the thick wooden table in front of her, drawing comfort from its density and size.

Orook stood just inside the door looking at Maria. She looked like a frightened and bewildered animal cornered by a predator. He decided that this was a mistake. As he turned and put his hand on the door handle, Maria spoke.

"If you leave, will they kill me?" she asked.

Orook closed his eyes, sighed, then looked back over at her.

"How old are you?" he asked.

"Well, I was 23 the last I recall - but if I really did spend 3 years traveling through space, then I guess I'm now 26," Maria said.

Orook hung his head. He then released the door handle and walked slowly over to the table in front of Maria. He pulled out a chair and sat down across from her. He looked down at the desk and waved his armband over the table. A rectangular section of the table suddenly lit up with a soft multitone glow. Orook touched the illuminated surface and navigated through the computer interface.

"Your name is Maria?" he asked.

"Yes," she said. "Thank you for not leaving."

"Are you now sufficiently calm to answer a few questions?" he asked.

"Calm?" Maria asked. "How am I supposed to be calm? I've been kidnapped by aliens, interrogated for what feels like weeks, and told nothing more than that something called a 'keeper' is going to come and take me home with him. Then, today, without any kind of warning or explanation, two men come and try to take me to some room where - no matter what that one guy says - they planned to execute me or otherwise dispose of me like an unwanted old horse. Then you show up and now I don't know if they still plan to kill me or -."

"Maria," Orook said calmly as he held up a hand to stop her rambling. "I see your point. Taking all of that into consideration, are you *relatively* calm enough to answer my questions?"

Maria looked at the man seated in from of her. His arms were positioned squarely on the desk, framing what Maria now believed to be a computer screen built into the table. His expression was distant, but not cold. She admired his perfectly tailored sapphire blue uniform which appeared to be made of an elegant but durable fabric which shimmered ever so slightly when he moved. His thick white hair was combed back and mostly tucked behind his ears. Only just enough of his hair fell free and loose around his face to soften the edges of his otherwise severely angular face. When Maria looked up into his stoic brown eyes, she began to feel calm. She took a deep breath.

"Ok, yes," Maria said. "I think I can answer a few questions."

"How did you know they were going to euthanize you?" he asked.

At this, Maria looked away as she thought about the answer to his question.

"It's hard to explain," she said. "It was as if I could hear - or maybe see - their thoughts, but it wasn't a sound... and it wasn't in words."

"Right, it is hard to explain," he agreed. "But your kind have a word for it. You call it 'telepathy.'"

"Right," Maria said. "It was as if all of a sudden, I just knew, and it was like a memory, except it hadn't happened yet."

Orook nodded.

"Most humans have the capacity to receive Pegasean thoughts after they have been here among us for a year or two," he said. "It is interesting that you would acquire the ability so quickly."

Orook then looked back down at the computer and continued perusing through Maria's records. Maria looked again at Orook's clothes. They were a shade of blue darker than any of the other uniforms she had seen thus far. Maria knew that the darker the Pegasean's clothing, the higher up they ranked in their career field and in Pegasean society as a whole.

"Can you stop them from killing me?" she asked.

"Yes," he said, without looking up from the computer.

Maria sighed with relief.

"Wait," Orook cautioned. "You asked if I could, and I can. You did not ask me if I would."

Maria tensed, then started to fidget with the sleeves of her sweater.

Orook looked at her assessingly. She did not look that much different than any of the others. She had long wavy dark hair and intense green eyes. She looked thin and frail, but that was to be expected after the long journey from Earth followed by three weeks in quarantine. She smelled, as all women from Earth smelled, like freshly turned soil and bubble moss. It was a smell he liked, but not one he could not live without.

"You must understand," he said. "The only way for me to stop them from dispatching you is for me to keep you... as what we call a 'companion.'"

"*Keep* me? As a companion?" Maria repeated, then closed her eyes and tried to see the words in his mind, the way she had seen the mind of one of the attendants. All she saw was a collage of images and words which did not make any sense.

Orook smiled, amused by the strained and perplexed expression on Maria's face.

At last, Maria gave up. She sighed as she opened her eyes and looked pleadingly up at Orook.

"Is anyone ever going to tell me what a 'keeper' is?" she asked.

"It is what I would be if I agree to host you," Orook said.

"And what would you do with me?" Maria asked.

"Frankly, I do not know. Not much I imagine. There is not a whole lot you can do as far as I am aware," he told her.

"What is that supposed to mean?" Maria asked.

Orook looked up at her and said, "Maria, you are a human from Earth. What exactly do you think you would be able to do here in Pegasea?"

"I don't know," she said. "I assume I would do some sort of work."

Orook shook his head. "While I do know of a few human women who work in relatively inconsequential jobs around the city, you would not be qualified to do much beyond the lowest level of work. We do not need you to work."

"Well then why the fuck did you guys bring me here?!" Maria asked.

"Calm down," Orook said.

Maria took a deep breath.

"Please just tell me - why am I here?" she asked. "Why was I taken from my home? Why am I being held captive?"

"You are not being held captive. You are being detained until you understand where you are and who we are. You are being detained so that you do not wander off into the wilderness and die. It is for your own safety," Orook explained.

Maria groaned.

"I do not want to waste my time explaining the whole history of the human project before I have even decided whether or not to keep you," Orook told her.

"Ok, alright," Maria said, remembering that it was not in her best interest to irritate this man.

Orook looked down and resumed looking through Maria's profile until he found the section describing her physical ability to adapt. Here he found that she had scored well. At the end of Maria's evaluation, there was a comment left by Pullmoo herself. It noted that Maria had an unusual brain abnormality. Orook's brow furrowed as he read the report provided by the First Biologist.

"Why would the First Biologist have any interest in a human brain abnormality?" Orook thought out loud.

"What?" Maria asked.

"There is something wrong - or different - about your brain," he said.

"Is that why they want to euthanize me?" she asked.

"No. The plan to dispatch you is based on the fact that you are not supposed to be here," Orook said. "You were not on the list."

"Well, in that case, just send me back to Earth, please," Maria said.

"That is not possible. You came here on the last transport ship arriving from Earth. The ships are being disassembled and repurposed as we speak," he told her.

Maria's heart sank as she absorbed that information.

"This anomaly in your brain is interesting," Orook said, more to himself than to Maria.

"What do you mean?" she asked.

"Never mind," he said. "It is of no concern."

"No concern? Why not?" Maria asked.

"It does not appear to affect your physical or mental health in any way," he said.

"Wait, are you talking about that thing where my brain sometimes reorganizes certain areas for no apparent reason and then goes back to normal?" she asked.

"That is not how I would describe it but let us assume we are talking about the same thing. What do you know about it?" he asked.

"Nothing," she said. "All I know is that it's weird and no one knows why I have this thing or what causes it."

"Fascinating," he said. "I am tempted to keep you just to study you."

27

"Please don't," Maria said. "Please don't study me, I mean."

Orook let out a long breath.

"The problem is that I am not particularly fond of humans in general," he said. "I do not see that any of you serve any real purpose here and I do not need company."

"Everyone needs company," Maria whispered.

"Maria, I...," Orook started to say, then stopped. An hour ago, even just thirty minutes ago, he had not cared one way or another about this woman. In the comfort of his apartment, the thought of her being euthanized had not phased him at all. Now he was suddenly feeling sorry for her and annoyed that he had been put in this position. He suspected that he was being manipulated and not necessarily for his own good. These thoughts and others raced through his mind until he decided.

"You have to make a choice now, Maria," he said. "You can come live with me, for the rest of your life, as my companion, or, you can be quickly and painlessly euthanized. I have never wanted a companion before, and I am not entirely sure I want one now. So, do not assume that living with me is the obvious choice over death. That said, these are your only two choices. There is no other place for you in our society or on our planet. Do you understand?"

"What is a companion?" asked Maria, surprised at her own daring to ask and kicking herself for not immediately saying "yes" to whatever it was.

"When you tried to read my mind a few minutes ago, what did you see?" he asked.

"Just a random bunch of images... I couldn't make sense of them," Maria admitted.

"There is no word in your language which adequately describes the relationship. All I can tell you is that you would live with me and keep me company," he said.

"Like a pet?" she asked.

Orook shook his head.

"No, not a pet," he said.

"Like a wife? Or a...," she asked.

"No, not a wife, or a girlfriend, or whatever else you are about to say," he said. "Again, there is no word for it in your language, because there is no such relationship on Earth. We are not the same species and we are not equals. What I *can* tell you is that you would have a status above that of an animal, so you would not be a pet."

"Would I be like a slave or servant?" Maria asked, still trying in vain to find a word.

"No, absolutely not," Orook said. "I suppose I might ask you to do a few household chores at some point, but no more than I do myself. Also, you would not be property. Humans have certain rights under our laws. In any case, I do not have the time or patience to go into detail about all that now. Make your choice."

"Ok, I agree to be your companion," she said quickly.

Orook nodded, then stood up to find the attendant and to reverse the order to euthanize Maria. He returned a half hour later holding two bands which looked like white and silver bracelets and a set of clothes, neatly folded in a pile, which were the same color as his own. He put these on the desk, then took one of Maria's wrist cuffs and tapped it with his armband. This caused the cuff to fall off Maria's wrist and into the palm of his hand. He then did the same with the other cuff and placed both cuffs on the desk. He replaced these with the new, lighter, bracelet-like bands.

"These are what they call 'training bands,'" he told her. "They do a lot of things, but mostly they monitor you during your first few months in the City. After you go through a final evaluation and pass a test, they will be removed, and you will be given an armband similar to mine, only smaller."

Maria twisted the wristbands around into a more comfortable position.

"You need to change into these before we leave," he said as he gestured to the stack of clothes on the desk. He then turned around and waited while she changed.

Maria picked up each article of clothing and tried to figure out how they were supposed to be worn. She did her best to put them on. When Orook turned back around and saw her tanged in a mess of fabric, he bit his tongue to keep from laughing.

"No, that is not right," he said, then explained that the bottom part was a kind of long skirt and should sit at her waist and go to her ankles. The blouse was designed to wrap around her and should be tied at her hip or in the back. The long sleeves of the blouse had slits going from the wrists to the elbows so that, later on, when she would have an armband like his, she would be able to access it without having to roll up her sleeves.

After Orook had finished explaining and turned back around, Maria took off both garments and tried again.

"Ok, I think I got it," Maria said.

Orook turned back around and approached her. He tugged and pulled at various parts of the ensemble, until it hung from her body in the manner intended.

"Ok, good, now put on your coat and shoes. Those should be easier, I hope," he said. Maria did so without needing any help. The coat was like any other full-length coat she had worn on Earth, except that it was significantly better made and more beautiful than anything she had ever worn before. Like her clothes, it was also sapphire blue, but made of a much thicker fabric. It was outlined with a subtle silver-blue trim that shimmered in the overhead light. The shoes were simple and sturdy, clearly designed for utility over style. When she was done fastening the clasps on the shoes, she stood up and looked at Orook. He nodded his approval. Without planning to do so, Maria suddenly wrapped her arms around him and hugged him tightly. She thanked him profusely and promised to be a good companion, whatever that was.

Orook sighed. "Let's not do this here," he said as he gently unraveled her arms from around his waist.

As they were leaving the room, Maria asked Orook if she could keep the sweater she was given in the Intake Hall. Orook shook his head "no" and motioned for her to hurry up.

CHAPTER 5

Maria had to almost jog to keep up with Orook's rapid stride through the hallway, out into the main hall, down a well concealed corridor, up two flights of stone stairs and then out into the open air. Maria gasped at the sudden burst of frigid wind in her face. She was used to the cold, but this was an extreme. It felt like the coldest day in the dead of winter back home, the kind of day when no one goes outside. Orook told her that they would need to walk about three kilometers to the nearest subrail station into the city. Maria quickly pulled the hood of her coat over her head and tucked her hands into her sleeves. She followed Orook as he started down the path, carved meticulously through the snow, without any further explanation or instruction.

Maria looked up occasionally at the back of Orook's head. He did not appear to be checking to see if she was still following him. She considered the possibility of escape. However, one look at the frigid and formidable mountain landscape told her that attempting to escape into this wilderness would only be an act of suicide. The cold air was biting as it whipped around her in violent gusts of wind. The rocky terrain to either side of the narrow path looked perilously unnavigable. She started to shiver violently as her face and ears turned numb. It was at this point that Maria noticed that, unlike hers, Orook's ears were protected by the same fluffy white peach fuzz that covered his neck, the tops of his hands, and the borders of his face. Obviously, he was far better equipped for this weather. By the time they reached the station, Maria wanted nothing more than to go to this man's house and stay there until spring. She did not care what he wanted at this point; just about anything would be better than staying out in this merciless cold.

At the end of the path stood a small structure, no larger than a bus station.

"We call these structures 'terminals,'" Orook said as he opened the door and ushered Maria inside and down a stairwell back underground.

Except for the conspicuous lack of rails or guide cables, the subrail station looked exactly like a subway station one might see in any metropolitan area on Earth.

"How does this train work?" Maria asked as she stepped inside the subrail car.

"Magnetic fields," Orook said simply, then directed Maria to sit down in one of the hard, bare seats.

Maria sat down and cupped her hands around her face as she tried to warm her hands and nose with her breath. Orook then sat down across from her and began reading messages off his armband. Maria wanted to say something to the man but could not think of anything to say. Despite his brusque manner, there was something about his calm, authoritative silence that she found comforting.

At the same time, Orook was feeling like a man who had just committed himself to a job for which he was wholly unqualified and uninclined to perform. Occasionally, he glanced up at Maria and tried to get used to the idea of having her around. At the moment, she looked frail, vulnerable and completely disoriented. He watched as she stared off into space, either in shock or deep thought, he could not tell which.

• • •

"This is my home," Orook announced as they reached the door to his sub-ground level apartment.

Maria stepped through the door and looked around. In many ways, the small home looked just like any other. Immediately inside the front door was a living room with a couch and an armchair upholstered in an earthy brown fabric. The largely bare walls were the color of Spanish moss and were all curved, as if the house were built of sections of a small silo fit into the bottom of a larger silo. Upon closer inspection, Maria noticed patches of white and pale green growing in rough patches along the walls.

"Why is there mold growing on your walls?" she asked.

"That is not mold. It is something more like lichen or air plants," he said. "We leave it alone because it produces oxygen, which improves the overall air quality indoors."

Orook hung up their coats as Maria continued to take in the room. Except for the conspicuous lack of windows, there was everything you might expect to see inside a home on Earth. To her right, she saw a path into what looked like a kitchen. To the far-left side of the living room there was a closed door which Maria assumed must lead to a bedroom.

"Are we underground?" Maria asked.

"Mostly, yes. But if you look up, you will see the sky," he said.

"Just like that room in the Intake Hall," Maria said aloud to herself.

"The roof is made of a special kind of cultivated transparent crystal and sits just above ground level," Orook continued. "The entire city of Pegasea is structured this way - with subrails and underground roads connecting every home and district. From above, the City looks a lot like a giant crystal snowflake."

Maria nodded.

"As you can see, we also have lights if we need them, which is not often. Even on overcast days, there is usually enough light to see," he said.

Orook then instructed her to remove her shoes before walking any further inside. Once she had done so, Orook gestured for her to follow him as he walked towards the kitchen. Here, he explained that, in winter, the Pegasean diet was limited to pre-prepared foods which were high in protein and fat and infused with vitamins and nutrients. He told her that these foods where made from what she might call "plants," many of which are grown in large greenhouses located throughout the city.

"You will eat the same food I eat," he told her. "Our biological needs are essentially the same, or similar enough, that we can eat the same food. We do not cook much, if anything, and especially not during the winter season, because it is just not worth the effort or resources. Most of our diet is boring and limited to liquid meals or pieces of something I suppose you might call 'bread.' We also eat a lot of something you will probably think of as tree nuts."

Maria had a lot of questions about all this, but by the time she started to ask the first one, Orook had already left the kitchen and was walking across the living room to the other side of the apartment. By the time she caught up with him, he was standing in the now open doorway to his bedroom.

"This is my bedroom," he said.

To Maria's surprise, she saw that the bedroom was larger than the living room and appeared to have another small, semi-circular room inside of it. This inner enclave did not appear to have a door. There was only a narrow break in the outwardly curving wall with a curtain drawn across it. Orook walked towards the room within the room. He pulled back the curtain and gestured for Maria to look inside. Maria looked in and recognized that it was another bedroom, smaller than the larger bedroom, but big enough to be comfortable. She saw that the room contained a set of shelves and drawers on each side, a bed, and what looked like a periscope to the outside. It was cluttered from wall to wall with boxes and other items. Aside from that, the space looked warm and inviting. Unlike the other walls of the house, the inside walls of this room were painted a soft yellow. Peeking out from behind the boxes, Maria could see that a pattern of small white and purple flowers had been painted along the base of the walls. The pattern broke at an archway inside the room. She craned her neck to try to see where it might lead.

"This is your room," Orook told her. "That break in the wall used to lead to a small bathroom. However, I removed the plumbing and turned the space into a large closet. I can turn it back into a small bathroom if you would like, or you can simply share mine. Every Pegasean home has one of these rooms. They used to be for children, before the Center Council decided that all children would be raised together in the Center of the City, by professional parents. In any case, human women tend to like them for the same reasons children do - they are cozy and private. After I clear it out, I will not enter your room without permission, unless absolutely necessary."

Maria nodded and thanked him.

Orook took something off a shelf in his bedroom and handed it to her.

"I think you have something like these on Earth," he said. "You call them iPads or tablets. It is, in essence, a portable computer. This one is simple to use. You can figure out how to use it on your own later. Among other things, it contains a lot of information about Pegasea and Pegasean culture, laws, and the Pegasean Rules of Order and Etiquette - or 'PROEs.' Please read as much as you can."

Maria turned the device over in her hands, looking for a button to turn it on or a port for a charge cord.

Orook tapped the screen with his finger to turn it on.

"It is solar powered," he explained. "Just turn it over and leave it out somewhere under the sunlight that comes in through the ceiling."

Maria nodded and placed the computer screen side down on a large ottoman-like storage unit at the foot of Orook's bed.

"Perfect," he said. "Any questions?"

While Maria had thousands of questions, she asked the one that was weighing most on her mind. "What is my purpose here? I know you said I would be your companion, but what will I do all day?"

Orook looked at her as he considered how to answer.

"Well, I suppose that is mostly up to you," he said. "Most of the other companions choose to do things together. They go to the exercise yard, or the companions' lounge. I'm not sure what else they do. You should ask them."

"Ok, but is there any way I can be more useful?" Maria asked.

Orook thought for a moment, then said "Actually, yes. Outside the bounds of the city, there are 'vocunines,' a somewhat intelligent species which is at odds with our kind. For reasons unknown to us, the vocunine consider humans to be something like sacred. They will not harm you, or any Pegasean who appears to be associated with you."

As he was explaining all this, Maria marveled at how easy it was for her to read his expressions and mannerisms. She was also surprised by the fluency with which he spoke her language. His English was unaccented and educated. He spoke it as if he had grown up down the street from her and attended the same level of education, and in the same areas of the country.

"How is it that you speak my language so well and speak it the same way I do?" she asked.

Orook scoffed as if the question was too stupid to warrant an answer. Maria wondered at this too. She wondered if his kind naturally scoffed like this, or if he learned this from the people brought here from Earth.

"You are not the first woman from Earth to come here, nor the first to come from an English-speaking country," he told her. "We learned your language, and its subtle variations, from the first women ever brought here. That was decades ago. You all bring over your language, mannerisms, expressions, and other things like that. Of course, we also have all of those things which are uniquely Pegasean. However, when we are in your presence, we assimilate. It is natural and nearly effortless for us. You, on the other hand, will not likely assimilate to our language because, well, you will never learn it. It is against Pegasean law to teach the City's language to humans and it is too complicated for you to learn on your own. You will, however, pick up some of our hand gestures. You will even be required to use many of them, according to the PROEs."

"What would you sound like if you spoke English with a Pegasean accent?" Maria asked.

"What a ridiculous question," Orook said.

"I'm just curious, geez!" Maria said, as she folded her arms across her chest.

Orook smiled at the child-like gesture.

"I would sound like this," he said, speaking in English with a Pegasean accent.

Maria uncrossed her arms, smiled and said, "It is a beautiful accent."

"Of course, it is," he said dismissively. "You will hear it a lot, but not from me. Now that you are outside of the Intake Hall, you will hear it when other Pegasean men speak to you."

"Why is that?" Maria asked. "I mean, if you are all able to assimilate as you just described."

"The answer to that question would require a rather lengthy explanation of Pegasean cultural norms which I would really rather not get into now," Orook said.

"Ok," Maria said. "Can I ask about something else?"

"*May* you - and yes," he said.

Maria blinked several times, flummoxed by the realization that an alien, on another planet, had just corrected her grammar. This moment, as well as many more moments to come, gave Maria such a sense of the surreal that she considered the possibility that she was, in fact, only dreaming all of this.

"Go on," Orook said. "If you have another question, ask it quickly."

"Um… right. Ok, so, how different are we?" she asked. "Genetically, I mean. You said we can eat the same food. We seem to be comfortable at the same temperatures, for the most part. You look like a human man."

Orook grimaced.

"We are not all that similar in appearance," he said. "In any case, you are correct in that we are genetically similar from an evolutionary perspective. Or, rather, we are similar in the way any given species is similar to the species which later evolves from it. We have the same number of chromosomes and a similar organization of genes. Does that surprise you?"

"If you really are aliens who evolved on a whole other planet, then yes," Maria said.

"Olrona is like Earth with respect to every characteristic relevant to the evolution of life. One would expect that the evolution of life on such largely similar planets would follow largely similar paths or patterns," Orook explained.

"Ok, if you say so," Maria said.

"It is not because I say so - it just is. That said, there are significant differences," he continued. "Beyond those differences, we have more symbiotic relationships with micro-organisms and are more amenable to subtle virus driven mutations and also what your geneticists on Earth call 'epigenetics.' Survival here is so arduous that even the pathogens we encounter are more likely to assist our survival, and thereby ensure their own, rather than threaten it. You will acquire many of these as well - in time."

Maria's eyes went wide with curiosity. She started to ask more questions until Orook raised a hand to stop the deluge of inquiry.

"We do not have time for all these questions," he said curtly. "What I will tell you is that, as similar as we may be, we cannot be considered the same species. There is no cross-breeding between our species. It is just not possible. The Center Council did some experimenting in this area at one time but gave up on it quite a while ago."

"Why...?" Maria started to ask.

"I cannot get into all that now. I have a meeting scheduled in half an hour," he said.

"Half an hour? How long is that?" she asked.

Orook sighed.

"I thought they would have at least explained our units of time to you at intake," he said.

"I was told that my keeper would explain all these things to me," Maria said.

Orook groaned, then said, "I should warn you now, Maria, I never asked to be a keeper and never wanted to be. I will try to explain as much as I can, but you will have to learn a lot on your own, ok?"

"Ok," she said.

"Right, well, our days are a little longer than days on Earth, about 33 Earth hours," he explained. "Each day is divided into 30 Pegasean hours, each hour into 60 equal minutes, which is divided into 60 equal seconds - just like on Earth. This should not surprise you, 60 is a very convenient number, divisible by 2, 3, 4, 5, 6, 10, 12, 15 and 30. In the end, our units of time are more or less the same, except that each unit of an hour, minute and second is roughly 10% longer. We work from the top of the seventh hour through at least the seventeenth hour. Since our days are longer, it may take you some time to adjust."

Maria nodded.

"What is your name?" she asked.

"You must never call me by name," he snapped. "You may call me 'keeper' or by any human term of respect or affection. That said, I am not particularly fond of any of the Earthly terms of affection. You should stick with 'keeper.'"

"Um…ok," she said.

"Now we must get going," Orook told her. "It takes 10 minutes to walk to the subrail station, then 10 minutes on the subrail to get to the meeting location. You might need your coat, but you will not need anything else. The streets are heated, but not to more than 10 degrees Earth Celsius."

CHAPTER 6

As they walked through the underground streets Orook explained the general layout of the city. He told Maria that the Center District was at the very inner most part of the city, and that several districts surrounded the center. He told her that each district had a District Center which served several nodes. From each node branched several streets, along which there were homes, training rooms, lounges, security stations, subrail stations, and utility rooms. As they walked, the streets became wider and more populated with other pedestrians. Maria became overwhelmed by all there was to see and hear. The streets were brightly lit by the mid-day sun pouring in on them from above. She noticed that all of the Pegaseans wore a similar type of clothing, but of different colors and shades. The clothing of some of them had embroidered symbols or patterns on their sleeves or around their collars. They all had snow white hair like Orook and the attendants at the Intake Hall. Some wore their hair short while some let it grow down to their shoulders or even down to their waists. Most of the ones with long hair wore it in braids or tied back in some way. They all had that same thin layer of fuzzy fur. Their ears were all long and steeply rounded at the ends, like a cross between a rabbit and lynx.

At some point Orook noticed that she was no longer paying attention to what he was saying. He sighed and waited for her to notice that he had stopped speaking.

"I'm sorry," she said. "It's just a lot to take in all at once."

"Ok, well, if for whatever reason we are separated, and you get lost, tap the homing beacon on your wristband."

Maria looked down at the bands on her wrists.

Orook took one of her wrists in his hand, turned it over, and pointed to a small symbol that looked a bit like a compass.

"It is this one," he said. "Once you turn it on, it will glow red when you walk in the wrong direction and blue when you walk in the right direction."

"What happens if I just stand still?" she asked.

Orook suppressed a smile, "let us hope that you never have to use it, ok?"

Once they were seated in the subrail car, Maria saw a bright orange button across from her and to the side of the railcar door. It had a symbol on it that looked a lot like a dog.

"What is that button for?" she asked.

"It is a vocunine alarm," he said.

"What exactly are vocunines? What do they look like?" she asked.

"In appearance, they look a lot like earthly wolves, only larger," he said. "But you must not think of them that way. Generally, they are as smart as humans, but less resourceful. They run on all fours but can stand up and uncurl their front paws. When they do that, their paws become more like hands. They can hold objects, including weapons."

"Like guns?" Maria asked in a tremulous voice.

"I suppose they could, but there are no guns anymore. At one time, every Pegasean had a gun-like weapon to protect themselves against the vocunines and Olronean intruders. They were never quite as powerful as Earthly guns. In any case, about 900 years ago, they were all destroyed." Orook said.

"Why?" asked Maria.

"Several reasons. One is that we all live in rather close quarters with crystal rooves over our heads. So, firing one indoors was extremely dangerous and usually very destructive. The second reason is that the Pegasean Center Council reached a kind of peace treaty with the vocunines. We agreed to destroy all of our high velocity projectile weapons, and they agreed never to attack a Pegasean woman," Orook explained.

"*All* high velocity projectile weapons?" Maria asked.

"Yes - you know, guns, bows, anything that projects an object at high velocity. I thought you were supposed to be smarter than the other women," he said.

"I know what the term means. I was just surprised!" Maria said defensively.

"We have other weapons," Orook told her. "They all require relatively close combat, but that is no matter. All Pegaseans are trained in such combat to the extent necessary to protect themselves. You will be too, to a lesser degree."

"Where are the vocunines? Where do they live?" she asked.

"They live in the woods and in the mountains all around us. We have sentinels who pace the walls around the City. For the most part, they keep the vocunines out of the populated areas. However, if one should breach the wall and infiltrate the streets, you should be prepared. And if you are in or near a railcar, press that button," Orook said and pointed to the orange alarm button.

"It is unlikely that a vocunine will deliberately harm you. However, it might try to take you out of the City in a misguided attempt to 'rescue' you," he said.

"What do I do if we are outside?" Maria asked.

"We will get to that when the time comes," Orook said.

"How often does a vocunine get into the City?" she asked.

"No more questions about them," he instructed. "There are other things I need to explain to you before we reach the meeting hall."

Maria groaned.

"Do not do that," Orook said.

"Do what?" Maria asked.

"Do not openly show annoyance with me or my instructions - at least not outside. I might come to tolerate it in the privacy of our home, but not in public. It is a clear violation of the PROEs."

Maria nodded, still annoyed, but determined to hide it.

"I am going to give you a crash course in the 'outside rules' - so pay attention," he said. "By 'outside' I mean outside the house, not the open outside. The 'outside rules' come from the larger set of PROEs, which are vital to our social structure, order and collective equanimity."

"Ok," Maria said.

"First, do as I instruct, always and without question. If you do not understand an instruction, you may ask for clarification, but do not argue. If you think that is unfair or demeaning to you in some way, get over it. Our society functions smoothly and efficiency at the grace of a rigid social structure that is in some ways egalitarian, but in other ways severely hierarchical. I will not get into all the complexities of it now, but there are certain basic rules which you must follow."

Maria started to ask a question, but Orook raised a hand to stop her.

"You must stop asking so many questions," he said. "I appreciate your inquisitive nature, but right now time is short, and you will have plenty of time later to research whatever questions you might have on your computer at home."

Maria bit her lower lip and nodded.

"Second, if another Pegasean asks you a question, or instructs you to do something, look to me first," he continued. "Give me an opportunity to answer for you, or to confirm or contradict the instruction. If I am not with you at the time, look at his clothing. If his clothing is as dark a shade as mine, regardless of the color or hue, follow his instruction. If it is a significantly lighter shade, use your own judgment. The color and hue of our clothing is based on what we do for work, our role within the operation of the City. Darker shades indicate higher rank and more experience or greater skill."

Maria nodded again.

"Human women are not allowed in the meeting hall. You will wait in the waiting room with the other companions. You may interact with them in any polite way you wish. When it comes to interactions between human women, for the most part, we allow you to make your own rules, unless you begin to abuse each other. However, to my knowledge, that rarely, if ever, happens. The women here are all relatively gracious and welcoming - they were either raised here or were selected from Earth based on such favorable characteristics."

Maria opened her mouth, then shut it again.

Orook sighed. "Go ahead, one question," he said.

"Where are all the Pegasean women?" she asked.

"Of course, you had to ask *that* question," he said.

"Only one Pegasean female is born for every 50 male Pegaseans," Orook whispered. "This wasn't always the case. About 1,500 years ago, there were roughly the same numbers of men and women. Then a virus, or something else, infected our species and disrupted the balance. Whatever it did, whatever its mechanism of action, it resulted in a drastic decline in the birth of baby girls. Our biologists study the phenomenon relentlessly, but have yet to identify a cause, much less a solution. The sudden decline of women caused a great deal of social upheaval, but that is a long story that I do not have time to tell you now."

"Do your women get married and have families like women on Earth?" Maria asked.

"Not exactly, no. During their childbearing years, they take many partners and are allowed to have one child with each partner. If a child she has with one particular partner dies, or is a girl, she can have a second child. This is all by design to ensure the continued genetic diversity of our population. Because there are so few of them, all women are required to have children. By law, no woman is permitted to keep any one partner for more than 5 years until after she meets her child bearing requirement. Most women will partner exclusively with one man until she becomes pregnant with his child. While she is pregnant or using fertility suppressants, she might entertain multiple partners concurrently. In any event, it is all up to her so long as she continues to bare children and ensures that no more than one child is born to each partner. If, for whatever reason, a woman is not inclined to accept partners, she can choose to be artificially fertilized every three years instead. The older women, the ones who have satisfied their reproductive requirement, will usually choose one partner to marry and then live at the very center of the city with their husbands. Only these older women and their husbands may serve on the Center Council, which is like your Supreme Court, except that it does everything. It makes the laws, appoints the district leaders and governors, and decides on all matters of high importance."

"Thank you for explaining all that," Maria whispered. "May I ask just one more really quick question?"

"Go ahead." Orook said. "If there is a quick answer, I will answer it. Otherwise, we have to move on."

"Can you move your ears? I mean, can you rotate them like a cat? Because they look a bit like the ears of a lynx or maybe a cross between a rabbit and a lynx," Maria asked quickly, hoping the question would not offend him.

This so surprised Orook that he could not help but laugh.

"Yes, I can rotate my ears," he answered, then quickly added, "No, I will not demonstrate it for you."

Orook then resumed his crash course on what he referred to as the "outside rules." But Maria's attention had drifted off again. She was starting to notice the absence of certain things, that had she been on Earth, she would have expected to see. There were no handicapped, poor or elderly Pegaseans, and no children.

CHAPTER 7

The subrail car slowed as it reached the station for District Center Two. As Maria and Orook stepped out of the railcar, Maria gazed in awe at all that she saw around her. They were still underground, but the ceiling was domed and climbed several stories above them. There were trees and other plants growing out of exposed patches of soil in the floor. The floor itself was tiled with perfectly laid marble-like pieces of various sizes and subtle shades of white, grey, and green, creating an intricate pattern throughout the entire district center. This place reminded her of an enormous indoor mall she visited once as a child. She could not remember much about the mall, except its size, and the fact that the large glass ceiling and indoor foliage made her feel as if she was outside. The same was the case here. She gazed around her like a child at an amusement park, almost colliding with various structures and other pedestrians. When Orook noticed this, he took her hand and pulled her close to him. This startled and unnerved Maria. His hand was warm but was holding hers entirely too tightly. She tried in vain to loosen his grip by wiggling her hand and her fingers.

"You're hurting my hand," she said at last.

Maria sighed in relief when Orook loosened his grip. Once they were within a block of their destination, he let go. She shook out her hand to help resume normal blood flow to her fingers.

"I am sorry if I hurt your hand," he said. "I did not know that you are so fragile."

"I'm not fragile," Maria protested.

"Sensitive, then," Orook said.

Maria rolled her eyes.

"I thought I told you not to do that," Orook chided.

"How did you know I rolled my eyes? You weren't even looking at me." Maria said.

"I have excellent peripheral vision," he told her.

"Are you seriously telling me that I can't roll my eyes in public?" Maria asked.

"No," Orook said. "What I *am* telling you is that you must not roll your eyes at me."

"That's not going to be easy," Maria muttered.

"Do I need to take you home?" Orook asked.

"Home?" Maria said dumbly.

Orook blinked at her, not comprehending why she would be so eager to go back to his house.

"Oh, right, you mean *your* home," she said.

Orook sighed, then said, "I understand that this must be all a bit disorienting for you, but you need to behave. Do you think you can manage to do that until we return to, well, the place you will soon come to think of as 'home?'"

Maria frowned, then nodded.

"Good, because we have arrived at the meeting hall," Orook said as he stopped in front of an ornately carved wooden door frame with frosted crystal doors. Maria ran her fingers over the carved wood and marveled at its beauty and artistry.

"It is orconean blue wood," Orook told her. "It is difficult to obtain and even more difficult to carve."

Maria nodded. This was not like any wood she had seen before. It was impossibly dark, with smooth lines of a lighter shade running along the grain and electric blue colored "veins" running parallel to the dominant grain. She could not understand how any tree could possibly produce a wood like this.

Orook waved his armband over the lock on the door and the door opened. They stepped inside and Orook greeted the meeting hall attendant, who responded by making the first gesture of respect. After the two men exchanged what Maria assumed to be pleasantries in their native tongue, Orook led Maria inside towards the companions' waiting room. At the door to the waiting room, Orook instructed her to wave her left wristband over the door lock. When she did, the door opened.

"Wait in here. I will come get you when we are done," he said, then walked away and into the main body of the meeting hall.

The waiting room reminded Maria of a church quiet room, where parents took crying or rambunctious children so as not to disturb the rest of the congregation. There were three other human women already seated in a loose cluster against the far wall. They were all dressed in the same color blue as she was, only a shade lighter. When they noticed Maria, they all looked up and smiled at her with genuine warmth as they gestured for her to join them. Cautiously, Maria walked towards them, then sat down, close enough to be social, but not quite close enough to join them.

"Oh, you poor thing," one of the women said. "You look positively terrified."

Maria smiled weakly at the women, who promptly stood up and walked over to her end of the room. The woman sat down next to Maria and introduced herself as "Rose."

"I'm Maria - and I'm ok. I just came from the Intake Hall," Maria said, shifting in her seat.

"Well, no wonder then," Rose said. "Don't worry, those fellas are straight - no one is gonna hurt you."

"Right," said one of the other two women. "So long as you're a good little girl and follow the rules."

"Oh, stop it, Alice," Rose snapped.

"It's easy for you Rose, you're from the South and you're..." Alice started to say.

"I'm *what?*" Rose said.

"Nothing," Alice said quickly.

"Go on, say it. It's easy for me because I'm what?" Rose persisted.

Maria stared at Rose who appeared to be attempting to set Alice's curly blond hair on fire using only her eyes.

"I swear you two," the third woman said. "If you have this argument again I will vomit. And then I'm going to scoop up the vomit and throw it in your faces."

Maria could not help but smile at the fearful and disgusted looks on the faces of Alice and Rose.

"She started it, Maddie. You heard her. You know she's always starting something," Rose said.

Maddie rolled her eyes.

"You two are the reason we aren't allowed to talk about race without supervision. You know that, right?" Maddie said, looking at Rose, then at Alice.

"Or abortion," Alice added.

"Or gender identity," Rose added.

"Wait, what do you mean?" Maria asked. "You can't talk about these things without supervision? What supervision? Why?"

"We - and by 'we' I mean you, me, and the other human women - are not allowed to discuss highly controversial subjects without keeper supervision. Hang out with these two long enough and you'll know why," Maddie said.

"They don't think we are capable of having a civil discussion without their help," Rose said bitterly.

"Yeah, as if they don't ever get into it with each other," Alice said.

"Right, but seriously Alice, when have you ever seen two Pegasean men break out into all out brawl in the middle of the District Center? Or start pulling each other's hair and -."

"Alright, that will do plenty, Maddie," Rose interrupted. "There be no need bringing all that up now. This ain't helping the new arrival."

Maddie looked at Maria and smiled. "Actually, you might not guess it from meeting them, but Rose and Alice are good friends," she said.

Maria looked at Rose, then at Alice. The two women shrugged in unison.

"I was born here," Maddie said. "But Rose and Alice came from Earth - about 40 years ago I think."

"*Forty* years ago?" Maria asked. "But you guys look so young, not more than 30."

"Didn't your keeper tell you? Once you get here, there are some viruses or something that keep us all from aging until we get to be over 300," Alice said.

Maria suddenly started to feel dizzy again. Meeting women who must be in their 70s, but looked no older than 30, struck at Maria's already crumbling walls of denial like a wrecking ball. The whole situation suddenly started to feel incurably surreal as dueling perceptions of reality collided in her mind. She stared blankly out into the meeting hall through a window in the wall dividing the companions from their keepers.

"Are you alright? You look a little faint," Maddie said as she came over and put a hand on Maria's shoulder.

Maddie's comforting touch steadied Maria just enough for her to get a grip on herself.

"I just...I just don't know why I'm here," Maria said. "What do they want from us?"

"Nothing much," Alice said. "They're just lonely. They can't have wives or girlfriends - not really anyway. They can't raise their kids or even have pets. So, they keep us around just to have someone there - you know, to talk to and stuff. Mine also likes to play with my hair, which creeped me out at first, but you can't judge them like you might human men - they're just different."

"I don't think my keeper wants any of that," Maria said.

"He must want someone to keep him company or else he wouldn't have requested a companion," Maddie said.

"He didn't request one," Maria said.

"What do you mean?" Maddie asked.

Maria then explained everything her keeper had told her about how she had not been on the list, and how he had not requested a companion. She also told them about how the men in the Intake Hall were about to euthanize her before her keeper showed up.

"That is really odd," Maddie said. "I don't even understand how something like that could happen."

Maria put her face in her hands.

"What the hell you doing Maddie?" Rose said.

"Sorry," Maddie said.

"Hey, Maria, listen," Alice said. "It's ok. You're lucky in a way. Your keeper is a big deal here."

"I don't even know his name," Maria said.

"It's Orook," Maddie told her. "But don't ever call him that. That's one of those rules you really can get in trouble for breaking."

"Yeah, he did tell me that much," Maria said.

"He's the First Engineer," Maddie continued. "Our keepers are all Second Engineers - so your keeper is our keepers' boss."

"Why does that make any difference?" Maria asked.

"Well, for one thing, it means he can call them all here on a social day and make them work instead of hang out with us," Alice muttered.

"Huh?" Maria asked.

"Don't mind Alice," Maddie said. "As much as she bitches about him, she adores her keeper. In fact, the whole reason she's in such a bad mood right now is because she would rather be with him."

"Really?" Maria asked and looked up at Alice.

Alice shrugged.

"They ain't all bad," Rose said. "Bossy, rude, arrogant and irritatin' as all hell, but -."

"But what?" Maria said.

Rose only gave Maria a thin smile.

"Rose plays the violin," Maddie said. "When she first came here from Earth, all she could do was cry over the fact that her violin was left back on Earth. So, her keeper made a new one for her - and he made it out of Orconean blue wood no less. He had to invent a new tool just to be able to carve the wood the way it needed to be carved. You should hear her play it - it's so beautiful it will make you cry."

"Wow," Maria said.

"They're all engineers," Maddie told her. "Rose's keeper works with manufacturing of special materials. My keeper is an electrical engineer and computer programmer."

"Do you know what mine does? I haven't had a chance to ask him, I've only been in the City for a few hours," Maria asked as she once again looked through the window into the meeting hall.

"Like Alice said, he's the boss. Orook is the First Engineer, so he does it all," Maddie told her.

"Is that why everyone keeps making that weird gesture to him?" asked Maria.

"Yes, it's their version of a salute I guess you could say, but not exactly," Maddie explained. "You're lucky, or special, however you want to look at it, that you were matched with him."

"*Lucky* might be pushin' it," Alice mumbled.

Rose stifled a laugh.

"Come on guys, knock it off," Maddie said.

"No, please," said Maria. "Let them tell me. I've had enough surprises for one lifetime. What is he like?"

"The word 'asshole' comes to mind," Alice said.

"Oh, for the love of summer, Alice!" Maddie said hotly.

Maddie then turned to Maria and said, "Don't worry. He is *not* an asshole. He's just a bit, well, stiff - and like I said, he tends to make our keepers work on social days, which is annoying."

"Oh," Maria said.

"Yeah, and he does it all the time," Alice added bitterly.

"Let's talk about something else," Maddie said with a sigh.

When no one volunteered an alternative topic of conversation, Maddie said, "Maria, how do you like Pegasea so far?"

"How do I like it?" Maria asked. "I don't know - I don't even want to be here. I want to go home, but my keeper told me that it's not possible because I was on the last transport. I was mostly miserable, scared and confused the whole time I was in the Intake Hall. What little I've seen of the city looks amazing, but it's just all so strange and new… it makes me feel dizzy."

An uncomfortable silence came over the room.

"I'm sorry," Maria said.

"Nah, none of that now," Rose said. "It's normal. You'll be alright though - you'll see."

The other two women nodded in agreement.

"What happens if you break the rules?" Maria asked.

"Most of the time they just scold you and give you a nasty look," Rose said.

"If you're real bad, they send you to remedial PROEs training," Alice added.

"What is that?" Maria asked.

"It's just this really boring class that goes on for days - where they remind you of all the rules and why they are important," Maddie said.

"Maddie goes about once every two weeks," Alice said with a smirk.

"Shut up," Maddie said.

Maria smiled.

"Don't worry," Alice said. "You're new and your keeper is like the president here, so you'll get away with murder for at least a lunar cycle or two."

"He's not like the president," Maddie said. "Pullmoo is more like the president. Orook would be something more like chief-of-staff - but there are no real parallels to U.S. government here."

"How would you know? You've never even been to Earth," Alice said.

"True. But I can read - can you?" Maddie retorted.

"Hey now," Rose said sternly, "we all know you're the smart one sugar - but you don't need to be like that. We get enough of that from the keepers."

"I know, I know," Maddie said. "Sorry, Alice."

Alice shrugged.

After a moment's silence, Maria asked, "So, is he nice? Orook I mean... aside from making your keepers work a lot?"

"I'm sure he will be nice to you," Maddie said. "And it's not like he's mean or anything - don't worry. We are not all too fond of him because he is a bit strict and demanding with our keepers, who are all subordinate to him. Honestly, though, none of us really knows Orook. But you don't have to worry - all Pegasean men are nice."

"Ok," Maria said, wishing Maddie had not told her twice not to worry.

Suddenly, another woman entered the room and immediately sat down and started crying. Maddie, Rose, and Alice immediately rushed over to the new arrival and enveloped her in affection and concern.

"What's wrong?" asked Alice.

"Go on, tell us," Rose said.

"I...I...," but the woman could not stop crying long enough to speak.

"Take a few deep breaths," Maddie instructed.

The bereft woman took a few heaving breaths and managed to get control of herself.

"I broke something important - some kind of model my keeper was working on. It was an accident! I thought it was one of those 3D puzzles he's always giving me! He was so mad he locked me in my room for an hour!" she told them all in one breath.

"Oh, it's ok, Jess. Nabook will forgive you. You know he will," assured Maddie.

"Of course, he will," said Alice.

"You know that's the truth," Rose added.

The comforting words seemed to work as Jesse started to calm down. While the women continued to sooth her, Maria heard Orook's voice coming from the meeting hall. She stood up to get a better view through the dividing wall window. Orook was standing now and looking clearly agitated as another man appeared to be explaining something to him. The man was gesturing back and forth between something on the table and the waiting room. Maria put the two scenes together and determined that the newly arrived engineer was explaining to Orook that his companion had broken whatever it was on the table. When the man was done explaining, Orook sighed heavily, looked from the broken object to the waiting room, then shrugged. Maria could not understand what they were saying or get any images from their minds at this distance. However, if she had to guess, she would say that Orook was telling the men that what was done was done and there was nothing they could do about it now. All the men then gathered up their things and left the table.

"They're coming back," Maria announced.

All three women stopped talking and looked at Maria. Jesse wiped her eyes and prepared herself for further admonishment before the door opened.

"Jesse?" called the man who had come with the broken object. Jesse jumped up and took the man's hand in both of hers. She began apologizing profusely and emphatically through her tears.

"It's ok. It's ok," he told her, looking embarrassed. "Jesse, stop, look at me, it's ok."

The two then walked away with Jesse clinging to the man's arm and still muttering her apologies. Each of the other women left as their keepers came to the door. Orook walked past the waiting room as he stared down at the broken object in his hands. Maria was first puzzled, then alarmed, as she watched him walk out of the meeting hall outer door and back out onto the street. Moments later, Orook came back in and headed straight for the waiting room.

"Time to go," he said as he opened the waiting room door.

"Did you forget I was here?" Maria asked, a little unnerved.

"Not exactly - I was just preoccupied," he said. "Our meeting was cut short because one of the companions broke the very thing we had gathered here to discuss."

Orook then gestured for Maria to come out of the waiting room. They then left the meeting hall. As they approached the District Center, Orook asked Maria if she was hungry. He then led her to a small structure which looked like a large coffee vending machine. Orook tapped a few instructions into an interface on the front of the machine, then waited while two glasses descended to a platform and filled with a pale green fluid. Maria hoped it was some kind of milkshake but judging from what she was fed in the Intake Hall, she did not think it was. Orook handed her one of the glasses and pointed to a small table and chairs under a nearby tree. Maria sat down at the table and took a sip of the drink. She grimaced at the taste, which was bitter and chalky.

"You will get used to it," Orook said.

"Don't you ever eat real food?" Maria asked.

"This is real food," he told her. "It is made from a fruit which is easily dried and stored over the winter. The first women to arrive here from Earth affectionately named it 'puke fruit.' We call it something else, of course, which translates to 'borcula eggs.'"

"What's a borcula?" asked Maria.

"A mythical creature from ancient Pegasean mythology. The fruit is purple with yellow spots - which matches the description of the eggs of a borcula as they are described in one of the ancient texts. You can read about it later if you want to know more. Did you enjoy meeting my colleagues' companions?"

"Sure," Maria said without enthusiasm.

"You should make an effort to become friends with them. Otherwise, you will quickly become lonely. I am usually gone at work all day," he advised. "And when I am not at work, I am usually running errands or visiting with my partner."

"Your partner?" Maria asked.

"Never mind that for now. Did you learn anything from the other companions?" he asked.

"I learned that you're the president of the city - or something like that," Maria said.

"I am *not* the president," Orook said. "We do not even have a president."

"Chief of Staff?" Maria tried.

"That is closer, but still not right," he said. "I am the First Engineer, which infers more authority than the title alone implies, but I am not an elected official or politician. There are no elected officials or politicians here. We are governed by the Central Council, District Councils, and by the Governesses. Please do not ask me to explain all that to you. Government structure is my least favorite subject."

"Who is Maddie's keeper?" Maria asked.

"His name is Etmook and he is a Second Engineer," he said. "Why do you ask?"

Maria shrugged, "What is his official title?"

Orook thought for a moment, then said, "I suppose if I had to translate it into English, it would be something like 'Second Engineer, Division of Electrical and Computer Sciences.'"

"That's a long title," Maria said.

"It is much shorter in Pegasean, which has a single word for 'Electrical and Computer Sciences,'" Orook explained. "Maddie's keeper taught her the Pegasean version to make it easier for her to formally introduce herself when need be. Your introduction is easy. You can simply say, 'my name is Maria, companion to the First Engineer.'"

"Does my whole existence and identity here revolve around you?" Maria asked, trying very hard not to sound derisive or sarcastic.

"The easy answer to that is 'yes,'" Orook said without apology.

"What is the hard answer?" Maria asked.

"The hard answer is more complicated," he said. "Obviously, you have your own mind and identity as a human woman. But in the eyes of the law and the City, you are primarily an extension of me. It must be that way or else you would be considered, well, dead weight. Life here is difficult and demanding. We cannot afford to sustain people who have nothing to contribute. This fact is actually written into our laws. The terminally infirmed and totally disabled are euthanized. The city simply cannot support them. Consequently, when the first women arrived from Earth, we had to change the law in order to create a place and a role for you. If we treated you like Pegaseans, you would have the lowest status, contributing something, but not much, to our society as a whole. However, the Pegasean men who took the first Earth women as companions did not like that idea. They wanted their companions to have a status closer to what they had, but not the same status, obviously. Eventually, a compromise was reached, one which resulted in a new kind of legal and social status, one which is unique to human women here. It is something that is better understood through experience than by explanation."

"This is fascinating... and disturbing," Maria said.

"Careful," Orook admonished, "you are bordering on heresy. You must never openly criticize anything about our laws or social rules. If you do, you could be judged to be a political activist. On Earth, such a label might be considered innocuous, or even noble. Here, it is the equivalent of being called a 'terrorist.'"

"Ok," Maria said as she shifted in her chair. "So, are there women from other countries here too?"

"Only other English-speaking countries," Orook said.

"Why did you limit your abductions to English speaking countries?" Maria asked.

"Efficiency," Orook said. "We focused our efforts on genetically diverse populations which all spoke the same language."

"Why?" she asked.

Orook rolled his eyes.

"What?" Maria asked.

"Figure it out yourself," he said.

"And how do you justify all this to yourselves?" she said.

"Justify what?" he asked.

"Kidnapping," she said.

"It was the only way to transport people here without alerting your governmental systems and scientists to our existence," he told her.

"Why so secretive?" Maria asked.

"Do you really have to ask that question?" Orook asked.

"I guess not," she said. "But what I really don't understand is how this planet could exist without anyone on Earth knowing about it. It can't be all that far away if it only took three years to get here."

"Olrona is hidden from your space exploring devices by an inner asteroid belt in our solar system. Some of your better astronomers likely have some suspicion of this planet's existence, but no way to know much about it," Orook explained.

"Well, I wish you had just left me on Earth," Maria said.

"Why?" he asked.

"Am I even allowed to say why?" she asked.

"Go ahead. I will allow you to speak your mind freely in this instance - since I asked the question. Just try to keep your voice down," Orook instructed.

"But that's just it," Maria said. "Why do I need your permission?"

Orook did not answer.

"You can't tell me why, can you?" she asked.

"I could, but we only just met a few hours ago, and you are overwhelmed and disoriented. I do not expect that any explanation I could give you as to why you need my permission to speak freely, would be helpful to you right now," he said.

Maria looked out at the people walking around the District Center. Within moments, she became entranced by the way the fractured light through the crystal ceiling danced above them. The scene was just close enough to home to be disconcerting. She could imagine herself sitting at a table in the food court of a large mall with natural lighting coming in through glass ceiling panels. The people walking around her now could easily be just busy shoppers. She closed her eyes and focused on the sounds around her, the smell of the air, the feel of the place. She willed herself to be back home and to wake up from this relentless nightmare.

"Are you ok?" Orook asked.

Startled, Maria turned back to look at her keeper, then started to fidget nervously with the ends of her shirt sleeves.

"It is not as bad as it seems," he said. "You might initially resent my dominion over you and our strict utilitarian ways, but you will get used to it. Also, despite what you might think right now, we are a generally kind and gentle people. I will never abuse my authority over you."

"It's not you I'm afraid of," Maria whispered. "You aren't the one who tried to euthanize me. What if I break too many of the rules? What if I piss off someone really important?"

"You do not need to worry about that now. You are the companion to the First Engineer. There are few people in this city objectively more important than me," Orook said with a smile.

"I don't like these rules you call the PROEs. I'm not good at being deferential and subservient," she said.

"Maria, again, try to relax. You will learn. And until then, and even after that, you will be forgiven for most minor indiscretions more readily than others," Orook said.

"Is that because of my status by proxy - because of my association with you?" she asked.

"Exactly," he said. "Now you are getting it."

CHAPTER 8

Back at what she would soon start to call "home," Maria sat in the living room armchair, fully engrossed in something she was reading on the tablet computer Orook had given her. Orook was busy clearing out her room and collecting blankets and other things she would need. When he had finished, he came into the living room and sat across from her on the sofa. She had not heard him coming or seen him when he sat down. When he spoke, she rattled and dropped the computer.

"Why are you so jumpy?" he asked.

"I'm not. I just didn't know you were there," Maria said as she bent down to pick up her computer.

"You will need to go shopping tomorrow," Orook said.

"Oh?" she asked. "For what?"

"You will need more clothes and different kinds of clothes. Those that you are wearing now are fine for every day casual dress, but you will need different clothes for exercise, sleeping, and other activities."

"I hate shopping," Maria said.

"Here, it is easy and painless," he told her. "You do not need any money and you can only wear one color."

"Really? No money?" she asked, intrigued.

"There is no money here. Not for anything," he said.

"How do you buy things?" Maria asked.

"There is no buying or selling. Everything anyone needs is available to them for the taking," Orook explained.

"But what stops someone from, I don't know, taking a hundred shirts?" Maria asked.

"Why would someone take a hundred shirts?" he asked.

"Ok, not shirts… but something scarce or valuable, like jewelry or something," she said.

"Our armbands keep track of what we take. If someone takes significantly more of something than his quota permits, an inventory manager will contact him and ask why he took more than he was expected to take. If there is a reasonable explanation, nothing happens. If there is no reasonable explanation, the items will most likely be confiscated. Here again, status makes something of a difference. There is a slightly higher threshold with respect to what I can take before an inventory manager is alerted. For most items, I am granted slightly more latitude with respect to what is assumed to be 'reasonable' or 'necessary' before my actions are called in question. Still, I would not be allowed to take, say, several orconean blue wood carvings from an art depot without someone knocking at my door demanding an explanation."

"There are art depots?" Maria asked.

"Of course," he said. "Ask Maddie to take you to one. I asked Etmook to send her over here tomorrow morning. She can help you find what you need and show you any places which might be of interest to you. I will not be home until later in the evening. In fact, depending on when you retire for the night, you might not see me again until the day after tomorrow. I am taking four of my Second Engineers out to Five Deaths."

"Five Deaths?" Maria asked, alarmed.

"Hmm, I apologize. That was a direct translation from Pegasean," Orook explained. "The human women call it the 'Spa Field.'"

"What kind of place could inspire such vastly different names?" asked Maria.

"It is an area about five kilometers from the City, where there is a cluster of natural steam vents like fumaroles," he explained. "The ground around the larger vents can be very unstable. The smaller vents often become inactive just long enough to become hidden under debris or snow. There are also nasty little creatures which sometimes live in them and… well, suffice to say, it is an extremely dangerous place to go if you are not familiar with it, or do not have a guide."

"I hope nothing happens to you," Maria said.

"Do not be silly," Orook said.

"Why is it silly for me to be concerned?" she asked.

"Because I know the place very well. As your people might say, I know it 'like the back of my hand,'" Orook said with a smile. This was one of the few expressions from Earth which he liked.

Maria nodded.

"I also asked Maddie to·help you start learning the Pegasean Rules of Order and Etiquette - the 'PROEs,'" he said.

"Oh, I can't wait," Maria sneered.

This earned her a disapproving look from Orook.

"Sorry," she said quickly.

"As I have said before, it is not so important here at home. However, you should practice these rules at all times for a while - until you know them by rote and by habit," Orook instructed.

"And by heart?" Maria offered.

"I am not particularly fond of that expression. It does not make any sense to me. How does one know something *by heart*? The heart pumps blood. It does not hold memories," he said.

"I think it just means that you know something so well that you do not have to think about it. Maybe it also implies that you remember it because you love it," Maria explained.

Orook thought about that for a moment, then said, "Well, if that is what it means, then I doubt there is anyone who knows the PROEs *by heart* - except maybe some of the sociologists. I certainly do not expect you to love them. I only ask that you learn them, memorize them, and apply them whenever we are outside or around other people."

Maria nodded.

When Orook was done laying out his plan for her for the following day, he excused her from his company. Maria went into the bathroom and changed into the night clothes Orook had left out for her. She saw that Orook had also left her a collection of what appeared to be toiletries in a small basket on one of her shelves. She picked up each item and turned it around in her hands. The labels were not in English and provided no pictures. She hesitated to use any of them, for fear she might inadvertently brush her teeth with shampoo or rub toothpaste on her hands. She would have to ask Maddie to explain it all to her tomorrow.

CHAPTER 9

The next morning, Orook took his four most trusted Second Engineers out to the surface that morning. He would teach them how to hear the ground. The requirement to teach the skill had long since been removed from the nursery school curriculum, but that made no difference to Orook. He lost one of his best electricians only three days before meeting Maria at the Intake Hall. The young man had dropped his land reader into a sink pit, then died in his efforts to retrieve the insidious device. Orook knew, better than few others in Pegasea, that the people of Pegasea had large ears for a reason. The terrain of this country was rough, treacherous, and always changing. It was a stirred pot of rock, crystal, ice and organic debris, all buried under a thick concealing layer of snow. This is why they all carried ground readers which could show them the ground under the snow and the pits and pockets of air or water under the ground. The readers also showed the relative densities of the stones and registered subtle movements and vibrations of unsteady masses. They were considered vital to survival out on the surface. Now he would tell these four loyal men to turn them off and trust him. He had no doubt they would do it, but they would not like it.

Four of the City's finest Second Engineers stood in a semi-circle facing Orook. Orook noticed that they each had a lock of their companions' hair either braided into their own hair or tied in a band around one wrist. This had, unfortunately, become a popular tradition now. The human women had come to believe that if they did this, it would better the odds of their keepers coming back from the surface alive. Orook found it silly, of course, but knew it did no harm.

"You want us to turn our ground readers off?" Etmook asked.

"Was I unclear?" Orook clipped.

"No, no sir," Etmook said, and blushed. He then quickly turned off his ground reader.

"You all need to learn how to do this without the assistance of a computer," Orook told them. "Our ancestors traveled over this ground without any such assistance, and so can we. The first thing you need to learn is how to activate your second inner ear. You probably do not even know you have such an organ, but it is there. It sits right on top of your primary inner ear. Since you have probably never used your second inner ear, you will need to activate it manually. Eventually, you will be able to switch back and forth effortlessly and even unconsciously."

Orook then instructed them to hold the base of one ear, at the point where it met their head, and tug up and back on it sharply. He told them they would hear a popping sound, which was normal. He advised them not to be alarmed when they were suddenly assaulted with a range of ultrasonic noise they had, up until now, been unable to hear. The men did as they were instructed and immediately gasped in surprise and discomfort. Etmook grimaced and covered both of his ears with his hands.

"That will not help you, Etmook," Orook said. "As you should know, ultrasonic waves travel through flesh."

"Where do the waves come from?" Etmook asked as he slowly removed his hands from his ears.

"There are several theories," Orook said. "We can discuss them another time if you would like, but not now. This is a field exercise, Etmook, not a lecture."

When the men had finally adjusted, Orook told them to leave the other ear in its normal sonic position until he instructed them otherwise, so that they could continue to hear his instructions. He then explained to them how the mountain and the ground beneath them was constantly emitting ultrasonic waves.

"But if the waves are coming from all directions, how can we possibly make sense of them?" Etmook asked. "The ground readers can only -."

"Etmook, your eyes can see using light coming from all directions and your sonic ear can hear sounds coming from multiple directions.

Our brains are far more sophisticated than the ground readers. Now, please, no more academic questions," Orook explained.

Slowly, Orook guided them to different locations and explained in detail how to interpret what they were hearing. He promised them that if they did this enough, an ancient and dormant part of their brains would come back to life. Once alive, that part of the brain would link their visual cortex with their second inner ear and they would literally be able to see through the snow and at least a short distance into the ground beneath.

The men, of course, had their doubts; but they trusted Orook unequivocally. They knew that Orook never used or needed a ground reader to travel even the most precarious areas on and around the mountain. This fact had contributed to his almost mythic status among the youngest of the engineers. If Orook was willing to teach them this extraordinary skill, they were certainly willing to learn.

CHAPTER 10

Meanwhile, Maria and Maddie strolled through the District Center Two at a leisurely pace. Maddie first took Maria to the garment depot, where an attendant took her measurements and a list of everything she required. He then asked her to wave her armband over a scanner on the counter. Maria was then told that all her new clothes would be delivered to her home within the next 30 hours. As they walked out of the depot, Maria said to Maddie, "Well, that was easy!"

Maddie laughed and said, "too easy, right?"

"Shopping could never be too easy for me," Maria told her.

"You're not like other new arrivals," Maddie remarked. "You didn't ask to try anything on - and you didn't ask about jewelry."

"Is there jewelry?" Maria asked.

"Yes, but not the way you might have had it on Earth," Maddie said. "Jewelry here is always handmade and personal - not something you pick up from a depot. A lot of the companions like to make necklaces and bracelets and exchange them among each other. This planet is full of stones which would be considered rare and precious on Earth but are just shiny gravel here."

"Orook told me that there are art depots," Maria said.

"Yep. There is one in this district center," Maddie told her. "Would you like to see it?"

"Sure," said Maria.

Maria was surprised when, upon entering the art depot, a human woman dressed in a pale shade of lemon yellow, trimmed with a darker shade of yellow, greeted them warmly and introduced herself as Clara.

"You work here?" Maria asked.

"Yes, I do," Clara confirmed.

"I thought human women aren't allowed to work," Maria said.

"Who told you that?" Maddie asked.

"Orook told me that we are not allowed to do anything important," she said.

"Oh, well, that is sort of true," Maddie conceded. "We are not allowed to work in any position above the fifth level."

"I'm a sixth level artist," Clara told them.

"That's cool," Maria said idly as she began walking around the depot, looking at different paintings and sculptures on display.

"Let me know if you want to take anything home," Clara said cheerfully.

"Oh, I don't know if I have a quota for art," Maria said.

"I can check for you," Clara offered. "Just come over here and wave your armband over the reader."

After Maria did as Clara instructed, Clara told her that she could take just about anything she wanted.

"Your keeper must not be too fond of art," she said. "He has only taken three drawings by second and third level artists over the past forty years."

"Does the level of the artist matter?" Maria asked.

"Yes, it does," Clara said "Each Pegasean, or his companion, is only allowed to take one work by the First Artist - that's one in a lifetime. They are allowed to take one by a second level artist every five years, one by a third level artist every year... and, well, you get the idea. There is no limit on how many works by a sixth level artist you can take home."

Maria nodded as she resumed looking around the depot.

"Why are some of the works by 'anonymous' artists?" Maria asked.

"That's a long story," Clara said.

"I would love to hear it," Maria said with a coaxing smile.

"Well, alright, if you are going to twist my arm," Clara said with mock exasperation. "There is this one human woman who is very, very good. There is a high demand for her work. This created a bit of a problem because, well, like I just said, there is no limit on how many works by a Sixth Artist a person can take. The city promoted her to

Fifth Artist, but that didn't solve the problem because the quota for work by a fifth level artist is pretty high - like two every lunar cycle. It got to the point where there would be people waiting outside the depot doors in the morning, pushing and shoving each other to be the first inside. It was pretty disgraceful. The city wouldn't stand for it."

"So, what happened?" Maria asked.

"Well, the city couldn't promote her any higher, because she's human. So, then the First Artist had the idea to start accepting anonymous work from low ranking artists who believed their work to be of a quality above their station. He announced to all of the artists that he would accept these anonymous works, judge their level, then release them to the depots as works by 'anonymous Third Artist' or 'anonymous Second Artist.' Of course, Sofia was the only artist who had any reason to do this."

"Is that the human artist's name - Sofia?" Maria asked.

Clara nodded.

"Does it bother her that she can't be promoted beyond the fifth level?" Maria asked.

"I don't think so," Clara said. "I never asked her, but I don't see why she would care. Her keeper is a Second Biologist, so it's not like she doesn't enjoy a higher status by proxy anyway. And she is the only 'anonymous' artist, so everyone knows her work - assuming they wouldn't be able to recognize it otherwise anyway."

"I see," Maria said.

"Who did this one?" Maria asked, pointing to a small painting of a snowman.

"Oh, that's one of mine," Clara said, blushing. "I'm not very good, I know."

Maria looked at the snowman and smiled. The snowman's arms and carrot nose were turned up towards a dark winter sky. Fluffy fat snowflakes swirled around the snowman, as if the wind was blowing them in wide circles around him, or as if the frosty man was dancing with them. The snowman looked so joyful that it made Maria smile. Clara was right though; the painting was not very "good" from a technical perspective. Regardless, Maria wanted it. It made her feel happy and reminded her of home.

"May I take this?" Maria asked, pointing to the snowman.

"Of course!" Clara said. "I will have it delivered to your house."

After Clara completed the transaction using Maria's armband, Maddie and Maria left the art depot. As they were leaving, Maria noticed a small wood carving on display on a shelf near the door. It looked to Maria as if it was carved from the same type of wood which Orook had identified as orconean blue wood. As they walked out the depot door and back into the main body of the District Center, Maria asked Maddie about the orconean blue tree and why the wood was so difficult to obtain.

"The trees grow at high altitudes on the mountains around here, but that is not the problem. The problem is that when the tree is injured, it does something which makes any Pegasean in the immediate vicinity suddenly feel overwhelmingly depressed and frightened. It also makes them hallucinate. It's really bad - or so I've been told. Any Pegasean who experiences it will never go anywhere near a living orconean blue tree again." Maddie explained.

"Why don't they just wear a mask or something?" Maria asked.

"I'm not sure, but I think it's because you can't just filter out whatever it is the tree releases. My keeper says it's not a chemical at all. He thinks the tree emits an electromagnetic pulse that screws with the Pegasean brain. He says that would explain why it doesn't happen after the tree is dead," Maddie told her.

"How fascinating," Maria said. "Does it affect us the same way?"

"It has an effect, but it's not the same for us," Maddie told her.

"How is it different?" she asked.

"Honestly, I don't know," Maddie said. "All I know is that there was this one woman who happened to be around when her keeper, who is a guardsman, accidently cut the trunk of one of those trees with his moon blade. She went completely nuts for about two weeks - kept babbling nonsense about the mountain and someone, or something, being held prisoner in the mountain. She eventually recovered though."

"Wow, that is really weird," Maria said.

Maddie nodded. She then took Maria to a few more depots to get essentials like a toothbrush and other toiletries. As she did, she explained to Maria how to tell the different between shampoo and toothpaste, and other important information. When they were done, Maddie took Maria to one of the vending machines that dispensed food and beverages.

"Oh god, please no," Maria said. "I don't think I can stomach anymore borcula Egg smoothies. I think I would rather eat the toothpaste."

Maddie laughed, then asked, "Is that all your keeper has given you?"

Maria nodded.

"Wow, he really is an asshole - no offense," said Maddie.

"None taken," Maria said.

"That is the worst food here. I mean, sure, it's supposed to be really healthy and good for you, but it's disgusting. This stuff is not so bad though," Maddie said and handed Maria a rectangular block of what might have passed for a vegan brownie. Maria eyed the thing warily before deciding to taste it. Her new friend was right, it was not nearly as bad as the borcula egg milkshake. It would be a stretch to say it tasted good, but it was at least tolerable. The two women sat at a table under a tree and "enjoyed" their selpuna cakes.

"Have you ever seen a vocunine?" Maria asked Maddie.

"Several times," Maddie told her.

"What are they like?" she asked.

"They're just big talking dogs," Maddie told her. "The keepers want us to think they are these big vicious beasts, but they're not. I mean, yeah, I know they sometimes kill a Pegasean on the surface, but sometimes dogs kill people. They really aren't as bad as the keepers say they are."

"My keeper says they can hold weapons," Maria said.

"I've never seen one with a weapon," Maddie scoffed.

"What do you do when you see one? I mean, what are we supposed to do?" Maria asked.

"Just pretend it's a big friendly dog and it will act like a big friendly dog," Maddie instructed. "You know, pet it, scratch behind its ears. If it doesn't go away, throw a stick."

"Seriously?" Maria asked.

70

Maddie nodded.

"Why do you think the vocunine consider us sacred? My keeper says no one knows why," Maria said.

"Well, I guess no one knows for sure, but there are theories. One theory is that, when the vocunines read the mind of a woman from Earth, they see her memories of her pet dog back home - and since they don't know what a dog is, they assume the woman is remembering a vocunine who worshiped her. Pullmoo is not convinced of that theory though."

"Who is Pullmoo?" Maria asked.

"She is the First Sociologist," Maddie said. "She really is like the president. She is the most powerful of all the Firsts. She is also the one who matches all the companions with keepers."

"Will I ever meet her?" Maria asked.

"Maybe at some point," Maddie said. "Your keeper is First Engineer, so he does occasionally have reason to meet with her - but I don't know if that means you will ever meet her."

Maria only nodded at this. After deducing that Pullmoo must have been the one who ordered the Intake Hall staff to euthanize her, she did not have any interest in meeting the woman.

After they finished their lunch, Maddie took Maria to the exercise yard and explained that they were required to exercise four days out of six, and to practice basic self-defense. She told Maria that they also had to take a fitness test at least once a year and that all the women hate it because it is difficult and unforgiving. Maddie then took Maria to the sparring yard, where the Pegasean men did their required hour a day of combat practice. She invited Maria to sit on a bench along the wall and watch.

"They used to have to fight a lot - when there were threats from other Olroneans from the outside. Now they only have to fight the vocunines," Maddie explained.

Maria watched several pairs of men sparring with long wooden poles. One of the men in the pair closest to the wall was wearing dark emerald green and the man he was sparring with was wearing a lighter shade of the same color. Another pair, farther off, were sparring with much more vigor and were wearing all white uniform and a red vest.

"Who are the men in white?" Maria asked. "Why do they have such low status?"

"They don't," said Maddie. "Those are surface guards. They have to wear white in the winter, as camouflage in the snow. The red vests tell you they are guards."

"Oh," said Maria. "Who are the guys in the emerald green?"

"They're presenters," Maddie said. "That's why they're just going through the motions. They know they will never go beyond the outer wall of the City. They're still competent, but their hearts aren't in it - you can tell, right?"

Maria nodded, then asked, "What are presenters?"

"They are like lawyers I guess. But they almost never take sides - they just present. There are no real trials here, not the way there are on Earth anyway. When something happens or when someone does something wrong, the presenters do an investigation and present evidence, facts and witnesses to the applicable Council. The Council then decides what to do," Maddie explained.

"Does that actually work?" Maria asked.

"I guess so," Maddie said. "Sometimes they do take sides, but only when the Council itself is divided. If the Council is divided on what happened, or what should be done about it, then they get two presenters to make presentations; one presenting in support of one view, another in support of the other. When that happens, then it starts to look a little like a trial on Earth. It's still called a 'hearing' though."

"Are there courtrooms?" Maria asked.

"Not really. They have large rooms like lecture halls. That is where the hearings are conducted," Maddie told her.

Maria was about to ask another question when Maddie yawned and told her that it was time for her mid-day nap. She was also starting to feel tired and agreed that it seemed about time to return home.

• • •

The next two lunar cycles were rather uneventful for Maria. She went to the exercise yard almost every day. She went to defense class and practiced what she was taught. At home, she spent many hours just lying on her bed staring up at the sky through the crystal ceiling, pretending she was back home on a park lawn or beach somewhere. When the silence and loneliness threatened to drive her mad with grief and longing to go home, she read. She read about Pegasea and her new home planet. Occasionally, but not often, she walked down the streets and looked for other women with whom to socialize. She often looked for Maddie but could never seem to find her. Sometimes she wandered the streets all day, not looking for anyone or anything in particular. On more than one occasion, she got lost and had to use her homing beckon to get home. Maria rarely saw Orook during this time. When she did see him, he looked exhausted and did not usually want to talk. More often than not, he simply came home and went straight to bed. When he did speak to her, it was usually to tell her to do something, or not to do something, or that she was doing something wrong. It got to the point where she tried to avoid him altogether, which was not difficult, considering how little time he spent at home.

CHAPTER 11

O ne cold winter morning, Maria awoke to a noise coming from one of her wristbands. The wristband was vibrating and softly pinging some kind of alarm. She looked up and saw a dark night sky untainted by even the threat of dawn. Concerned, and a little alarmed, she stepped outside her enclave to find Orook standing just outside her room. The sudden sight of him startled her.

"I need you to come to the surface with me. I am going up to a cave in the mountains. This is very dangerous because if a vocunine traps me in that cave, it will most likely kill me. I need a human woman to stand outside the cave entrance and keep watch. Do you think you can do that?" he asked.

"What time is it?" Maria asked.

"Look at your wristband," Orook said.

Maria looked down at her wristband and saw that it was not even seven hours into the new day. After doing the calculation in her mind, she figured that the current time in Pegasea was something like the equivalent of 5:30 A.M. on Earth.

"Are you still converting to Earth time in your head?" Orook asked.

"No," Maria lied.

"Do not lie to me. It is cowardly and counterproductive - and gravely insulting to me. Also, you are exceptionally bad at it," he said.

"Why do you say I'm bad at it?" she asked.

"Because you blink excessively when you lie," Orook told her.

"Ok, fine, yes, I still convert to Earth time in my head," Maria said, annoyed. It was way too early in the morning for this kind of banter.

"Well, stop," he said. "You need to become fluent in our time."

"Ok, ok," Maria said with a yawn.

Orook looked at her as if she was a defective pet.

Seeing his expression, Maria's face flushed with a combination of shame and anger.

Orook took a deep breath and tried again.

"Maria, listen to me. I need you to come with me into the mountain. I need you to keep watch while I go into a cave. Do you understand?" he asked in a condescending tone.

"Yes, I get it," Maria snipped.

"When we are out there, you need follow close behind me. You need to step exactly where I step. You must do exactly what I say, Maria. It is not about the PROEs out there. If you do not follow my orders out on the mountain, you could, and probably will, die." Orook told her.

"I understand," she said soberly.

Orook looked at her as if still trying to decide whether or not this was a good idea.

"Are you strong enough for this? Physically, I mean," he asked.

"I think so," Maria said. "I've been doing all the required exercise and defense training for two lunar cycles now."

"Good," he said.

It took Orook at least an hour to get ready to go, then another half hour for him to get Maria ready. They had to put on winterized clothes and wear special boots. They packed up all kinds of equipment, some of which Maria recognized as typical hiking gear and some she had never seen before. Orook wrapped a white scarf around Maria's head, nose, mouth and ears. The last thing they put on were full length white over-coats and gloves.

"When I tell you to, hold on to the loop in the back of my coat, but never ever pull on me unless you want to kill us both. You hold on just to make sure you do not lose track of me, never to keep from falling, do you understand?" Orook asked.

"I do," she said.

When they stepped outside into the open air, Maria was surprised by how well insulated she felt. As they walked, she felt almost warm, but not quite. Maria concentrated hard on following Orook's exact footsteps. She marveled at how he seemed to know where to walk without any signs or equipment to guide him. They walked, and at times climbed, for what felt like hours before they reached the mouth of a narrow cave into the side of a nearly vertical wall of solid stone.

"I need to go in there," Orook said and pointed to the mouth of the cave. "You need to stay here and be on high alert for vocunines. If you see one coming, holler into the cave immediately. Keep constant watch. Look in all directions, but do not follow a pattern. If you get into a pattern of say, looking right to left and back again, they can sneak up on you. So be unpredictable with your watch. That is not as easy as it sounds. You can fall into a pattern without even realizing it."

"I understand," she said.

"Do you, Maria?" Orook asked fiercely. "Because if you fail in this, I could die."

"I understand!" she repeated.

Orook took a deep breath. He seemed hesitant to enter the cave.

"I can do this," she said.

This reassurance did not comfort Orook much, but he went into the cave anyway. Maria did as she was instructed and kept a constant watch, which she actively varied so she would not get into a pattern. Unfortunately, it was not enough. Just as she was looking left, a vocunine dropped down and landed at her right, as if the animal had fallen from the sky. Maria, startled by the vocunine's sudden appearance, jumped, then quickly regained control of herself. She took one long stride to put herself between the vocunine and the mouth of the cave. She then hollered to Orook to warn him. When Orook did not respond, Maria hollered again.

"Don't worry dear angel. I know the man in there," the vocunine said casually, as if he and Orook were old friends.

The animal looked so much like a dog from Earth that Maria was stunned to hear it speak. She noticed, with some relief, that the animal's tail was wagging, and that it appeared to be smiling at her. When it cocked its head to look at her, the gesture was so strikingly similar to the way her own dog on Earth used to look at her, that Maria felt home sick. Unconsciously, she reached out her hand to pet the beast, then quickly pulled back. She did not know if Maddie was entirely right about these creatures. While it looked harmless, friendly even, Maria felt something else emanating from the creature. Was it malice or just hunger? Maria could not be sure, but whatever it was, it made her gut ache and her heart pound.

"Don't be scared my lovely, I would never hurt one of you," said the beast, "and please, I would be honored if you pet me."

Something told Maria not to pet the vocunine. She remembered Orook's warning, back on the day she first met him, not to mistake these beings for dogs. And yet Maddie had told her that this is what they wanted. Torn with indecision, Maria stood statuesque with her hand outstretched half way between herself and the vocunine.

As if the animal could read her mind, it said "you are afraid for your man in there. You should be."

At hearing the animal confirm her fear, Maria's blood went cold and she recoiled even further. Slowly, the vocunine approached her. It then gently pushed its huge head against her ribs and began moving her aside.

"Stop!" Maria shouted. "You must not go in there!"

The sudden strength of the woman's voice gave the vocunine pause.

"Why not?" it asked.

"This is a sacred place," said Maria with authority. "This is not just a cave, it is a passage into the soul of this mountain. If you spill blood inside, you will disgrace and defile the mountain and your soul will be marred for all eternity. If you kill the man inside the cave, you will never be admitted to heaven."

The vocunine looked up at her as if it only understood half of the words she had just said. Then, after staring at her for a long time, it slowly backed away.

"Thank you for warning me my angel," said the beast. "I will kill the man out here."

Maria did not much like the idea of that either, but at least Orook would not be cornered at the end of a dark narrow cave. Just as she was about to issue yet another warning to her keeper, Orook bolted out from behind Maria and away from the mouth of the cave.

As soon as the vocunine saw Orook, it changed. Maria watched in stunned fascination and horror as the animal's long hackles slowly rose, its lips curled, its eyes narrowed, and its stance widened. It was like watching a man turn into a wolf under a full moon, except that instead of starting out as a man, the beast had started out as a friendly looking Siberian husky. The change was none-the-less just as drastic and terrifying.

The vocunine growled maliciously at Orook, who stood motionless next to the mouth of the cave. Maria looked from her keeper to the vocunine, then back again. Slowly, she stepped between them. She then took hold of the side of Orook's coat so that she could hold on to him while remaining between him and the angry beast. Orook then began to walk along the side of the rock face, heading back to the City along the same path they had come. As they walked, the vocunine paced menacingly alongside them. Maria noticed that while Orook was remarkably sure footed on this terrain, the skill of the vocunine was on a whole other level. The beast practically danced alongside them, never once looking down at the ground.

"Why do you hide behind your guardian? Don't you want to face me? We have a score to settle you and me," the vocunine snarled at Orook.

Maria wondered how it was possible for the creature to growl and speak at the same time.

"You killed my father. Then you killed my wife. She had just had cubs. Three of them. They were still pink with her blood when you slaughtered her," the vocunine said to Orook.

If any of the vocunine's words had any impact on Orook, Maria could not see it. Her keeper only continued to walk steadily forward, as if he could not hear the vocunine's accusations.

"They died because of you - all three of them. It is not fair that you only had one child for me to kill," the animal whined.

For an instant, Orook's step faltered.

"I ate him you know," said the vocunine. "I... tore... him... apart. I relished every chunk of flesh and splinter of bone. Then I licked his blood off the snow."

Orook suddenly stopped and Maria jolted to a halt. She looked up at him expectantly.

"Obviously, this animal wants desperately to die," he whispered to her.

Orook then turned to the vocunine and said, "You must first allow me to make the woman safe. Then, I will face you, over there." He pointed to a tree off about 300 meters from the side of the mountain. After the vocunine nodded in agreement, Orook lifted Maria up by her waist and sat her on an outward reaching cleft of stone.

"Stay put," he told her. "The ground may change, but you will be safe up there. Just sit tight."

Trying not to panic, Maria quickly asked him what he was going to do and how she would get home.

"Relax, even if by some stroke of dumb luck he manages to kill me out there, he will not hurt you. In fact, he would probably help you get back to the City," Orook explained quickly. He was gone before Maria had a chance to respond.

As soon as Orook left Maria safely perched on a stable cleft of rock, he began speaking to his vocunine challenger in Pegasean. It didn't matter what he said, he just needed to keep talking. The only way he could prevent the vocunine from seeing his mind was to keep speaking aloud in his native tongue. So, he talked to the beast as he pulled what amounted to a small taser from his inside coat pocket. He told the vocunine that, at the time he killed his wife, he had not known she had just given birth, or that she was just protecting her cubs when she attacked.

"Stop talking," the vocunine said. "I can't tell if you're lying when you just keep talking."

Orook stopped talking to let the animal see the truth in his mind. Unfortunately, the vocunine saw more of the truth than Orook had intended. He saw the truth of Orook's words, but also the truth of the fact that even if Orook had known about the cubs, he would have killed their mother anyway. Enraged, the vocunine flew at Orook. Orook managed to leap out of his path in time but stumbled and fell back onto a large crystal bolder sheathed in ice and silt. That was alright though. This was the boulder Orook had wanted to find. It was composed of the perfect sort of crystal for what he needed to do.

Maria, who saw Orook fall, cried out. She pleaded with the vocunine to leave the man alone. Hearing her plea, the animal paused to consider what Maria might be trying to communicate to him. It did not take long for him to determine that her concern was no longer for his soul, but only for the life of the Pegasean man he was about to kill. This did not surprise the vocunine. As messengers from heaven, the sacred women from Earth were kind and compassionate creatures. He lamented having to kill this man in front of her.

"You know what I hate most about your kind?" Orook asked, as he covertly felt around the boulder for an exposed patch of crystal. "You are too emotional. What great loss is it to you if you lose a few cubs? Your women can give birth to several kids at a time. And you have no shortage of females either. How special could any particular one of them possibly be?"

At this the vocunine stood up on its back legs and uncurled its front paws. Orook found what he was looking for just in time. He dropped his ears out of their ultrasonic range and touched the taser to an exposed patch of crystal. As soon as he did this, the boulder erupted in sound that now only the vocunine could hear. All Maria heard was a series of faint clicking noises. What the vocunine heard was the equivalent of a jet engine starting at full throttle less than a meter away. It so startled and disoriented the animal that it fell over and whined miserably. He turned away from Orook and scrambled away from the source of his misery. Orook stood up and pursued the vocunine, watching and waiting for him to make a fatal error. The sudden burst of ultrasonic waves essentially blinded the vocunine to the precarious terrain beneath him. His back legs fell to opposite side of an exposed stone. Moving quickly, Orook locked both hands together and struck down hard on the rump of the animal, shattering its pelvic bone against the hard stone beneath. The animal howled in agony but could do nothing. It was helpless now. Without pity, Orook waited a moment to make sure the vocunine was completely disabled. He then turned away and walked back to Maria.

"What have you done?" she said, staring at the limping, whining animal Orook had left to die.

"What does it look like?" Orook said bitterly.

"You can't just leave him like that," Maria said.

Orook did not answer. He only reached up and pulled her down off the stone.

"Walk behind me now," he instructed.

"Keeper, please, I beg you, don't just leave him there like that," Maria pleaded.

"What exactly do you want me to do? Call for a rescue crew?" Orook scowled. "And then what? Should we treat it for its wounds and release it back out onto the mountain - so that it can try to kill me another day?"

"No, of course not," Maria said. "But look at him, he's suffering terribly. What if it takes him days to die?"

Orook gritted his teeth. Maria saw the thought in his mind. She saw that Orook could have killed him outright but had chosen not to. Orook wanted the animal to suffer.

"You told me that the Pegaseans are a kind and gentle people," she whispered.

Orook sighed and stopped walking. He looked down at the ground around Maria's feet and assessed its stability.

"Stay here," he instructed. "Do not take a single step, just stand right where you are."

Orook then made his way back to the dying vocunine. It was slowly crawling its way back to the mountain, scraping its abdomen along the rocks and dragging its back legs behind it.

"Come to finish me off have you?" hissed the animal.

"If you would like, yes," Orook said.

"I can see in your mind that the angel has shamed you," said the vocunine.

"They do not know you the way we know you." Orook countered.

"You know nothing," he growled.

"Then why do the Earth women live with us and not you?" Orook challenged.

"You are holding them captive," said the vocunine.

"And how does one hold an angel captive?" Orook asked.

The animal looked up at Orook and sneered, "with love and lies and dark magic."

"Do you want me to put you out of your misery or not?" Orook asked.

"I want to die in the cave, inside the mountain," the vocunine said.

"Am I supposed to wait while you crawl your way back there?" Orook asked coldly.

The vocunine did not respond. He only kept crawling towards the cave.

"I do not have time to wait. The human woman will die from cold if we get stuck out here after dark. You know that." Orook told him.

"Go then," said the vocunine.

Orook looked down at the wounded animal and felt a pang of guilt. Then remembered what had led him to confront the animal in the first place.

"Are you really the one who killed my son?" Orook asked. "Or did you just say that to provoke me?"

"Does it matter now?" the animal asked.

"Yes," Orook said.

"Yes, I killed him. It was my right to kill him. You killed three of mine when you killed their mother," the beast told him.

Orook grit his teeth, pulled out a knife, and drove it through the animal's heart. He then wiped the blade clean against the fur on its back. When he returned to Maria, he did not tell her what happened, and she did not ask.

CHAPTER 12

O nce they were safely back at home and comfortably warm and dry in their everyday clothes, Orook sat down on the sofa in the living room. Maria stood halfway between the living room and the bedroom, unsure of whether or not she should join him. She wanted to go back to her room, but something told her that would be rude. Unable to decide, she stood fidgeting with her shirt sleeves and occasionally shifting her weight from foot to foot.

"Maria, what are you doing?" Orook asked, annoyed with her nervous bird-like movements. When she failed to respond, he politely asked her to sit down or leave the room.

"Did I do the right thing? I mean, I know he snuck up on me, but I don't know how. I did exactly what you said," Maria blurted.

"You did fine," he said.

The affirmation helped calm Maria.

"How did you manage to lie to the vocunine?" Orook asked. "They can read minds."

"I didn't lie," Maria told him. "In that moment, I genuinely believed that if he had killed you in that cave, his soul would be tarnished - because it would not have been a fair fight."

Orook nodded and said, "well done." He then gestured for her to sit down. She sat in the armchair positioned cattycorner to the opposite end of the sofa from where Orook was seated.

"How old was your son when you lost him?" Maria asked.

"He was only 25 Olronean years old - which is roughly the same age in human Earth years," Orook told her. "I had only just met him about two lunar cycles earlier. We are not permitted to meet our children until they turn 25. It felt like an eternity, waiting for his 25th birthday. And when it finally came, I was so happy and so proud - as if he had been laid in my arms as a newborn that day."

"I'm so sorry," Maria whispered.

"And yet you shamed me into providing his killer with a quick and painless death," Orook said bitterly.

Maria tensed in her seat and resumed fidgeting with her arm bands.

Seeing her reaction, he said, "I am sorry. That is not fair. It was my choice - and you were right. Cruelty serves no noble purpose."

"I understand though," she said. "If it had been my child, maybe I would want to be cruel too."

They sat in awkward silence until Orook said, "I have another son, he is 5 and lives in the nursery."

"How old are you?" Maria asked.

"I am 75. But you have to understand how Pegaseans age. We come of age only a bit more slowly than humans. We are considered adults at 25 and fully matured by 35. We then stop aging altogether until we reach about 350, give or take a decade. After that, we age rapidly, then die within 5 years. That is the way it will be for you now too. At the Intake Hall, you were introduced to the same viruses that prolong our lives by interrupting the aging process. However old you are now, you will not age again until the last few years of your life," Orook explained.

The idea of that was too much for Maria to get her head around. She could not imagine living even 100 years.

"Why aren't you allowed to see your children until they are adults?" she asked.

"The Central Council determined that the primary source of discordance among Pegaseans was rooted in subtle differences in values and views held by individuals, and that these differences either arose or cemented in childhood. The Council then decided that all children should be raised together, in the same place, by the same people, and taught the same views and values. It was also determined that raising all the children together would make the most efficient use of resources. Lastly, this method of child rearing prevents the Pegasean mothers from showing favoritism towards one or a few of their many children. As you can imagine, no woman with fifty children could possibly love them all equally. The sociologists found that a child's awareness of his mother's favor, or lack thereof, was psychologically damaging all around," Orook told her.

"Ok, but...," Maria started to protest before Orook stopped her.

"I do not like it either. I can tell you that here, in the privacy of our home, but you must never repeat it outside these walls. Understood?" he said.

"Yes," Maria confirmed, then said, "May I ask, who is the mother of your sons?"

Orook closed his eyes and let out a long breath.

"I'm sorry, never mind, I shouldn't have..." Maria stammered.

"No, you committed no offense," Orook assured her. "I am not upset with you or the question. This is simply not an easy thing for me to talk about. I do not have much time left with her. Her name is Linoo. She is a Second Sociologist and the governess of our District. We are at the end of our term. I suspect she will formally terminate our partnership before the next lunar cycle."

"Is that why I was paired with you?" Maria asked, avoiding his eyes.

"Almost certainly," Orook said.

"But it's not the same, is it? I mean, I still don't get what this relationship is supposed to be exactly, but I'm pretty sure I'm not supposed to be that kind of partner," she said.

When Orook saw her blushing, he smiled faintly and said, "No, you are not supposed to be that kind of partner, but you do soften the blow of sudden loneliness. I am sorry you were taken from your home planet, then threatened with death. All the same, I am glad you are here."

Maria knew the polite thing to say would be that she was happy to be here. But the truth was that "happy" was probably not the right word. If she could have gone back home that very second, she would have. She missed her dog and her old bed. She missed coffee and real food. She missed a lot of things. On the other hand, she did not have to worry about paying back her student loans anymore - and at least that was something. Also, she was on another planet, with aliens, talking dogs, and giant crystal mountains. She could not deny that it was all rather exciting.

"This is a fascinating place and you're a very interesting man," was the best she could come up with to say.

"Thank you for being polite," he said. "I do hope that you will come to enjoy yourself here."

Maria nodded, but was doubtful.

CHAPTER 13

The Pegasean week consisted of six days; five work days and one social day. Under the Pegasean Rules of Order and Etiquette, Pegasean men are expected to spend most of their social days with their partners or companions. Men without partners or companions are expected to congregate with each other and interact socially, doing anything other than work. Orook usually worked on social days anyway or spent them with Linoo. On the social day following Maria and Orook's trip to the mountain cave, Orook finally took the time to explain all of this to Maria.

"It's ok. Go see Linoo. I don't mind," Maria said cheerfully.

"I was not asking for your permission," Orook clipped.

Maria's face turned red with anger and embarrassment. Seeing this, Orook tried to be more gracious.

"Thank you, though," he added. "I appreciate your understanding."

Maria took the platitude for what it was worth and wished him well. Truthfully, she did not enjoy the thought of spending an entire day in his company. It was not that she did not like him. She just could not seem to relax around him. He was too rigid. There were too many rules to remember.

"If you would like, you may come with me," Orook suggested.

Maria's eyes went wide.

"Let me clarify. You may come with me to her door, introduce yourself, and then go off on your own to a companion lounge or something. You should get out of this apartment every once in a while. Today is a social day. You should do something social," he explained.

Maria agreed to his suggestion and went with him to Linoo's home. She was curious about Linoo and wanted to meet her. When Linoo opened the door to them, Maria's jaw dropped just enough to be conspicuous. Linoo was the most beautiful woman Maria had ever seen in life or in pictures. Linoo's long white hair framed a face with high cheek bones and baby blue eyes that lit up when she smiled. The governess was draped in a dark lavender dress and stood with a poise and elegance which was completely foreign to Maria.

"It is rude to stare," Orook chided.

Maria blinked, then held out her hand and said, "I'm so sorry. My name is Maria."

Orook pushed her hand back down to her side, then made a circular movement with his hand, prompting her to finish her introduction.

"Oh, sorry, my name is Maria and I'm the first companion's engineer... I mean, I'm the First Engineer's companion. No, wait..."

Linoo burst out laughing, which only made her more beautiful and more distracting.

Orook put his hand to his forehead and sighed.

"It's ok, sweetheart," Linoo said. "I know who you are, and I am delighted to meet you."

Maria looked at Orook, then to Linoo, then back again.

"What am I supposed to say now?" she asked Orook in a whisper.

Orook closed his eyes and said, "Just make the second gesture of respect."

"The second?" Maria asked.

"It's ok, Orook. Let her go. We have other things to do," Linoo said with a sly wink.

Orook looked at Maria and said, "Never mind, just go before you inadvertently insult her."

"Thank you," Maria said, and was happy to leave them.

"I swear Pullmoo matched me with her out of spite," Orook said after greeting Linoo with a kiss.

Linoo shook her head slowly as she pulled Orook towards her until his body was flush with hers. She pushed a strand of his hair behind one ear and tenderly stroked his cheek.

"I'm going to miss you after today," she said with genuine regret.

"Me too," Orook said with a much deeper sadness.

• • •

While Orook and Linoo enjoyed their last day together as partners, Maria traveled back towards her home street. She decided to walk rather than take the subrail, so that she could explore more of her district. As she walked, she noticed a companion lounge about a kilometer from home. Through the lounge's large windows, Maria saw Maddie sitting inside. She picked up her pace, excited to see a familiar face. She slowed down when she noticed that Maddie appeared to be crying. She was sitting crumpled in a chair with her face buried in her hands. Maria then suddenly felt a brush against her shoulder as Etmook flew past her towards the lounge. Maria watched as Etmook rushed to Maddie and fell to his knees in front of her. She saw Etmook gently pull Maddie's hands from her face. He spoke quietly to her at first, then more loudly. Maria ducked behind a support beam closer to the lounge and tried to hear what they were saying.

"Maddie, you're my wife and I love you. I don't care what the City says about us. We are partners forever," Etmook told her. "Why do you think I made us those rings?"

"We're just pretending to be," Maddie argued. "We're not really."

"Oh? Then why have I never partnered with a Pegasean woman? You don't think they want me? Do you not see how handsome I am?" He said, trying to make her smile.

"You *are* pretty cute," Maddie said, still sniffling.

"Cute? I'm gorgeous!" he said and tossed back his hair with exaggerated vanity.

Maddie laughed and wiped her eyes with her sleeve.

"I only want you Maddie," he said. "Whatever is wrong with your ears, I don't care, ok?"

"You won't let them take me away?" Maddie asked.

"Never!" Etmook said.

"What if you can't stop them?" Maddie asked.

"Oh, I can stop them," he said with a smile. "I run the entire security grid. I could let in every vocunine on the mountain. I could lock everyone in their bathrooms. I could…"

"Ok, ok, shhh," Maddie said, hushing him with her finger and a smile. "Someone will hear you. And there are no locks on the bathrooms."

"Well, then I'll put locks on all the bathrooms - just in case," he said with a straight face.

"We have to be careful," Maddie cautioned. "We might say a key word that triggers surveillance."

"First of all, I am the one who sets those key words, so I know what they are. Secondly, no one monitors the companion lounges," Etmook said. "They think you humans are all idiots."

"You don't?" Maddie asked.

"How can you even ask me that?" he said. "If I thought you were an idiot, why would I have taught you Pegasean? Or PEG 6? Why would I invite you to help me with my work? Why would I be here on my knees, in a companion lounge, breaking at least 7 different PROEs and 3 AERs, just to beg you to come home?"

Maria saw Maddie look up and scan the street outside the lounge. A moment later, Maddie looked back down at Etmook and smiled as he whispered something into her ear. Maria then watched in disbelief as she saw Maddie and Etmook embrace and kiss as if they were both going off to war. As if they both suddenly felt Maria's eyes on them, Maddie and Etmook turned and saw Maria staring at them from behind the stone pillar across the street.

"Oh no," Maddie said. "I think we've been caught."

"I better go," Etmook said.

"Don't worry. I'll talk to her," Maddie reassured him.

"Please do," Etmook said, wide eyed. "If I have to go through remedial PROEs training again, I swear Maddie, I'll put a fucking poison dart in my eye."

Maddie laughed loudly at this, then waved enthusiastically to Maria.

Maria entered the companion lounge just as Etmook was leaving. Etmook nodded cordially to Maria as he passed.

"I thought men weren't allowed in the companion lounges." Maria said.

"They're not," Maddie said flippantly. "Etmook is just a bit of a rebel."

"I thought rebellion was frowned upon here." Maria said.

Maddie's shoulders dropped. She frowned as she said, "Yeah, it is."

"It's ok," Maria said quickly. "I didn't mean it like that. I didn't mean to interrogate you. I'm just surprised is all."

Maddie looked pleadingly at her.

"I swear I won't tell anyone!" Maria said. "Who would I tell anyway?"

"Um, maybe your keeper, his boss," Maddie suggested.

"We don't have that kind of relationship," Maria said. "He held my hand once - but I'm pretty sure that was only to keep me from getting lost in the District Center."

"Really?" Maddie asked, not sounding terribly surprised.

Maria nodded.

"Well, most keepers and companions aren't like me and Etmook. You shouldn't compare yourselves to us. We're outliers. In fact, if anyone knew the way we are with each other, we might be separated," Maddie said.

"You can trust me," Maria said. "In fact, it's nice to see that at least one of these guys is sorta normal."

Maddie smiled and allowed herself to relax.

"Did Etmook say he made you rings?" Maria asked. She wanted to ask Maddie why she had apparently escaped to the lounge to cry, but she did not want to pry.

Maddie smiled, "Yeah, he did."

"May I see yours?" Maria asked.

Maddie looked down at her hands, which appeared to be completely unadorned. She then rubbed the hem of her sleeve at the base of her ring finger until a ring slowly became visible. She held up her hand to show Maria.

"Whoa!" said Maria. "That is really cool."

"It's some kind of special material Rose's keeper invented. It's perfectly translucent from all angles. So, it's pretty much invisible. But if you apply friction to it, like I just did, it becomes visible for a few minutes," Maddie explained. She then hid the ring under her other hand until it became invisible again.

"Why would the city not want you and your keeper to be in love? Or get married?" Maria asked.

Maddie shook her head. "We're not supposed to be romantic with each other or treat each other like equals. That's not what companions are supposed to be."

"I see," Maria said.

"It's not what you think though. It's not a gender thing. It's a species thing. The dozen or so human men here don't have it much better. They're kept in some secluded part of the City and are only here to produce sperm to impregnate companions with baby girls, who will be raised to be companions for the next generation. Don't get me wrong. I'm sure they're not mistreated or anything. I'm just saying, our diminished status isn't because we're women - it's because we're human."

"I know," Maria said with a sigh.

"I'm sorry you're stuck with a lousy keeper," Maddie whispered.

"He's really not all bad," Maria said. "I think he tries to be nice - at least sometimes. It's hard though. There are just too many rules. Most of the time I just try to avoid him, so I don't have to worry about accidently offending him or violating the PROEs in some way. So, I guess it's partly my fault - but how are we supposed to get to know each other if I can't even say his name?"

"Your keeper is particularly fond of the rules," Maddie said absently.

"Not all of them. He really wants to see his son," Maria said before remembering that she was not supposed to share that information.

"I can't believe they don't even get to raise their own children," Maddie said. "It makes me almost glad I'm not Pegasean. I can't imagine having my babies taken from me to be raised in a nursery where I can't even see them until they are adults."

"What about the human babies? the baby girls? Can their mothers see them?" Maria asked.

"The rules are more relaxed in the human nursery because, well, we're not as important," Maddie said. "So yeah, the human mothers can visit their kids in the after-school hours. They can even stay overnight with them sometimes. When they get to be about 17, they can either keep going to school or start doing some kind of simple work. When they turn 25 they are matched with a keeper. Pullmoo does all the matching. But if a match doesn't work out, they can be re-matched until they find a good fit."

"It all sounds so reasonable," Maria said sarcastically.

"You better watch that," Maddie said. "Sarcasm like that is a violation of the PROEs."

"You're one to talk, Mrs. Etmook," Maria said.

"Touché," Maddie said with a smile.

The two women sat in comfortable silence until Maddie asked, "Hey, do you want to hear about a prank Etmook pulled on your keeper?"

"More than anything in the world," Maria said, her eyes bright with intrigue.

"So, one time - I don't remember exactly why - Etmook was really annoyed with him. So, he programed the security zone around your house to pick up the word 'love' as a level 1 key word. That means that, every time your keeper said that word over the intercom, the door to his house would lock. It was brilliant because he was seeing Linoo all the time back then. Every time he talked to Linoo to arrange a date, and ended the call with 'I love you,' his front door would lock, and he couldn't leave the house until security came to let him out," Maddie said.

Maria laughed and asked, "Did he get caught?"

"No, of course not," Maddie said.

"How did he escape getting caught? I would think they could trace that sort of thing," Maria said.

"Normally they can, but I designed a self-terminating programming glitch to do the trick," Maddie said.

"*You* did?" Maria asked, impressed.

"It was nothing," Maddie said. "Their computer system has virtually no protection against malicious code because they just don't need it. I mean, who is going hack into it? -the vocunines? Etmook could have written the worm himself, but he wanted me to learn, so I did."

"There is no threat from the inside? ...or from other of their kind outside?" Maria asked.

"Not anymore - not since the last of the Olroneans outside the city died out. Now there are only pranksters like Etmook. Nothing serious. You have to remember, they are all bred and raised from birth to be good law-abiding citizens," Maddie explained. "Etmook is as rebellious as they get and even he is more talk than anything else."

"I don't think you are giving him enough credit," Maria said.

Maddie shrugged and said, "Etmook loves your keeper like a father, you know. I even think his pranks are, on some level, like a cry for attention."

"It's probably best not to over analyze things like that," Maria advised.

"Yeah, you're probably right," Maddie conceded.

"I wish I could see the nursery," Maria told Maddie.

"No one is allowed in there except the parents and the guards - and sometimes an engineer who needs to get in to fix something." Maddie told her.

"How would that work - with an engineer I mean?" Maria asked.

"One of two ways - either one of the parents or teachers places a work order through the security system, or, the engineer places a request because he received a maintenance alert from a remote monitor," Maddie explained.

"I see," said Maria.

"*Although,*" Maddie continued.

"What?" Maria asked.

"Well, your keeper has technical access to just about everything, everywhere, all the time - because he's First Engineer. When he took you from the intake hall, did he program your training bands to restrict your access?" Maddie asked.

"I don't know," Maria said. "Why?"

"Because when a companion is taken from the Intake Hall, her training bands are initially set to have all the same access as her keeper - so she can go where he goes. That's the default. Keepers with higher levels of access are supposed to manually place restrictions on their companions' training bands. But knowing your keeper, he probably forgot - or just never thought about it," Maddie said excitedly.

Maddie stood up suddenly, then took Maria's hand and led her out of the lounge.

"Where are we going?" Maria asked.

"To my house," Maddie said.

When they arrived at Maddie's house, Maddie waved her own armband over the door and let them in.

"Keeper!" Maddie called out excitedly.

"Ugh, you know I hate when you call me -," Etmook started to say before he looked up and noticed Maria.

"Oh, you have company," he said.

"Don't worry my love. She's cool," Maddie said quickly.

"I am cool," Maria confirmed.

"Well then," he said. "How can I help you ladies?"

"We need you to scan her training bands," Maddie told him. "We want to know if her keeper restricted her access after intake."

"Oooo, this sounds like fun," Etmook said as he walked over to Maria. He took one of her wrists and waved his armband over her training band.

"Well?" Maddie asked eagerly.

"Well, well, well, looks like Maria has the keys to the City on this pretty little bracelet." Etmook said with a smile. "No restrictions."

Maddie clapped her hands together and bounced on the balls of her feet.

"Not so fast, beautiful. Having technical access is fun and all, but there is not much she can do with it," Etmook warned.

"What do you mean?" Maddie asked.

"I mean… where is she going to be able to go without someone immediately knowing she is not supposed to be there?" Etmook asked.

Maddie frowned.

"It's still cool, though" Etmook said, sounding apologetic.

"What about the nursery?" Maria asked.

"Hmm," Etmook said. "You could probably go to the human nursery without any problems. There are companions there all the time seeing their kids. But I don't know about the Pegasean nursery. That might be dangerous. Security is very tight over there. You will be able to get in, but once there, if someone sees you -."

95

"Thanks for the warning," Maria said as she turned to leave.

"Where are you going?" Maddie asked.

"Um, I probably shouldn't say, right?" Maria said.

"Right!" Etmook said as he took Maddie's hand to keep her from following Maria. Maddie did not have to ask why he had stopped her. If Maria really was reckless enough to trespass into the Pegasean nursery, she might find herself in real danger. Maddie tried to warn Maria before she left, but Maria did not seem to be listening.

"Thank you!" was all Maria said before closing the door behind her as she headed out into the street.

CHAPTER 14

After they had made love for what would turn out to be the last time, Orook and Linoo sat in Linoo's bed and held each other as they talked.

"So how is your new companion?" Linoo asked.

"She has some marginal utility as a look-out for vocunine I suppose," Orook said.

"Oh, please stop. You are making me jealous," Linoo said facetiously.

Orook groaned. "Well, what do you want me to say?" he asked.

"Just tell me what she is like - the good things," Linoo said.

"She is sweet and a bit child-like in a nice way. She is full of awe and wonder about everything. She is also eager to please despite her superficial petulance," Orook reported.

"She sounds perfect for you," Linoo said.

"*You* are perfect for me," he said softly as he gently twisted a lock of her hair around his finger.

Linoo shook her head and said, "You would like to think that, but I'm not."

"How so?" he asked.

"You know I don't want to get married. I'm not like your sister. I could never wait 100 years to marry one man. Just the thought alone is depressing," she said.

"Ok, but what I do not understand about our laws is why there has to be a time limit. Why can we not stay partners forever? We have contraceptives for men," Orook thought aloud.

"You know why," Linoo said. "There is only so much time in a day my dear. There are other men waiting. I can't keep hangers-on around for too long."

"Is that what I am?" he asked.

"Oh, Orook, you know I do love you - just not in the way you want me to." Linoo said gently.

"You used to," he whispered.

"That was a long time ago," she said.

Orook started to argue, but Linoo refused to engage.

"Let's talk about something else," she said. "Tell me more about Maria. Something is bothering you about her. That much is obvious. What is it?"

"The woman is terrified of me. She hides in her room all day or darts around the house like a nervous animal. When I try to talk to her she tenses up as if she expects me to throw something at her. It is starting to get on my nerves - and that only makes it worse. Because, apparently, I am even more terrifying when I am annoyed," Orook confessed.

"Well, that much is true. But she should know by now that you aren't going to hurt her, right?" Linoo asked.

"She saw me kill a vocunine the other day. I am sure that did not help." He said.

"Oh, Oroo, why would you do that in front of her?" Linoo asked.

"It was the one who killed our son," he explained.

Linoo nodded approvingly.

"Honestly though, I do not think that is why she is afraid of me. It is something else, but I do not know what it is," Orook said.

"Maybe she's not actually afraid of you. Maybe she is only intimidated by you, and afraid of this whole new world in general," Linoo speculated.

"I suppose that is possible. Either way, she has to lighten up. Her anxiety around me is annoying," he said.

"Maybe you need to let her see another side of you," Linoo suggested.

"Hmm... which side do you prefer?" he asked as he brushed the tip of his nose against her cheek.

"Stay focused, Orook. This is serious," Linoo chided as she playfully batted him away.

"Ok, what do you suggest I do?" he asked.

Linoo leaned back on the wall behind her bed and thought. She tried to remember the first time she had warm feelings for Orook. When it came to her, she smiled.

"Remember when we were both little kids in school and the teacher told us about something on Earth called a 'water fountain?'" she said. "He told us all about these beautiful water fountains that the Earth people build in their District Centers and parks. He showed us pictures too. I was so enchanted by them. I cried when he told us that there were no water fountains in Pegasea."

"I think I remember this," Orook said. "During the exploration period, I built you a small fountain in a crystal bowl."

"I can still see it when I close my eyes. It was beautiful," Linoo said.

"I do not think you are remembering this correctly. It looked more like a malfunctioning toilet," Orook said.

"That is when I fell in love with you," Linoo said, ignoring his alternative account of the model fountain.

"Are you sure? As I recall, it exploded about five minutes after I showed it to you," Orook reminded her.

"It did not explode! It just kind of... fell apart," Linoo said.

"Well, it fell apart with quite a bit of enthusiasm then - so much enthusiasm, in fact, that the table caught fire and the guards were called in," Orook said.

Linoo laughed and said, "That's funny Orook. You're funny. I bet Maria doesn't know you can be funny."

"It is not something I am proud of," he said.

Linoo smiled and shook her head.

"I am not going to build her an exploding fountain," Orook said. "And besides that, I do not need - or even want - Maria to fall in love with me. I only need her to get along with me well enough for us to pass our compatibility exam."

"The compatibility exam is more difficult to pass than you might think," Linoo warned. "You're correct when you say that she doesn't need to be in love with you - but you both need to at least be fond of each other. It requires a bit than just getting along."

Orook moaned. "What is the point of all this?" he asked. "Even if I manage to win her over, what will I do with her? She is human. All she can do is read and ask questions."

"That is not fair. They can do all sorts of things. Many of them have low level jobs or play instruments in the District Center during the social day parties. Others make jewelry or knit blankets. They do all sorts of things," she told him.

"Sounds riveting," Orook said.

"Ok, well, wouldn't it be nice to have a friend who is always there for you?" Linoo tried.

"Sure," Orook said as he continued to toy with ends of Linoo's long hair.

"In addition to that, you do know that the human women have all the same parts we have, right?" Linoo asked.

"So?" Orook asked.

"Seriously, Orook?" Linoo said.

Orook grimaced.

"Oh stop," Linoo said. "They are not all that different from us."

"Ok, well, even if I could get past her... well, let us just say, even if I wanted to do that with her... I thought it was illegal for keepers to do that with their companions," Orook said.

"Well, technically, yes. There is a general prohibition. But all such general prohibitions have exceptions. You need to read the actual law," Linoo advised.

"I would rather not," Orook said. "As the humans like to say, sometimes ignorance is bliss."

"Suit yourself. I hope you like knitted blankets," Linoo said.

"Do you think a lot of men do this with the human women? I wonder how many of my engineers are joining with their companions," Orook thought out loud.

"Darling, I think it's safe to assume that most of them do," Linoo said.

"Well, I have never heard any of them talking about it," he said. "And it certainly seems like something men would talk about."

"Yes, but, as you pointed out, it is generally prohibited," Linoo said. "So, they keep it quiet. No one wants to be interrogated by what

Pullmoo calls the 'love police.' Even if they followed the law to the letter, who wants to sit in a room and explain the details of how they followed all the rules and met all the requirements?"

"Sounds like a lot more trouble than it could possibly be worth," Orook said.

"Well, it sounds like you and Maria are a long way off from that anyway," Linoo said as she waved away his expression of distaste.

"I would rather do it with you," Orook said as he kissed her exposed shoulder and neck.

Linoo smiled and returned his affection.

A few moments later, Orook's armband began to vibrate. It only did this when he was receiving an urgent message. He quickly flicked his wrist to answer to call.

"This is First Engineer Orook, what is the problem?" he asked.

The caller's voice came loud and clear through Orook's armband, "I'm sorry to disturb you sir, this is Second Body Biologist Hanook. There has been an incident. You need to come to the Body Biology Center immediately. She is ok, but you need to take her home."

Linoo looked at Orook, concerned, then spoke to the caller. "Hanook, this is Linoo, Governess of District Two, where Orook lives with his companion. Please tell me what happened," she said.

The caller then proceeded to explain that Maria had managed to access the Pegasean nursery. When she was discovered there, a guard darted her with a tranquillizer in order to stop her from interacting with a child.

At hearing this, Orook covered his face with his hands as he tried to control his anger. Linoo thanked the caller and told him that Orook would come to fetch Maria immediately.

"You better go," Linoo said as she started to get dressed.

Orook drew his hands down his face.

"How did she get into the nursery?" he asked through gritted teeth.

"Relax, Orook," Linoo said, "I'm sure there is an explanation."

"*Why* would she go to the nursery?" Orook asked.

"You will have to ask her that," Linoo said. "But the most likely reason is simple curiosity. You read her profile. She is a highly curious creature."

Now Orook started to get dressed too, all the while trying not to show his fury.

"Try not to be too angry with her, Orook," Linoo warned. "I know that this must be upsetting for you, but you must remember that she is only human."

"Maybe so, but she is not all *that* stupid. She knew what she was doing," Orook countered.

Their last kiss was unfortunately brief and tense as Orook hurried out the door.

CHAPTER 15

Less than an hour after being darted by the guard, Maria slowly regained consciousness in the examining room of a Pegasean physician. She squeezed her eyes shut, then opened them again, trying to clear her blurred vision. When she realized that her wrist bands were firmly attached to the arms of her chair, she immediately struggled to pull them free. As if it was nailed to the floor, the chair would not budge. Maria screamed. Moments later, Hanook came into the room and motioned with his hands for her to quiet down.

"What's going on?!" Maria asked.

"It's ok, Maria," Hanook said. "You're ok. I'm what your kind call a 'doctor.' You may call me 'Doctor' if you like, ok?"

Maria looked him up and down. He did not look like a doctor. The bright terracotta color of his uniform made him look like more of an escapee from a high security prison of the sort back on Earth.

"If you can relax, I'll turn off the magnets and explain what is happening. Can you do that Maria? Can you relax?" he asked.

"I'm getting a little tired of being told to relax," she said. "What is it with you people and the drugs and the restraints? Just how dangerous do you think I am?"

Hanook smiled. "Maria, if you follow the rules -," he started to say.

"Yeah, yeah, I know," Maria said. She then let out a long breath and forced herself to smile at Hanook.

Hanook watched her for a moment longer, then walked over to her and touched his armband to the top of her chair. The arms of the chair released their grip on Maria's wristbands and her arms fell free to her sides.

"You were in the nursery. Do you remember that?" Hanook prompted.

"Yes," she said. "A child came up to me and reached up his arms to me. I think I thought he wanted me to pick him up. But then, I don't know, I don't remember anything after that."

Hanook nodded.

"Very good," he said. "You only lost a few seconds then."

"What happened in those few seconds?" Maria asked.

"It appears that you bent down and reached for the child. One of the teachers pulled the alarm. An on-duty guardsman arrived immediately, saw what was happening and disabled you with a tranquilizer," he told her.

"Why?" she asked.

"Well, Maria, you had no business in the nursery. The guard did not know who you were, why you were there, or what you were about to do to that child," Hanook explained.

"So, he shot me?" she asked.

"No, he darted you, with a blow dart," he corrected. "And you're very lucky that he noticed your training bands and considered that you might just be lost. He could have used a lethal dart."

Maria sighed and wondered just how many more times she would narrowly escape death at the hands of these Pegaseans before she reached her next birthday.

Hanook then tested her pupils with a pen light and read her pulse off her wrist band.

"You seem ok," he said. "Now just sit here please, while I go notify your keeper that he can take you home now."

About ten minutes later, Hanook returned with Orook. The undisguised fury in Orook's eyes sent a chill down Maria's spine.

"Let's go," he said, then turned and walked out of the room.

Stunned by the incensed tone of his voice, Maria felt momentarily unable to move. She looked up at Hanook as if asking him for help.

Hanook gestured with his head and eyes that she needed to follow her keeper. Maria let out a long breath, then forced herself to get up and walked quickly to catch up with Orook. Once they were back home, Orook instructed her to go to her room and to stay there until he called for her. She tried to meet his eyes and apologize, but he refused to look at her.

"Do not test me right now Maria," he said coldly. "You should just be thankful that I am not a violent man."

Maria, remembering the incident with the vocunine, walked quickly to her room and closed the curtain. From insider her enclave, she could hear Orook speaking to someone in Pegasean. Maria recognized the voice as Linoo's. They must be speaking through the intercom, Maria thought.

"How long can a human go without food or water?" Orook asked.

"Oh stop," said Linoo.

"I am serious," Orook said. "How long can I keep her in her room?"

"Don't keep her in there for too long," Linoo said.

Orook groaned.

"I mean it. Let her out before the end of the day. That's an order," she insisted.

"Ok, ok," Orook said dismissively.

"You need to prepare her for the hearing tomorrow," Linoo advised.

"Is a hearing really necessary? What are the charges?" he asked.

"You are being charged with trespass by proxy, meddling with a child, and reckless use of your security clearance," she said.

"Are you serious? They think I told her to go to the nursery?" Orook asked.

"It could have been worse, darling," she said. "One of the parents wanted you to be charged with kidnapping and abuse of power over your companion."

"This is ridiculous. Why would I want to kidnap a child? And I have no idea how she was able to use my security clearance," he said.

"You neglected to restrict her access after you took her from the Intake Hall. Her wristband still has its default security settings, which are simply the same as yours. Assuming that, after the hearing, the Council is convinced that this was a mere oversight on your part, the current charges will be dropped and replaced with a charge of companion neglect." Linoo explained.

Orook's face went pale, and he admonished himself for his negligence.

"There is another problem - or complication rather," Linoo said. "The child who approached Maria was our son."

This information left Orook momentarily speechless.

"Orook? Are you still there?" Linoo asked.

"How… how can that be?" he stuttered. "There are hundreds of children in the nursery. Why him? Why would he approach her?"

"That is exactly the problem," Linoo said. "Even the Council members who would otherwise be happy to drop all charges, with or without a hearing, are bothered by this apparent coincidence. They know how you feel about the City's child rearing policies. You have submitted several poignant memorandums on the issue."

"But I would never…," Orook protested.

"I know. And I think they know too. But that is why there is going to be a hearing. The matter needs to be discussed in an open forum. It will not be an adversarial hearing. Lenook will simply present the facts and question the witnesses before the Inter-District Council. For purposes of the hearing, Lenook won't take a side. The Council will then determine what charges are fair and supported by the evidence. I'm sure they will want to hear from Maria and the teachers."

"What a mess," Orook said with a sigh. "If I had known she would be this much trouble, I would have left her in the Intake Hall or euthanized her myself."

"Do you really mean that, Orook?" Linoo asked.

"No, I do not really mean that," Orook admitted.

"I do not think I like this side of you Orook," she said.

"What side?" he asked.

"This cold and bitter side," Linoo said. "It doesn't suit you."

"Linoo, I do not have time for this nonsense. Half of Node 43 is without running water between the third and fourth hour of the day. The intercoms in Node 56 continue to beep every time -."

"Orook, stop," Linoo interrupted. "You need a break. You haven't taken a restoration period in the past five years. You need to delegate more of your responsibilities. You have at least twenty highly qualified second engineers at your command, plus many more third and fourth engineers under their command."

"The Council is going to suspend me from work. I am sure of it," he said.

"You will be fine," Linoo said.

"Will you be moderating the hearing?" he asked.

"Unfortunately, no," she said. "The hearing will be before the Inter-District Council, and I represent one of the involved Districts. I'm the mother of the child; and, as you know, I was with you when all this happened."

"Right," Orook said.

"You're lucky I was able to convince the Center Council that they didn't need to get involved. You know how they are about anything involving the nursery or children." Linoo added.

"Indeed. Thank you," he said.

"You can thank me by following my order to release your companion from her room before they add a charge of companion abuse to the list. I also strongly advise you to at least make some attempt to reconcile with her before tomorrow."

Orook scoffed at her latter suggestion.

"Oroo… don't be stubborn," Linoo admonished in a gently parental tone.

"When will I see you again?" he asked.

"Orook, you know we can't see each other anymore - not like that anyway," Linoo reminded him.

"We could still run away together. I could build us a house in the mountain. We can live off the snow toads and steam grass," Orook suggested wistfully.

"Don't tempt me, Oroo," Linoo said. "Now go make up with Maria and get some rest. You don't want to look haggard for the hearing tomorrow."

• • •

Orook waited until the very last hour of the day before calling for Maria to come out of her room. Stalling for time, Maria asked if she could first go to the bathroom. Orook waved his hand towards the bathroom and let her go. When she came back out into the bedroom, Orook had to stop her from immediately returning to her room.

"What are you doing?" he asked. "I would think you would be happy to be out of there."

Maria stopped walking but did not respond.

"Do you even understand why I am so upset?" Orook asked.

"I'm sorry. I know I must have embarrassed you," she said.

"*Embarrassed* me?" he said through gritted teeth. "I do not get *embarrassed*. You could never possibly embarrass me. You can, however, *inconvenience* me. And that is what you have done, Maria. Thanks to your little escapade today, you and I will have to spend the entire day at a hearing tomorrow. I can only hope that the hearing will not steal a second day from me."

"A hearing?" Maria asked, trembling in response to the unbridled hostility in his voice. "What... what have I been charged with?"

"*You* will not be charged with anything. In general, the City does not charge humans for their indiscretions. Their keepers are charged," Orook explained.

"But that's not fair," Maria protested. "It's my fault."

"Of course, it is your fault!" Orook said. "Unfortunately, the law here, in its infinite wisdom, does not allow a human to be held accountable for any actions over which she is not supposed to have any control - regardless of whether or not she actually had control over those actions at the time."

Maria looked confused, but Orook did not care. He could not remember the last time he had allowed himself to get this angry at anyone. Linoo was right. He was acting out of character. He took a deep breath and did his best to calm down.

"The point is, Maria, you broke the law. Do not try to tell me you did not know that you are not allowed in the nursery," he said in an even tone.

Maria looked down at the bare floor as she fussed with the ends of her blouse.

"Now I have to waste my time defending myself against several criminal charges which are utterly ridiculous. That is why I am angry. And there is nothing you can do about it now. So, you can say that you are sorry all you want. You cannot give me back all the time I am going to lose because of this, much less the time I have already lost," he said.

"What are the charges?" Maria whispered.

"That is none of your concern," he said.

"I promise it won't happen again," Maria offered.

"That is a certainty," Orook told her. "I have restricted your security clearance. You cannot go past the end of the block unless I am with you."

Orook stared at Maria as she wrapped her arms around herself and continued to look down at the floor. Intellectually, he knew that this was the moment when he should tell her that part of the reason he was so angry was because she put herself in danger; because she could have been hurt or killed by the guardsman. He could almost hear Linoo's voice in his head, telling him to apologize for being so harsh. He frowned at the thought of what Linoo would think of him if she knew just how indifferent he was to Maria's misery at this moment. Why was he so angry? This was not like him. Then, suddenly, he knew. This pathetic human woman had seen his son. She had been only inches from him. The boy had reached his arms up to her. His anger was being stoked by envy - and shame. She had gotten closer to his son than he ever had. And why? Because she dared to break a vile rule he did not have the gall to break himself. It was just not fair.

"I am at least partly to blame," he said in an eerily vacant voice. "As soon as you arrived, I should have restricted the security clearance on your wristband."

Maria did not respond. She had not had anything to eat or drink since that morning. When Orook saw her sway on her feet, he helped her sit down on a storage compartment at the foot of his bed. He then brought her a liquidized meal from the kitchen. She took it and drank it without thanks or complaint, then handed him the empty glass.

"May I go back to my room now?" she asked dully.

Orook looked at her, now finally a little concerned.

"What is wrong?" he asked.

"I just want to go home," she said.

"You are home," he said.

"No, I mean home, home… I miss my dog," Maria said in a daze.

"Oh, you mean Earth?" Orook asked.

Maria nodded.

"You do not want to go back there," Orook said. "The whole planet is ripe for an apocalyptic global climate shift that will wipe out most of the human population. That is why the transports will not go back there anymore. The data collected by the Center Council predicts that the country you were from will be buried in half a kilometer of ice and snow within the next five to ten years. It will take several decades, if not centuries, after that for the planet to warm back up enough to sustain any significant level of life. Trust me. You are better off here."

Maria turned up her face to look at him. Her eyes were wide with shock and disbelief.

"Did you not know this?" Orook asked softly.

It was now all too much for Maria. She blinked a few times before her head dropped and she fainted. Orook managed to catch her just before her head hit the floor.

CHAPTER 16

The next morning, Orook and Linoo waited in a small private room within the larger Inter-District Hearing Hall. They both sat at one side of a small desk and waited for the presenter to come and brief them on what would happen at the hearing.

Lenook, a Second Presenter for the City and Orook's future brother-in-law, sat in his office with Maria. Lenook was assigned to all inter-district cases and controversies. He interviewed Maria and several witnesses from the nursery that morning in preparation for the hearing. After he had finished collecting and sorting through all of the available evidence, he stopped working and looked up at Maria, who looked tired, dazed and obviously traumatized.

"It's going to be ok," he assured her.

Maria nodded weakly.

"Are you sure you do not want to be placed with another keeper?" Lenook asked.

"Why do you keep asking me that?" Maria asked.

"Because you look like hell," Lenook told her.

"It's not his fault," Maria said.

"Oh, I'm pretty sure it is," Lenook said without thinking.

Maria looked up at him sharply.

"I didn't mean it like that," Lenook said, putting up his hands in surrender. "I'm convinced he didn't use you to try and break into the nursery. I'm just saying, no companion should have to be as miserable as you look right now."

"Well then convince the Council to drop the charges," she said.

"You know I can't take a side in this," Lenook said. "But I do expect that even an unbiased presentation of the facts and evidence here will be sufficient to convince the Council to let him off with what amounts to a warning."

"Thank you," Maria said.

"Ok, now wait here while I go talk to your keeper and the governess," Lenook said.

When Lenook walked into the private room where Orook and Linoo had been waiting, he didn't look happy. He glared at Orook as if he was clearly guilty of the pending charges and several others.

"How is Maria? What did she say?" asked Linoo.

"Oh, don't worry about that," said Lenook. "She blames herself for everything. She insists you had nothing to do with any of it. She has no idea who the boy is or why he approached her. She is racked with guilt and miserable."

Orook sighed with relief.

"So why do you seem so unhappy?" he asked.

"Because, dear brother-to-be, I would have preferred a witness who has not been both physically and emotionally traumatized within the past 12 hours."

Linoo looked sharply at Orook, who insisted that he had no idea what Lenook was talking about. Linoo asked Lenook to explain.

"Ok, well, let's review, shall we?" Lenook began. "First, she is darted with a tranquilizer and loses consciousness. She wakes up and finds herself bound to a chair in an examination room. This, you should know, is terrifying for people from Earth - especially after they have been, in essence, kidnapped by aliens. Fortunately, Hanook, the kind body biologist who released her from the chair, managed to calm her down. But then her keeper shows up, obviously livid with her. He shows no concern for her, or even asks her about what happened. All he does is walk her home in silence and sentence her to her room where she is forced to remain for almost 7 consecutive hours."

"Orook!" Linoo said, as shocked as she was angry.

"Wait, it gets better," Lenook continued. "After he finally does let her out, he wastes no time explaining to her just what a curse she is on his life. She tries to apologize, but he won't let her. When the poor thing says she misses Earth, he decides that *this* is the perfect moment in which to tell her that the entire human race is destined for extinction, or close enough to it. That is when she passed out."

"Is that what Maria told you?" Orook asked.

"Well, not exactly. Being the kind soul that she is, she tells the story in such a way that casts you in a far less boorish light. For example, she insists you didn't force her to stay in her room. Regardless, I know what really happened because I know *you*," Lenook said with genuine disdain.

"I did not leave her in her room all that long. And I thought she already knew about Earth," Orook countered.

Lenook did not believe him, but it did not matter. Orook was in luck. One of the teachers provided a convincing theory as to why Orook's young son had approached Maria. The theory was that Maria resembled a popular character in a series of children's stories. And, in fact, when Lenook looked at the pictures of this character, he could certainly see a resemblance. There were also witnesses who claim that there were other children who had turned and started heading in Maria's direction upon seeing her. The fact that Orook's son had just happened to be the child closest to her at the time did seem to be just a coincidence. Lenook was not about to tell Orook any of this before the hearing though. He decided to let Orook sit and worry for just a few more hours. This was the least he could do for Maria.

· · ·

Following the hearing, which lasted less than three hours, the Inter-District Council decided that Maria had gone to the nursery on her own and without any prompting, or permission, from Orook. However, they also determined that Orook was entirely responsible for the fact that Maria was able to get into the nursery, and for the fact that she was apparently unaware of just how serious a trespass into the nursery would be taken by the City. They admonished him for his negligence and suspended him from work for two weeks. During this time, he would commit himself to teaching Maria everything she needed to know about life in Pegasea. If, at the end of the two-week suspension, Maria passed her citizenship test, and if they both passed their compatibility exam, all would be forgiven.

CHAPTER 17

B y the time they got home from the hearing, Orook had resigned himself to his fate and was ready to move on. He loathed not being able to work, but there was nothing he could do about it now. He had already begun making plans in his head for the upcoming weeks. He began speaking these plans out loud before he realized that Maria was no longer in the room with him. Orook went to the bedroom and heard Maria moving around in her room. Orook sat down on the corner of his bed closest to her enclave.

"Maria, what are you doing?" he asked.

"I'm leaving," she said.

After hearing the Council's decision, Maria decided that she would rather risk death of cold out on the surface than spend all day, every day, with Orook for two uninterrupted weeks.

"To go where?" Orook asked.

"Anywhere but here," Maria said.

"Maria, have you not learned by now that you cannot just go wandering off? There are places in the City you are simply not allowed to go. The guardsman might not be as astute next time. You could be hurt, or worse," he told her.

"I'm leaving the City," Maria said. "I'm going to the surface, to the outside. I'll take my chances with the vocunines."

"You are being irrational," he said. "For one thing, I have already restricted your access around the City. You cannot even get close to any door to the outside. Even if you could manage to find your way up to the surface, you would not last a day. The vocunines are not your problem. They might even try to help you, but they would fail. You do not know how to navigate the land, find food or water. You would most likely die of exposure in less than a day."

Maria stopped packing but did not otherwise respond to Orook.

"Please come out, Maria," Orook said, trying to sound as conciliatory as possible.

Eventually, Maria came to the curtain, then ventured a step out into Orook's bedroom. She stood just outside her room, arms folded, looking anywhere but at her keeper.

"Do you know the Pegasean gesture for apology?" Orook asked.

"Yes," she said, then demonstrated the gesture.

"Yes, that is one of them," he said. "But that one is specifically an apology for failure to recognize another person's status, knowledge, or experience. Or, it can also be used as an apology for insubordination, negligence or inadvertent error. In any case, there is a separate gesture for an apology for doing inexcusable harm to another."

Orook then touched his palm to his chest, then flipped his hand so that his palm faced downward.

"That is the second gesture of apology," he said. "It is intended to show that the status of my inner person - my soul, I guess you could say - is diminished," he explained.

Maria half rolled her eyes, then made the gesture to him.

"No, no, no," Orook said as he waved his hand as if to erase her apology. He then made the gesture again, trying to more clearly indicate that he was making the gesture to her.

"You are apologizing to me?" Maria asked.

"Yes," he said. "I hurt you. And now, in retrospect, I see that the degree to which I hurt you was unjustified and possibly even callous on my part."

Maria looked at him and saw the sincerity in his face.

"Is there a gesture for forgiveness?" she asked.

Orook gestured for her to come closer to him. Maria walked tentatively over to him. He then took her hand and put her palm to her chest, then flipped her hand up the opposite way, so that her palm faced upward.

Maria smiled weakly, then collapsed into his arms and burst into tears. It was pathetic, and she knew it. But she could not help herself. She was not just crying because of the fiasco at the nursery. She was crying for Earth, for her dog, and for everything she had lost. She cried for all her confusion and frustration. She cried for every reason for which she had refused to cry before now.

Surprised and confused by Maria's sudden embrace, Orook initially froze in place. She was holding him and sobbing into his shoulder. He had never seen her cry before and did not know why she was doing so now. Gradually, he relaxed, then began to stroke the back of her head as he tried to understand what was going on inside her troubled human mind. Why was she seeking comfort from him now? Was she still upset about Earth? As he tried to answer these questions, he recalled a kind of psychological disorder which can occur in humans when they are held captive. The disorder causes the captive human to become sympathetic, or even loving, towards her captor, as a kind of defense mechanism. He wondered if Maria was suffering from this disorder now. If so, he knew he would have to tell Pullmoo and Maria would most likely be removed from his house, at least temporarily. As he was thinking about all this, Maria got control of herself and looked up at him. Seeing the pensive, worried look on his face, she asked, "What's wrong?"

"I think you might have Stockholm Syndrome," Orook said, in the same tone he might have used to diagnose an ear injection.

Maria blinked at him, then chuckled softly as she dried her face with the sleeve of her shirt.

"You do not think so?" he asked.

Maria shook her head.

"Besides the fact that such a diagnosis does not usually come from the would-be captor, I do not feel as if I'm being held captive," Maria said. "Or, even if I am, I'm a captive of circumstance, this horrible planet, and the draconian laws of this City. I don't think of you, in particular, as my captor."

"Not even when I kept you in your room for eight straight hours before the trial?" Orook asked.

"When you what?" Maria asked.

"You do not remember?" Orook asked. "I was very angry, and I told you to go to your room and stay there."

"Yeah, but, it's not like you locked me in," Maria said. "My room doesn't even have a real door - just a curtain. I stayed in there because I was embarrassed and because I felt terrible about getting you in trouble. You weren't actually holding me prisoner in there."

Orook decided not to disabuse her of that perspective and quickly changed the subject. "So, what would you like to do during these next two weeks," he asked. "I'm all ours - by order of the Inter-District Council."

"I don't understand. Is this how they are punishing me?" Maria asked.

"Ouch," Orook said dryly.

"You know what I mean," Maria said. "Is having to be supervised by you constantly for two weeks - is that my punishment for what I did?"

"No. It is my punishment for - allegedly - neglecting you," he said.

"That does not make any sense," she said.

"You still do not understand," Orook said. "They see you as something like a child. They do not hold you responsible for this. They blame me and my failure to - well, whatever it is I am supposed to be doing as your keeper."

Maria clenched her fists.

"I'm not a child," she said through gritted teeth. "I'm a grown woman. Why does your government insist on treating me like some kind of infant who can't make decisions or be responsible for my actions? It's very frustrating."

"Would you rather they have sentenced you to electric shock torture?" he asked. "Because that is the punishment for intentional trespass into the nursery and unauthorized physical contact with a child. That is how you would be charged if you were considered a responsible individual acting independently of any authority other than your own."

"But I didn't touch him," Maria said.

"That is only because the guardsman darted you before you could. I know you have this silly system on Earth where, by some twisted logic, a person is punished less severely if they happen to fail at the commission of a crime. You call it an 'attempted' crime and you consider it a less severe offense. We do not reward people for incompetence here. If you show the will and intent to commit a crime, whether or not you succeed makes no difference," Orook explained.

"That actually makes more sense," Maria admitted.

"Of course, it does," Orook agreed. "Everything we do makes more sense. That is why we do not let humans do anything important here. Your kind are all either unintelligent or irrational, or both. You are, as a species, emotionally and mentally unstable. Your ethics are irrational as well. That is why you must follow our instructions and do as you are told."

"*Our* ethics are irrational?!" Maria said. "Didn't you just tell me that the City uses *torture* as a punishment?"

"Maria, use your head," Orook instructed. "We do not have the space or resources to jail people. So criminal punishments are designed to be short lived but painful and memorable. If you put your emotional reaction aside, you will agree that a few hours of pain, no matter how bad, is a lot more humane, and practical, than being forced to spend twenty or more years in idle confinement."

Maria started to tense and fidget as she looked nervously around the room.

"Ok, listen," Orook said, "it almost never actually happens. People here do not often break the laws. In fact, I cannot even remember a time in the past fifty years when anyone has been sentenced to anything more serious than remedial PROEs training."

This did nothing to ease Maria's growing discomfort and fear.

"I'm sorry. I should have stopped at electronic shock torture. I can see that I have now terrified you with the thought of remedial PROEs training," he said with a smile.

Maria almost smiled. Was he trying to be funny?

"Can you just trust me?" he said. "We need to get past this so that we can prepare for your citizenship test and our compatibility exam."

"Ok, ok, so, how do we pass these tests?" Maria asked.

"Your test is easy," Orook told her. "You just have to study the PROEs and the AERs. You basically just have to memorize them."

"Ok, I can do that," Maria said confidently. She had, in fact, spent most of her life studying and memorizing information in preparation for one exam or another.

"The compatibility evaluation is what we really need to work on," Orook thought aloud.

"You don't think we're compatible?" Maria asked as she started to nervously shift her weight from foot to foot again.

Orook suddenly reached out and grabbed her at the elbows.

"Stop that!" he said.

Maria's eyes went wide, and she froze. Orook then quickly released her and apologized.

"Maria," he said. "You have to stop doing that."

"Doing what?" she asked, her eyes still big with shock.

"This bouncing around and twitching every time we are in a confined space together. It is driving me crazy," he confessed.

Maria folded her arms as if trying to physically still herself.

Orook sighed.

"Maria, are you afraid of me?" he asked.

Maria dropped her arms, suddenly disarmed by the genuine concern in his voice.

"Afraid of you? Why do you think I'm afraid of you?" she asked.

"You are always tense and fidgety around me. You actively avoid coming anywhere near me. You do not even sit next to me on the sofa," he said.

"I just hugged you," she countered.

"You had an emotional meltdown. As soon as you composed yourself, you backed away from me again," Orook said.

"So, what do you want me to do?" Maria asked.

"I just want you to relax. I am not going to hurt you. I would think that would be obvious by now. If I did not hurt you after you robbed me of my last few hours with Linoo, then it seems highly unlikely that I ever will. Can you not see that?" he asked.

"I'm so sorry," Maria said.

"Let us not go through all the apologies again. I just want to move on, so we can pass these tests and I can go back to work, please," Orook pleaded.

"I'm not afraid of you," she said. "It's not like that. I just, I don't know how to act around you. I'm always afraid I'm going to offend you, or break a rule, or whatever. Everyone around you is so stiff and deferential. It's like, I don't know, it's hard to explain."

"Ah, so Linoo was right - you find me intimidating, is that it?" Orook asked.

"I find everything here intimidating, but yes, you in particular maybe. It's also being cooped up in here all the time. I'm just really stressed out." Maria explained.

"I see," said Orook. "Well, listen, try not to worry about offending me when we are at home. I do not care so much about the PROEs when we are alone. You must never call me by name, not even in private. That rule is not a PROE; it is an actively enforced rule. But that is the only one you have to follow when it is just you and me here. Otherwise, you are not one of my engineers. You do not have to see me as your boss or overlord or anything like that, alright?"

Maria nodded, this was helping.

"And I will broaden the range of your security clearance after these tests are over," he promised. "There are certain places you simply must not go, but I will give you as much freedom as I can."

"I appreciate that," Maria said.

"Our summers are short, but very pleasant," he continued. "There are areas on the surface, within the walls of the City, where the rocky ground has been filled in and stabilized. When the temperature warms up, you will be able to go out to those areas, the parks, and enjoy yourself - either with or without me."

"Oh, that sounds great," she said with a long sigh.

"Do you think you could sit down now?" Orook asked.

"On your bed?" Maria said with real apprehension.

Orook made an exasperated sound, then closed his eyes and reminded himself to be patient.

"I suppose part of the problem here is that you just do not know me very well," he said. "I have no use for subtlety. If I had something untoward in mind, trust me, you would know. Besides that, it is illegal for me to show that kind of interest in you."

"What kind of interest?" Maria asked.

"Forget it - just sit down," he said. "I am not going to touch you."

"Ok," Maria said, then down next to him on the edge of the bed.

"Linoo says you need to see another side of me," Orook thought aloud. "I think that means that you need to see me in a context where I'm not the boss or the highest-ranking citizen in the room. So, I need to take you with me to meet someone who ranks above me."

"Pullmoo?" Maria suggested.

Orook cringed and said, "no, anyone but her."

"Linoo?" Maria tried again.

"No, I do not think that would work," he said. "She does not necessarily rank above me. She can give me orders because she is the governess of the district in which we live. Outside our district, she ranks below me."

"Well, who ranks above the First Engineer?" Maria asked.

"Technically, in times of peace, only the First Mathematician," he said.

"Can we meet with him?" she asked.

"Her - the First Mathematician is my sister," he said. "And yes, we can meet with her. I think she would probably like to meet you actually."

Orook looked down thoughtfully at Maria who was now smiling up at him.

"Maria, of all the places in the City you could have gone with unlimited security clearance - why did you go to the nursery?" he asked.

Maria shrugged.

"Tell me," Orook insisted.

"I...I honestly do not know for sure. I just got this sudden impulse to go there. I had a dream about it a few nights ago," she confessed.

"What kind of dream?" he asked.

"Just one of those crazy stupid dreams where nothing makes any sense - some kind of talking tree telling me I should go to the nursery because I might find something important there," Maria said.

Orook stared at her.

"What?" Maria asked.

"Ok, well, stop taking orders from strange entities which appear only in your dreams," he said. "I am surprised that I would even have to give you that instruction."

Maria blushed, then nodded.

"Alright, well, it is late and we both need to get some sleep. It has been a long day," he said.

Orook stood up then and gestured for Maria to do the same.

"Should I... I don't know. Do you want me to hug you good night or something?" she asked.

"No, no, I think once was enough for today," he said. "Maybe tomorrow, if you feel so inclined."

"Ok, good night," she said as she turned to head back to her room.

• • •

Once she was safely tucked away in her bed, Maria felt better. For the first time since she had arrived on this planet, she felt the first inkling of hope that she might not be completely miserable for the next 300 or more years.

CHAPTER 18

The next morning, over two bowls of the frothy swill the Pegaseans ate for their morning meal, Orook told Maria that, unfortunately, they would not be able to meet his sister, Wilamoo, until the next day. He explained that Wilamoo had a report to give to the Center Council in the afternoon, and that she would be busy preparing for the meeting all morning.

"I have another idea - something we can do today instead," he said.

"Ok," Maria said.

As they were getting ready to leave, Orook reminded Maria that she should try to walk a pace behind him. He also reminded her that there were many places where humans were not allowed to go, and others where she would only be allowed unless accompanied by a Pegasean man or woman. He warned her against speaking to any Pegasean unless first spoken to and advised her to, in general, speak quietly and only to him. Maria had heard all of these rules before and was starting to get annoyed.

"Just out of curiosity, are there separate restrooms and drinking fountains for humans and Pegaseans?" Maria asked bitterly.

Orook, who had an encyclopedic knowledge of all of Earth's history, grit his teeth and tried not show his annoyance at the question.

"Have you been spending a lot of time with Alice and Rose?" he asked.

"No, why?" she asked.

"I ask because Rose has been known to compare our PROEs to the Jim Crow laws of your former country. Such a comparison is, of course, ridiculous and offensive," he said.

"It's not that ridiculous," Maria said. "There are a lot of similarities."

"There are none," Orook said.

"How can you say that?" she persisted. "They both do nothing more than reinforce the perceived inferiority of one group of people to another group."

Orook closed his eyes and shook his head.

"The Jim Crow laws served no legitimate purpose - they were asinine rules constructed by petty and emotionally deformed humans," he said.

"So, what are you saying?" Maria asked. "That the PROEs are not asinine because they serve some legitimate purpose? Seriously?"

Orook pinched the bridge of his nose between his eyes.

"Maria," he said. "If your dogs on Earth could walk, talk, and hold objects, would you not give them rules, or try to train them? - so that they would not interfere with your everyday work and activities? The PROEs exist to keep you from wasting our time or energy, or both. You walk behind us so that we can lead you. You wait to be spoken to so that you do not speak without purpose. You are not permitted in places where your presence could disrupt our work, or where your lack of understanding or your limited sensory perceptions might put you in danger. So, yes, they serve several very legitimate purposes."

Maria rolled her eyes.

"Ok, so why is sarcasm against the PROEs?" she asked.

"Not all sarcasm is against the PROEs, only needlessly derisive sarcasm - because it is distracting and offensive without purpose," he explained.

"Ok, why am I not allowed to call you by name? Or even say your name in your presence?" Maria tried again.

"As I have already told you, that rule is a law, not a PROE," Orook said.

"The Jim Crow laws were laws, not rules of etiquette," she said.

"Honestly, I do not know the purpose of that rule," he conceded. "I am sure there is one. We are simply not privy to it."

"And that doesn't bother you?" Maria asked.

"Why would it?" Orook asked.

"You just explained to me how all these rules have a legitimate purpose and that their purpose is what justifies them. So, doesn't it bother you when you don't know the purpose of one of them?" she asked.

"Not necessarily," he said. "Here in Pegasea, sociology and psychology are considered sciences just like any other. I would assume that the purpose of that particular rule is rooted in one or both of those. Since those professions are outside my area of expertise, I do not expect to understand everything about them."

"And you're ok with that?" Maria asked. "It doesn't bother you that there might be a rule, or several rules, the sole purpose of which is to manipulate you psychologically? And even if that possibility alone doesn't bother you, doesn't it at least make you wonder if a lot of these other rules don't have a greater sociological or psychological purpose which is left unstated? You say you view these disciplines as a science, ok, fine - but what if some other discipline did something similar? What if the body biologists put something in the water without telling anyone what it was for or what it did? Wouldn't that bother you?"

Orook looked at her without responding. He did not want this conversation to continue. She was getting too close to some of his own misgivings about some of the rules.

"You can walk beside me if you hold my hand," he said at last, then held out his hand to her and smiled warmly.

This certainly was not the response Maria was expecting. She tried to see his mind but could not completely understand what she saw there. It was something like a wall, and a warning, or maybe just a request, that she walk away from it.

"Ok, keeper, whatever you say," Maria said with a wry smile as she put her hand in his.

• • •

"The subrail is going to be crowded this morning because it is a work day," Orook warned as he and Maria waited at the station.

When the subrail car arrived, all but one of the seats were taken. Orook offered Maria the one remaining seat, but she declined. She was tempted to make a snarky remark about not wanting to waste a seat which could otherwise be used to by a Pegasean but chose to bite her tongue instead. They were operating under the "outside rules" now.

Just like a subway car on her home planet, there were rails and poles in the center of the car for standing passengers to hold onto. At each stop, more and more Pegaseans boarded and the space became more crowded.

"How many people live in the City?" Maria asked Orook.

"Close to 15,000 Pegaseans and approximately 9,000 humans," he said.

"Are there other Cities with your kind?" she asked.

"No, we are the last," Orook said.

"What happened?" Maria said.

"I will explain all of that when we get to where we are going," he told her. "In general, it is considered rude to talk about such things on a crowded subrail shuttle."

Just as he said this, more Pegaseans boarded the shuttle.

"Why are there no companions traveling in this subrail?" Maria asked.

"During work days, most companions stay within their nods, or within a few blocks of home. Even the ones with jobs tend to stay within their own district," Orook explained.

At the next stop, when even more people boarded the subrail, Orook maneuvered himself around Maria so that they could occupy less space and so that he could shield her from the encroaching crowd. Standing this close, she noticed that the top of her head barely reached his chin. When she tilted her head back to rest her neck, it touched the top of his chest.

"Why do you smell like pears?" she asked.

"I have no idea," he said.

"Do Pegaseans wear cologne?" she asked.

"Of course not," he answered.

"Deodorant?" Maria asked.

"That is not necessary," Orook told her. "This downy fur we have, which I am sure you have noticed, has anti-bacterial properties. So, we do not acquire the kind of bacteria which causes body odor on humans."

Maria looked at his face and neck. The peach-fuzz like fur was thickest at the tips of his ears, then thinned out towards his face. There was only a barely visible amount of it on his forehead, down the bridge of his nose, and around the area where a beard might otherwise be. All Pegaseans seemed to have a similar, but slightly varied, pattern of down. The Pegasean women had more around their cheeks and had none around their jaws. All the Pegaseans had a similar pale to light olive colored skin. Maria herself was just barely a shade darker than Orook.

"Do all Pegaseans have white hair?" Maria asked.

"In winter, yes," Orook said. "In summer, we change. About a third of this downy fur sheds off. What is left of it, along with the hair on our heads and eye brows, changes color."

"Like an ermine?" Maria asked.

"Something like that," he said.

"What color does yours turn in summer?" she asked.

"Hmm, what would be your guess?" Orook asked playfully.

Maria thought for a moment.

"What color is the ground in summer?" she asked.

"All sorts of colors - different shades of blue, green, brown and grey," he said.

"Do you get spots or stripes?" she asked.

At this, several of the Pegaseans standing around them suppressed smiles or even laughter. Maria's face flushed with embarrassment.

"It is ok," Orook told her. "They think you are cute - like a child."

This did not make Maria feel any better.

Orook leaned into her ear and whispered, "When you were on Earth, did you ever see an arctic fox in summer?"

Maria shook her head.

"Well, then I guess you will just have to wait and see," he said with a smile.

Still feeling self-conscious, Maria remained quiet until they reached their destination.

After they got off the subrail, Orook led Maria into the Center District Commons. As usual, Orook walked at a fast pace which was not easy for Maria to match. When she nearly tripped over a step in the road, she asked Orook if he could please slow down.

"I could," he said, "but I think you need to practice walking faster."

Maria stopped herself from groaning, remembering the outside rules against openly showing annoyance with her keeper. She made a mental note to express her annoyance later, when they were back home.

"Good job," Orook said.

Maria gave him a puzzled look.

"You did not show any annoyance with me after I made that obnoxious comment," he explained.

"Does that mean we can slow down?" she asked.

Orook nodded, and did in fact, slow his pace to match Maria's.

They stopped in front of a door with a sign on which something was written in Pegasean. Underneath the Pegasean writing was the English translation "Game Center." Maria had not been to a Game Center before and asked Orook what it was.

"I think the name is pretty self-explanatory," he said as he moved his armband over the lock and opened the door.

Inside, Maria saw what looked more like a training camp for astronauts than a Game Center. She looked around and saw dozens of display monitors paired with interactive devices and isolated booths containing what she guessed were some kind of virtual reality systems. She also saw off-set rooms which looked a little like large racket ball courts. These rooms all had various types of controls and devices which Maria could not identify.

"Wow, I didn't know this was here," Maria said in awe.

"Companions are not allowed in here without their keepers or at least another Pegasean," Orook told her.

"Why?" Maria asked, doing her best to sound only curious.

"Almost everything in here is potentially dangerous to humans," Orook explained. "Humans used to be allowed in here unaccompanied. However, after several companions hurt themselves, the rules were changed."

"What happened? How did they get hurt?" Maria asked.

"I would rather not recount each and every incident, but I will tell you that there was one woman who got into one of the imposed reality units and ended up in the Body Biology Center for three days.

For some reason, one which I am sure only a human could possibly understand, she asked the machine to simulate an encounter with a dragon." Orook told Maria.

"What happened?" Maria asked.

"Can you not guess?" Orook said.

"Does the machine actually inflict wounds?" Maria asked.

"No, it does not inflict actual wounds. However, it can - and does - inflict the sensation of pain through the device you wear to play the game. It can create a rather aggressive sensation of pain, pleasure, pressure, extreme temperatures and so on, directly inside your central nervous system through remotely mapped synapse stipulation. By various synchronized mechanisms, it can cause a great deal of physiological stress which can potentially cause very real kinds of stress injuries," Orook told her.

Maria had no idea what remotely mapped synapse simulation might be, but she understood the general idea - the game could make you feel things and feel them intensely.

"What exactly happened?" Maria asked again.

Orook gave her a look as if he was trying to assess whether or not she really couldn't figure that out for herself. After seeing Maria's blank expectant expression, he asked, "Maria, do you and I have the same understanding of what a *dragon* is supposed to be?"

"I don't know," Maria answered.

"Well, in my mind, a dragon is a menacing creature from human folklore which resembles a giant winged predatory reptile. It is portrayed in stories from Earth as a sinister beast with enormous teeth and claws, an impenetrable armor of scales, and keen senses. I think it's also supposed to breathe fire too, correct?"

Maria nodded.

"So, what do you think happened?" Orook asked.

"Did it hurt her? - or did the machine simulate the dragon hurting her?" Maria asked.

"Yes, and mortally so, before it ate her - several times and in several different ways," Orook told her.

"Why several times?" Maria asked.

129

"Because it's a game!" Orook said, annoyed. "Like your video games on Earth, if you die in the game, the game starts over."

"Right, but...," Maria started to say before Orook interrupted her.

"This woman from Earth could not cope with this level of sensory manipulation. It was too real for her. She panicked and stopped believing it was only a game. During the three long hours she was essentially trapped in the imposed reality unit, the dragon found several gruesome ways to hunt her down, dismember her, toss her broken body around, and all sorts of nasty things you would expect a dragon to do. She is lucky the pain alone did not kill her," Orook said.

Maria's face went a bit pale at hearing this. She asked "Why would the game inflict so much pain? Couldn't the same thing have happened to a Pegasean?"

"No Pegasean I know is dumb enough to summon a dragon without first setting a lot of safety parameters," he said. "However, your other question, about the machine inflicting pain, is valid. You asked why it has that capacity. The answer is - because you cannot create a perfectly authentic artificial experience without every aspect of that experience. Pain, or at least discomfort, is an aspect of every experience. For example, suppose you asked it to simulate walking barefoot along a beautiful warm beach. If you did not occasionally experience the discomfort of stepping on a sharp stone or seashell, the experience would not be as authentic. Even if you wanted to experience something as innocuous as a university library on Earth, it would not feel truly real if the machine did not simulate the discomfort of a hard wood chair you might sit down in - or cause you to sneeze when you went down into the dusty old archives. At any given time, whether you realize it or not, you are experiencing some minor levels of pain or discomfort throughout your body. Most of the time, we are not even consciously aware of them. However, you *would* notice if they were all suddenly absent. Both Pegasean and human brains process far more information than the small fraction of which we are consciously aware. Every little bit of that information comes into play when the brain makes a determination of 'real' verses 'not real.' So, the machine has to simulate all of it. It cannot just selectively leave out the sensory input you do not think you want. If it did, the experience would not seem real. Do you understand?"

"I do." Maria said. "That all makes perfect sense. But shouldn't there be a fail-safe somewhere? I mean, shouldn't the user be able to set a maximum pain level or something like that?"

"There is," Orook said curtly. "This woman either forgot to set it or failed to set it properly. Either way, this is why we do not let humans in here without supervision."

"I see," Maria said with a soft sigh.

"That was just one incident with one kind of game," Orook said. "There were others."

"I don't want to know," Maria said.

"No, you probably do not," Orook agreed.

When he noticed Maria start to fidget as she looked warily around at everything in the room, Orook added, "Relax, I will not let you experience being mauled by any mythical Earth creatures."

"Thank you," Maria said.

"Come on," he said, taking her hand again. "What I want to show you is better than those simulators - at least in my opinion."

Orook then led Maria to the back of the Game Center where there was a white door with a sign written only in Pegasean. Orook took a card from a box hanging on the wall next to the door and slid the card into his armband. He then took off his shoes and instructed her to do the same. After he unlocked and opened the door, he held it open for Maria to step in after him. She looked cautiously inside before stepping over the threshold. As soon as she stepped into the room, her feet sunk into the floor as if she had stepped into a thick bed of freshly loosened soil. She noticed that the room was perfectly circular. The walls and ceiling looked impossibly smooth and white. When she looked down, she saw that she and Orook were standing in a bed of very tiny, perfectly spherical, white beads. She bent down to get a better look at them. Then she tried to pick one up. When she did this, several came up together in a string, as if they were all tiny magnets. This much alone delighted Maria. She loved magnets and started wrapping the string of beads around her fingers. Then she knelt down and started to build them up into piles, then shaped them into more complicated shapes. Orook watched her for a while, amused, before saying her name to get her attention.

"These are really fun," she said.

"Indeed. Would you like me to turn them on now? Or is this enough for you?" he asked.

Maria was not sure how to answer the question. She was happy just playing with all the tiny little white magnets.

When she did not answer, Orook asked her what her favorite, harmless, animal on Earth was. He then quickly corrected his "was" to "is" after seeing the look of distress on her face over his use of the past tense.

Maria thought for a moment, then said, "I like rabbits."

Orook then spoke out loud to the room in Pegasean, except for the word "rabbit," which he said in English. Within seconds, the round wall around the room disappeared and she suddenly found herself looking out onto a grassy meadow. Then the tiny white marbles at her feet begin piling up into short narrow lines, then turned different shades of green and yellow until they looked like grass. Maria waved her hand over them and watched as they responded just like blades of real grass. When she looked up, she saw a rabbit, formed from the same tiny spheres, which had turned various shades of brown and grey to give the illusion of fur. Maria reached out her hand, and the rabbit sniffed at her fingers. Maria was speechless for several minutes.

At last she asked, "Can I pick it up?"

Orook nodded.

Maria picked up the rabbit and cradled it in her arms. She touched its head and stroked its ears. The rabbit responded in every way she would expect a domesticated rabbit to respond. She turned to Orook, her eyes wide with joy and awe. She didn't have to tell him how delighted she was.

"What else?" Orook asked.

"What else can it do?" Maria asked.

"It can create an interactive model or diorama of just about anything," Orook told her.

"Can we see somewhere else on this planet?" Maria asked.

"Of course. Where would you like to see?" he asked.

Maria shrugged.

"Well, like Earth, most of the planet is water. There are only a few habitable areas on a few land masses. Most of these are inhabited by formidable predators like the vocunine. There are none of my kind living outside Pegasea," Orook told Maria.

"Why?" she asked.

"That is a long story," Orook said.

"Do we have time? I would like to hear it," Maria asked.

"We have all day," he said.

Maria bounced gently on her feet. She liked this room a lot and told Orook so.

Orook smiled and said, "Me too."

CHAPTER 19

Maddie knocked on the door to Pullmoo's office and waited nervously for the most powerful person in Pegasea to appear on the other side. When the door opened, Pullmoo greeted her with a warm and welcoming smile.

"Please come in my dear," Pullmoo said. "Sit wherever you like."

Maddie looked around briefly, then sat down on the sofa across from Pullmoo's desk. Pullmoo walked over, sat down, and beamed at Maddie. Maddie shifted in her seat in an attempt to conceal her effort to put an inch or two more space between herself and the First Sociologist.

"Uh… so… my body biologist, Hanook, told me that I needed to talk to you," Maddie said.

Pullmoo nodded and circled her hand, encouraging Maddie to continue.

"There is something wrong with my ears," Maddie said. She then explained that, one day after Etmook came home from one of Orook's navigation lessons, he had tugged on her ear as he explained what Orook had taught them.

"And all of a sudden, my hearing in that ear went all crazy," she said. "I heard all these weird sounds - or at least I think they were sounds. It was frightening and strange. I don't know if I can even describe it."

"There is nothing wrong with your ears," Pullmoo said.

"But when I…," Maddie started to argue.

"Maddie, you have a second inner ear, just like I do - just like Etmook does," Pullmoo told her.

Maddie shook her head. "That's not possible," she said. "I know that humans can acquire some adaptations due to the acquisition of microbial organisms native to this planet, but they can't just grow a second inner ear."

"No, they cannot," Pullmoo agreed.

Maddie sighed. Pullmoo was doing that annoying thing Etmook always did to her. She was letting Maddie feel her way around in the dark before turning the on lights. Why did they all have to be like teachers?

"Please Pullmoo," Maddie said. "Just tell me what is going on. I haven't slept well in days. I don't want to figure it out myself."

"You are both human and Olronean my darling - human and *Pegasean* to be more precise," Pullmoo said.

Maddie shook her head again. "No, that can't be," she said. "Humans and Olroneans are different species. They can't produce viable young."

"And yet here you sit, the daughter of a Pegasean man and a human woman," Pullmoo said as she held out her arms as if presenting Maddie to an incredulous jury.

"Is this some kind of joke?" Maddie asked.

"When I joke, I'm funny. Is this funny, Maddie?" Pullmoo said.

"No, definitely not," Maddie said. "Would you please explain this to me then. I don't understand. How did I happen?"

"Well, the lines between species aren't always so black and white - especially when there is a great deal of genetic diversity within the species themselves. Pegaseans are not particularly diverse, genetically speaking. However, humans are quite diverse. The first human women we took from Earth were taken from all over the planet and intended to represent the spectrum of human genetic diversity. Some of these women were just the slightest bit closer to Pegaseans, genetically, than the others. The difference was not enough to render them the same species, but in at least one woman - your mother - it was enough to allow her to become pregnant with you, Maddie," Pullmoo explained.

"Where is she now?" Maddie asked.

"Unfortunately, she died in child birth," Pullmoo said. "The delivery was difficult. Something must have happened which caused a small amount of your blood, or other bodily fluid, to pass into her body. This caused an unexpected immune reaction in your mother.

It was incredibly fast and severe. The Body Biologists were unable to save her. I'm sorry, Maddie."

Maddie only nodded as she stared at the bare wall behind Pullmoo's desk.

"Am I able to have children?" Maddie asked.

"To be frank," Pullmoo said. "We do not know. As soon as you hit puberty, you were implanted with a contraceptive to make sure you never conceived."

Maddie closed her eyes and clenched and unclenched her fists.

"Don't be angry Maddie," Pullmoo said. "I know it might not seem fair, but it was for your own good."

"May I, respectfully, ask you why I have been living as a human?" Maddie said. "Why was I not raised as a Pegasean - or as the hybrid that I am?"

Pullmoo took a deep breath. "First, please know that your father and I agonized over this very question," she said. "We knew that there was no way to raise you as both. The Center Council usually does whatever I advise it to do, but in this case, there was no way they were going to create a third type of social status to accommodate only one person. The City was still in the process of adapting to the new status created by the introduction of human women to our citizenry. Creating yet another level of complexity so soon would have been too much."

"Ok... but why did you choose to raise me as a human rather than a Pegasean woman?" Maddie asked.

"I had to plan for the eventuality that your mixed status would become widely known," Pullmoo said. "At the time, I believed that the people of this city would respond more sympathetically to a half-Pegasean woman forced to live as a human, than they would to a half-human woman living as a Pegasean."

Maddie looked away as she tried to conceal her irritation.

"I made up for this, at least in my mind, by matching you with Etmook," Pullmoo said.

"How did matching me with Etmook make up for anything?" Maddie asked.

"Well, for one thing, he was always a bit of a rebel. I knew from the start that he would only begrudgingly ask you to follow the PROEs outside your home," Pullmoo said. "I knew he would teach you Pegasean, in violation of the law. I knew he would involve you with his work and do his best to treat you as an equal. After all, he too is a romantic. From the time you were both just children, I knew that you would be perfect for each other. I like to think that by matching you with Etmook, I gave you the best of both worlds. Maybe I am deluding myself, but that is what I like to think. What do you think, Maddie?"

"Honestly?" Maddie asked.

"Yes. Please, speak freely," Pullmoo said.

"I'm angry," Maddie confessed. "And yes, I know that is not fair to you. I know that you only did what you honestly believed was best for me. It's just... well, I don't know. I guess I would have liked to have some say in the matter."

"That is the human in you talking," Pullmoo said.

"Well, I was raised human - so whose fault is that?" Maddie said with half a smile.

"You have a delightful ability to let yourself feel, but then to just as easily detach from your emotions," Pullmoo said. "I wonder if this is a consequence of your unique mix of human and Pegasean qualities."

Maddie took a deep breath, then smiled at Pullmoo.

Pullmoo picked up Maddie's hand and kissed it. She then gently touched Maddie's ears and frowned. "It broke my heart to ask the surgeon to trim your ears," she said.

"That's ok," Maddie said. "Etmook likes my 'stubby' ears - as he calls them."

"You are being kind Maddie," Pullmoo said.

Maddie shrugged.

"Who is my father?" she asked.

"I can tell you, but Maddie, you must never repeat any of this to anyone. Do you understand?" Pullmoo said gravely.

"I understand," Maddie said.

"Knowledge that it actually is possible for a human woman to have a child with a Pegasean man would change the way all Pegasean men in this City feel towards their companions and would cause a detrimental degree of emotional and psychological confusion," Pullmoo said.

"How? Why?" Maddie asked.

"To make a long story short - as your kind like to say - the relationship of a companion and a keeper, as it is intended and should be, is incompatible with any possibility of reproduction between them," Pullmoo explained.

"Huh? Why?" Maddie asked.

"That is all I am willing to explain to you right now, Maddie," she said.

"May I tell Etmook?" Maddie asked.

"If he doesn't already know, yes, you may tell him," Pullmoo said.

"How would he know?" Maddie asked.

Pullmoo shrugged.

"Ok, well, I promise not to tell anyone except Etmook - I am sworn to secrecy," Maddie said. "Now who is my father?"

"Second Body Biologist Hanook," Pullmoo said.

Maddie's eyes went wide with sudden realization.

"So that's why he is always coming up with lame reasons to call me into the Body Biology Center!" she said. "Honestly, I thought he had it in for me. He tells me every other year that I failed my fitness test - even though I'm always sure I passed. Whenever I challenge the results, he comes back and apologizes, saying he misread the data or some bullshit like that."

Pullmoo smiled and nodded. "I hope you will forgive him for the deception," she said. "He just wants to see you and talk to you as much as he possibly can without giving away the secret."

"Why are you telling me all this now?" Maddie asked.

"We always knew we would have to tell you eventually. We just wanted to wait until you were well settled in the life we planned for you - so that you would not be tempted to agonize over whether or not a different path would have been better," Pullmoo explained.

Maddie nodded, then sighed heavily.

"What is it my dear?" Pullmoo asked.

"It's just a lot to process," Maddie said.

"Don't over think it," Pullmoo advised. "For all intents and purposes, you are human. Try not to imagine what life would be like if you were Pegasean - it will only cause you grief."

Maddie shrugged. "You are right about pairing me with Etmook - at least to some extent," she said. "It would be a lot harder if you had paired me with someone rigid, like Orook."

Pullmoo smiled. "That reminds me," she said. "I wanted to ask you - how is Maria doing?"

"You paired her with Orook," Maddie said, as if this was all there was to say.

"Yes, I know," Pullmoo said.

Maddie shrugged, then told Pullmoo that she had not seen Maria since before Maria's trespass into the nursery. "What happened at the hearing?" she asked.

"Oh, I made sure nothing much came of it," Pullmoo told her. "I just needed a reason to suspend Orook from work."

Maddie narrowed her eyes at Pullmoo. "You planned for Maria to go to the nursery?" she asked.

"Not quite," Pullmoo confessed. "I planned for her to get Orook into trouble. As it turned out, you did more than I did to bring that about. In fact, my only contribution to the whole ordeal was the apparent coincidence of Orook's son being the first child to reach her once she was there."

"How did you manage that?" Maddie asked, intrigued.

"Have you ever heard the human expression that goes 'a magician never reveals his secrets?'" Pullmoo asked with a furtive smile.

"Alright, never mind," Maddie said. "But will you tell me why you matched Maria with Orook? She's so nice and Orook is so... well, you know."

"Oh stop," Pullmoo said. "You do not know Orook the way I know him. He might come across as cold and heartless, but he's nothing of the sort."

"So, you think Maria will be happy?" Maddie asked.

"Eventually," Pullmoo said confidently. "She is almost certainly smitten with him by now."

"But will he ever love her?" Maddie asked.

"I suspect that she will grow on him," Pullmoo said. "I cannot say if they will ever become as close as you and Etmook. Believe it or not, there are some things even I can't predict."

"Or control?" Maddie asked with a cynical smile.

"Indeed," Pullmoo agreed. "Even now, I am in the delightful presence of my favorite reminder of that fact."

"You are infuriatingly unflappable. You know that, right?" Maddie asked.

"I have to be my dear," Pullmoo whispered with a distant smile.

CHAPTER 20

B ack in the Game Center, Orook instructed the circular room to display a scene from the early days in the long history of his kind. Within seconds, Maria was standing in an ancient farm land being worked by people who looked like Pegaseans.

"We started off in much the same way early humans started out on Earth," Orook explained. "We started with farming and agriculture, then began making foundries and factories. Back then, the ratio of men to women was roughly one to one, as it is among humans on Earth."

As Orook continued to speak instructions to the room in Pegasean, the room responded to each command, taking Maria through the evolution of the Olronean people and their various civilizations throughout the planet. At one point, Orook spoke a command to the room which resulted in the appearance of two Olronean children, holding each other by the elbows and pressing their foreheads together. Orook told Maria that, at one time, the Olroneans used mostly only telepathy and hand gestures to communicate.

"Back then, the Olroneans barely spoke," he said. "There are several reasons for this. One of them is that when our ears are in the position required for ultrasonic hearing - which is somewhat similar to echolocation used by Earth bats - we are unable to hear ordinary sound. This means they could not hear each other talk while using both ears to navigate a rough or mercurial terrain."

"Why does the ground move and shift so much?" Maria asked.

"We do not know why the ground moved so much outside the mountains back then," Orook told her. "We are talking about tens of thousands of years ago. The planet was very different then. The ground moved everywhere - even in the desert. Currently, the ground is relatively still except in these mountains around Pegasea."

"So, they had to have both ears in the ultrasonic position all the time?" Maria asked.

"Most of the time, yes. We can leave one ear in one position and one ear in the other position, but it is not as effective," he said. "In any case, the skill was mostly lost as civilization grew and advanced. The ground stopped moving and stopped emitting ultrasonic waves - it stopped 'speaking' to us. Eventually, the Olroneans stopped using their second inner ear."

"But you use yours out on the mountain, right?" Maria asked.

"Yes. The mountains here speak, the land speaks," he said. "Unfortunately, the children are not taught how to listen to the ground."

"Why not?" Maria asked.

"Very few Pegasean citizens ever have reason to go beyond the outer city wall," he told her. "Thus, the skill is considered unnecessary. Regardless, I have been teaching it to my Second Engineers because I personally think it is important."

"Why does the ground around Pegasea 'speak,' but not in other places? Why only here?" she asked.

"No one knows for certain why the ground of the mountain moves or why it speaks. What we do know is that where it moves, it speaks and where it speaks, it moves. I once thought it might have something to do with the lithosphere of this planet - but any explanation at that depth would not explain why it all stopped everywhere but here," Orook said.

Maria watched Orook's brow furrow as his brain worked. After a few moments, he chuckled to himself.

"What?" she asked.

"I was thinking about the vocunine and what they believe - which is silly," he said.

"What do they believe?" Maria asked with a smile.

"They believe that the ultrasonic waves and the ground movements are caused by a god-like creature living deep inside the mountains," he said. "This is why they refer to the Eye of Olrona as Mount Olympus, the home of the gods. I believe they stole that name from your people.

Maria's smile faded instantly.

"What kind of creature?" she asked.

"It is not a talking tree, if that is what you are worried about," Orook teased.

"Are you sure?" Maria asked.

"Quite," Orook said. "Now, let us move on, shall we?"

"Ok," Maria said.

"As I have explained before, for various reasons, we evolved a lot faster than humans on Earth - intellectually, philosophically, and technologically," Orook said as he resumed his presentation on the history of the early Olronean people.

Orook explained that once the Olroneans drove most of the more menacing predators into the wilderness, they were able to build large cities, that enjoyed rapid technological development. He told her that the Olroneans began going into space long before the Pegaseans began making trips to Earth.

"The technology had already been developed by the time Pegasea came into existence," he said. "All we had to do was build the transports. This took some time, of course, but it was only a matter of repeating what had already been done."

Orook then explained that, approximately 2,500 years ago, the birth rate of baby girls began to drop off at a relatively slow, but alarming rate. The room then created what looked to Maria like a sophisticated medical science research lab. Orook explained that Olronean scientists determined that men were still producing sperm with the expected ratios of male and female chromosomes. He told Maria that for a long time, the source of the problem remained a complete mystery. Eventually, a team of Body Biologists managed to produce some evidence that the problem was being caused by a virus-like pathogen of unknown origin.

"We still do not know exactly what it is or how it works," Orook said. "Every time our scientists manage to isolate a protein or virus they suspect to be at the root of the problem, it appears to disassemble itself before it can be properly identified."

"There are things our scientists can't figure out either," Maria said. "In fact, before you guys kidnapped me, a biologist friend of mine told me the sperm production in men all around the planet is declining and no one knows why."

"You were not kidnapped. You were rescued," Orook said.

Maria did not appreciate his reminding her of the imminent demise of humankind on Earth. She was, however, grateful that he had not gone into an oration about how unevolved humans can be easily confused by strange phenomenon, but that it takes something truly extraordinary for the Pegaseans, or Olroneans, to be baffled.

"At first, our population did not suffer much because around this same time period, our life spans were starting to get longer and longer," Orook went on. "As I explained to you previously, we have an explanation for this phenomenon. There is a virus, a viral family actually, which interrupts the aging process and prolongs our natural lives."

Maria nodded.

Orook proceeded to tell her that when their populations did start to crash, the Olroneans panicked. The room suddenly filled with menacing shades of red, orange and black as figures of Olroneans attacking other Olroneans filled the room. In one part of the room, Maria watched what looked like several men approaching a woman on a hospital bed. Maria started to move towards this part of the room before Orook suddenly gave the room a sharp command. Maria jumped as everything suddenly went white again and all the beads fell in a rush to the floor, making a sound like rain.

"I am sorry," Orook said to Maria. "That is *not* what I intended to show you."

He then quickly gave the room another command and six pairs of Olroneans appeared around the room. Orook told Maria that at the height of violence and depravity among the Olroneans, six kind men and six brave women left their home cities and banded together, determined to find somewhere on the planet they could be safe and live in peace.

"It was not easy," Orook told her soberly. "Back then, and even now, it was rare to see six women in one place. They were hunted by groups of Olronean men who did not believe that a woman should be allowed to choose just one mate. To some degree, that sentiment is understandable under the circumstances. However, the way they went about imposing their ideas was unspeakable."

Maria only nodded.

"These are the twelve founders of Pegasea," Orook told her. "They found an odd geological formation deep in the mountains - a flat area of relatively soft stone approximately 200 square kilometers in size. In the stone were thousands of circular trenches, as if cut out of the ground with a giant pipe. They made their homes in these trenches."

"Is that why all the walls of your house are curved?" Maria asked.

"*Our* house," Orook corrected. "And yes, that is why the walls are curved."

"I wonder what created all those trenches," Maria thought aloud.

"There are several theories I can tell you about later," Orook said. "First, let me finish my history lesson."

"Ok," she said.

"Once these twelve founders established themselves, they sent out secret messages to others, inviting them to come join them," Orook continued. "The city grew slowly over the first few hundred or so years. The outer wall was built to keep out unfriendly Olronean outsiders."

The room then created a model of the whole city of Pegasea spread out over the entire floor of the room. Maria walked to the edge of the room and found a place to stand where she would not interrupt the model.

"As I told you before, from an aerial view, the entire City of Pegasea looks a bit like a giant crystal snowflake," Orook reminded her.

Maria marveled at the model of the city spread out before her. It was beautiful. She could see the City Center and the roads and subrails which branched out from the City Center to the District Centers, then branched out from the District Centers to the various nods.

"What is a 'nod?'" she asked. "Is it like a neighborhood?"

Orook nodded, then circled half way around the room before he stopped and squatted down. He pointed to a spot about two-thirds of the way down the model, in a direction towards the City Center.

"That is the street on which we live," he told her.

Maria walked over to where he was positioned and looked down the length of his arm to see where he was pointing.

"I see it," she said.

Orook then stood up, gave more commands, and the model of the City shrank as steep majestic mountains rose up all around it. Orook explained that the City is well hidden and almost impossible to access on foot.

"Not that it matters much now," he said soberly. "The Olronean population outside the City declined rapidly until it ultimately disappeared entirely."

"Wow," was all Maria could say.

CHAPTER 21

B y the time they got home, Maria was exhausted. She wanted to crawl into bed and take a nap. She was headed in that direction when Orook stopped her.

"Wait," he said.

Orook then opened a drawer in one of the walls flanking the living room and pulled out a box about the size of three university text books stacked on top of each other. Orook handed the box to Maria.

"You may have these," he said.

"What is it?" Maria asked as she lifted the lid. When she looked inside, she saw that the box was filled with the same tiny white beads as the ones she had seen in the round white room in the Game Center. When she saw that they clung together like tiny magnets she smiled joyously as she looked up at Orook.

"They are just extras from the prototype. They do not do a whole lot outside of the room," Orook tried to tell her.

Maria didn't care. She loved them anyway.

"Thank you!" she said as she started to pinch them into little peaks within the box. Maria then started to walk back to her room before she thought better of it. It seemed rude to just go hide in her room again.

"What do you plan to do now?" she asked.

Orook had turned to the wall and was doing something with his armband that Maria had never seen him do before. Suddenly, a large section of the bare wall lit up and displayed pictures and text in Pegasean.

"Whoa," Maria said. "What is that?"

"Please do not tell me that you have never seen a computer monitor, or at least a television, before," Orook said.

"Of course, I have - but how did it just come out of nowhere?" she asked.

"It has always been here Maria," he said patiently. "When I turn it off, it becomes the color of the wall. Since it is built into the wall, when it turns the color of the wall, it becomes virtually invisible - that is by design. Most Pegaseans find large black rectangles to be unaesthetic, if not ominous."

"Oh," Maria said.

Orook smiled. "You are tired. Go to sleep," he said.

Maria nodded as she yawned.

• • •

Maria emerged from her room several hours later.

"How was your nap?" Orook asked.

"Wonderful," she said. "I'm sorry I still get really tired in the middle of the day. I don't know why."

"It's like jet-lag," Orook explained. "Our days are longer. Not to mention, you spent three years on a space ship. Sometimes it takes a year to fully adjust."

"How do you know the term 'jet-lag'?" Maria asked.

"I thought I already explained that to you," Orook said.

"I know, but...," Maria started to say before Orook interjected.

"I have a perfect memory, Maria," Orook told her. "And I can assimilate any language, dialect, accent, cultural cues, verbal customs, mannerisms, and so on. My recall of the term 'jet-lag' is hardly impressive. The fact that I roll my eyes in annoyance is more impressive as far as proficiency in Earthly communication skills goes."

"If Rose were here, would you speak to her with a Southern accent?" Maria asked.

"I could, but I would not," Orook told her. "To deliberately assimilate the communication style of another man's companion is offensive to her keeper."

Maria gave him an inquisitive look.

"Among Pegaseans, it is a kind of invasion. The closest analogy I can make is to that of a man going through another man's private things, or rather, through his companion's private things. Assimilation of another's language and nuances of communication is considered a highly intimate act. If you read the PROEs manual every once in a while, you would know that. An exception to this is when a body biologist or presenter does it to make a human feel more comfortable or at ease," Orook explained.

"So, if I ever meet Rose's keeper, he will speak to me with a Southern accent?" Maria asked, trying to understand how this all worked.

"Or in a Pegasean accent - as all the other men do when they speak to you," Orook explained.

"I see," Maria said. "And this is because the Pegaseans view assimilation as a form of one-way intimacy."

Orook nodded.

"Is that why humans are not allowed to learn Pegasean?" Maria asked.

"Maybe," he conceded. "However, there is another far more likely reason. Pegasean is a beautiful language. Why would we want to suffer through hearing you butcher it?"

"Why is it that I can only see your mind every once in a while?" she asked.

"You only see what I allow you to see or want you to see," he said. "The only way you can perceive my thoughts is if I put them in a certain place in my mind. That is the best I can do to explain it in English. Granted, occasionally, if I want you to know what I am thinking, my thoughts will go to that place without my conscious effort to put them there. However, that rarely happens. The vocunines are different. They do not need any help. They can somehow access our thoughts even if we do not put them in that place. The only way to stop them is to speak out loud in your native language. I do not know how it works, but doing that somehow interrupts their access, or interrupts the signal, however you want to think of it. It is difficult to explain in your language."

"Why can't you read my mind?" she asked.

"Seriously?" Orook asked. "Do you have any capacity for deductive reasoning at all? Because if I have to explain absolutely everything to you, this is going to be a very long two weeks."

Maria frowned. "Ok, let me guess, humans don't have that place in our minds... or something like that?" she ventured.

"You have that place in your minds, but you do not know how to put thoughts there," he explained.

"Can it be learned?" Maria asked.

"I do not know," Orook said. "You would have to ask Pullmoo. She is the expert in all of those sorts of things."

Maria sighed. She wanted to keep talking to him, but his tone was so harsh. When he turned back to the computer monitor on the wall, she started to walk back to her room.

"Do not go back to your room," Orook said without turning away from the monitor. "Sit here on the sofa. We can look at pictures or watch one of those videos you call 'movies' from Earth."

"I don't want to annoy you," Maria said.

"Then stop asking questions without first at least trying to figure out the answers yourself," Orook suggested.

Maria nodded and walked back towards the sofa. She stopped in front of it, unsure of how close to him she should sit. At seeing her indecision, Orook reached out and pulled her down onto the sofa so that she was seated next to him.

"Thank you," she said.

Orook nodded and said, "You are welcome."

CHAPTER 22

As Orook flipped through various images on the monitor, Maria looked at his arms and what she could see of his neck and shoulders, wondering if his downy fur was as soft as it looked.

"May I touch you?" Maria asked.

"Touch me where?" Orook asked cautiously.

"I just want to touch your fur. I'm curious. It looks so soft," Maria said.

Orook held out his right arm to her. She ran her hand down the length of his forearm.

"It really is very soft," Maria remarked.

"Is that why you like rabbits?" Orook asked.

Maria nodded, "yes."

"May I have my arm back now?" he asked.

"Yes. Sorry. Of course," Maria said, blushing as she quickly let go of him.

"At least you are not afraid of me anymore," Orook said.

"I was never afraid of you," Maria insisted.

Orook did not respond as he turned his attention back to the monitor.

"What are we going to watch? or look at?" Maria asked.

"I have not yet decided," Orook told her. "To be honest, I have not used this thing in a while."

"Do you have pictures of yourself when you were a kid?" Maria asked.

"I think I do actually," he said.

It took a minute or two for Orook to find the pictures. After he found them, Orook showed Maria a picture of himself when he was an infant. Maria saw that his "baby fur" was much thicker and fluffier than it was now. His infant ears were proportionately much larger and stuck out past the top of his head. Of course, Maria cooed and told him how ridiculously cute he was.

"All Pegasean babies are cute. It is the ears and the white fur - it makes all babies look like bunnies," he explained, then winked at Maria.

Maria rolled her eyes as she smiled.

Orook then changed the picture to one of a young Pegasean boy and girl, holding hands as they laughed and played outside in what must have been summer.

"That is me," he said, pointing to the little boy.

"Who is the little girl? Is that your sister?" Maria asked.

"No, my sister is much older than me. We did not grow up together. I only knew her as a child because she frequently came to visit me in the nursery. Because each Pegasean woman has at least 50 children over her lifetime, everyone has a lot of half-siblings and half-cousins. In fact, there is someone in the Center Council whose full-time job is to make sure that no one inadvertently partners with someone who is too closely related to them. Double-siblings are rare because Pegasean men are only allowed to have a second child if the first one is a girl - or if the first boy dies," Orook told her.

"Yes, I remember you told me that," Maria said, "So who is the little girl in the picture with you?"

"That is Linoo," Orook told her.

The sadness in his voice as he said her name reminded Maria of why, whenever she broke up with a boyfriend, she destroyed every picture she had of him. This thought led to the terrible realization that she had no pictures of anyone from Earth, not even of herself. While it was only a small part of all she had lost, it felt like so much more. She took a deep breath and tried to hide her upset.

"What is wrong?" Orook asked and Maria told him. Orook then asked Maria if she had a cell phone with her at the time she boarded the space ship.

Maria shook her head.

"I am sorry," he said. "Did you have a boyfriend back on Earth? Is that why you are upset? We could have an artist recreate a picture from your memory if you would like."

Maria did not answer.

"Why are you avoiding my question?" Orook asked.

Maria blushed.

"This is interesting," Orook said. "Whether or not you had a boyfriend back on Earth is of no interest to me. However, the fact that you do not want to admit to it is amusing. Why are you being so evasive?"

"Why don't you use your superior deductive reasoning skills to figure it out," Maria said sarcastically, then crossed her arms.

"Ok…," Orook said. "I think you had a boyfriend and that he was married, or engaged, or otherwise someone whom you had no business cavorting around with."

Maria frowned.

"Am I right?" Orook asked.

Maria only turned her face away from him.

Orook nodded to himself. Of course, he was right.

"I didn't know he was married when I met him," Maria said defensively.

Orook tried not to smile as he said, "So, it is not just the Pegasean rules of order and etiquette you do not like - you did not like Earth's rules either."

This made Maria feel angry, then sad, then ashamed. She curled up into a ball and buried her face in her arms. Orook looked at her. He had upset her and would have to undo this somehow.

"I was only teasing you. I did not mean to hurt your feelings," he said, unconvincingly.

When Maria did not unfold, Orook sighed. He did not have the patience for this, but he knew he needed to try. If he could not win her over, they would surely fail their compatibility evaluation and he would probably be suspended from work for an additional two weeks.

"Do you miss him?" Orook asked.

With her face still buried in her arms, Maria considered the question. Surprised to realize that she did not miss the man at all, Maria lifted her head and said, "no."

"You must have broken a lot of hearts on Earth," Orook said, making a weak attempt at flattery.

"Oh, shut up," Maria muttered, but at least she was smiling now.

"You are beautiful. Especially your eyes. They are the color of burning copper sulfate," he said.

"That is the nerdiest pick up line I have every heard," Maria said, laughing.

Orook closed his eyes and shook his head.

"To be clear, I am *not* flirting with you," he said. "When I say you are beautiful, I mean that you are aesthetically pleasing to the eyes - like a nice painting or a blossoming tree."

"Gee, thanks," she said.

Orook smiled, then quickly turned back to the monitor and continued to show Maria various other pictures from his childhood and beyond. He even showed her pictures of himself with some of the other engineers.

"Hey! Is that Etmook and Maddie?" Maria asked excitedly in response to one of the pictures.

"The two on the right? Yes," Orook said.

Maria smiled at the picture. Even in this stiff formal photo, taken at some event which could have been an awards ceremony, you could tell they were in love.

"How did you recognize Etmook?" Orook asked.

"I met him, remember? That first day when you had me wait in the companions' room in the meeting hall," Maria explained quickly.

"But you did not recognize the other keepers. Why did you recognize him?" Orook asked.

Maria suddenly became nervous. Why was he interrogating her about this?

"Um, well… I don't know… I must just remember him in particular because he's so handsome," Maria lied.

Orook looked at her with suspicion, then said "I will not deny that Etmook is a good-looking man, but you are obviously lying to me, why?"

Maria's heart began to race. She didn't know what to say, or what was safe to say.

"Just tell me," Orook said, trying to sound harmless. He then let Maria see his mind, which was free from any anger or worry.

"I saw them outside one day," Maria said, prevaricating only a little.

"And…," Orook prompted.

Maria shrugged.

"They were kissing and stuff," she said.

Orook shook his head disapprovingly.

"They really shouldn't do that in public," he said.

"There was no one else around," Maria said.

"You were around," Orook countered.

"Why does that matter?" Maria asked.

"It is a PROEs violation, or maybe several violations, depending on what you mean by 'and stuff,'" Orook told her.

"To do it in public or to do it at all?" Maria asked.

Orook made an exasperated sound.

"Enough of this," he said. "You are going to start reading the PROEs Manual now."

Orook then turned off the monitor and stood up. He instructed Maria to get her computer out of her room and bring it to him. After she did so, he touched the screen and maneuvered through the device until it clearly displayed the PROEs Manual. He then handed it back to Maria.

"Start reading," he instructed. "I've locked it to this one source, so you can't read anything else until you get through it."

With a groan, Maria started walking back to her room, computer in hand.

"No, do not go to your room," Orook instructed. "Sit in that chair you like out here in the living room."

Maria bristled. She opened her mouth to tell him to stop bossing her around, then closed it again.

"I just want to make sure you do not fall asleep," Orook explained gently.

"Ok, dad," Maria muttered.

Maria saw Orook's ear twitch.

"You are not a child, and you are certainly not my child," he said firmly but not unkindly

Maria sighed and braced herself for another lecture about the inferiority of humans. To Maria's surprise, Orook did not lecture her. Instead, he asked, "Was there anyone on Earth from whom you willingly and graciously took instructions? Were there people who, in any sense, ranked above you? - like a boss, a professor, or a coach?"

Maria nodded and said, "I had a lot of professors. I also had a boss where I worked at the coffee shop, but no one ever took him seriously. He was an idiot."

"Ok, well, maybe it would help you to think of me as you would one of them - as one of your professors," he suggested.

Maria considered this for a moment, then said, "Actually, that might fit. Except for the holding hands part - it would be weird and inappropriate if I ever held a professor's hand as much as I held yours today."

At this Orook smiled and said, "Ok, but aside from that - does thinking of me that way help you?"

"Help me what?" she asked.

"Help you to follow my instructions without becoming bitter," he explained.

"It might," Maria conceded. "I will try."

"Thank you," he said.

Faced with few other options, Maria started to read the PROEs Manual. She fell asleep no less than three times before it was actually time to go to bed for the night. Fortunately, Orook woke her up each time.

CHAPTER 23

In a cave deep in the mountain range surrounding Pegasea, the alpha vocunine of the mountain pack howled into the cold and windy night, calling all those loyal to him. Once the entire pack had gathered obediently in the cave, the alpha told his pack about the Pegasean called "Orook." He recounted Orook's crimes with hostile condemnation. He began by reminding them that Orook had killed their previous pack leader when he set off explosives in the northern ridge in order to build a water reservoir for the City of Pegasea. He conceded that he did not believe that Orook had intended to kill his brother. Regardless, his actions had shown a complete lack of respect or concern for the vocunine. The alpha then recounted to his pack what Orook had done to the vocunine who happened to be the alpha's youngest, and favorite, nephew and his nephew's wife.

"He used trickery to blind my nephew to the ground!" cried the alpha. "Then he broke his back and left him to die a slow and shameful death. Then after the angel shamed him for his brutality, this wretched man offered to end my nephew's life. This brave and noble vocunine refused the man's offer and expressed his wish to die inside the mountain, an honorable place to die. But the killer refused him his dying wish by stabbing him in the back!"

The pack's growls first intensified, then turned to howls and whines of lament.

"We must end this man," the alpha told them. "Enough is enough!"

The pack yelped in agreement and comradery with their leader.

"When the cold breaks, we will breach their city wall and confront their leader, the one they call Pullmoo," the alpha told them. "We will demand she give us Orook, or we will rip them all apart!"

Again, the pack voiced its agreement. Some of them even stood up on two legs as if getting ready to storm the city that very moment.

"Their guards can hold off one or even a few of us, but they can't stop us if we all attack at once," the alpha said confidently.

"What about the human woman who guards the man called Orook?" asked one of the pack members.

The alpha thought for a moment, then said, "We will demand her as well. We will set her free. She will be grateful to us and reward us in heaven."

The pack nodded in agreement with this plan as well.

The alpha then discussed with his pack the details of their plan to storm the city of Pegasea at dawn of the first day of spring.

• • •

Back inside the city, Maria tossed and turned in her bed as the Prisoner once again invaded her dreams. Once again, she saw the cave and the tree that spoke into her mind until she could not stand it anymore. She sat up and rubbed her temples, then got up and walked out of her room. She looked over at Orook's bed and saw that he was awake.

"I'm sorry, did I wake you?" Maria asked.

"Yes, I heard you talking in your sleep," he said.

"Yeah, I do that sometimes," she said, looking down at her bare feet on the cold tile floor.

Orook got up out of bed and walked to the kitchen. He returned a minute later and held his hand to Maria.

"What is it?" Maria asked as she looked at the small leaves in his palm.

"This is an herb that helps quiet loud dreams," he told her. "Chew them slowly. It will help."

"Ok, thank you," Maria said as she took the leaves from him.

Orook nodded, then returned to bed and soon fell back to sleep.

Maria sat down on her bed and chewed the leaves as she looked out her periscope to the outside. The full moon was bright and allowed her to see a bit of the surface world above her. She could just barely see buds beginning on the trees and her heart leapt at the thought of the approaching spring.

CHAPTER 24

The next morning, Maria woke up with a tentative new joy at the thought of spending another day with Orook. She had gone to bed the night before feeling about her keeper the way she always had - a kind of begrudging respect and admiration, mixed with gratitude and an inexplicably profound level of trust. Then, seemingly overnight, something had changed, ever so slightly, but maybe just enough. As she showered and got dressed, she mentally explored the shift in her mind and in her heart. By the time she walked into the kitchen for breakfast, she thought she knew what had happened - she was starting to like him.

When Orook saw her, he handed her a bowl and a glass. She stood holding it, just watching him, until he gestured for her to sit down. When he spoke, she listened to the sound of his voice. As she began eating her breakfast, she stared at his clothes and his hair and wondered about who he really was - what he was thinking and feeling.

At the same time, Orook was wondering why Maria had suddenly become so uncommunicative. This woman who, just the day before, could barely go ten minutes without asking six questions, was suddenly quiet.

"Are you ok?" Orook asked as he took Maria's empty dishes from her.

"I'm fine, why?" Maria answered.

"You have been very quiet this morning," he said.

"I have?" she asked dully.

Orook gave her an assessing look, then decided not to press the issue. They needed to get going.

"Well, I am certainly not complaining. We should go now. My sister is expecting us in about half an hour," he said.

"I'm ready," Maria said cheerfully.

• • •

The subrail was not as crowded as it had been the day before and Maria and Orook were able to sit down for most of the way to Wilamoo's home. When they arrived, Orook reminded her to stand one pace behind him as he knocked on the door. It was less than a minute before the door opened. In front of them stood a Pegasean woman, about the same height as Orook and dressed in black clothing trimmed in blue and silver.

"Oroo!" the woman exclaimed with a broad smile. Maria watched in fascination as Orook made a rather elaborate gesture of respect which Maria had never seen before. Maria could not clearly see what he was doing because his long over coat concealed the details of his motions. Orook and Wilamoo then hugged like old friends.

"And who is this?" asked Wilamoo in English, looking behind him to Maria.

"My name is Maria, companion to the First Engineer," Maria said robotically, then bowed. She looked to Orook for confirmation that she had done the right thing.

Orook sighed softly, then said, "The introduction was correct, but you do not bow. You are supposed to…"

"Oh, leave her alone, Orook, we're all family here," Wilamoo said.

Orook only shook his head and muttered, "She's never going to learn."

"You never learned either Oroo. That is why the Center Council appointed you First Engineer. The rules are much easier when you're at the top," Wilamoo teased as she winked over Orook's shoulder at Maria.

Turning to his companion, Orook said proudly, "Maria, this is Wilamoo, First Mathematician of Pegasea and my double sister."

"Double sister?" Maria asked.

"We have both the same mother and the same father," Wilamoo explained as she beckoned them both inside, "and please just call me Wilamoo."

Maria stepped into Wilamoo's home to find a warm and inviting atmosphere. There were flowers on the end tables and plush rugs covering most of the floor. This house seemed so much brighter than Orook's, which was perpetually dim in the winter months. Maria noticed, as she walked past Wilamoo and into the living space, that Wilamoo was clearly pregnant.

"Whose is it this time?" Orook asked, eyeing her prominent baby bump.

"Who knows? Who cares?" Wilamoo said dismissively. "The nurses knock me up with someone new every time. If it's not Lenook's, it makes no difference to me."

"How much longer before you two can get married?" Orook asked.

Wilamoo blew out a long breath, then said "Well, it all depends on how long it takes me to fulfill my reproductive requirement. This will be my 42nd son. So, I only need to have a few more boys. However, as you know, I still don't have any daughters. So, it's hard to say. I sure hope I don't have to wait until the very end of my child bearing years."

Orook smiled, then said, "You must love him a lot."

"With every fiber of my being, as the Earth women like to say," she said.

"Am I invited to the wedding?" Orook asked.

"Only if you stay out of trouble," Wilamoo said with a grin.

Orook narrowed his eyes at Maria.

"Don't blame her, Oroo," Wilamoo admonished.

"You sound like Lenook and Linoo," Orook muttered.

Maria wanted to change the subject.

"Why did my keeper make that fancy gesture when he first saw you?" she asked, then tried to imitate the gesture.

"Sooo many reasons," Wilamoo answered as she playfully shoved Orook. He allowed himself to stagger from the blow. Maria had to smile. She had never seen Orook look so happy or so relaxed.

"It is the third gesture of respect." Orook told Maria. "Wilamoo and I are both Firsts, but she is a mathematician. Mathematics ranks higher than engineering. It ranks higher than all other professions because it makes all other professions possible. It is the enemy of chaos and provides rules to all things that are real. That would be reason enough to warrant the second gesture of respect. The fact that she is my elder sister requires an additional level of respect."

"And it goes like this...," he added, then demonstrated the movement where Maria could see what he was doing.

"You seem to enjoy doing that," Wilamoo said, teasing him.

"Well, how often does a man of my distinguished status have occasion to make such a gesture?" he countered, with mock bravado.

"Do all Pegasean brothers and sisters act like this with each other?" Maria asked, hoping she didn't sound rude.

"No, we're special," Wilamoo said dryly.

"*Very* special," Orook agreed.

"And yet, when was the last time you bothered to come visit me?" Wilamoo asked, looking sternly at Orook

"I came over just last...," Orook started to say.

"*Not* counting the occasions when you only came to give me a math problem to solve? Or a model or simulation to run?" Wilamoo interrupted.

"You know how it is," Orook said. "There is never any time."

"Excuses, excuses," Wilamoo said dismissively. "It took an order from the Council to get you here, just admit it."

"He really *is* always working," Maria said in an attempt to defend her keeper.

"Thank you, Maria," Orook said with a trace genuine gratitude.

"In any case, I've decided to punish you for not visiting me more often you by inviting Lenook to join us," Wilamoo said triumphantly.

Orook groaned, "*Why?* You know the man loathes me."

"You are exaggerating. He just doesn't know you very well and that is no one's fault but your own," Wilamoo chided.

"I like the Second Presenter. He seems kind," Maria said, still not sure when she was allowed to say the name of a Pegasean man.

"You may say his name so long as he is not here and so long as there is no chance of him hearing you say it. It is the same with my name. If you want to talk about me with your human friends, you are free to say my name among them, so long as I never hear you say it. Do you understand?" he asked.

Maria nodded.

"Well, now that we are all clear on that point, why don't we all go sit down in the kitchen? Lenook will be here soon and I have a wonderful meal for us," Wilamoo instructed cheerfully.

When Maria walked into the kitchen, which was small but cozy and brightly lit, she saw drying herbs hanging on the walls and colorful dish rags stacked neatly next to the sink. On the kitchen table, she saw place settings for four people. In the center of the table was the closest thing to real food Maria had seen since she left Earth. There was what looked like actual bread, cheese, and a bowl of some kind of berries and nuts.

"Oh, wow!" said Maria. "Where did you find real food?"

"During the winter, when such things are scarce, there is a place in the Center District Commons where you can get one of these things once every lunar cycle. If you don't avail yourself of the luxury in one lunar cycle, you get a kind of credit which carries over into the next cycle. And, well, my brother never uses his, so he gave his credits to me. We are going to have what amounts to a feast in this City - in winter at least," Wilamoo explained.

"It looks wonderful," Maria said eagerly and thanked Wilamoo profusely.

Lenook arrived as Wilamoo was pouring water flavored with a native herb into each glass on the table. He walked into the kitchen, greeted Wilamoo with a kiss on the cheek, then smiled at Maria. He only glared at Orook.

"What now?" Orook asked.

"Nothing," Lenook said, then smiled. "Your companion looks much happier now. It must be the food. Or is this simply the first time you have let her leave her room since the hearing?"

"Stop it," Maria said hotly. "You are being rude."

Lenook and Orook turned in unison to look at Maria, clearly surprised at her tone.

"I'm sorry," Maria said quickly.

"That is quite alright," Lenook said slowly. He then turned back to Orook and made the first gesture of apology. Maria did not understand why he used the first gesture rather than the second. Orook, however, understood perfectly well and did appreciate the subtle insult. By using the first gesture, Lenook was apologizing for his failure to recognize Orook's accomplishment or skill in winning Maria's loyalty. He was not apologizing for what he had said.

Once they were all seated, they began eating and the mood gradually lightened. Maria told Lenook and Wilamoo about her and Orook's trip to the Game Center and about the pictures Orook had shown her when they got back home. Eventually, Lenook became convinced that Orook actually was making an effort to be a better keeper. He then sincerely apologized to Orook and the tension between the two men eased.

"You know Pullmoo would have found a way to suspend you from work one way or another," Lenook told Orook.

Orook sighed, "I suppose you are right. She and Linoo have been hounding me to take a restoration period for years."

"Why does it seem like Pullmoo controls everything that goes on around here?" Maria asked.

"She doesn't control everything," Wilamoo told her. "Only the Center Council can change the laws. In fact, any and all significant City-wide decisions require the Council's approval."

Lenook gave Wilamoo an incredulous look.

"What?" Wilamoo asked.

"You know as well as I do that the Center Council does whatever Pullmoo tells it to do," Lenook said, in a tone suggesting only admiration for Pullmoo.

"But why?" Maria asked again. "I mean, how did she get into such a position of power? Is the First Sociologist always the most powerful person in the City?"

"Not usually," Orook told Maria. "Usually, the First Mathematician is the most powerful - but my sister has no use for power. She also adores Pullmoo."

"*You do?*" Maria asked.

"Absolutely," Wilamoo said. "She is the most intelligent person in the City, by far. She could have been a First of anything. She could have been First Mathematician or First Engineer if she had wanted to be. She is also the most kind and gracious person I have ever met."

Maria looked to Orook to see if he agreed with what his sister had just said.

"I agree that Pullmoo is the most intelligent person in the City," Orook said, answering Maria's unspoken question.

"More intelligent than you and Wilamoo?" Maria asked.

Both Wilamoo and Orook nodded "yes."

"Should I be insulted that she didn't ask if Pullmoo was more intelligent than me?" Lenook asked, and they all laughed.

"Why are you so interested in Pullmoo?" Wilamoo asked.

Maria clenched and unclenched her fists briefly. Orook observed her subdued anger with keen interest.

"Well, she almost had me killed," Maria said, trying in vain not to sound angry.

"I'm sure she knew what she was doing. She always has a plan," Wilamoo said dismissively.

"A *plan*?" Maria said bitterly. "So, I'm supposed to just trust her then, is that it? Is that what you all do? You just accept her decisions because she has a plan? Don't you see what she has done - what she continues to do? She and the Center Council choose who you are, what you do and who they will love. She allows the Center Council to rip babies from their parents' arms to be raised in an orphanage you like to call a 'nursery.' She is an evil manipulative bitch."

"Maria…," Orook said softly as he discretely and gently squeezed her hand under the table. Maria hung her head, suddenly embarrassed by the sudden awkward silence she had brought down on the run.

"My dear, that was incredibly rude," Wilamoo said at last. "I'm not much of a stickler for the PROEs, especially among family, or in the privacy of my home, but I do expect people to behave decently. I certainly don't appreciate you speaking so unkindly, and with such blatant hostility, about someone I respect and whom you have never even met. You should be ashamed."

Maria apologized in a voice barely above a whisper.

"Wilamoo," Orook said, "While I certainly don't condone Maria's bad behavior, she does have at least some justification for resenting the woman. Pullmoo really did have an order out to euthanize her."

Wilamoo nodded, then said to Maria, "I understand, and I accept your apology. However, you must never speak that way about her, or anyone else for that matter, again - at least not in my house. Do you understand?"

Maria nodded and promised she would not.

• • •

After dinner, Lenook suggested that they all play a Pegasean game of cards.

"You play cards?" Maria asked. "Like the way we play cards?"

"Well, obviously, our playing cards are different," Lenook said. "But yes, the way we play is similar - at least in that the games involve a combination of change and strategy."

"May I play?" Maria asked.

"Of course," he said.

Lenook and Wilamoo then showed Maria the cards, which each had a color and a number. They then explained the rules of the game they all agreed to play. Like the Earthly game of Hearts, the game was a game played with teams. Naturally, one team consisted of Wilamoo and Lenook while Maria and Orook made up the other team. As the game progressed, Maria became more and more frustrated with Orook's apparent resignation to their ultimate defeat. After losing the third round, she cleared her throat and politely asked her keeper if she could have a word with him in private.

Orook looked to his sister.

Wilamoo casually gestured her dismissal of him from the room, then placed her cards down on the table in a neat little stack.

Lenook gave his fiancé a furtive smile as Maria and Orook left the room.

"Maria, what is this about?" Orook asked as he closed the door to the kitchen behind them.

"Do you want to win this game? Or are we just playing to pass the time?" Maria asked.

Orook's brow raised, then narrowed.

"Why do you ask?" he said.

"Because you're not even trying," Maria whispered.

Orook folded his arms.

"How would you know?" he asked.

"Oh, come on!" she said. "Just how dumb do you think I am?"

"Maria, all humans are dull," he said.

Maria grit her teeth and glared at him.

"And exactly how many humans have you known besides me?" she asked.

"I do not need to know many of you," he said. "I have seen the data. Every human is given an intelligence test. If she is born here, she is tested several times throughout childhood and at least once after she comes of age. You were tested shortly after you arrived here from Earth. Granted, you received the highest score attainable on the human intelligence test - but that only means that you are about as smart as a human can be expected to be."

"Wait a minute," Maria said. "What do you mean I scored the highest on the *human* intelligence test?"

"You scored 100. The test for humans only goes to 100. The test for Pegaseans goes up to 200," he explained.

"Give me the test for Pegaseans then," she demanded.

Orook stared at her for a long moment before saying, "It's written in Pegasean."

"So, translate it for me," Maria said.

"Alright," Orook said. "But we cannot do this now. Wilamoo and Lenook…"

"No. I want to take it now," Maria insisted.

Orook frowned.

"Please," Maria added.

Orook took a deep breath, then went into the kitchen and asked Wilamoo and Lenook if they would mind taking a brief hiatus from the game they were playing. He explained that Maria wanted to take the Pegasean intelligence test.

Lenook grinned and said, "You will need the English translation. I just happen to have it on my computer."

"Why would you…," Orook began to ask.

"Maria is not the first human woman to express an interest in taking the Pegasean test," Lenook interrupted.

"What is the highest score achieved by a human?" Orook asked.

"That I cannot tell you," Lenook said. "What I can tell you is that the median score for a Pegasean is between 120 and 130, while the median score for a human woman is between 90 and 100. The most intelligent humans can score within the median range for Pegasean. The most intelligent Pegaseans will score between 190 and 200."

"What did you score?" Orook asked with a crooked smile.

"I could tell you, but I am afraid that doing so would disrupt the delicate balance of our relationship," he said with a wink.

"Boys," Wilamoo said. "It doesn't matter what either of you scored because I scored higher than both of you."

"Only by five points," Orook said.

"Only four in my case," Lenook said under his breath as he pulled out his tablet computer and brought up the test before handing it to Orook.

Outside in the living room, Maria chewed her nails as she paced back and forth in front of Wilamoo's sofa. She wondered what was taking her keeper so long. Just as she was working up the nerve to go into the kitchen and ask, Orook came out through the door holding Lenook's tablet computer in one hand.

"In theory, the test has no time limit," he said as he held the device out to her. "However, the faster you answer the questions, the higher your score."

"Explain how that works," Maria said. "How the scoring works... how the questions are scored and how time is taken into account."

After Orook explained the scoring system, Maria sat down on the sofa and started the test. She found all the easiest questions and answered them immediately, then moved on to progressively harder questions until exactly 36 minutes had passed. She then stopped the test and handed it to Orook.

"You did not finish the test," he said. "You did not answer all of the questions."

"I don't have to answer all of the questions," she said.

"True, but...," Orook started to say.

"Just score it," Maria said.

Orook looked at the screen and pressed the button to process the results. His eyes went wide when a score of 144 displayed on the screen.

"You cheated," he said.

Maria sat back, crossed her arms and grinned triumphantly.

"I am serious," he said. "You manipulated the scoring system."

"Are you saying that I out-smarted the Pegasean intelligence test?" Maria asked.

Orook struggled to suppress a smile.

"Alright, ok," he said. "I concede that you are smart - not as smart as me, but that would not be a fair comparison even if you were Pegasean."

"I know you are smarter than me," Maria said. "Why do you think I like hanging out with you? It's certainly not because of your charming personality."

Orook knit his brow. "You like spending time with me?" he asked.

"Well, yeah," Maria said. "Back on Earth, well, not to brag or anything - but I was usually always the smartest person in a room. You might think that's a good thing, but it's hard sometimes. I didn't have a lot of friends... it was hard to talk to people, you know?"

Orook smiled, then sat down next to her.

"Yes, I do know," he said. "And not to brag myself - but it is often like that for me among my people as well. Granted, the range of our intelligence is narrower, but still... I understand."

Maria looked at him, then unfolded her arms.

"I apologize for underestimating your intelligence," he said. "In my defense, you make a lot of stupid decisions that seem inconsistent with an intelligent mind."

"Yeah, I know," she muttered.

"Why is that?" he asked.

Maria shrugged. "Sometimes I do things without thinking," she conceded.

Orook shook his head and said, "your species is very strange."

"Well, in any case...," Maria said, "will you stop playing this card game as if your partner is an idiot? Can we play to win now?"

"Yes," he said. "As long as you promise to think."

• • •

On their way home, Orook noticed that Maria had again become uncharacteristically quiet, as she had earlier that morning. It seemed like every time he looked in her direction, she was either staring at him or blankly at the floor.

"Do you know why I did not admonish you for your opprobrious outburst against Pullmoo?" he asked as they got off the subrail and walked down the street towards home.

"I don't know what 'opprobrious' means," Maria said dully.

"It means hateful," Orook said. "Now tell me why I did not scold you."

Maria sighed, then, paraphrasing from the PROEs manual, she said "because when a companion requires admonishment, her keeper is expected to give a kind of right of first refusal to the highest-ranking person in the room. If that person doesn't admonish the recalcitrant companion, then the keeper is expected to admonish her."

"Very good," Orook said, "you really have been reading the manual."

Maria nodded.

Once they reached home and went inside, Orook told Maria that there was another reason he had not admonished her.

"Oh? What is it?" Maria asked.

"I am not so fond of her myself," Orook said with an affectionate smile.

CHAPTER 25

In the late morning of the next day, now on the third day of Orook's suspension, Maria was sitting in the living room, in her favorite plush brown armchair, trying to read the last thirty pages of the PROEs manual. She was not making much progress because she kept having to read and re-read the same words over and over again. She could not concentrate. Orook was sitting on the sofa and was busy tinkering with what looked like some sort of complicated three-dimensional puzzle, or maybe a complex valve or switch plate of some sort. She watched his dexterous hands manipulate the numerous moving parts and wondered about his objective with the thing. Maria let her eyes wander from his hands to his well-toned arms and shoulders, then up his neck to his face. She took in the sight of his thick hair, which he left a bit ruffled now that he had nowhere to go. She followed the line of his jaw and his aquiline nose. His raw sienna colored eyes seemed to almost glow with concentration. When she closed her eyes, she thought about his smell, a subtle mix of aromas like that of sliced pears and sawdust. This could not be happening, she told herself. She must be ill, or confused, or maybe it had simply been much too long since she had been with a man. As she squirmed and rotated in her chair, she tried to force herself to think about something else. When this proved futile, she decided that if she was ever going to finish reading the PROEs manual, she would need to at least take a long cold shower or spend some time alone in her room.

"Can I take a break?" Maria asked.

"*May* you take a break - and no, you may not," Orook said as he continued to manipulate the complicated device in his hands.

"Why not?" Maria whined.

"Maria, you just took a break an hour ago. I might also add that you have done nothing but stare at me for this past hour," he said.

Maria blushed, then groaned.

"What is going on? You are not usually this difficult," he said.

"I'm not being difficult," Maria said as she sunk down in her chair and stared at the door.

"Why have you been ogling me?" he asked.

"I wasn't *ogling* you - I was just looking at you," Maria said. "There isn't a whole lot else to look at in here."

"Hmm, well, please try to concentrate," he said.

Maria made a show of turning her attention, such as it was, back to the PROEs manual.

A few minutes later she asked, "So, are we ever allowed to interact with the human men of this city?"

"No," he said.

"Why not?" she asked.

"Why do you think?" Orook asked.

"Because it would be fun, and you guys hate fun?" Maria said.

"Did we not have fun at the Game Center? Or at my sister's house?" Orook asked.

"Yeah, we did, but that's not the kind of fun I'm talking about," Maria said.

"Human reproduction is tightly controlled here," he said without looking up. "If human men and women were allowed to join together at will, there would be no way to make sure that mostly girls are born - or that they would all be born healthy and otherwise compatible with life here."

"Is that what you call it? Joining?" Maria asked.

Orook nodded.

"Well, back on Earth, we often join just to join, not necessarily to procreate," Maria said.

"That is true of us too," Orook told her. "After our second son was born, and there was no longer any further procreation permitted between us, Linoo and I still joined frequently during the mating season."

"You have a mating season?" Maria asked.

"Yes. We get restless in the late spring and early summer, then the impulse dies down over the course of the winter months," Orook explained.

"So, if you are only allowed to partner with a Pegasean woman once, and only for 5 years, what do you do the rest of the time?" Maria asked.

"Maria, why are you asking me these questions?" he asked.

Maria shrugged.

"How do your kind join? Is it the same way we do?" Maria asked.

Orook sighed, then put down his device and looked at Maria.

"What?" Maria said, avoiding his eyes.

"You really do need to finish reading the PROEs manual," he said.

"I can't," Maria said.

"Why not?" Orook asked.

"Because I'm *restless*," Maria said.

"Well, what would you like to do to remedy this problem?" he asked.

"You're supposed to be really smart, right?" she said. "What do you think I want to do about it?"

"I already told you that human women are not permitted to interact with the few human men in the city," he said.

"Well, am I allowed to *interact* with your kind?" she asked.

Orook raised an eyebrow at her.

"Are we allowed to?" she added quietly.

Orook smiled as he stood up and walked over to Maria's chair. He took the tablet computer off her lap and placed in on the end table. He then took her hand and lifted her to her feet. When he put his arm around her waist and kissed her, Maria's knees buckled so badly she had to steady herself on the arm of the chair.

"Wow," he said. "Maybe you should have asked me sooner."

Maria, who was feeling slightly dizzy now, only nodded. She let him lead her back to the bedroom.

"You human women like to do this in the dark, right?" Orook asked. Without waiting for a response, he pressed a button on the wall near the door to the bedroom. The room went dark as the crystal roof gradually turned opaque. Maria looked up and marveled at the effect.

She was momentarily distracted as Orook deftly undid the knot at the side of her blouse. The rush of cold air at the small of her back shocked her back into semi-coherence. Orook put his arms around her and covered her exposed skin with his hands. It was the most physical contact she had had with anyone since leaving Earth and she all but melted under his touch.

"So, is it really all the same?" she asked as her brain started to shut down.

Orook nodded as he gently stroked her back with the tips of his fingers. He waited for her to give in to her desire. He did not have to wait long.

• • •

Several hours later, Maria woke up alone in Orook's bed, feeling more rested than she had in a very long time. His bed was a lot more comfortable than hers - which had originally been designed for a Pegasean child. She found her clothes and got dressed before walking back into the living room.

"Feeling better?" Orook asked. He was fully dressed and had obviously been working at something the entire time Maria had been sleeping.

Maria nodded, then sat back down in her favorite chair. Orook walked over to her and handed her back her computer.

"Do you think you can finish your reading now?" Orook asked.

Maria nodded.

Feeling a little more focused now, Maria found where she had left off in the manual and continued reading. When Maria got to the last chapter of the manual, she learned that all public displays of affection between keepers and companions, other than hand-holding and brief hugs, were violations of the PROEs. There was also a long footnote which explained that, in general, joining between Pegaseans and humans was prohibited under the City's Actively Enforced Rules (the City's criminal code). It was also illegal for a Pegasean man to make any kind of sexual advance on any human woman. The only exception was if a companion indicated, in advance and in no uncertain terms, that she desired to join with her keeper. Even then, there was a requirement that the companion show continued interest in the activity throughout the encounter. If at any moment she expressed a desire to discontinue the activity, or even simply remained still for more than 20 seconds, the rules required the man to stop and walk away. When and if that happened, he was not permitted to show annoyance or disappointment at her change of heart.

Maria read on to learn that the basis of the general prohibition, as well as the numerous conditions placed on the exception, was the undeniable power differential between keepers and companions, and between Pegasean men and human women in general. The text noted that, initially, joining with human women, or even showing any interest in doing so, was outlawed entirely. This law was based on the idea that the power and authority Pegasean men had over human women made true consent impossible. However, the law was instantly unpopular among all parties involved. Additionally, it turned out to be nearly impossible to enforce since no human woman was willing to accuse her keeper of any wrong doing. In the one and only case where a keeper and companion were actually caught in the act, the companion of the accused keeper insisted that she had coerced him. She then refused to eat until the Center Council agreed to drop the charges against her keeper. After much debate, a compromise was made between the law makers and the Pegasean men who kept companions. The general prohibition against propositioning human women, or joining with them, remained the law - but with an exception added to it. If the specified conditions were met, then joining would be permitted. During these debates, the wishes of the human women were heard by the Center Council, as was required by the PROEs, but were not officially factored into the final decision.

Maria looked over at Orook, who was engrossed in whatever it was he was doing.

"This is ridiculous," she said.

"What is?" Orook asked.

"This rule that keepers can't show any interest in joining," Maria said.

Orook shrugged.

"I don't make the rules," he said.

"But you follow them," she said.

"Of course, I do," Orook said. "Try to finish the manual before you go to bed."

"I'm almost through it," Maria told him.

"Good," he said.

Maria quickly read through the rest of the last chapter until she got to the last paragraph which addressed sleeping arrangements for keepers and companions. Under the PROEs, and under the Actively Enforced Rules, a keeper was strictly forbidden from asking his companion to share a bed with him, or even suggesting that she do so. The only circumstances under which a companion was permitted to sleep in her keeper's bed is if she was terribly uncomfortable in her own bed and requested to sleep with him in his. By this time, Maria was so annoyed with these rules that she almost threw the computer across the room. Instead, she simply turned it off and set it on the end table.

"These rules are absurd - and kinda insulting," Maria said.

"Would you rather we have free reign to abuse you in any way we desire?" Orook asked.

"Those are not the only two options," Maria said.

"In practice they are," Orook told her. "As the manual explains, the power differential makes it very difficult to define 'consent.'"

"If I didn't want to join with you or sleep in your bed, you would know," Maria said.

"Would I?" Orook asked.

"Of course, you would," Maria insisted.

"Well, we can get into this debate another time," he said. "I am tired and am going to bed."

"I'm not sleeping with you," Maria said.

"Suit yourself," Orook said.

CHAPTER 26

The next morning, as they cleaned up after breakfast, Orook told Maria that he had plans to meet Lenook in the sparring room. He explained that even though he was not required to attend sparring practice during his "vacation," his sister had asked him to help her fiancé, Lenook.

"He is an inexcusably weak fighter," Orook said.

"Why does he need to be able to fight? Do the vocunine attack the city often?" Maria asked.

"No, not often," Orook said. "However, when they do attack, we need to be ready. Also, in addition to the vocunine, there are even more ferocious predators in the lands past the mountains. Granted, these have yet to come near the city, but that does not mean they never will."

"What kinds of predators?" Maria asked.

"Never mind them for now," Orook said. "In any event, you should be practicing too. You will come with me today. The men's sparring room is next door to the human's defense practice room."

After they had changed into their practice clothes, Orook told Maria that it would soon be warm enough to go outside and visit the parks at the surface.

"Really?" Maria said, excitedly.

"Yes, today is the first day of the spring," he told her.

• • •

In the sparring room, Orook found Lenook standing idly out on the practice room floor, twirling his bō like a baton. Lenook waited as Orook carefully inspected the bō in his hands and tested it for weaknesses.

"Oh, come on Orook, it's just a big stick," Lenook said. "How much diagnostic testing could it possibly require?"

Orook glared at him, then hit the bō he was holding hard against a bench along the practice room wall. The weapon broke into splintered pieces. Orook looked at Lenook and said, "You were saying?"

Lenook groaned.

Once Orook finally found a practice weapon that met his approval, he joined Lenook on the practice mat.

"You are holding your bō incorrectly," Orook said.

Lenook sighed and repositioned his hands.

Orook advanced on Lenook, who moved quickly to block Orook's strikes. It was all he could do to keep Orook at bay. After twenty minutes, Lenook was exhausted and out of breath.

"Ugh, Orook!" Lenook panted. "Why are you trying to kill me?"

"If I was trying to kill you, you would already be dead. You are terrible at this," Orook said.

Orook then deliberately hit his bō against the knuckles of Lenook's left hand, which was gripping the bō at an odd angle.

Lenook wailed.

"What the fuck is wrong with you?" Lenook shouted in English.

"You are pathetic. What does my sister see in you? I have sparred with human women who were more adept at this than you," Orook scolded in their native tongue.

"I am a *presenter*," Lenook said. "We aim to *avoid* conflict - and preferably without excessive physical exertion."

"And what happens if the vocunine invade the City?" Orook challenged.

"I will hide behind you," Lenook quipped.

Orook wacked Lenook's legs with his bō. Lenook yelped as he fell to the floor.

"You have to get better at this," Orook said.

He rubbed his bruising shins as he spewed profanities at Orook.

"If I try, will you stop hitting me?" Lenook asked.

"Let me put it this way, if you do not try, I will most certainly keep hitting you. Your only chance of me not hitting you is if you try - and try a lot harder," Orook said.

"You can't make me do this," Lenook said.

"Maybe *I* cannot, but Wilamoo can," Orook reminded him.

Lenook groaned and stood back up. Despite his best efforts, he could barely keep up with Orook. After an hour, Orook told him they could stop for the day, but that they would need to practice together at least four days a week if he was ever going to improve.

"Why can't I just carry a blow dart with me at all times?" Lenook asked.

"As if anyone would trust you with a blow dart," Orook said.

CHAPTER 27

F ully dressed in the deep royal purple of the First Sociologist, Pullmoo strode out onto the surface land just outside the bounds of the inner city. The edge of her skirt collected dew from sprouting clover as it danced in the warm spring wind at her heels. She refused a Guardsman's escort as she approached the mountain king, the alpha vocunine, Borkane.

"You come out to me alone?" he snarled. "Do you mock me?"

"What are your demands?" Pullmoo snapped.

Standing down on all fours, the king's head came level with Pullmoo's.

"I could bite your head off right now," he growled.

Despite Borkane's enormous size and formidable stance, the Pegasean woman faced him with no more reservation than if she were confronting a petulant child. When Pullmoo smiled, the king's bravado shattered before her intrepid eyes like glass coming against stone.

"We want the one you call Orook, and the human woman who protects him," Borkane said.

"Why?" Pullmoo asked.

"He killed my brother. He slaughtered my nephew and his wife. He left their children to die. We will not stand for any more of his brutality," cried Borkane.

"And you expect me to just hand them over to you?" Pullmoo clipped.

"We will destroy this city if you do not," the alpha snarled.

"I am tempted to let you try, but I'm afraid you might do just enough damage to annoy me," Pullmoo hissed.

The alpha growled and took a menacing step towards her until Pullmoo could feel his hot breath on her face. Unyielding, Pullmoo stared deeply into the animal's cold blue eyes as if seeing past them and into his mind,

"There is a story I once read in one of the sacred books from Earth. It is a rather interesting story. Would you like to hear it?" Pullmoo asked.

The alpha narrowed his eyes but did not answer.

"In this story, there were two warring tribes of men. Each morning before the ongoing war would resume, the strongest of the one tribe of men came out between the lines of battle and challenged the men of the other tribe to produce their strongest warrior. It was understood that if his challenge was met, and if he was defeated by the challenger, the war would end with victory going to the challenger's tribe." Pullmoo told him.

The king listened with keen interest.

"What do you say we recreate this story here, Borkane, between us," Pullmoo challenged. "You agree to fight my most skilled guardsman and whichever of you comes out of it alive shall have his way."

"If I win, you will give me Orook and the human woman?" he asked.

"Indeed," Pullmoo said. "And if my First Guardsman wins, well, you will die, and your pack leaves my city in peace."

Borkane looked at Pullmoo and read every corner of her mind. Once he was convinced that this was not a trick, he agreed. Then, remembering what Orook had done to his nephew, he said, "You must agree - no magic weapons, no tricks. We each choose one weapon and we fight on leveled ground."

"So be it," Pullmoo said as she waved a dismissive hand at the king.

Pullmoo then turned and walked back towards the entrance to the body of the city, not once turning to look at the mountain king left smoldering at her back.

CHAPTER 28

After Orook and Lenook showered in the men's washroom, they got dressed in their ordinary clothes and walked over to the women's practice room. They sat down on a hard, wooden bench against the wall and waited for Maria.

"Before you met my sister, did you have a human companion?" Orook asked.

Lenook turned to look at Orook.

"Why do you ask?" Lenook said.

Orook shrugged.

"I did have a companion," Lenook said. "Lindsay was her name."

"What happened?" Orook asked.

Lenook took a deep breath and closed his eyes.

"Please do not tell me she was euthanized," Orook said.

"No, no, nothing like that," Lenook said. "Lindsay wanted nothing to do with me after I told her that I was in love with Wilamoo. She put in a request to be re-matched immediately. I begged her to stay. I told her that Wilamoo had no problem with me continuing to be her keeper - but it didn't matter."

"Why did she react so poorly?" Orook asked.

"Honestly? Are you that oblivious?" Lenook asked.

Orook turned to look at the Second Presenter.

"Lenook, do I need to remind you of your status relative to mine?" Orook cautioned.

With mocking exaggeration, Lenook made the first gesture of apology to Orook.

"I know nothing about human women," Orook said. "If Lindsay had grown so attached to you, why would she request to be rematched?"

"Human women are not like Pegasean women," Lenook explained. "They are jealous creatures. Lindsay could not tolerate sharing me with another woman - she cried herself to sleep every night until Pullmoo found her another keeper. I felt terrible - and not just for her. I loved her too. I was very sorry to see her go."

"How could she expect you to choose her over a Pegasean woman?" Orook asked.

"Maybe it is my fault," Lenook said. "Perhaps I should have stopped joining with her after I partnered with your sister. But how could I have known Wilamoo would ask me to marry her? Pegasean women don't usually choose a husband until they are much older, if ever."

Orook's brow furrowed as he turned to look out at the practice room floor. He watched Maria attempt to block her instructor's repetitive blows as he thought about what Lenook had said.

"Are you concerned?" Lenook asked. "Has Linoo had a change of heart? - or have you managed to win the heart of some other Pegasean woman?"

"No and no," Orook said.

"What is troubling you, then?" Lenook asked.

"Lenook, do the human women have any kind of defenses against being, well, imposed upon?" Orook asked.

"Unfortunately, no," Lenook said. "That is why the city is so protective of them. They are entirely vulnerable. Why do you ask?"

"Why do you think?" Orook whispered.

"Ah, well, I am happy for you too then," Lenook said.

Orook closed his eyes and shook his head.

"Relax Orook," he said. "Almost all keepers and companions join with each other. Granted, some do it more often than others, but almost all of them do it eventually or at some point."

"How would you know?" Orook asked.

"I have done countless compliance and compatibility evaluations. I have also done numerous enforcement interviews to make sure companions aren't being taken advantage of by their keepers. Altogether, I've seen and interviewed hundreds of pairings of Pegaseans and humans," Lenook told him.

"Those interviews must be uncomfortable," Orook said.

"They are not so bad," Lenook said. "Most of the time it is quite obvious that no one is being physically or emotionally abused. In my whole career as a presenter, I have only seen one keeper and companion fail to follow the rules - and they are a bit of special case anyway."

"Maria resents a lot of the rules. She finds them silly and even a bit demeaning," Orook told him.

Lenook shrugged.

"There is something nice about having her around," Orook thought aloud. "I have never lived with anyone before. It is nice - not being alone."

Lenook nodded.

"Linoo has never slept in my bed, or even been to my house," Orook said.

"That is not unusual," Lenook said. "Wilamoo only started coming to my house after she asked me to marry her - never while we were only just partners."

"Will Maria eventually ask to sleep in my bed?" Orook asked.

"I doubt she will ever ask you. If she wants to, she simply will," Lenook said.

"Is that ok?" Orook asked.

"If she does it all on her own, yes. However, you must never ask her to. If you do, we might end up having one of those uncomfortable interviews," Lenook said and playfully elbowed Orook in the ribs.

• • •

Just as Maria was coming out of the women's shower room, a blaring siren filled the sparring hall and the street outside. Red and white lights flashed ominously in sync with the alarm. Orook and Lenook shot up to their feet and looked around the room and then cautiously out to the street. Maria stood frozen in place, half way between the shower room exit and the wall where Orook and Lenook had been waiting for her. She stood in place as she looked around nervously. Orook looked down at his armband as he walked quickly towards Maria. Lenook followed closely behind him. They both read an emergency message which informed them that a pack of a hundred or more vocunine had breached the city's outer wall.

"What is going on?" Maria asked.

"A pack of vocunine has breached the wall," Orook told her.

Maria's eyes widened.

"What do we do?" she asked.

"Lenook, you should go to Wilamoo's house in the Circle of Mothers," Orook instructed. "It is heavily fortified. Also, under the treaty - assuming they intend to honor the treaty - they will not go there."

"And if I happen to encounter the beasts on my way there?" Lenook asked.

"In that case, you better pray a guard is around to save you," Orook said. Then, seeing the genuine fear on Lenook's face, he added, "Do not worry, they have yet to come into the body of the city. They are positioned within the wall but appear to be waiting for something."

"What will *we* do?" Maria asked as she took her keeper's hand.

Orook looked down at her hand in his, then looked back out at the street, now quickly filling with people.

"We will go home," Orook said as he laced his fingers into hers. "If they are here to cause damage, they will not go to individual homes. They will go to the district centers, or somewhere more densely populated."

CHAPTER 29

B ack at home, Maria and Orook watched the wall monitor and waited for further instructions from the Pegasean City Guard. Within twenty minutes, a guardsman dressed in a blood red uniform arrived at the door. The guard quickly introduced himself to Orook, made the first gesture of respect, then explained that Orook and his companion would need to come with him to the surface.

"Why?" Orook asked.

"I will explain on the way," said the guard. "Now please hurry."

Orook and Maria hurried to keep pace with the guard who, speaking to Orook in Pegasean, explained the challenge Pullmoo had put to the alpha vocunine. He told Orook that, as part of the terms of the agreement, he and Maria would need to be held at the surface until the conclusion of the fight between the First Guardsman, Vartook, and the alpha vocunine. As the guard explained all this to Orook, Orook quickly translated the essence of what he was saying into English for Maria's benefit.

Furious, Maria let go of Orook's hand. She stood, fist clenched, staring at the street for a moment, then turned and stridently headed back home.

Orook and the guard stopped and looked back.

"Do you need me to go after her?" asked the guard.

"No, wait," Orook said, then jogged to catch up with his companion. When Orook reached Maria, he took her arm and turned her towards him. She tried to pull away, but he was too strong. His grip held firm as she seethed.

"Maria, we have to go!" Orook said.

"I won't!" Maria shouted.

When Orook saw tears forming in her eyes, he loosened his grip but did not let go.

"Listen to me Maria," he said. "There is no reason to be afraid. Vartook is the First Guardsman. He is the most lethal entity on this mountain. There is not a vocunine alive that could possibly defeat him."

"That is not the point," Maria spat.

Orook's brow furrowed.

"What do you mean?" he asked.

"I'm sick of being used this way," Maria barked. "How many times am I supposed to be a pawn in this woman's games?"

Orook slowly let go of Maria.

"You know I am not fond of Pullmoo either," he said with a sigh. "However, the current situation is not her fault or her doing. The alpha vocunine demanded that the City hand us over to him. If she refused, he told her that he and his pack of over a hundred angry vocunine were prepared to attack the City. This deal Pullmoo has made - she is saving us and the City."

Maria stopped shaking her head only long enough to wipe her eyes with her sleeve.

"It would make more sense to be angry with me," Orook said. "They are here because of the way I killed that vocunine. You were right Maria, I never should have done that to him. I profoundly offended the alpha and the entire pack. Now, because of *my* lapse in judgement, they have come seeking revenge. I am sorry."

"No. You went back," she said. "You put a knife in his heart."

"That was only damage control," Orook said. "I am sure that when the other vocunine found him, they knew exactly what had happened. There were likely even witnesses to the whole thing. They are always watching everything we do at the surface - and they are everywhere."

"I'm not angry with you," Maria mumbled.

"Come on," he said as he took her hand. "Despite the unfortunate circumstances, I am personally looking forward to seeing Vartook fight the alpha. You might also enjoy seeing him in action. His skill is unrivaled."

Maria looked up and past Orook, to the austere guardsman standing resolutely less than a block away. She watched the guardsman look down at his armband, then pull something from his waistband before he started walking towards them. Maria took a deep breath, then nodded.

"Alright, alright, I'm coming," she said loudly for both Orook and the guardsman to hear.

• • •

Once they were out on the surface, Orook explained to Maria that they were now in one of the outdoor parks within the city's outer wall.

"We just walked out of terminal two, which is the closest such terminal to our home. You should remember where it is so that you can come back here on your own once the weather warms. The ground here has been leveled and stabilized. Look around and you will see buds on the trees and the ground cover peeking up through the soil," he said.

Maria was too busy looking for the mountain king to take in any such banal signs of spring. When she saw Borkane, she gasped, then tugged on Orook's sleeve and whispered, "That vocunine is at least three times the size of the one you killed."

"Indeed, he is *at least* that much larger," Orook said.

"And you are sure that the First Guardsman can defeat him? - single-handedly?" Maria asked.

"Of course," Orook said.

Their escort then directed Maria and Orook to a park bench where they were to wait until the fight was over. Maria brushed debris from the crystal bench before taking a seat. She crossed her arms and looked down at the ground at her feet. There were, in fact, little sprouts of something coming up through the loose moist soil. She began counting them just to keep her mind busy while they waited.

"Now that you are here, Vartook will be out in a moment," the guard told them.

Moments later, a stately Pegasean man in a crimson uniform emerged from the terminal. Orook nudged his companion, then pointed his chin in the direction of Vartook.

"That is Vartook," Orook told her.

"He is no bigger than you," Maria whispered.

"He is a little taller," Orook said. "But that is not important. He is no less than three times faster and stronger than me. I assure you."

Maria noticed that Vartook was carrying a menacing looking object in one hand. It was a bladed weapon shaped on one side like a crescent moon, with a large indent in the blade's outer curve. To Maria, the blade resembled that of a bat in flight, with a thick handle where the bat's feet might be.

Vartook stopped as he approached Pullmoo. Maria noticed that the First Guardsman made no formal gesture of respect. He only gave a cordial bow of his head, like a gentleman greeting a lady. Maria watched as Pullmoo appeared to be giving the man instructions. At first, Vartook nodded along with whatever Pullmoo was saying. He then suddenly shook his head vehemently. Maria could not hear what they were saying. Regardless, it was obvious to Maria that Pullmoo was telling Vartook to do something that he did not want to do. However, as Pullmoo continued to talk, Vartook's expression gradually relented until at last he nodded slowly. The First Guardsman then made his way over to Borkane, who was now pacing around the center of the park.

Vartook took his place and stood with both hands holding his weapon casually down in from of him. He kept his eyes on the alpha as the beast approached. When the two were squarely facing each other, Vartook bowed to the mountain king. Borkane sneered, then stood up on his hind legs and glared down at Vartook. Now towering over the Pegasean, he quickly pulled his sword from its harness on his back and swung it down on Vartook. With a speed and strength Maria could hardly believe was possible, Vartook blocked the rushing sword with his blade, catching it in the notch of the blade's outer curve. He then slid the blade down the length of the sword until it reached the hilt. With one quick movement, Vartook turned the blade and slashed it down and around, severing off one of the alpha's fingers and severely wounding two others. The beast made a sound of pain and anger but did not drop his weapon.

Maria could not watch this. She hid her face in the sleeve of Orook's uniform. Every few seconds, she heard a kind of yelp from the alpha until her curiosity forced her to look up. She watched as Vartook skillfully and gracefully maneuvered around the beast. He blocked, dodged and evaded the alpha's every move. She noticed that every time the two got close enough, Vartook slashed at the vocunine. After she watched Vartook do this several times, Maria started to understand that each time Vartook slide his blade against his opponent, he was deliberately cutting him just enough to hurt and to draw blood. He was not yet trying to mortally wound the beast.

"What is he doing?" Maria asked.

"I do not know," said Orook, who seemed equally puzzled.

"How is he keeping the vocunine from reading his mind?" Maria asked.

"The guardsmen are trained to fight is such a way that does not require much, if any planning or thinking in advance. They simply do not think any thoughts for the vocunine to read, or do not think any that would be useful to the vocunine. Sometimes they think of something completely unrelated to the fight or sing a song in their heads. They then rely on muscle memory, reflexive movements mastered in training, and instinct, to act as needed in each moment. It is an extremely difficult skill to master," Orook explained.

"Wow," Maria said, admiring the First Guardsman as she watched him react instantly to every move the vocunine made.

Without warning, Vartook rushed directly at the vocunine, then leaned backwards and slid across the ground underneath the animal. Maria saw the glint of his blade flicker for an instant as he passed under Borkane's wide stance. The blade was so sharp and quick that Borkane felt little more than a sting. Neither Maria nor Orook understood exactly what Vartook had done until a bloody chunk of flesh fell from the underside of the vocunine and hit the ground with a wet thud. They both gasped upon the realization that the First Guardsman had just castrated the beast. It took the king himself a few moments longer to come to the same realization. When he did, he looked around furiously for his assailant. Vartook stood behind the animal, composed as he waited for this very reaction. When the alpha lunged at him, Vartook waited until Borkane was nearly on top of him, then spun rapidly to one side, holding his blade out and against the animal's neck as he did so. The mountain king was now only moments from death as his blood rapidly vacated his body through fountaining eruptions from the wound in his neck. Once Vartook was certain that the alpha vocunine had taken his last breath, he carefully wiped the bloody blade with a cloth. He then attached the weapon to the belt of his uniform such that its outer curve pointed down towards the ground. Silently, he walked back to Pullmoo as the other vocunine slowly circled around their fallen king and howled with fear, grief and defeat. As he approached, Pullmoo instructed several other guardsmen to keep watch over the grieving vocunine and to make sure they all left the city limits within the hour.

"We need to go express our gratitude now," Orook said to Maria.

Maria sat paralyzed as she stared at the corpse of the alpha vocunine. She said nothing as Orook prodded at her to stand up, then took her hand and led her over to Pullmoo and Vartook.

"Thank you, Vartook, you have saved my life and that of my companion," Orook said as he made the second gesture of gratitude to the First Guardsman.

Orook then turned to Maria and was about to give her instructions on how to properly express her gratitude when she suddenly got to her knees before Vartook. As Orook looked on in perplexed silence as she reached the palm of her left hand out to Vartook's weapon. She then deliberately ran the palm of her hand against the outer curve of the down turned blade. Blood ran down between her fingers as she opened and closed her fist several times until her entire palm was covered in blood. Maria then pressed her bloody palm to the left leg of Vartook's uniform. Vartook's jaw dropped as he stared down at Maria. He then looked over at Orook who only mirrored the guardsman's befuddled expression. Pullmoo, who was now beaming down at Maria with approval and admiration, spoke first.

"The woman from Earth has bestowed on you a great honor Vartook - the highest honor, if I recall correctly," she said.

"I can see that," Vartook managed to say as he reached down to Maria, took her unmarred hand and lifted her to her feet.

Orook remained speechless. His capricious companion had just made the third gesture of gratitude to the First Guardsman of Pegasea.

191

CHAPTER 30

After they arrived home, Orook washed the blood off Maria's hand, applied medicated ointment and bandaged her self-inflicted wound.

"Where did you learn of the third gesture of gratitude?" he asked.

"I read about it in the PROEs Manual," Maria said proudly.

"Are you entirely clear on its significance?" he asked.

"It means I owe him my life," she said.

"Yes, that is the gist of it, but do you understand exactly what it means?" Orook asked.

"It means that I am indebted to him. If he ever needs anything from me, he just has to ask, and if I'm able, I will oblige," Maria said.

"It does not have to be something he *needs*," he said.

"So?" she said.

"Maria, he could ask you for anything, and I mean *anything*. He could ask you to kill me and you would be obligated, under the oath you just made, to either do it or die trying," Orook explained. "He can ask you to commit a crime. If he did, and you committed the crime, he would not be charged for it - you would be. Or, at least, that is the way it would work if you were Pegasean. Since you are the first human in history to perform that gesture, I am not sure how it would work legally."

"Why would he ask me to kill you? - or to commit a crime?" Maria asked.

"That is not the point Maria," Orook said. "The point is that no one, and I mean *no one*, has performed the third gesture of gratitude in over a thousand years."

"A *thousand* years," Maria repeated.

Orook nodded.

"Well, the manual really should have mentioned that," Maria said. Orook suppressed a smile.

"Are you upset with me?" Maria asked.

"No, not at all," he said. "To be honest, I am impressed. To make a gesture like that requires a special kind of courage and humility."

"Really?" Maria asked.

"Yes. That, and, well, Pullmoo is not easily surprised by anything anyone does - but you certainly surprised her today," Orook said.

Maria's expression turned grave.

"So, back when people still made the third gesture of gratitude, what kinds of things where they asked to do?" she asked.

"Actually, in most cases I have either read or heard about, the recipient of the gesture immediately asked for something trivial - like a kiss on the cheek or a small gift. It would be something symbolic like that. Then the giver of the gesture would not have to worry about when their debt might be called in, or what the recipient's demand might be," Orook told her.

"Why didn't Vartook do that?" Maria asked.

"Probably because he was just too stunned to think of it," Orook said. "Again, it has been over a thousand years since the last known use of the gesture - and to my knowledge, it has never been performed by a human."

"Why did people stop using it?" Maria asked.

"Honestly, I do not know," he said.

"What do you think he will ask of me?" Maria asked.

"Most likely nothing," Orook said.

"I hope he doesn't ask me to commit a crime," Maria said, thinking out loud.

"Perhaps I should not have said anything. I did not intend to cause you this much anxiety. Do not worry. He will not ask you to do anything you do not want to do," Orook said.

"Are you sure?" Maria asked.

Orook shrugged.

"I do not have Pullmoo's gift for predicting what people will or will not do. What I do know is that Vartook is a kind man. I do not see any reason why he would make an unkind request," he said.

"What if I refuse to do whatever it is he asks of me?" Maria asked.

"Tradition would dictate that you take your own life in that case. Otherwise, technically, he is allowed to take it for you," Orook told her.

Maria's face went pale at hearing this.

"Relax," Orook said. "That is most certainly not going to happen. Even if Vartook makes a request of you, which I doubt he will, he would certainly not call on the ancient laws to compel you. Besides, if it ever came to that, I am sure the Center Council would intervene."

Orook's lack of concern over the matter eased Maria's anxiety.

Wanting to change the subject, she asked, "What do you think Pullmoo told Vartook to do? I mean - what do you think they were talking about right before the fight?"

"I think it is safe to assume that she asked him to draw out the fight and humiliate the alpha. Of course, like I explained earlier, she could not have asked him to do anything too specific - since the guardsman cannot have a plan in mind as he engages in the fight. However, she could have asked him for something more general - like to prolong the encounter, or to be cruel," Orook said.

"Why would she do that?" Maria asked.

"Most likely to strike a blow at their collective consciousness and group identity. It might also have been, in some way, to show that she condoned what I did to the alpha's nephew," Orook said wearily.

Maria grimaced.

"It makes me a little sick to think about it, honestly," Orook said.

"It looked like Vartook did not want to do things that way," Maria said.

"I am sure he did not," Orook agreed.

"Then why did he?" Maria asked. "Did Pullmoo order him to?"

"No, she does not have the authority to give orders to the First Guardsman - no one does," Orook told her. "Pullmoo must have just convinced him that she…"

"…had a plan?" Maria finished for him.

Orook looked up at Maria and was troubled by the intensity he saw in her eyes.

CHAPTER 31

After Maria and Orook expressed their gratitude to Vartook, the First Guardian escorted Pullmoo back to her office. When they reached her door, Vartook asked if he could speak with her privately.

"Of course," Pullmoo said, and gestured for him to come inside. She then closed the door behind him and sat down at her desk. Vartook sat down in a chair opposite her desk.

"What can I do for you Vartook?" Pullmoo asked.

"I will be coming upon 170 years of age this summer," he said.

Pullmoo nodded and gestured for him to continue.

"I have no children," he said.

"That is because you have yet to partner with a Pegasean woman," Pullmoo said.

"Yes, I know," he said.

"So how can I help you? Would you like me to make a recommendation?" she asked.

Vartook shook his head.

"You have someone in mind then?" she said.

Vartook nodded,

Pullmoo waited for him to continue. When he failed to elaborate, she asked him if he had asked this woman to partner with him.

"Not yet," he said.

"I see. Well, it is rather simple," Pullmoo said. "You simply have to ask her. You are the First Guardsman. Any woman in the City would be delighted to have you. I would be very surprised if anyone declined your request. In fact, I'm sure that even Linoo would move you to the top of her waiting list."

"I'm not interested in Linoo," he said.

"Well, whoever it is, you have no reason to be shy," Pullmoo said with a reassuring smile.

Vartook shook his head and looked down at his folded hands.

"How can I help?" Pullmoo asked.

Vartook looked up at her with pleading eyes.

"*Me?*" Pullmoo asked.

Vartook nodded.

"I must be losing my edge," Pullmoo muttered.

"You hoped for better?" Vartook asked.

"No, no," Pullmoo said quickly. "There is no better man than you Vartook. You know that."

Vartook smiled.

"I was referring to my professional abilities," Pullmoo explained. "This is the second time today that a person has surprised me. The First Sociologist aims to never be surprised by anything anyone does."

"Was the first surprise what the First Engineer's companion did? - the third gesture of gratitude?" Vartook asked.

"Yes," Pullmoo said as she leaned back in her chair and steepled her fingers. She stared past Vartook in silence as she thought about Maria and the vocunine.

"So... what is your answer?" Vartook asked.

As if startled out of a trance, Pullmoo looked up at him and blinked several times.

"Vartook, why me?" she asked. "I can count on one hand the number of men who have requested to partner with me. Most of my children were conceived in the Body Biology Center. I do not have much time for partners. You shouldn't expect much."

Vartook looked down at his hands. He did not dare tell her that her lack of suiters was at least partly due to his subtle but ever-present interference.

"Do you remember when we first met?" he asked.

Pullmoo closed her eyes as she recalled the memory.

"You were only 8 years. I was only Fourth Guardsman back then, in my late 40s," Vartook recounted.

Pullmoo nodded, remembering.

"To this day, no one knows how you did it - how you managed to slip the City Guard and get outside the outer wall," Vartook mused.

"And no one ever will," Pullmoo vowed.

"I found you," he said. "You were hunkered down in an old abandoned security outpost far outside the City, at the edge of the valley. I swear you had set up no less than a hundred snare traps all around the outpost. It took me hours to make my way inside."

"I still can't believe you found me," Pullmoo said, shaking her head.

"When I opened the door and saw you inside, you were badly bruised and scratched up - your clothes were torn, and your hair looked like you had been struck by lightning. But your eyes - your eyes were as clear as a summer's day. You looked straight at me - no fear, no regret," Vartook said.

"I had no reason to be afraid," Pullmoo said.

"Pullmoo, you were a little girl and you had been out in the wilderness for almost a week. You should have been terrified," Vartook countered.

Pullmoo shrugged.

"I had to carry you kicking and screaming all the way back to the City." He continued. "I still have the scar on my arm where you bit me."

"I should probably apologize for that," Pullmoo said.

"I've loved you ever since," Vartook confessed. "Obviously not romantically at first - you were just a kid. But after you were grown... and still now..."

"This is all very touching, Vartook," she said. "But if all you are saying now is true, why have you waited so long to tell me?"

"Do you remember what you said to me as we finally made it back to the outer wall of the city?" he asked.

Pullmoo closed her eyes but did not answer.

"You told me that if I forced you back inside that wall, a part of you would die, and you would never forgive me," Vartook lamented. "After we were through the wall, you suddenly became very still. Then you told me, in a voice so cold that, to this day, it haunts my dreams, that you would hate me forever."

"I'm so sorry you took that so seriously Vartook," Pullmoo said. "I was just a child. I don't hate you. In fact, I don't think I ever hated you. You were just doing your job. How could you not know that I would grow to understand that some day? More than that, you probably saved my life."

Vartook shook his head.

"You don't know what you were like - even then - the intensity in your eyes and in your voice. You have a way of saying things that makes them sound so final, and so irrefutable," he said.

"Alright, Vartook, have it your way," she said.

"Is that a yes? Will you partner with me?" Vartook asked.

"Yes," Pullmoo said. "Unless, of course, you come to your senses before we consummate the partnership."

"My senses are just fine," Vartook said with a charmingly seductive smile.

For the first time in her adult life, Pullmoo blushed.

CHAPTER 32

Over the next few days, the weather warmed, and the sky grew brighter. Virtually overnight, Orook, as well as the other Pegaseans, underwent their seasonal changes. They lost half their winter fluff and what was left of it darkened to various shades ranging from slate gray to black. Their hair and eyebrows also darkened. The morning after the change came over Orook, Maria nearly failed to recognize him. Upon seeing him for the first time that morning, Maria gasped and stepped back. Orook was standing in front of the living room wall monitor. He chuckled at Maria's reaction before returning his attention to the monitor. Maria looked him over before making her way over to him.

"You look so different," she said. "Your hair is dark brown now."

Orook nodded as he navigated through different windows on the monitor.

Maria touched his now bare forearm.

"You look human," she remarked.

Orook frowned.

"Well, except for your ears," Maria conceded.

"This happens to all Pegaseans in spring," Orook reminded her.

"What are you looking at?" she asked.

"This is a schematic of the City - and those little dots are remote monitor indicators of various states of system health and stability," he explained as he touched the monitor to focus on different nodes and districts within the schematic.

"Is anything wrong? - with the systems, I mean," Maria asked.

"Surprisingly, no," Orook said. "Maybe Linoo was right, maybe I can trust my Second and Third Engineers to take care of things - at least for a week or two."

Maria nodded, but she was not really paying attention. She was stroking his arm and marveling at how much his appearance had changed.

Orook looked down at her and asked, "Why are you stroking my arm like that?"

Maria quickly folded her arms and looked back up at the monitor.

Orook smiled.

"Maria, if you are desiring my affection, you need to be more explicit," he said.

"Why?" she asked.

"You read the law. I am forbidden from touching you unless you make your wishes known 'in no uncertain terms'," he said, quoting the PROEs manual and the law.

"Ok, so, what exactly does that mean?" she asked, annoyed.

"Well, you could just state it plainly," he suggested.

"That's stupid," Maria muttered.

"Why are you so shy about this sort of thing?" he mused.

"I'm not shy," she snapped. "I just think this is ridiculous."

"Maria, these rules exist to protect you. I am surprised you are unable to see that," Orook said.

"It just makes everything very awkward," she said.

"Why?" he asked.

"It just does," she said.

"I do not understand," Orook said.

"Keeper, do you have intention of assaulting me or forcing me to join with you?" Maria asked.

"Absolutely not," Orook said. "The very thought is abhorrent to me."

"Ok, I believe you," she said. "So now why do we have to follow these stupid rules?"

"If for no other reason, because we will both be asked a lot of questions at our compatibility evaluation. Following that, the city conducts random compliance checks," he told her.

"Is there any reason we can't just lie?" she asked.

Orook shook his head disapprovingly.

"It's none of their business!" Maria seethed. "They have no right to ask us those kinds of questions."

"Maria, aside from the fact that I believe it is wrong to lie, Pegaseans *cannot* lie to other Pegaseans - not in person anyway," he told her. "We have too many involuntary tells. And we can see each other's minds."

"I thought you had control over what another person could see in your mind?" Maria said.

"Normally, yes, but when we lie, the truth goes to that place in our minds where others can see it - the very act of lying causes that to happen involuntarily," he explained.

"Is that how I was able to read the minds of the men in the Intake Hall? - the ones that were preparing to have me euthanized?" she asked.

"Did they try to lie to you?" Orook asked.

"They told me they were taking me to see a doctor," Maria said.

"Hmm..." he said. "That was not strictly a lie. Still, one of them must have believed it was a lie or else you would not have been able to see the truth in his mind."

"Fascinating," she said.

Orook nodded.

Maria stared at him as she recalled her time in the Intake Hall and the terror she had felt in that moment she knew those two men intended to kill her.

"Thank you for not leaving me there," she said.

"Yes, well, you are not the only victim of Pullmoo's manipulations," Orook said with half a smile.

Maria sighed.

"Well, in any event, we should get ready to go practice," he said.

"Do I have to go to defense practice every morning?" she asked.

"You have to go at least four days a week. Yesterday morning was the fourth time you have gone this week, so no, you do not have to go today," he said.

"Is that your rule or the city's rule?" Maria asked.

"Both," he said.

"Can I learn how to spar?" she asked.

"You can, and you may," he said. "Do you want to?"

Maria nodded.

"Then go get ready - you can spar with Lenook. He is about your speed," Orook said.

CHAPTER 33

When Maria and Orook arrived at the practice room, they found Lenook sitting on a bench reading messages off his armband and chuckling at whatever he was reading.

"You're going to spar with Maria today," Orook said as he approached the bench.

Lenook looked up and smiled at the two of them.

"Oh, thank the stars!" he said. "I can't take much more sparring with you. You're a merciless tyrant."

"Do not be too happy about it," Orook cautioned. "Human women might not be strong, but they can make up the difference with sheer enthusiasm once they get the hang of it. They also lack our Pegasean affinity for form or nuance, which means they can be difficult to predict."

"I'm not sure if I should be insulted or flattered," Maria said.

"Neither," Orook said. "I am only warning Lenook that sparring with you might be more of a challenge than he would like it to be."

Orook then handed Maria an aluminum bō and began to show her the fundamentals of how to use the weapon offensively - something she was not taught in her self-defense training. Some of his instructions required demonstrations during which he put his hands on her arms, shoulders or hips and guided her through the movements. The physical contact made it difficult for Maria to concentrate. Every time he put his warm hands on her hips or shoulders she had to fight to stay focused. Orook pretended not to notice as Lenook struggled to contain his amusement.

"Why are you torturing the poor woman?" Lenook mused.

Orook ignored him as he continued to teach Maria the basics of sparring with a bō. Once he had completed his tutorial, he told

Lenook and Maria to face each other on the mat and begin. At first, Maria hesitated, reluctant to strike at Lenook. Taking full advantage of her hesitation, Lenook struck Maria several times. Maria's anger quickly supplanted her timidity. Maria blocked his next blow, then struck back. As they continued, Maria's intensity grew until they were both exhausted and badly bruised.

"Well done," Orook said.

"Thank you," Lenook said.

"Not you - her," he corrected.

After they all showered and changed, Orook invited Lenook to join them in the District Two surface park. Lenook politely declined, explaining that he already had plans to go to the park later with Wilamoo.

As Orook and Maria walked down the street to the stairwell up to the surface, Maria asked, "Why do all of your names end in 'ook?'"

"In Pegasean, the root word 'ook' means 'man.' The start of each name has some significance or meaning that makes the name unique," Orook explained.

"What does the beginning of your name mean?" Maria asked.

Orook searched his mental dictionary of English words for an appropriate translation.

"It comes from the Pegasean word 'ore' which means 'true,' but not 'true' as in the opposite of 'false.' It might be closer in meaning to the English word 'sincere' or 'integrity.' It is difficult to translate precisely," he explained.

"So, does 'moo' or 'noo' mean woman?" Maria asked.

"No, those are simply two gender neutral root words for 'person'," Orook said.

"Do you ever have nicknames?" she asked.

"Men do when we are boys," he told her.

"What was yours?" she asked.

"Oroo," he said.

"That's cute," she said.

"All boyhood nicknames are created more or less the same way - by dropping the 'k' at the end of the boy's real name. There is some variation on this of course. For example, Lenook was called 'Leo' because 'Lenoo' sounds too much like a woman's name," Orook explained.

"What does 'len' mean?" Maria asked.

"Joy," he said.

"What about Etmook's name? Is 'etm' a word in Pegasean?" she asked.

"No, but 'etma' is a word which means 'shimmer,' like a 'shimmer of light.' He was called 'Etmo' as a boy," he said.

Maria continued to ask Orook about the meaning of each of the various Pegasean names she could recall until Orook said, "Maria, are you trying to trick me into teaching you Pegasean?"

"No," she muttered.

"Why the sudden interest in our names?" he asked.

Maria shrugged.

"Am I allowed to call you by your boyhood name?" she asked.

"No," Orook said. "Personally, I wouldn't mind it. Linoo still calls me 'Oroo.' However, it is against the law for you to call me that - because it is still considered my name."

Maria frowned.

"Why do you dislike calling me 'keeper?'" Orook asked.

"It's just so impersonal," Maria said.

"I think that is the point," he said. "I am not a sociologist, but if I had to guess, I would say that the intent of the rule is to keep you from thinking of me as an equal."

Maria sighed as she let go of his hand and dropped a step behind him. They walked in silence for several blocks before Orook said, "I can understand why you are confused. This relationship we have has an odd sort of duality to it."

"I'm not confused," Maria said. "I'm frustrated."

"Maria, I tried to warn you - when we first met in the Intake Hall. The relationship you and I have is not like any relationship you might have had on Earth."

"That's because it's sick," Maria mumbled.

Orook slowly came to a stop and turned to face his companion.

"I know, I know - I can't say that sort of thing in public," Maria said.

"I am going to let it go- just this once - because I can see that you are troubled. I fear that you are frustrated because you want to see me as a kind of partner which I can never be to you," he said.

"I... it's not...I don't know," Maria stammered.

"How did you end up on that transport ship?" Orook asked.

Maria looked up at him with wide eyes.

"You were not on the list. You were not brought aboard by the transport team. So how did you end up on that ship?" he asked again.

"Do I have to tell you?" Maria whined.

Orook assessed the woman in front of him, taking in her deflated posture and generally miserable appearance.

"No, you do not have to tell me," he said. "However, I am going to insist that you talk to one of the sociologists - which are also psychologists here. You need help."

"Ok, whatever," Maria said.

Orook put a gentle hand on her shoulder. Despite her conscious effort not to recoil, Maria knew he must have felt her muscles twitch, because he quickly removed his hand.

"Hey... have you ever wondered what the vocunine eat?" he asked.

"No, not really," Maria mumbled.

"There is an animal which lives in the lower areas of the mountains and in the meadows around the mountains - imagine a cross between a goat and a chinchilla," he said.

Maria's brow furrowed as she remembered something she had seen back at the Intake Hall.

"I might have seen one of those, a dead one, in a freezer in the Intake Hall," she said.

"Why would you have been shown such a thing?" Orook asked with a frown.

"I was in denial about being on another planet. One of the attendants thought it might help me come to grips with my new reality," she said.

"Why didn't he just show you the night sky? The stars should have convinced you," he said.

"He tried that," Maria told him. "Apparently, I don't know much about stars."

"Well, in any case, if you like rabbits, you will probably like cloud-jumpers. They are the primary source of protein for the vocunine.

We eat them too, but not nearly as often or as much. We keep small herds of them in enclosures just outside the parks. The inventory staff, and sometimes the biologists, collect their milk to make cheese."

"So - they are like cows?" Maria asked.

"In terms of their purpose, yes. However, they look nothing like cows and they move more like goats," he said.

"Are they nice?" Maria asked.

"They are very docile, if that is what you mean," Orook said. "Would you like to see them?"

"Yes," Maria said. "Do they have any defenses against predators?"

"They can jump rather high - and perch themselves on impossibly narrow ledges, just like mountain goats. They also have a defense similar to chinchillas on Earth. They are covered in a fine dense fur which conceals where their body begins and the fur ends. When something tries to bite them, the fur releases from the skin and the attacker is often left with nothing but a mouth full of fur," Orook explained.

"That's neat," Maria said. "Can we see them now?"

Orook nodded, then smiled, relieved that he had at least succeeded in distracting her.

• • •

Maria took a deep breath of fresh air as they stepped out of the terminal into the park. She closed her eyes for a moment as she enjoyed the unfiltered sunlight on her face and the smells of blooming trees and the buoyant clover-like ground cover at her feet. When she opened them again, she saw Orook gesturing for her to follow him. He then led her to a structure at the park's far end and showed her what the human women called "cloud jumpers." Maria found the name to be apt. They were fluffy and round like chinchillas, but with long thin muscular legs like a giraffe. They leaped and jumped around the enclosure like young goats. As Maria approached them, she found them to be delightfully friendly and playful.

"Can they talk?" Maria asked.

"No, of course not," Orook said.

"What do they eat?" Maria asked.

"All sorts of things that grow on the mountains and in the valleys and meadows around the base of the mountains. They eat things which resemble lichen, moss, grass and whatever else they can manage to digest. They can also find food in some of the caves which have hot springs inside of them. The warm water from the spring, and any sunlight shining through some of the more transparent crystal rocks creates mini-ecosystems inside the mountains, were plants and such can and do grow in abundance," Orook explained.

"Can… uh, *may* we see one of those?" Maria asked.

"Which is it?" Orook asked. "Are you asking if we are able to see one? - or if we are allowed?"

"Keeper, are you testing my resolve not to show annoyance with you in public?" Maria asked.

Orook suppressed a smile.

"I will take you to one, but not today. Today, I intend to catch up with my colleagues," he said, and pointed to a group of men dressed in engineer's blue, congregated at the other end of the park.

Maria followed Orook as he started walking towards his subordinates.

Half way there, Orook stopped and said, "Why don't you go spend some time with Maddie?"

He then pointed to Maddie, who was lounging in a bright green and yellow hammock stretched between two trees, some distance away from the gaggle of Second and Third Engineers. Delighted to see her friend, Maria readily agreed, then jogged across the park to join Maddie.

• • •

When the Pegasean engineers saw their boss approaching, they all brightened, genuinely happy to see him.

"We've missed you," said Etmook as he reflexively made the first gesture of respect.

"Oh?" Orook said. "How have you all been fairing without me?"

Orook's question was met with an enthusiastic but discordant mix of confident reassurances and grave concerns.

"Ok, ok, one at a time - tell me everything," Orook said with a smile.

CHAPTER 34

Maddie wiggled awkwardly as she made room for Maria in the hammock. They both laughed as they struggled to find a comfortable orientation in the stretchy suspended material. No matter how they positioned themselves, they inevitably ended up squished together somewhere in the middle of the hammock.

"Should we just go find a bench?" Maria asked.

"Why? Do I smell?" Maddie asked.

"No! You smell great - I mean you smell fine," Maria said, trying not to giggle as the hammock continued to sway and press them together.

"I love these things," Maddie said. "The material is super strong, but it still breathes - so you don't get hot."

"Well, we'll see," Maria said. "I'm not so sure they are meant for two."

"Oh, it's fine," Maddie said as she reached over the edge for a rope on the ground.

"What are you doing?" Maria asked as the hammock tilted until they were nearly perpendicular to the ground.

"I'm getting the pull rope, so we can swing!" Maddie grunted.

Maria squealed as they rocked and rolled back to equilibrium after Maddie had hold of the rope and returned to the center of the hammock.

Once they were settled and gently swinging in time with Maddie's tugging on the rope, Maria rested her head back and stared up into the blue sky through the trees.

"This is nice, actually," Maria said.

"Umm, hmm," Maddie agreed.

The two women then commenced sharing their experiences over the past few weeks. At a break in the conversation, Maria craned her neck to look up at the outer city wall. It was an impressive structure which took full advantage of the natural rock cliffs of the surrounding mountains.

"Why have the Pegaseans never tried to leave the city?" she asked Maddie.

"They do," Maddie said. "You even left the city once - with Orook. Isn't that when he killed that vocunine you told me about?"

"Yes, but that's not what I mean. I mean, why have they never tried to *live* outside the city? Certainly, this can't be the easiest place on the planet to live?" Maria clarified.

"It's too dangerous," Maddie told her. "You wouldn't believe the crazy things that live beyond the mountains - like the ruekars."

"What are ruekars?" Maria asked.

"Trust me, you don't want to know," she said.

"Ok, but I'm sure the Pegaseans know how to make traps, guns, and poisons - so why don't they just clear out these ruekars and other predators and start a settlement?" Maria asked.

"It's not that easy. Besides, there are just too few Pegaseans left to start another city. In order to keep their population constant, each woman has to have at least 40 or 50 kids over her life time. They would have to have even more than that in order to grow their numbers. I suppose it's possible because they are fertile for about 200 years and their gestation period is only about 10 to 11 months - but who wants that kind of pressure?" Maddie explained.

"I see," Maria said. "Has anyone ever survived outside the city?"

Maddie shrugged, then said "I've heard a few stories about people leaving the city and never coming back. And of course, everyone knows about Pullmoo."

"What about Pullmoo?" Maria asked.

Maddie gave her a look.

"What?" Maria asked again.

"I can't believe no one has told you the story about how she left the city when she was only eight," Maddie said. "You really need to hang out with the other companions more."

"She left when she was eight?!" Maria said.

Maddie nodded, "No one knows how she managed to pull it off, but she survived for almost a week before Vartook found her and brought her back."

Maria shook her head as she tried to imagine Pullmoo as a little girl.

"She's not all bad you know," Maddie said.

"Whatever," Maria said. "Let's talk about something else."

"How are you and your keeper getting along?" Maddie asked.

Maria groaned.

"That bad, huh?" Maddie said.

"No, it's not like that… it's just, ugh, it's hard to explain," Maria said.

"Is he being nice to you?" Maddie asked.

"As nice as an arrogant prick with an overblown sense of decorum can be," Maria said.

"Funny, though, how your eyes sparkle when you talk about him," Maddie teased.

"Shut up," Maria said with a smile.

"It's ok, you know," Maddie said. "Pullmoo knows what she's doing. If you don't love him now, it's pretty safe to assume you will soon enough."

Maria's smile faded as she considered her true feelings for Orook. She was comfortable with her feelings of admiration, respect, gratitude, and even attraction towards the man - but love? Then again, what could love be that was anything more than all of those feelings put together?

"Do you and Etmook ever get in trouble for breaking the rules?" Maria asked.

"We used to get in trouble all the time," Maddie confessed. "We were even separated once."

"Used to?" Maria asked.

"Yeah, not so much anymore - thanks to Lenook," Maddie told her.

"How did Lenook help?" Maria asked.

"Once he started conducting all of our evaluations, we stopped failing them," she said. "But he made us promise to follow the rules whenever there are other people around. We try, but maybe not as hard as we should."

"That was nice of him," Maria said.

Maddie nodded.

"I wish Orook and I didn't have to worry about the rules at home," Maria thought aloud.

"The problem with your keeper is that he would probably follow most of them even if he wasn't worried about getting caught," Maddie said.

"True, but you have to admit, there is something admirable about that," Maria said. "He has a lot of integrity."

"True to his name," Maddie said, proud of her own clever play on words.

"Yeah, he told me that 'ore' means 'true' - or something like 'true.'" Maria said.

"It sort of does, but it's difficult to translate precisely," Maddie said.

Just as Maria was about to ask Maddie a question about that, Orook's face appeared above them, startling both women.

"Are you ready to go home?" Orook asked as Maria struggled to sit up in her fabric chrysalis.

"It would be nice to stay outside a little longer," Maria confessed as she gave up trying to right herself.

Orook put a hand on the edge of the hammock and tilted it, along with the two women, towards him. He looked down at his armband, then at Maddie.

"If I broaden your security access so that you can travel between here and home without me, do you promise to stay with Maddie and not go wandering about the City?" Orook asked seriously.

"Yes," Maria said.

Orook looked from Maria to Maddie, then back again.

"Why would I risk getting in trouble and stuck at home with you for another two weeks?" Maria scoffed.

Orook nodded, then reconfigured Maria's security clearance so as to give her the access needed to go between their home and the park. Once this was done, he paused for a moment, reconsidered, then made one final change.

"Ok, I have broadened your security access. However, I have set it up such that you either have to be with me or Maddie in order to go anywhere past the end of our street," he explained.

"Thank you," Maria said.

"You trust me that much?" Maddie asked.

"Are you saying I shouldn't trust you?" Orook asked.

"No," Maddie said. "I was just asking. I'll keep her out of trouble if you want."

"Alright then," he said to Maddie, then turned to Maria and told her to be home before dusk.

CHAPTER 35

Pullmoo sat in her office, contemplating the vocunine. As she thought, she moved a pink crystal stone, polished by years of wear, smoothly between her fingers. She watching it catch the light as it appeared, then disappeared, over one finger, then under the next. Once she was confident of her plan, she called Vartook and requested that he meet with her as soon as possible. He was at her door within less than a half hour.

"Just come in!" she shouted.

Flummoxed by the lack of formality, Vartook stared at the door for a moment, then down the hallway in both directions. He quickly moved his armband over the lock and let himself in. As soon as he was inside and had shut the door, he said "Pullmoo, it's one thing for me to let myself into your private home, but this is your office."

"I don't care," Pullmoo clipped.

Vartook frowned.

"I apologize," she said. "That was insensitive. I know you are an exquisitely ceremonial man and such informality makes you uncomfortable. From hence forth, I shall come to the door."

"It is not for my sake, Pullmoo," he said. "No one should be seen allowing themselves into your office. It is a security risk."

"Of course," Pullmoo said.

"Now, what can I do for you?" Vartook asked.

"I want you to go out into the mountains and talk to the vocunine," she said.

"May I ask why?" Vartook said.

"I want you to convince them that this feud between the vocunine and the Pegaseans must end. We have an opportunity now that Borkane is dead. Most of the vocunines' lingering animosity towards us has been maintained by his stubborn bloodline of dull-minded behemoths," Pullmoo explained.

"Is that why you asked me to humiliate Borkane?" Vartook asked.

"It is most of the reason, yes," she said. "However, I think you might have misunderstood what I meant by 'humiliate.' I only needed you to establish, beyond a shadow of a doubt, that you are the superior fighter. I wanted you to make that point painfully obvious - which you did."

"I see," Vartook said, then muttered, "I wish I had understood that nuance at the time."

"No, you were brilliant. You could not have done better," she said.

Vartook shrugged.

"Borkane was the largest and strongest of his lineage thus far. He was also the least intelligent," Pullmoo continued. "His son, Solomane, is no golden retriever, but is the first in his bloodline to be smaller than his father. Either that or he is not really Borkane's biological son. In any event, he is highly intelligent - for a vocunine - and is the presumed heir to Borkane's 'thrown,' if you will."

"What is a golden retriever?" Vartook asked.

"It's a kind of Earth dog - but never mind that," Pullmoo said quickly.

"What of Borkane's mate, Solomane's mother?" Vartook asked. "There no rule among the vocunine that the alpha be male. The alphas usually are males, because they are bigger, but..."

"I don't know much about her," Pullmoo interrupted. "The only thing my informants have been able to tell me about her is that she is of average size and relatively reclusive for a vocunine. This alone is enough information to allow us to assume she will not be taking Borkane's place."

"Alright," Vartook said.

"I want you to make sure Solomane becomes the next alpha," Pullmoo said.

Vartook knit his brow as he looked past Pullmoo and tried to imagine how he might go about such a task.

"I will give you all of the information I have about the vocunine on these mountains," Pullmoo said. "It is more information than you currently have, and it might help."

"Pullmoo, with all due respect," Vartook said, "Why do you presume to have more information about the vocunine than I do?"

"I suppose that is a fair question," she said. "I presume to have more information because I have gone about collecting my information in a very different way and for very different reasons. But this is not a competition. I certainly have no intention of challenging you for the position of First Guardsman."

"If you did, it would not be a fair fight," Vartook said with a smile. "I would be too distracted."

Pullmoo closed her eyes and shook her head.

"I know, you do not like it when I flirt with you," Vartook said.

"That is not strictly true," Pullmoo said with smile. "In this case, you misread my expression. I was imagining what it might be like to fight you and the mere thought was terrifying."

"We don't use lethal weapons in the professional challenges," he said. "We wear padded uniforms and there are judges who…"

"Let us return to the original purpose of these meeting before we get too far off the trail here," Pullmoo said. "We need Solomane to be the new alpha," Pullmoo continued. "This will go a long way towards tipping the balance."

"The balance of what?" Vartook asked.

"The vocunine are currently in a very fragile emotionally state. They are teetering on the border between adoring us the way they did long ago and hating us more than they ever have before. The side to which they fall is critical to the success of my grander plan. We need to make sure they fall towards adoring us - so that we can return to the way things were, long ago, before the baby girl crisis," Pullmoo explained.

"Are you talking about back when the vocunine and the Olroneans lived together?" he asked.

"Yes, but they did more than merely coexist," she said. "Our species evolved alongside each other for tens of thousands of years. We are weaker without them, as they are without us."

"I do not imagine that this is a very commonly held opinion among our citizenry," Vartook said.

"Only because no one consciously remembers the way things used to be," she said. "Vartook, do you know the origin of the third gesture of gratitude?"

"No," he said.

"It troubles me to think that I might be the only person left in Pegasea who knows the story," Pullmoo said.

"Then tell it to me, my love," Vartook said.

Pullmoo's eyes softened as she smiled at the First Guardsman.

"Did it ever strike you as odd that the bloody hand is placed at the level of the recipient's knee or calf? Why there?" Pullmoo asked.

Vartook leaned back in his chair and folded his arms as he considered.

"I never thought about it before," he said, "but now that you ask, yes, it does seem odd. I do not know of any other gestures at that position."

"The vocunine always had hands which curl into paws - but they could not always stand up on two legs. That is why," she said.

Vartook looked up through the ceiling as he tried to imagine a vocunine of average size performing the gesture to an Olronean or Pegasean. He then nodded to himself.

"But why would this gesture in particular, and not the others, be designed to accommodate them?" he asked.

"Ah, but why, my dear, do you assume that the gesture originated with our kind?" Pullmoo asked as she sat up in her chair and rested her elbows on her desk.

Vartook shrugged.

"The gesture was essentially invented by the vocunine," Pullmoo explained. "Many thousands of years ago, their species was once on the brink of extinction, just as ours is now. At some point, the last of their kind retreated to this same mountain range. They survived well enough for a while until a pack of ruekars found them. When the slaughter began, the cries from the vocunine echoed through the mountains and were heard in a nearby village of early Olroneans. The Olronean men followed the cries of the vocunine until they arrived on the scene of the massacre then under way. Disgusted by the brutality of the ruekars, the men killed them and thereby saved the lives of the very last of the vocunine. There was blood everywhere. So much so that it ran over the ground beneath the vocunine's paws. When the vocunine approached the men, and touched them in an instinctive show of gratitude, they left a hand print of blood. And this is when the vocunine and the Olroneans began a long and meaningful friendship that would last for thousands of years to follow. It is also the origin of the third gesture of gratitude."

"How interesting," Vartook said.

"I have no doubt that, at the time Maria made that gesture to you, she was completely oblivious to the significance of it. All the same, it could not have been more perfect," Pullmoo said.

"And you had no part in this?" Vartook asked. "You did not tell her to do this?"

"I wish I could take credit for this one, but I cannot," Pullmoo confessed.

Vartook leaned over and rested his arms on his knees. He stared at Pullmoo's rug as he replayed the scene in his mind. Shaking his head, he said, "What a strange thing for a human woman to do."

"Indeed," Pullmoo said.

"Why did we stop using the gesture?" he asked.

"We stopped using the gesture around the same time the vocunine turned on us," Pullmoo told him. "It was too painful a reminder of the comradery we lost, and the reason we lost it. When the hapless young Maria performed that gesture to you, it was deeply reverent to both you and the vocunine - and her innocence and naivety only made it more so."

Vartook nodded, then said, "I was rather moved by it. I have saved many lives in my lifetime, but I had never received that gesture before - not that I ever expected it."

"So, will you help me, Vartook?" Pullmoo asked. Will you help us, the city, put right our relationship with the vocunine by ensuring that Solomane takes his father's place as alpha?"

"I will do what I can," Vartook promised.

CHAPTER 36

Maria arrived home at least an hour before dark that evening. She and Maddie had spent much of the day strolling through the park. They had gone to the District Center for food, where they met up with a few other companion women. Maria tried to be social, knowing that she would need friends if she was going to survive the next 300 or so years in Pegasea. At the time she arrived back home, Orook was sitting on the sofa fumbling with the same strange device she had seen him working on a few days ago. His concentration on the object was such that he barely noticed her as she came through the door.

"What is that?" Maria asked as she sat down next to him.

"It's a puzzle," he said as he narrowed his eyes at some misaligned section of the object.

"Is it fun?" Maria asked.

"Like any difficult puzzle, it is fun until it is infuriating," he said.

"May I see it?" Maria asked.

"Be my guest," Orook said as he handed her the puzzle, then explained the goal.

Maria turned the puzzle over in her hands several times.

"This is impossible," she said.

"So it would seem," he chuckled.

Maria handed the insidious device back to Orook.

"Did you eat dinner with Maddie?" he asked.

Maria nodded.

"I made you an appointment to speak with one of the sociologists," he told her.

"Ok," she yawned.

"You're meeting with Pullmoo tomorrow evening," Orook said.

"What?!" Maria shouted as she jumped up from the couch.

Orook looked up at her with wide eyes.

"I am *not* meeting with *her*," Maria spat.

"Maria, I understand why you do not like her, but Pullmoo is the best psychologist in the city. You should be flattered. It is not her job to counsel trouble women from Earth. That job is usually assigned to the Fifth or Sixth Sociologists. I was quite surprised to discover, after I put in the request, that she had assigned herself to you. She must have some special interest in your mental state," he said.

"Oh, I'm sure she does," Maria hissed.

"Maria, you are acting like a child," he said.

"I won't go!" Maria insisted.

"You will," he said.

"You can't make me!" Maria said as her eyes began to moisten with tears of rage.

Orook's eyes became distant as he looked upon her in silence.

"I won't go," she repeated.

"Maria, please do not defy me," he whispered. "There is nothing I want less than to demonstrate the means by which I can compel you to follow my instructions."

Tears began to roll down Maria's face as she asked, "What are you talking about?"

"Give me your wrist," he said.

"Why?" Maria asked as she tucked her hands under her arms and stepped away from him.

"You asked me what I was talking about. If you give me your wrist, I will show you," he said.

Maria shook her head.

"Ok, I will tell you then," he said. "There is a mechanism on one of those bands which will inflict varying degrees of pain down your arm and into the rest of your body. I can trigger that mechanism at any time using my armband."

Maria's face went pale as she took another step away from him.

"You wouldn't do that to me," she whispered.

"Do you really want to test that hypothesis?" he asked.

"I would never trust you again," she said.

"That is an odd thing to threaten me with, considering it does not appear as if I have your trust now. I am telling you that you need to speak to Pullmoo and yet you are refusing to go," he said.

"But that's not because I don't trust *you*. I don't trust *her*," Maria said.

"Do you not see how that might be the very root of the problem?" Orook asked. "Regardless of how you, or I, feel about the woman personally, refusing to trust her is counterproductive. She does, in essence, run this city. You have a level of distrust and hostility towards her that is unhealthy and which, in my opinion, is impeding your ability to adapt. I do not know how she could possibly have known but Pullmoo must have some insight into this fact. I assume that this is why she answered my request personally."

Maria fidgeted with her wristband, as if subconsciously trying to remove it. Seeing this, Orook second guessed his decision to show her that most hideous of its functions.

"You are probably right though," he said as he stood up from the couch. "I doubt that I could ever bring myself to use that thing."

Maria continued to stare at the floor as Orook retreated to the bedroom. As soon as he was gone, Maria sat back down on the sofa. She picked up one of the cushions, pressed it to her face and screamed. An hour later, Orook found her asleep in the living room, curled up into the sofa like a hibernating animal in its winter burrow. Slowly and silently, he scooped her into his arms and carried her to her room. He placed her on her bed and covered her with a blanket. As he turned to leave, he heard her mumble something in her sleep. He turned back to her and placed his hand on her forehead until she quieted.

"What a mess you are," he whispered before leaving her room and drawing the curtain behind him.

CHAPTER 37

L ate in the evening of the following day, Maria numbly readied
herself to go to Pullmoo's office. Orook explained that he would
take Maria to the City Center and then escort her to Pullmoo's office.
Maria remained silent as he explained that he would drop her off, then
pick her up whenever Pullmoo notified him to do so. Maria was silent
the entire way there.

When they arrived at the door to Pullmoo's office, Maria stood
waiting with her arms folded petulantly across her chest. When
Pullmoo opened the door, Maria looked away as Orook greeted her
and gestured his respect. She refused to make any introduction or
cordial gestures to this woman. Pullmoo pretended not to notice and
simply stepped aside to allow Maria into her office. Maria walked in
and wordlessly sat down on the same sofa where Pullmoo and Maddie
had recently exchanged secrets.

After Orook left, Pullmoo pulled up a chair across from the sofa
and sat down at a comfortable distance across from Maria.

"Maria, do you know why you are here?" she asked.

"Because my keeper thinks I need psychological help," Maria spat.

"Do you think you need psychological counseling?" Pullmoo
asked.

"No," she said.

"Orook tells me that you are having trouble adapting," Pullmoo
said.

Maria glared at Pullmoo.

"Yeah, and what if I don't want to adapt?" she said.

"That would be most unfortunate," Pullmoo said.

"For you or for me?" Maria asked.

"Both," she said.

"Do you really intend to counsel me here?" Maria asked. "Or have you simply come up with a new plan to use me in some way?"

"Perhaps a little bit of both," Pullmoo said with a smile.

"What is the plan *this* time then?" Maria seethed.

"You don't need to know that," Pullmoo said.

"Fuck you," Maria said. "I don't want to be part of your wretched plans anymore."

"Everyone is part of at least one of my plans Maria," Pullmoo told her. "Besides that, you don't have much of a choice in the matter."

"I don't have much of a choice in anything apparently," Maria said.

"True," Pullmoo said.

"I hate you," Maria hissed.

"Why?" Pullmoo asked.

"Because you're evil," Maria said.

"Hmmm, that is a new one," Pullmoo mused. "I have been called a lot of things, but evil? I think you flatter me."

"Flatter you?" Maria said with wide eyes.

"To be evil requires a complete disregard for the ethical values of one's culture and society. To be truly evil, a person would have to have a will and an ambition wholly detached from the concerns and opinions of others. Such independence and personal strength of will is considered admirable among your kind, is it not?" Pullmoo asked with a twinkle in her eye.

"What? No!" Maria snapped.

"Oh? Forgive me then, I must not completely understand the human value system," she said.

Maria narrowed her eyes at Pullmoo.

"Cut it out," Maria said.

"Cut what out?" Pullmoo asked.

"You *know* why what you are doing is wrong. Or, at the very least, you know why I think it's wrong," Maria said.

"Yes, I know why you think it is wrong. Obviously, I disagree. As I am sure your keeper has told you, we apply the sciences of psychology and sociology as we would any other science. For some reason, this is difficult for your kind to accept in practice - despite the fact that you do it all the time, only with far less competence. That incompetence is likely due, in no small part, to your inane belief that applying these sciences deliberating and methodically crosses some sort of mercurial ethical boundary," Pullmoo said.

"Look, you can call it whatever you like," Maria said. "And you can justify it a hundred different ways - that's the beauty of a utilitarian system, isn't it? Any cost-benefit analysis can be skewed in any direction depending on the ultimately subjective value you put on each outcome. I'm not as dumb as you think I am - and I'm sure you have endless explanations and justifications for everything you do. But none of it matters because it's still just wrong."

"Is that what the tree in your dreams told you? What the Prisoner told you?" Pullmoo taunted.

Maria's face flushed.

Pullmoo raised an eyebrow at her.

"Why would you ask me that?" Maria asked through gritted teeth.

"Just curious," Pullmoo said. "It sounds like something a vocunine might say. Or, rather, something a vocunine might feel. They are not so apt at putting such things into words."

"Are you trying to insult me?" Maria asked.

"What do you think?" Pullmoo mused.

Maria stared at the First Sociologist as she tried to understand what this woman was trying to do with her, or to her.

"Why are you screwing with me?" she asked.

"Besides the fact that it amuses me?" Pullmoo asked.

"Yes, besides that," Maria seethed.

"Because it will help you loosen the bonds of your former world and let go of your current value system," Pullmoo said. "You need to open your mind."

"Open my mind? Seriously?" Maria said. "Open it to what? - to the idea that it is ok for me to be treated like a dog, or a child? - ok for me to be used as some sort of security blanket for a grown man? I don't think so."

"Why not?" Pullmoo asked.

"Why not?" Maria repeated. "Ugh! How do you not see how sick this all is? I get that you guys are all really smart and advanced or whatever - but I'm not an animal. You and I are not all that different. So, if it's all so great - why don't *you* be Orook's companion?"

"Oh, my dear, that would be most inappropriate and counterproductive," Pullmoo chuckled.

"Why?" Maria asked.

"For one thing, the companion role cannot be filled by a Pegasean," Pullmoo said. "But let me cut all this short by simply telling you that I do understand why you resent being assigned to a submissive role. I am well aware of the fact that women on your planet were oppressed for a very long time and that many of them still are even now. I can certainly understand how and why you must feel as if you are being forced back under that same sort of oppression…"

"That's not it at all," Maria interjected. "Obviously you guys aren't sexist against women of your own kind."

"Well, then what is it?" Pullmoo asked.

"Oh my God!" Maria said, letting out a long breath. "You are a fascist! In every way! You control every aspect of people's lives. No one here has any real choices or any real freedom. You take children from their parents! And this rigid social hierarchy you have - it's sick. And I don't know what exactly is going on with us, the human women, and this whole keeper-companion relationship you've created, but it's not right - and I don't mean just because it's morally reprehensible. There is something else wrong about it. I can't wrap my head around it, it's mostly just a feeling. But whatever it is, it's wrong… somehow, it's not right…"

Pullmoo smiled as Maria trailed off.

"You know exactly what I'm talking about, don't you?" Maria accused.

"Well, first of all, you are giving me credit for a lot of decisions I did not make and had no part in making," Pullmoo said. "I am only 130 years old - much too young to have played a role in the decision to raise the children collectively. As for our social hierarchy, much of that was established long before this city, or I, even existed. I was involved in the development of the keeper-companion arrangement, but, well, again, I might remind you of the unsavory alternatives."

"Whatever," Maria muttered. "Why do you care so much about what I think anyway? Or how I feel?"

"I only care to the extent that it affects our First Engineer. Despite how he might seem to you, he is perilously soft-hearted. He is genuinely concerned about your emotional and psychological health," Pullmoo said.

"What do you want from me?" Maria asked. "I can't help how I feel."

"Of course, you can," she said.

Maria drew her hands down over her face as she groaned.

"I can help you," Pullmoo said.

"I don't want your help," she snapped.

"Don't be so hasty. I have a lot of power in this city. There is almost certainly something within my power which I could do to help make life here a bit easier for you," Pullmoo said.

"Can you let Orook see his son in the nursery?" she asked.

"No," Pullmoo said

"Can you let me call Orook by his name?" she asked.

"No," Pullmoo said.

"Well, could you at least let him kiss me without an engraved invitation?" Maria asked.

"Actually, that I might be able to do," Pullmoo said.

"Really?" she asked.

"Yes, but I must caution you Maria, the means to this end could have unintended consequences," she warned.

"How so?" Maria asked.

"I can grant immunity, to a Pegasean man, from prosecution under a particular law. However, I can neither change the law itself nor create a new law. Only the Central Council can change existing laws or make new laws."

"Ok…," Maria said.

"So, the problem is, in order to give you what you want, I would have to grant Orook immunity from prosecution under the law prohibiting all such salacious interactions with human woman, but I cannot redefine the law itself. Of course, I would have to write the immunity papers such that they only applied to any would-be offense committed by him against you."

"Right," Maria said. "So, what's the problem?"

"Let me put it bluntly," Pullmoo said. "If I gave Orook that immunity, technically, there would be nothing under the law specifically prohibiting him from forcing himself on you. There is no separate law prohibiting the assault of a companion. There is no need for such a law because the general prohibition, with its one well defined exception, covers joining by force and all other such torrid acts and unwanted advances. Do you understand? So, we are faced with a kind of all or nothing situation."

"I see," Maria said.

"So, I must ask you - how important is this to you? And, how much do you trust him?" Pullmoo asked.

Maria pinched and rubbed the bridge of her nose as she thought.

"If you do give him this immunity, can it be taken back?" she asked.

"Yes, but not instantly and not without good reason," Pullmoo said.

"Well, I want you to do it anyway," Maria said.

"Are you sure?" Pullmoo asked.

Maria nodded.

"I can't even imagine him doing anything like that to me," she said.

"Neither can I," Pullmoo agreed. "But you never know. We've been wrong before."

"What do you mean?" Maria asked. "Who is 'we?'"

"Another time," Pullmoo said as she stood up and walked over to her desk. She pulled out a piece of paper and wrote on it for several minutes. Maria watched as Pullmoo completed the document with her signature and placed a kind of seal at the bottom. Pullmoo then rolled up the paper and slid it into a tube.

"Why the fancy paper and packaging?" Maria asked.

"Because unlike an electronic document, this is impossible to forge or duplicate," Pullmoo said.

"It would also be easy to destroy," Maria added.

"Indeed," Pullmoo said.

Pullmoo then called Orook and instructed him to come retrieve Maria.

CHAPTER 38

When Orook arrived at Pullmoo's office, Pullmoo stepped outside into the hallway and closed the door behind her. She wanted to speak with Orook privately before he took Maria home.

"Well?" Orook asked.

"You and Maria have at least one thing in common," Pullmoo said. "You both seem to believe that I am an evil witch determined to enslave you all."

"In that case, I have once again underestimated her intelligence. I will have to apologize to her," he said with a smirk.

"Indeed," Pullmoo chuckled.

"So, tell me, what is wrong with her?" Orook said.

"Absolutely nothing," Pullmoo said.

"Then why is she having so much trouble adapting?" Orook asked.

"She is suffering from something which, on Earth, would be referred to as 'culture shock.' It will pass. She will be fine. In the meantime, she asked me to give you this." Pullmoo said, then handed Orook the cylinder holding the immunity papers.

"What is it?" Orook asked.

"A spell to reverse all of my dark magic," she said with a grin.

"If only such was possible. What is it really?" Orook asked again.

"She asked me to grant you immunity from prosecution under the law which prohibits the propositioning of, or joining with, human women. The immunity papers I've just given you are strictly limited to any would-be offense against her, and her alone. So, don't go hounding any other human women," Pullmoo said.

"Why would she ask you for this? Has she accused me of -" Orook started.

"No, of course not," Pullmoo said.

"I do not understand," he said. "I thought her problem was that she resents my control over her life - how does giving me *more* control help her?"

"Ironic, isn't it?" Pullmoo mused.

"How does she still not understand that the law is there to protect her?" He asked. "I have explained this to her several times."

"Orook, she understands the intended purpose of it. However, she also understands that the law creates a kind of barrier between the two of you. That might not have been the law's original intent - in fact, I doubt it was back then - but the effect is all the same. It prevents you from treating her the same way you would a Pegasean women," Pullmoo explained.

"How could I possibly treat her like a Pegasean woman?" he asked. "Did you explain to her why Pegasean women are different from human women?"

"No, I thought I would let you have that honor," Pullmoo said.

Orook groaned.

"Orook, I need your assurance that you will not abuse this immunity I have given you," Pullmoo said.

"Abuse it? I do not even want it," he said.

"Then by all means, burn it for all I care," Pullmoo said. "However, I advise you to keep it for however long it may take to prove to your stubborn companion that you are not being brainwashed by me or the city - that you are acting, or not acting, of your own free will. Becoming convinced of that *will* help her adjust."

Orook nodded.

"Now, go home," Pullmoo instructed. "Tell no one of this. Explain to your companion that this immunity I have given you must be kept in the highest confidence. I will make sure that you are never evaluated by the love police or asked any of those uncomfortable questions at your compliance evaluation. If either of you tell anyone about this, I will have you both flogged. Do you understand?"

"I do," he said.

Orook looked down at the ornately embossed cylinder, which he held gingerly between his hands at each end. He rotated it slowly with his fingers, as if it were a poorly constructed pipe bomb that could explode at any moment. He then tucked it into an inside pocket of his uniform and thanked the First Sociologist for her assistance.

Pullmoo then opened the door to her office and called Maria to come outside and go home with her keeper.

CHAPTER 39

When they arrived home, Orook studied Maria as she took off her shoes. He took the cylinder with the immunity papers out from his pocket and held it out to Maria.

"Maria, why did you ask Pullmoo for this?" he asked.

"Well, it wasn't my first choice - or even my second," she said.

"What was your first choice?" he asked.

"I asked her to let you see your son," she said.

Orook let the cylinder drop from his fingers as he stared at Maria.

"Why would you ask for *that?*" he asked.

"Because you want to see him - and you should be allowed to. It's cruel to keep a father from his child," she said.

"That was very generous of you," he said as he picked up the cylinder.

"Then I asked her to let me call you by your name, but she said she couldn't do that either," Maria said.

"Human women cannot be granted immunity," Orook explained. "Also, calling a Pegasean man by his real name is one of only a few offenses which doesn't commute from a companion to her keeper. So, if you were caught doing that, I wouldn't be able to help you either."

Maria shrugged.

"The immunity she gave you was the third and last thing I asked for," she said.

"Well, you should not have - it was a reckless request. That law is there to protect you," he said as he put the immunity papers in the back of a drawer in the far wall of the living room.

Maria rolled her eyes.

"Why would you want to put yourself in such a vulnerable position?" he persisted. "This makes no sense to me."

"Am I really in any more vulnerable a position now that I was before?" she asked. "Are you planning to take me on the floor any second now?"

"Of course not," Orook scoffed.

"Pity," Maria teased.

Orook closed his eyes and shook his head.

"Maria, what do you want from me?" he asked.

"I just want you to be normal," she said.

"What is normal?" Orook asked.

"Just treat me the same way you would a Pegasean woman," Maria said.

"I can't do that," he said.

"I get why you can't outside the house - but why can't you in private? When it's just us?" she asked.

Orook sighed.

"Well?" she persisted.

"I really did not want to be the person to explain these things to you," Orook said.

"What things?" she asked.

Orook took a deep breath and told her to sit down.

"You are not like a Pegasean woman," he began.

"I know, I know, I'm weak and stupid and in every way inferior," Maria moaned.

"No, that is not the sort of difference I am referring to," Orook said. "Pegasean women have natural defenses against being abused by men. They have a very dynamic vaginal wall that is designed to encourage welcomed partners and dissuade unwelcome intruders. When they feel threatened, angry, or are in pain, there is a defense mechanism that kicks in - and the wall goes from soft and pliable to firm and coarse. It starts out like fine sand paper. But in extreme circumstances, it can turn into something more like a bed of small clawed thorns. As you can imagine, this means that any partner of a Pegasean woman has to be a bit careful. Most of the time, it's not an issue or even a concern. That said, every Pegasean man has either heard stories about, or experienced himself, the unfortunate consequences of ignoring the signs and trigging that defense mechanism. Even if it is only a small trigger, the effect is memorable. Unfortunately, the Pegasean women have no conscious control over it."

Maria stared at Orook with wide eyes.

"Are you serious?" she asked.

Orook nodded.

"Has this... have you ever experienced this defense mechanism?" Maria asked.

"Only once," Orook said. "One time when I was with Linoo, one of her braids got caught on my armband. I'm still not exactly sure what happened, but at some point, I inadvertently ripped out several strands of her hair. The sudden sharp pain she felt triggered her defenses. I did not suffer too badly. The wound healed in a few days."

Maria shuddered.

"No wonder you guys are so cautious," she said.

"That was just a fluke," Orook said. "It all happened too fast for there to be any warning. In almost all other circumstances, there are plenty of warnings. We do not need to be overly cautious or gentle. We only have to pay attention."

"Ok, but what does any of this have to do with me?" Maria asked.

"When the first women from Earth arrived in Pegasea, and the body biologists informed the Pegaseans that human women had no defenses, they were horrified. It was unimaginable to us. That is why the Center Council became extremely protective of your kind. In fact, at first, the Center Council insisted that all of the Earth women be kept in the Intake Hall. They also prohibited Pegasean men from interacting with the Earth women at all. This gravely insulted the Pegasean men," Orook told her.

"Of course, it would," Maria thought aloud.

"So much so, in fact, that it caused the closest thing to a riot this city has ever seen. It was not that the Pegasean men were particularly desperate to interact with the women from Earth, it was the insult of being prohibited from doing so. They were hurt and heartbroken over the fact that the Pegasean women still thought of them all as potential rapists. Even when the Center Council conceded and allowed the human women into the body of the city, as you know, it was strictly illegal to so much as voice any kind of desire for them." Orook told her.

"And this is the same Center Council that set up the whole keeper-companion relationship?" Maria asked.

"Maria, do you know where those terms originated?" Orook asked.

"No," she said.

"They came from a time when the vocunine lived among the Olroneans," he told her. "Back then, the relationship between vocunine and Olroneans was something quite different than what it is now. They lived with us the way dogs on Earth live with humans. Only, the vocunine were so much more than mere pets. They can speak, as you know. They have hands and they can assist a person in just about any task. They were true companions to the Olroneans - and they called them their keepers. The Center Council adopted this terminology, in part, to encourage a strictly platonic relationship between Pegasean men and human women."

Maria covered her mouth with her hand.

"Oh my god," she said. "That's it, isn't it?"

"What is it?" Orook asked.

"That is why we are here!" Maria said. "You miss the vocunine. You took us in to replace *them*."

Orook closed his eyes and shook his head.

"That is ridiculous," he said. "We have gone on just as well without the vocunine for quite some time now. We do not need them."

"Yeah, right," Maria said.

"Just stop," Orook warned.

"Alright, ok," Maria said putting up her hands. "So, what happened? Why did they become your enemies?"

"First, you must understand that, before the baby girl crisis, there simply was no such thing as rape on this planet," he explained. "In fact, no Olronean language even had a word for it. Since the very origin of our species on this planet, no man ever had anything to gain, and quite a bit to lose, by forcing himself on a woman - the thought was never entertained. That is the way it was for thousands of years, through all recorded history. But when the birth rate of baby girls became critically low and women became scarce, well, the remaining women were often married or otherwise not willing to have dozens of children with different men. The Pegasean women have adapted and have managed to keep our population staple. However, it took them a while to come to any kind of agreement with respect to how this should be done. Back then, women were like women on Earth, they married and had a few children with one man, or maybe two if she divorced and remarried. Even though the longevity viruses had already started to lengthen our lives, they still could not imagine having as many children as the Pegasean women do now. Even if they were able to contemplate a life of 325 or more years, they simply were not willing to suddenly start mothering a multitude of children with different men."

"I can understand that," Maria said.

Orook nodded, then continued, "All the same, the rest of the Olronean populace was in a panic. For reasons I have already explained, these women could not easily be forced to have more children by other men."

"So, what happened?" Maria asked. "Did they threaten them?"

"Maria, why do ask such inane questions? When a woman is threatened, does she not become afraid? Or at least angry? Why do you think the presence of a threat would reverse her defenses rather than heighten them?" he asked.

"Sorry," Maria said. "I guess I didn't realize that this defense mechanism responded so strongly to emotions. But if reproduction was the issue, why didn't these women simply agree to be artificially inseminated by a doctor?"

"Some of them did," Orook said. "And those women were left in peace at first. But the depravity and aggressiveness of the Olronean men only deepened as the crisis peaked. Also, Olronean women are not easily impregnated, by any means, when they are highly stressed and only marginally willing. Their wombs are also very responsive to stress - although obviously in a different way. Eventually, many of the men simply got tired of dealing with all these obstacles. They began capturing women and bringing them to corrupted hospitals where they were first sedated, then rendered unconscious. Suddenly everything these men wanted to do became a lot easier. The natural defenses of an Olronean women can be shut down very easily while she is unconscious. This was the dawn of the darkest days of Olronean history. Just about every remaining woman left on the planet was eventually put into an induced coma, raped and impregnated against her will. Many of them were probably experimented on as well."

"What happened to them?" Maria whispered.

"They all died," Orook said. "It took maybe ten years. In many cases, the vocunine companion of a captured woman would track her down and attempt to rescue her. When this happened, the vocunine would be shot and the woman, if she was still alive, would be returned to her chemical prison. In other cases, some women awoke from their coma just long enough to realize what was happening and killed themselves. Often, it was a vocunine companion who managed to bring them back to consciousness. Some of the women who killed themselves also ended the lives of several others. They must have assumed, as was probably the case, that these other women would also rather die than be used as slaves. This was more than their vocunine companions could bare. Many of them refused to leave their keepers even after they had died. No one knows exactly how many women were lost in all, but it was tens of thousands at the very least. The loss of these women marked the beginning of the end of the Olronean populations outside of Pegasea. The female Olronean population never recovered and eventually died out. A few hundred years later, the last of the male population died out."

"Wow," Maria said.

"During much of this time, the women in Pegasea were safe because the people here are civilized and kind," he said. "However, the story of what happened to those other women had a terrible impact on everyone. This is why the vocunine now hate us. From their perspective, the Olronean men brought a whole new kind of evil into the world. They do not hate Pegasean women as much, but they still hold them partly to blame, for not at least trying to stop it. It does not seem to matter to them that no one in Pegasea participated in that atrocity, or condoned it, or could have possibly done anything about it."

Maria only nodded.

"Now do you understand?" he asked. "In our eyes, the human women are a lot like those unconscious Olronean women - completely defenseless and vulnerable."

"But it's not the same. I'm not unconscious," she said.

"You might as well be," he said.

Maria rolled her eyes.

"You just do not understand," Orook said. "Even if you have no fear of me physically forcing myself on you, you are failing to appreciate the countless other subtler ways I could compel you, or manipulate you, into doing what I want. What if I refused to take you to the places you wanted to go unless you agreed to sleep in my bed? What if I told you that you will eat nothing but your least favorite foods unless you acquiesce to my desires?"

"You're not that kind of guy." Maria said.

"How would you know what kind of guy I am?" Orook asked.

"Well, I've been living with you for several months now. I think I have some idea," she said. "And besides that, if sleeping with you means I never have to eat another borcula egg slurry again, I would be more than happy to make that deal."

"You see, that is exactly what I am talking about," he said. "That is the sort of thing the law - the one you just gave me immunity to - is designed to prevent."

"I was kidding!" she said.

"Were you?" he asked.

"Yes! Geez, I'm not *that* easy," she said.

Orook raised an eyebrow at her.

"Shut up," Maria muttered.

"I think I know why you are failing to see this from my perspective," he said.

"Oh?" Maria said as she folded her arms.

Orook sat down next to her and smiled from one corner of his mouth.

"What?" Maria said. "Why am I unable to see whatever stupid point you are trying to make?"

"I think it must be because you cannot even imagine a moment in which you do not desire me," he said.

"Oh my god...," Maria said.

"I promise you," he said. "There will come a day when you do not find me so -"

"Shut up!" Maria said as she shoved him hard in the shoulder.

Orook laughed.

"Why can't you just be normal?" she asked.

"I am trying to be normal right now," he said.

"Wow," she said. "So, is this how you are with Linoo?"

Orook shrugged.

"How did you manage to get with her anyway?" Maria asked. "No offense, but she seems way out of your league."

"We fell in love when we were just kids - before either of knew she was 'out of my league' as you put it," Orook told her.

"When did she fall in love with you?" she asked.

"According to her, it happened one day in school... there was a small explosion, the table caught fire... it was mess," he said.

Maria stared at him with wide eyes.

"Oh Maria," he said. "Do not compare our relationship to the one I have - or had - with Linoo. You are a wonderful woman, but it is just not the same. That is not entirely a bad thing either. Unlike Linoo, you are stuck with me forever."

Maria sighed.

As they sat in awkward silence, the sunset sky bathed the room in an amber glow. In the dimming light, Orook noticed that Maria was unconsciously fidgeting with her wristband again.

"Give me your right wrist," he said as he sat down next to her and held out his hand.

Reluctantly, Maria put her wrist in his hand. Orook then used his armband to release and unlock the wristband on her right wrist. He slid it off over her hand and looked at it for a moment. He then snapped it in two and tossed it onto the end table. Seeing Maria's surprised and puzzled expression, he said "You don't need that one. It is only needed for restraint and discipline. You need the other one though, that has your access chip and that homing device I showed you."

"Thank you!" Maria said.

Orook nodded.

"I would like to sleep in your bed," she said. "But not because you took the wristband off! I honestly just find your bed far more comfortable - seriously."

"Of course," he said.

CHAPTER 40

A thick morning fog rose from the early spring rain as Vartook ventured out onto the mountain alone. He was never more thankful for his second inner ear than he was that morning, navigating over wet rock and mud, through an ominous mountain mist that rendered his eyes almost useless. He walked slowly and deliberately as he followed the rough trails, if they could even be called "trails," Pullmoo had shown him on a map. According to her, these trails were frequented by the more dominant members of the mountain vocunine, the ones most likely to challenge Solomane. The smaller and more obsequious vocunine preferred to navigate over the rocks or through the labyrinth of caves throughout and beneath the mountain. Vartook's plan was to find Solomane's would-be challengers and convince them, one way or another, that it was in everyone's best interest that they abandon any ambition to become the new mountain king.

Just when Vartook was starting to doubt the accuracy of Pullmoo's information, he sensed a presence on the rocks above him and to the right of the trail. He stopped and stood still as he waited for his stalker to appear. Concentrating intently on his surroundings, he took in every sound and every shift in the air around him. At last, from behind the mist, a shadowy figure came down from the rocks and stepped out onto the path. The shadow approached, then stopped at a safe distance ahead of the First Guardsman.

"What are you doing here?" the shadow asked.

"My name is Vartook and I am the First Guardsman of Pegasea," Vartook said.

"I know who you are," quipped the shadow. "I asked what you are doing here."

"Can you not see my mind?" Vartook asked. "Are you not a vocunine?"

"Your mind is muddled to me," said the shadow. "Maybe you do not know yourself why you are here."

Vartook wondered why the creature behind the mist, which could only be a vocunine, could not clearly see his mind. Perhaps this particular vocunine suffered a defect which prevented it from doing so.

"I am looking for vocunine who might seek to be alpha of the mountain pack," he offered.

"Which pack?" asked the shadow.

"How many packs of vocunine are there on this mountain?" Vartook asked.

"I do not know your Pegasean numbers - but there are at least as many packs in these mountains as I have fingers and toes," it answered.

Vartook looked with wide eyes out into the fog all around him, astonished. Could there really be that many?

"Which pack was led by the one known as Borkane?" Vartook asked.

"All of them," said the shadow.

"I do not understand," Vartook said.

"My grandfather, father of Borkane, united all of the vocunine packs on and around the mountains by challenging the alpha of each one - except that he didn't kill them, as was the normal way of taking over a pack. Instead, he asked for their... I don't know the word..."

"Allegiance?" Vartook suggested.

"What is that?" the shadow asked.

"It is like loyalty, but more than that," Vartook explained. "If your grandfather is the father of Borkane, are you Borkane's son? Or his nephew?"

"I am his son. I am Solomane," he answered.

Vartook said nothing.

"You were not expecting to find me out here," Solomane said.

"No, I was not," said the guardsman. "I am pleasantly surprised."

"Pleasantly?" asked the vocunine.

"Yes," Vartook said. "My partner believes that you will make a fine leader for the vocunine. She has sent me out here to ensure that you are not challenged for the position of alpha."

"That is most strange," remarked Solomane.

"What is strange?" asked Vartook.

"All of it," he said.

"We believe that you might be more open to the possibility of a truce between the vocunine and the Pegaseans," Vartook explained.

Solomane approached Vartook, then stopped and sat down on the ground in front of him. Vartook saw the animal clearly now, and saw that this vocunine, while still substantially larger than even the largest dogs on Earth, and a bit larger than most of the vocunine he had seen over the course of his long years as a guardsman, was still less than half the size of his fallen father. While keeping one hand on his weapon, Vartook bowed his head in greeting. Solomane laughed at the gesture in the soft rumbling way that all vocunine laugh, with a sound like a deep hiccupping purr. Vartook had never heard the sound before and took a step back, fearing the animal might be sick.

"You have never heard a vocunine laugh before, have you?" Solomane asked.

When Vartook did not answer, Solomane looked up at the man with cold, distrustful eyes and said, "You have never let one of us live long enough in your presence, have you?"

Vartook looked down at the ground and sighed.

"Do not pretend to be remorseful," Solomane sneered.

"I pretend no such thing," Vartook said. "It is my job to protect my city. Yes, I have killed many of you over the course of more than a hundred years. However, I invite you to hear my heart and see my mind, now, as I tell you that I have not once enjoyed doing so."

Solomane stared at Vartook for a long moment, assessing the man fully, then said, "And what happens if I become king and I am not who you think I am? What if I am not interested in peace between your people and mine?"

"That would be unfortunate," Vartook said.

"You would kill me then?" Solomane asked.

"Only if you gave me reason to," he said, holding Solomane's eyes.

"Your kind are no good," said the vocunine. "The Olroneans are evil and vile and have no respect for anything... not even the Prisoner."

"I am *Pegasean*," Vartook intoned. "We left the Olroneans to die at their own hands almost a 1,000 years ago."

"How noble of you," Solomane scathed.

Vartook grit his teeth, then calmed himself. This is pointless, he thought. Pullmoo was naive if she really thought that peace between the vocunine and the Pegaseans was possible. He turned his back to Solomane and started walking back down the trail to the city. Solomane followed Vartook, keeping pace with the man at a safe distance behind him.

"Why are you following me?" Vartook asked.

"Curiosity," the vocunine answered.

Vartook said nothing as he continued to walk resolutely towards home.

"Your woman will be displeased with you if you give up this quickly. What will you tell her? That I was rude to you?" Solomane taunted.

Vartook's well trained ears heard the layered emotions in Solomane's words. Slowly, he came to a stop, then turned to the mountain. He let his gaze trace the crystal boulders on up into the overhanging mist.

At last, Vartook turned to Solomane and said, "It is true that the Olroneans did terrible things towards the end of their civilization. But we are different. The Pegaseans are different."

"Perhaps," conceded Solomane. "But my mother told me never to trust any of you. As did my father... but he was a fool."

"There is no forgiving what those men did, but I am not one of them," Orook continued. "The founders of Pegasea came to this mountain to escape those men and their kind. Why does this not mean anything to the vocunine?"

"Because we see it as cowardly. Your fathers and grandfathers should have fought them," Solomane said.

"That would have been suicide," Vartook snapped.

"A noble death all the same," Solomane countered.

"Let me ask you something, Solomane," Vartook said. "If Pullmoo had put you to the same challenge to which she put your father - if you had been the one who had to face me - would you have accepted the challenge?"

"No," Solomane said.

"And why is that?" Vartook asked. "Were you not equally outraged by Orook's actions against your kinfolk?"

Solomane whined quietly and hung his head.

"Do not feel ashamed," Vartook said. "You understand what I am saying. There is no point to engaging in a fight you cannot win."

Solomane nodded slowly.

"Solomane, are you smarter than your father?" Vartook asked.

"Yes," he said.

"Then you must see the futility in continuing this feud between our species. There is nothing to gain from it," Vartook said.

Solomane looked up at Vartook and searched the guardsman's eyes.

"This must be the will of the Prisoner," he said.

"What is?" asked Vartook. "And who is this Prisoner you keep referring to?"

"The ruekar have come to the valley," Solomane said in a rush.

"Why are you telling me this?" Vartook asked. "A few of them come to the valley every year."

Solomane shook his head.

"This is different. This is not a few wandering young males," Solomane explained. "There are hundreds of them now - whole troops of them."

Vartook swallowed as he unconsciously tightened his fingers around the handle of the crescent blade at his waist.

"When did you first see them?" he said softly.

"The day before Borkane broke into the city wall," Solomane said. "I wasn't there because I didn't want to play along."

"Play along?" Vartook asked.

"My father was enraged by Orook's actions - that much is true. But his bigger plan was to move the pack into the city itself, where he thought we could all hide from the ruekar. It was a very stupid plan. I tried to tell him it was stupid, but he wouldn't listen," Solomane explained.

Vartook's mind began to race. He looked in the direction of the valley, even though it was too far to be seen from his current position, even on a clear day.

"Why are the ruekar gathering in the valley?" Vartook asked.

"I do not know," said the vocunine. "But I think it must be because they have grown so much in number, they need more land to spread out... more food to hunt."

"That could be," Vartook said.

"Or it could be the Prisoner called them here," Solomane thought aloud.

"I insist you tell me what this Prisoner is," Vartook said.

"The Prisoner of Mount Olympus, the Silent Speaker, the Heart of the Mountain," Solomane said, as if at least one of these names should be familiar to Vartook.

"Is this some kind of vocunine god?" Vartook asked.

"Maybe," Solomane said.

"Maybe?" Vartook repeated. "What kind of answer is that?"

Solomane looked squarely into Vartook's eyes as he said, "It is the only answer I can give you."

The two then stood in an awkward silence for some time, each unsure of how to proceed. After several minutes, Vartook asked Solomane if he had any intention of attempting to avenge his father's death. Solomane stifled a laugh before assuring Vartook that he had no such intention.

"We do not avenge a fair death," Solomane told him.

"That is fortunate," Vartook said. "There has been enough blood shed between our people."

Solomane agreed.

"And you must leave my challengers alone," he added.

"I had no intention of harming them," said Vartook. "I was only going to advise them against challenging you."

"And if they failed to heed you?" Solomane asked.

Vartook said nothing.

Solomane shook his head, then said, "If I am to assume the position of alpha, I must do so honestly."

"It is good to know that you have such an honorable spirit," said the guardsman.

"But you did not know this before meeting me," said the vocunine. "So why do you and your woman want me to be king? Do you think I will follow your instructions like an obedient Earth dog? Because we are not dogs, and I will not..."

Vartook put up a hand to stop Solomane from saying any more.

"Solomane, that is not why we want you to lead the vocunine," Vartook said. "Now listen to me. We both have bigger problems now. The Pegaseans and the vocunine are both civil societies compared to those rapacious little monsters. There will be no bargaining with them, no truce, no treaty. Do you understand? The choice has been made for us now. The feud must end, and it must end now."

"You don't need us," Solomane muttered.

"Maybe not - but what if we do?" Vartook said. "You and your kind most certainly need us. You can hide in the caves at night, but how will you hunt? As soon as the weather warms up enough for the ruekar to roam the mountain, you will have to hide all day long. In the peak of summer, even the nights might be warm enough for them to roam the mountains. What will you do then?"

Solomane whined in fear and misery at the thought.

Vartook bent at the waist and looked straight into Solomane's eyes.

"The vocunine were much stronger when they lived among my people," he said. "Together, our species drove the ruekar into the wastelands of this planet, where they belong. Let us try to repeat their success - at least enough to keep them off these mountains and out of the valley."

Solomane nodded, but still looked miserable. Vartook wanted to say something more encouraging to the vocunine, but he was too busy trying to keep his own fear at bay. The ruekar were formidable creatures. Individually, they were small, no bigger than a small Pegasean child. However, a troop, or any small group of them, could move in concert with each other, with a singleness of mind like that of a flock of birds or a school of fish. They had teeth like scalpel blades and claws like sharpened fish hooks. Their furless skin, which hung on their bodies in loose folds, could change color and texture as quickly and artfully as Earth's cuttlefish. Their only apparent weakness was an intolerance of any climate that was either too cold or too dry. Vartook imagined that this is why the ruekar were staying in the valley for the time being. It was still early spring on the mountain. The air above the valley was still too cool and dry for the ruekar. They were safe for now, but not for long.

"Have you ever fought a ruekar?" Solomane asked.

"On occasion, I have had to deal with one of them," Vartook said. "But I have never had to battle more than one at a time."

"Could you fight a troop of them?" Solomane asked.

Vartook thought for a moment, then nodded.

"Are you sure?" Solomane asked.

"I am," Vartook said plainly. "However, I would not want to fight a large troop of them. If I did, I would not likely walk away from the experience completely unscathed. I imagine that fighting a troop of them would be like fighting off one of those shape-shifting reaper spirits from vocunine legend."

"How are you going to protect the city?" Solomane asked.

"First, I will need to ask the city's tailors and engineers, to design a more protective uniform for myself and my guardsmen," Vartook told him. "Beyond that, I will need time to think and prepare. We will need to assess the entire city for weaknesses. We let some of our guard down when the last of the Olroneans died off. Most of the vocunine are large and not too sly. We could always see or hear you coming. The ruekar are different. We will need to block every hole and gate every pipe. It is going to be an enormous undertaking. Everyone in the city will have to prepare in some way."

At that, Vartook resumed walking back to the city. When he noticed that Solomane was no longer following him, he turned back and said, "Why are you just standing there? Come on, we need to get started now."

The vocunine prince looked up at him, perplexed.

"Solomane, tell me the truth now - can you not see my mind?" he asked.

Solomane's ears drooped as he looked away from the First Guardsman.

"Solomane… can you see my mind at all?" Vartook asked again.

"A bit," Solomane said quietly. "But my species has been slowly losing this ability as we have been speaking more to each other in the Earth language more and more over the past several generations. Some of us are still strong with it, but not many."

"What is the limit of it?" Vartook asked. "How much of my mind can you see?"

"I think my ability is only as good as yours," Solomane confessed. "With your kind, I can see what a man wants me to see and I can see when he lies…and sometimes when his emotions are strong."

"Ah," said Vartook. "That is the limit of our telepathic ability as well."

Solomane's ears fell.

"Do not worry yourself over it," Vartook said. "Once you ally yourselves with my people, you will no longer need to have that advantage over us."

Solomane's ears lifted a bit.

"You must come back to the city with me," Vartook told him. "I will train you to fight, as will my Second Guardsman. We will train you all day, every day, until you are the best. Once you have established yourself as the new alpha, or king, or whatever it is they call you now, you will command the vocunine under your reign to join with the Pegaseans, as you will have by that time."

When Solomane opened his mouth to speak, Vartook held up a hand and said, "The choice has been made for you - for all of you - and for us as well. The city might likely survive a ruekar attack, but it will not fare well for the experience. The vocunine will most certainly suffer in the extreme, if you survive at all. There is only one option for you and your pack. Borkane was right, you need us. You will need to either move into the city or gain our help in fortifying your dens in the mountain caves. Either way, you and your pack have no choice but to end your feud with us. Do not mistake me, we will benefit as well. The vocunine are far better than we are at navigating the mountain terrain.

You have other talents as well - all of which we will use to our collective advantage in the coming struggle with the ruekar."

Solomane stared at Vartook for several moments before he slowly stood up and walked to Vartook's side. Vartook looked down at the vocunine and was suddenly filled with a celestial sense of fate and something else. It was the sort of feeling he had when he found something he had not known he had lost. Only this feeling was something stronger and deeper, as if that something lost was no mere misplaced object, but a piece of his soul.

CHAPTER 41

"Are you allowed, under your laws, to train me in Pegasean methods of combat?" Solomane asked as he and Vartook reached the outer city wall.

"There is no law, that I know of, which would forbid me from training you, or from providing you with a weapon. Also, as First Guardsman, my word is law when it comes to any matter related to city security. Not even the Center Council has any authority to command me with respect to the particulars of such matters," Vartook said with smile.

"That is a lot of power for one man," Solomane remarked.

Vartook looked down at Solomane and smiled.

"We will first train inside the city walls, in one of the parks," he said. "Once you are comfortable, we will train out here, on the mountain."

Solomane nodded.

"Follow me," Vartook instructed. "I need to introduce you to the other guardsmen."

"Now?" Solomane asked.

"Yes," Vartook said.

Compelled by the authority in Vartook's voice, Solomane followed Vartook along the path towards the closest gate in the wall. When they reached the gate, Vartook called up to his guardsman stationed on top of the wall above the gate. He explained that the vocunine at his side was a friend and ally and was not to be harmed or questioned. This puzzled the guardsmen, but they said nothing. They knew better than to question their commander without invitation to do so. Vartook then used his armband to open the heavy stone door through the wall. Once they were inside the wall and in the park, Vartook sent a message to all of his second level guardsman. He directed them to come meet with him in the park closest to the third western facing gate and to do so as quickly as reasonably possible. He then sat down on a park bench and waited for them. Solomane was pacing nervously in a wide circle around the bench.

"Solomane, stop that, you're making me dizzy," Vartook said with a chuckle.

"Really?" Solomane asked.

"No - but stop it anyway. Come, sit here by me," he said.

Solomane abided his command and sat on the ground at the guardsman's feet. Vartook felt an inexplicable urge to put a comforting hand on the nervous vocunine's head but was unsure of how such a gesture might be received.

"I won't be insulted if you touch my head," Solomane said.

"So, you do have some telepathic ability left," Vartook said.

"That was not telepathy," Solomane told him.

"What do you mean?" Vartook asked.

"That was just, I don't know how to say - putting things together. I heard the muscles in your arm start to move and I saw you glance at the top of my head," Solomane tried to explain.

"So Pullmoo was right. You *are* smart," Vartook said.

Solomane waggled the back of his head, a gesture which was the vocunine equivalent of a shrug. A moment or two later, Vartook put his hand between the animal's ears and stroked his thick fur. The feel of the fur between his fingers awoke something in Vartook which, paradoxically, felt like a powerful memory he simply could not recall. He stared blankly into nothing, trying to catch the thought or the feeling, or whatever this experience was; he could not tell for sure.

The sight of the two of them, the vocunine sitting at Vartook's feet, with Vartook's hand on the animal's head, perplexed Sitook, the first of Vartook's Second Guardsman to arrive in the park. So strange was the sight, in fact, that the guardsman stopped walking towards them and stood some ways off. He waited there, staring at them, as if waiting for a hallucination to pass and reality to return. Sensing the man's presence, Vartook looked up out over the mostly empty park. At the same time, Solomane lifted his head and did the same.

When Vartook saw the discomposed Second Guardsman standing ideally at the edge of the park lawn, he stood up and gestured for his subordinate to come towards them.

Sitook gestured his respect to Vartook as he approached, then stood staring at Solomane as if he had never seen a vocunine before this moment.

"Solomane, this is Sitook," Vartook said, "Sitook, this is Solomane."

Sitook, unsure of the etiquette appropriate for the situation, simply nodded and waited for Vartook to explain.

"I will explain when the others arrive," Vartook said. "How are Kim and Leah?"

Sitook blinked at Vartook several times before telling him that his and Altook's companions were doing well.

"They asked us to tell you that they are happy for you," Sitook said, "... for you and Pullmoo I mean."

"They are kind," Vartook said with a smile. "Please give them my regards and more."

Sitook just continued to stare at Solomane, hardly listening to Vartook.

Altook was the next guardsman to arrive. The rest of Vartook's second in command arrived in quick succession thereafter. Once they were all present, Vartook stood up and explained everything that he had learned from Solomane. As he did so, the Second Guardsmen stood in attentive and disciplined silence. However, as soon as Vartook finished and asked if there were any questions, they exploded with questions and concerns. Vartook put up his hands in a calming gesture.

"There is no need to panic," Vartook said in a pacifying voice which betrayed not a trace of his own growing state of alarm.

Altook did his best to conceal his terror as he asked, "What are we going to do?"

"We have at least three full lunar cycles before the temperature and humidity over the city rise to any level the ruekar find tolerable," Vartook said. "In that time, we will prepare, and we will help the vocunine prepare as well. We will work together, as our species did for thousands of years before the founders of Pegasea first broke ground on this mountain."

Vartook then told his men the story Pullmoo had told him about how the Olroneans and the vocunine first became allies and the origin of the third gesture of respect. After hearing this story, and in light of the imminent threat posed by the ruekar, it did not take the Second Guardsmen long to warm to Solomane. Similar to what Vartook had experienced, after each Second Guardsman had an opportunity to speak and interact with Solomane, they all felt a similar, though less intense, instinctual recollection of their shared ancestral history. Within an hour, they began to readily, and even joyfully, give Solomane advise and demonstrations related to combat. Among themselves and with Solomane, they began discussing and debating what kind of weapon would best suit the vocunine.

"Let us wait on that point," Vartook interjected. "We need to evaluate his strengths and weaknesses first - as well as his talents and natural rhythm in fighting - before we can even begin to speculate about weapons."

The Second Guardsmen all nodded in agreement with their commander.

"When will the other vocunine come to join us?" Sitook asked. "When will Solomane assume command of the pack? How many are there in the pack? I ask this because we will need to train them all - or at least, all of the males and child-less females."

Vartook looked towards Solomane, allowing the vocunine to answer the question himself.

"You keep saying 'pack' as in one pack - but it's not just one pack," Solomane said. "It is many packs - we are like a kingdom now, divided into territories, then further divided into packs. Like I told your alpha, my grandfather united all the vocunine packs on and around the mountains by challenging the alpha of each one and prevailing. Borkane was not just an alpha, he was more like a king and I am his oldest son, which makes me a sort of prince. We got these words - 'king' and 'prince' - from the human women. My home den is in a cave within the mountain you call the 'Eye of Olrona' but which we call 'Mount Olympus' - which we also got from the human women... and inside Mount Olympus is..."

"Ok, so how many of you are there?" Sitook interrupted.

"I do not know Pegasean numbers very well," Solomane said.

"What about Earth numbers?" Vartook asked.

"Earth numbers are easy, since they go up by sets of fingers," Solomane said confidently.

Sitook gave Vartook a quizzical look.

"I think he means that Earth numbers are base ten," Vartook told him.

Sitook nodded, then asked, "ok, tell us in Earth numbers - how many vocunine live on and around this mountain range?"

Solomane appeared to think for a moment, then said "at least five sets of ten- sets over again three times."

Sitook sighed.

"He means five times ten to the third power," Vartook translated.

"Five thousand?!" Sitook said. "How did we not know there are so many of them?"

"To my knowledge, we never bothered to count them - or estimate their numbers," Vartook said.

"Commander, with great respect, I must ask you, how can we train so many of them in just a few months?" Sitook asked.

Vartook considered for a moment, then said, "I will discuss this with Pullmoo and others, we will think of something - maybe we can recruit some of the better fighters as honorary guardsmen. Etmook is at least as skilled with a bow as any of you. I honestly do not know why he is being wasted as an engineer. In any event, the point is that there are others who might be able to help us."

Sitook nodded but remained skeptical.

Vartook then dismissed him and the other Second Guardsmen.

"Return to your posts, I will keep you all informed of any new developments and decisions. Also, please, speak of these matters to no one - not even your companions or partners," Vartook said firmly. "News of this must come at the right time and be delivered by the right people. Delivery of such news is best left to the sociologists."

The guardsman all nodded their assent and agreement, then bid farewell to Solomane before departing. After they left, Vartook called Etmook and asked him if it would be possible for him to fashion something with an access that could be worn by a vocunine. Etmook, perplexed, asked Vartook why he would ask for such a thing. Normally, Vartook would consider such a question, coming from an engineer, to be insolent. However, Etmook, as the engineer in charge of the city's electronic security system, enjoyed a kind of unofficial blended position somewhere between engineer and guardsman. Consequently, whenever it came to matters of security, Vartook tolerated most of his questions, as he might do if Etmook were one of his Second Guardsmen. Thus, he explained the situation to Etmook, who then assured Vartook that he would be able to provide what he needed and would gladly bring the device to him as soon as possible.

As promised, Etmook met Vartook in the park within less than two hours, holding a circular object which looked a lot like a companion training band, only thinner and lighter. He stayed with Vartook and Solomane until he was sure that the band would fit around the vocunine's wrist, that it worked, and that it was not likely to fall off. Etmook was not entirely happy with how it fit the vocunine. It looked uncomfortable and he suspected that the device was restricting his wrist movement to at least some degree.

"It's not perfect," Etmook said, frowning. "It would be better if he could come to my workshop where I could custom fit something for him."

Vartook shook his head and said, "this will do for now. You can work on making a better one tomorrow."

Solomane needed to return to his pack before nightfall and Vartook did not want to let him go without access back into the city. He did not know exactly why this was so important to him. The more time he spent with Solomane, the more he began to recognize a growing sense of foreboding when it came to the mountains beyond the city wall. It was more than just the ruekar in the valley. He knew now that this feeling had started days before he ever met Solomane, and even before he battled with Borkane.

Solomane noticed Vartook's growing unease and fought back an impulse to adopt the man's fear and anxiety.

"We will survive," Solomane said.

Vartook nodded, then said "I will train you quickly. My guardsmen will train the rest of your pack. We will be ready."

Solomane pressed his large head into Vartook's chest and sent a message of gratitude and trust to the man's mind. Vartook nodded appreciatively, then walked with Solomane to the outer wall, where the two new comrades bid each other farewell until the next morning.

CHAPTER 42

The day before the last day of Orook's suspension, Orook received a message from the Inter-District Council notifying him that his two-week suspension would end the following day, provided that he and Maria passed their final compatibility evaluation and provided that Maria passed her citizenship exam. A few minutes later he received another message stating that Second Presenter Lenook would arrive at his home the afternoon of the following day to conduct the evaluations. Orook's brow furrowed as he read the second message. He was surprised that Lenook was going to be conducting their exams. Usually, these kinds of routine exams were left to the Fourth Presenters. He was still mulling this over as he went to the bathroom and turned off the hot water supply to the shower. Maria, who was in the shower at the time, cried out in shock when the ice-cold water hit her body. She uttered a stream of profanities as she scrambled to turn off the water. She then wrapped herself in a towel and stepped out of the shower to find Orook waiting expectantly.

"Did you turn off the hot water?!" Maria growled.

"Yes," he said. "I have told you, repeatedly, not to use the hot water for more than five minutes. It is wasteful to use it for longer than that. If you are unable to discipline yourself to stay within the time limit, I will put a timer on the valve."

Maria groaned.

"Please get dressed," he said, ignoring her resentful glare. "Lenook is coming here tomorrow to administer our exams. You need to review the PROEs manual this morning and maybe again later this evening."

Maria rolled her eyes.

Orook folded his arms and stared down at her until she sighed and nodded. Maria then got dressed and sat in the living room. She brought her computer into her lap and sighed heavily as she turned it on.

"We will do something more fun later," Orook promised, as he put a glass of juice and a selpuna cake on the end table closest to her.

Maria sipped the juice and tried not to look as unhappy as she felt.

"What is wrong?" Orook said. "Certainly, reviewing the PROEs manual cannot be *that* painful."

Maria looked up at him and wished he could read her mind. Despite the immunity Pullmoo had given him, he still never showed any form of unsolicited affection towards her much beyond a friendly hug or taking of her hand. It was getting to the point where Maria was beginning to believe that perhaps she had misjudged him. Perhaps his feelings for her were exactly as they appeared - conspicuously nonexistent.

"Just promise me," she said, "that after I pass this test, I will never have to read this thing again."

"I cannot promise you that," Orook said as he circled around to the back of her chair.

Maria groaned, then shouted when the back of her chair suddenly rotated backwards. Orook gently rocked the chair on its hind legs until Maria looked up at him. He smiled mischievously down at her, then leaned over and brushed his lips against her cheek.

"I promise," he whispered. "If you pass this test, I will let you have your way with me for as long as you want."

Maria scoffed.

"You are such a pain in the ass," she muttered as she turned back to her computer and commenced studying for her exam.

• • •

Pullmoo listened with rapt attention as Vartook reported on his recent encounter with Solomane.

"I realize that I have gone a bit beyond the scope of what you asked of me," Vartook said without apology.

"Ah, yes, you have once again exceeded my expectations," Pullmoo said, beaming at him.

"At some point, you might have to raise your expectations," he said with a wry smile.

"Very true," Pullmoo agreed, then leaned back in her chair and looked away, suddenly deep in thought.

"What is it?" Vartook asked.

"This information about the ruekar is troubling," Pullmoo said.

Vartook agreed.

"Why have so many of them come out to the valley?" Pullmoo thought aloud.

"I don't know," Vartook said.

"So, what is the plan now?" Pullmoo asked.

"I think we need to take them into the city," Vartook said. "As crazy as it sounds, I think we need to take them all in. First, my guardsman will train those of them with the most potential as fighters. We should then place these trained vocunine in the homes of the Pegasean women, yourself included. The rest we should place throughout the city, in homes with men who are amenable to the arrangement. There are more than enough homes in the city to accommodate them all. Food and other supplies may become a concern at some point, but we can address that later, once the ruekar retreat for the winter. I only hope there are enough men willing to host them."

"There will be," Pullmoo said.

"How can you be so sure?" Vartook asked.

"For the same reasons I know that you and Solomane will bond with each other quickly, if you haven't already," Pullmoo said.

"I believe we have - even if I don't know why," he conceded.

"Some of our citizens will be more reluctant at first than others. The human women will help. Generally speaking, they like the vocunine and are likely to encourage their keepers to at least meet them at the gate. Once they agree to meet, I suspect things to go smoothly from there," Pullmoo said.

"You are assuming that at least most of the vocunine will be willing to come live with us in the city," Vartook said.

"Well, they don't have much of a choice at this point - if what Solomane says about the Ruekar is true," Pullmoo said. "But you are right, I expect at least some of them to be reluctant. They will be putting themselves at our mercy."

"I hope the other men take to the vocunine as quickly as I took to Solomane," Vartook said.

"They will," she said.

The two sat in silence for several minutes before Pullmoo asked, "do you want to know a secret?"

"Only if it is one of yours," Vartook said with a warm smile.

Pullmoo stood up and walked over to the couch, then sat down next to her partner.

"When I was a girl, I befriended a young female vocunine," she told him. "I loved her dearly. I used to sneak out and meet her in the mountains as often as I could. We would play together out there - and swim in the water of the Mouth of the Mountain Queen.".

Vartook shook his head at her childish recklessness, even as he smiled at the thought.

"I've always loved the vocunine," Pullmoo admitted. "Well, not so much Borkane and the likes of him, obviously. But the others - they are kind and loyal beings. I've always been determined to find a way to bring this feud between our species to an end."

"We are all so fortunate to have you guiding us in these matters," Vartook fawned.

Pullmoo waved her hand at his flattery and said, "You don't know that yet. It may very well turn out that I end up getting us all killed."

Vartook shook his head.

"In any case," Pullmoo continued. "May I assume that Solomane will stay with you, in your home? He will need to move back and forth as he plays diplomat for a while, but after that?"

"That is my wish, yes, if he would like," Vartook said.

"I imagine it has been a bit lonely for you at home - all this time you went without a companion or a partner," Pullmoo said.

At this Vartook blushed and looked away from her. Pullmoo did not understand this reaction from him. For one thing, Vartook, like her, never blushed. She narrowed her eyes at him and tried to see his mind. When she could not see what he was thinking, she asked why he suddenly seemed embarrassed.

"I'm not embarrassed," Vartook said. "I just… well… I do not know if it is appropriate for me to tell you… or my place to tell anyone for that matter."

"Tell me what?" Pullmoo asked.

"Only that I have not been entirely lonely," Vartook said, unable to meet her eyes.

"Well, now you must tell me. Out with it Vartook. I demand to know," Pullmoo said with exaggerated authority.

"Ok, alright, I will tell you," Vartook began as he held up his hands in surrender. "Some time ago, two of my Second Engineers discovered that they enjoyed each other's physical company more than they did that of their companions from Earth - if you know what I mean."

Pullmoo nodded and said, "Yes, that happens. How old were they at the time?"

"Oh, I don't know - maybe 40 or 45?" Vartook guessed. "In any case, the problem was that they both already had companions from Earth whom they adored in a platonic way, and who also adored them. Their companions did not want to be matched with other keepers and the two guardsmen did not want to turn them over to the district sociologist. They all wanted to stay together. Their solution was to move into two adjacent homes and asked a few engineer friends of theirs to connect the homes via an archway - to, in essence, construct a two-bedroom home. Once that was done, the two men moved into one bedroom and their two companions moved into the other bedroom. This way, the men could still watch over and take care of their companions and everyone was happy."

"Ok…," Pullmoo said. "What does any of this have to do with you?"

Vartook blushed again, then took a deep breath and continued, "The two women, the two companions - well, they still, occasionally, wanted a man's affection so to speak. And according to them, my Second Guardsman helpfully suggested that they visit with me whenever they experienced such desires. Of course, no one consulted with me first before the first one showed up at my door late one evening. You can imagine how uncomfortable I was at first."

"I take it you got over that discomfort," Pullmoo mused.

"Well, yes… once I understood the situation, I didn't see the harm in it," he confessed.

"Is that it? That is your big secret?" Pullmoo asked.

"Yes - most of it," Vartook said hesitantly.

Pullmoo stared at him expectantly, then gestured for him to go on.

"So, every so often, one or the other of them kept me company for a day or two," Vartook continued. "This went on for years. Then one evening they came over together. You can imagine my surprise when they…"

Pullmoo, bit her lower lip, trying not to smile, then put up a hand to stop him.

"You need not go into great detail my love," she said. "Some things are best left to the imagination."

When Vartook looked up and saw her bemused expression, he asked, "You find all this amusing, do you?"

"Forgive me Vartook," she said. "It is just that I never would have imagined you to be so… well, I do not know exactly how to put it. I want to say 'accommodating' but that does not quite cover it. In all my years as First Sociologist, you are my only blind spot. You repeatedly surprise me - and I have no idea why that should be."

"I would like to think it is because I am the only man you have ever been in love with," Vartook said with a smile.

Pullmoo doubted that was the reason but did not tell him so. She only smiled back and asked, "so do these two lovely ladies still visit you?"

Vartook frowned and said, "no, no, of course not."

"Why not?" Pullmoo asked.

"That would not be right. I am your man now," Vartook said.

"That is sweet of you to say Vartook, but whatever the nature of the relationship between a particular keeper and his companion, it does not usually change when he partners with a Pegasean woman - mostly because the partnership is temporary, and the companionship will continue long after the partnership is over," Pullmoo explained.

"But I am not their keeper," Vartook said. "In fact, they do not need keepers anymore. They only stay with Sitook and Altook because they are all dear friends and want to stay close. Soon after they moved into their new arrangement, I had the two women trained as sixth level guardsmen. They started out mediating minor domestic disputes and squabbles between the other companions in their district. They then became so proficient with the monitoring systems that they were recently promoted to fifth level guardsmen. I believe that entitles them to their own homes and allowances, correct?"

"If they are now Fifth Guardsmen, then yes, they are eligible," Pullmoo answered. "Of course, they would have to pass a series of tests and show that their work hours are up to standard… along with a dozen or so other requirements."

"Of course," Vartook agreed.

"Now that you are telling me all this, I think I know of these women," Pullmoo said. "Many years ago, one of my Second Sociologists asked me to approve a customized design for a guardsman trainee uniform for a pair of human companions whose keepers were Second Guardsmen. He started with the traditional sunset pink uniform of the sixth level guardsman, then edged it with the much deeper red hue of the Second Guardsman."

"Yes, that sounds like what they wore as trainees and also as sixth levels," Vartook confirmed.

"They are a good team," Pullmoo said idly. "I remember a time they broke up a particularly nasty fight between two companions at their home district center."

"Yes, I heard stories about that," Vartook confirmed.

Pullmoo sat pensively for a few moments before asking, "Vartook, who will keep you company after our partnership ends?"

"Please, let's talk about something else," Vartook said with a sigh, then brought one of her hands to his lips and kissed her knuckles.

"Of course," Pullmoo said gently. "I will just have to ask you to marry me some other time."

Vartook looked sharply up at her with wide eyes.

"I understand if you do not want to accept, because…," she started to say before Vartook gathered her in his arms and hugged her so tightly she could barely breathe.

"Your answer is 'yes,' I take it," Pullmoo choked as she struggled for air.

CHAPTER 43

In the afternoon of the following morning, Orook quizzed Maria on the PROEs as they waited for Lenook to arrive. Maria felt drained and defeated but answered all his questions correctly.

"I am impressed," he said. "You really are good at studying things like this."

"It's apparently all I'm good at - or good for," Maria mumbled.

"That is not true," Orook said.

Before Maria could argue, Lenook arrived at the door. Orook walked to the door and let him in. They greeted each other and spoke rapidly in Pegasean for a few minutes before Lenook took a seat in the living room.

"How are you doing today?" Lenook asked Maria in English.

Maria shrugged.

"Don't worry love, this will not take long," he said with a reassuring smile.

He then took a tablet computer out from a hidden sleeve in the front of his uniform. He turned on the device and brought up a screen with the official seal of the city, then waved his armband over the display. Maria watched and waited as he navigated through a series of what looked forms.

"Why are you the one conducting these evaluations?" Orook asked. "Isn't this a bit below your station?"

"Normally it would be," Lenook confirmed. "However, the First Presenter and I have struck a kind of bargain. Part of that bargain is that I may request assignment to any case I choose, and he will not question my results or conclusions."

"And what does the First Presenter get out of this?" Orook asked.

Without looking up from the computer, Lenook said, "He gets to keep his position as First Presenter."

"You agreed not to challenge him for his position?" Orook asked.

Lenook nodded.

Orook looked at Lenook as if seeing the man for the first time.

"And the First Presenter is sure that he would lose to you in a challenge," he asked.

Lenook looked up at him and smiled.

"What's wrong Orook?" Lenook asked. "Does the thought of me rising to a similar status as yourself frighten you?"

"Engineering ranks above presenting. Even if you became the First Presenter, you would still rank below me," Orook scoffed.

"Yes, of course," Lenook said dryly as he turned his attention back to his computer.

"Why did you ask to be assigned to our case?" Maria asked.

Lenook looked up at her and smiled.

"Well, normally, I do not take cases involving friends, because I try to avoid any appearance of impropriety. However, I do often assign myself to what the people on Earth might call 'high profile' cases. I also take controversial cases and any case Pullmoo asks me to take. You two love birds fit all three of those categories."

"Oh," Maria said.

"Is this to ensure that we pass?" Orook asked. "If so, I must object. I will not be party to that sort of corruption."

"Absolutely not," Lenook said. "When Pullmoo asks me to take a case, it is because she needs a customized evaluation - not customized to ensure that you pass, - customized to ensure that you do not fail for a stupid reason, or for a reason that should not apply to you."

"Was it Pullmoo who asked you to do all of Maddie and Etmook's evaluations?" Maria asked.

Maria laughed at Lenook's exaggerated expression of mock surprise.

"Why would Etmook and Maddie need a customized evaluation?" Orook asked.

"I am not at liberty to disclose that information," Lenook said. "Maria is not even supposed to know that they have a customized evaluation."

Orook looked at Maria, who only shrugged.

"So, when do we begin the evaluations?" she asked. "Which one do we do first?"

"We can begin now, and we can do either one first. Which one do you prefer to do first?" Lenook said.

"I think I would rather do the citizenship evaluation first - if that's ok with my keeper," Maria said, looking at Orook.

"That is fine," Orook said.

Lenook then politely asked Orook to leave the room. He explained that, since Maria had some telepathic ability, protocol dictated that no one, other than the examiner, be in the room with her when she took the test. Orook then excused himself to the bedroom. Lenook noticed that as soon as Orook was gone, Maria started to fidget nervously with the folds in her skirt.

"May I assume that you have read the PROEs manual?" Lenook asked.

"Yes," Maria said.

"And the AERs - the Actively Enforced Rules?" he asked.

Maria nodded.

Lenook then proceeded to ask her a series of questions regarding the PROEs and the AERs. The first of these were very easy. Maria answered these without hesitation. The questions became more difficult as the exam went on.

"Give me an example of a situation where a companion may refuse a command given to her by her keeper?" Lenook asked.

"Any situation where the command would require her to act in violation of an actively enforced rule," Maria answered.

"And what must she do in such a situation?" Lenook asked.

"She must state the specific rule and how his command would require her to break it," Maria said.

Lenook waited, then prompted, "anything else?"

"Oh, she has to offer an alternative, if there is one, or otherwise express that she is not unwilling to follow his command, only unwilling to break to the law - or something like that," she added.

"Close enough," Lenook said with a smile. He noticed that the frenetic energy of Maria's fidgeting had increased considerably since they had started. He put down his computer and suggested that they take a break.

"Ok, why?" Maria asked.

"Because I think you're getting nervous," he said.

"It's weird because I never get like this for exams," she said.

"Oh? Why do you think this exam is different?" Lenook asked.

"I don't think it's the exam itself," she said. "I just don't like the PROEs. They make me feel…"

Lenook waited for her to finish.

"I don't know." Maria said. "It doesn't matter."

"You can tell me," Lenook said. "We're on break now."

"I just don't think the difference between humans and Pegaseans is so huge that all these demands for deference and outward showings of submission are necessary," she said.

"You do know that expressing that opinion is a violation of the PROEs, right?" Lenook asked.

"Yes… no, wait, no it's not," Maria said. "I'm allowed to answer any question from a Second Presenter, or the First Presenter, completely and honestly, even if doing so would otherwise violate the PROEs, if he or she asks me the question while we are both in my home."

"Well done," he said.

"So, we're not really on a break, are we?" Maria asked, a little annoyed.

"We are," Lenook said. "I was just giving you an opportunity to get extra credit in case you miss too many of the difficult questions coming up."

"Oh, ok, thanks," she said.

"Did you ever have a companion?" Maria asked.

Lenook looked at her quizzically, then slowly nodded.

"What happened to her?" Maria asked.

"Why would you ask me about her, Maria?" Lenook whispered.

Maria shrugged.

"You're not like the other Pegasean men," she said. "You don't make me feel like a second-class citizen. I just wondered if that was because you never had a companion - but I guess you have."

"Do the Pegasean women make you feel that way?" he asked.

"Good point," Maria said. "Yeah, they aren't any better. I think they try to be nicer about it, but that almost makes it worse."

"I don't mean to disillusion you here Maria, but part of being a good presenter is knowing how to make other people feel comfortable. Some people feel most comfortable when they feel equal to others, some feel more comfortable feeling superior, and some actually prefer to feel inferior. I knew, from the moment I met you, that you are a person who prefers to feel equal to others," Lenook explained.

"Oh," Maria said with a sigh.

"That does not necessarily mean that I feel superior to you, Maria," he added quickly. "Frankly, I rarely bother to assess a person as generally inferior or superior to me. Oh, sure, I will occasionally make a determination like that when it comes to one particular skill or another. But when it comes to judging people as a whole, there are only two categories of people in my mind - there are people I like and people I don't like."

"And which of those do I fall into?" Maria asked.

"So, far, I would say that you are in the people-I-like category," Lenook said with a smile.

Maria tried to smile, but her face would not cooperate.

"Don't get too comfortable there though," Lenook warned. "I've been known to re-categorize people quickly and with impunity. Just ask your keeper."

At that, Maria did smile.

"Now, can we get on with this exam?" he asked.

Maria nodded and they proceeded with the rest of her citizenship exam. When it was over, Lenook told her that she had passed and congratulated her. He then asked her to fetch Orook from the bedroom. Once Maria and Orook were both back in the living room, Lenook asked if they wanted to take a break before proceeding with their compatibility evaluation. They both declined, eager to get the ordeal over with.

"Alright then," Lenook said as he tapped something into his computer. After a few moments, he looked up at Maria and asked, "If you could go back to Earth right now, would you?"

Maria frowned, then looked at Orook.

"What does that have to do with our compatibility?" she asked.

"Just answer the question, please," Lenook said.

"But I don't know," Maria said. "I can't answer that."

"It is ok, Maria," Orook said. "I will not be hurt or insulted if your answer is in the affirmative."

Maria swallowed hard, then looked away as she thought about the question.

Getting impatient, Orook said, "Maria, in these past two weeks we have spent together, not a day has gone by in which you have not, on multiple occasions, expressed longing for Earth or for something on Earth. You miss everything about that horrible planet. You miss your friends and the food - especially something called 'burritos' from a restaurant down the street from where you used to live. You miss going to class and jogging outside in the park outside your apartment. You miss the smell of cut grass, the feel of a paper textbook in your hands and sitting in front of a window on a sunny day. You miss the clothes you used to wear and the sound of bicycle bells. You recalled for me, with great nostalgia, the way your apartment used to smell around dinner time - how several of your former fellow tenants were from the country of India and the smell of the spices saturated the air for at least a block around the building. You miss swimming in a pool and laying out in the sun in your favorite swim suit. You miss your dog - 'Oliver' was his name, right?"

Maria turned to look at Orook, surprised by the detail of his recall.

"Do not be flattered," he said. "I remember everything - whether I want to or not."

"Orook," Lenook said, "I really need her to answer the question."

Maria continued to think about the question and about Earth and all the things Orook had mentioned.

"Is it true that Earth is doomed?" she asked Lenook.

"Yes, but for purposes of the question, let us pretend that it is not. Would you go back?" he asked.

"If I say 'no,' are you going to ask me why?" she asked.

Lenook thought for a moment, then shook his head.

"No," she said. "I would not go back."

"Is that because you love your keeper?" Lenook teased.

"No, it's not," Maria said, then quickly added, "I'm not saying I don't love him... that's just not the reason."

"What is the reason?" Lenook asked.

"You promised you wouldn't ask me why!" she said.

Lenook held up his hands in surrender, then looked back down at his computer. He massaged his chin with one hand, then looked up at Orook.

"Orook, why did you remove and destroy the training band for her right wrist?" he asked.

"It was unnecessary," he said.

"That is not a complete or honest answer," Lenook said.

Orook averted his eyes.

"It was used at least once - to restrain her to a chair after she was caught in the nursery," Lenook said. "So, obviously, it was not completely unnecessary. Second, if that was really the reason, you would not have destroyed it. You would have only taken it off and returned it to inventory."

"She hated it," Orook snapped. "It made her feel like a prisoner - and that made me hate it."

Lenook nodded approvingly.

"Are all the questions going to be like this?" Maria asked.

"Like what?" Lenook asked.

"Questions that make us uncomfortable," she said.

"These questions make you uncomfortable?" Lenook asked, feigning innocence. "I'm so sorry. Would you rather I ask you questions about joining?"

"No!" Maria and Orook said in unison.

Lenook laughed. "Actually, I think I'm done. You passed," he said.

"Seriously?" Maria asked.

Lenook nodded, tapped something into his armband, then told Orook to take Maria to the District Center tomorrow and have her training band exchanged for a companion's armband.

"Ok," Orook said, "When can I return to work?"

"Theoretically, you may return to work immediately," Lenook told him. "However, I should remind you that tomorrow is a social day."

"Yes, but I always work on social days," Orook said.

"And that brings me to another matter we need to discuss," Lenook said.

"What do you mean? What else is there to discuss?" Orook asked.

Lenook took a deep breath as he looked at Maria, then back at Orook. Maria interpreted this as a signal that maybe she should leave. She started to stand up.

"Where are you going?" Orook asked.

Maria paused half way between standing up and sitting and looked at Lenook.

"This matter has nothing at all to do with your lovely companion," Lenook said.

"Alright, well, Maria, if you would like to leave you may, but you may also stay if you like," Orook said.

After a moment's hesitation, Maria sat back down, curious to hear what Lenook had to discuss with Orook.

"Two days before your suspension, ten of your twelve second level engineers filed a group grievance against you," Lenook told Orook. "The grievance falls under my jurisdiction because the ten individuals who signed the grievance come from six different districts, which makes this an inter-district matter. As you know, I am the lead presenter for all inter-district matters."

"A grievance? for what?" Orook asked.

"You can't guess?" Lenook said.

"Honestly, no," Orook said.

"Really? You don't have even the faintest idea?" Lenook asked.

"I think I know," Maria said, trying to be helpful.

Lenook smiled.

Orook gave Maria a chilling look of forewarning.

Now afraid to speak, but feeling that she needed to defend herself, Maria opened her mouth, then shut it again.

"Go ahead Maria," Lenook said. "I'm curious to see just how obvious it is to everyone but your keeper."

Maria only shook her head and said, "I should not have said anything."

She then looked at Orook and apologized for her lack of respect.

After a moment of awkward silence, Lenook continued.

"They are accusing you of breaking the rules regarding requiring subordinates to work on social days," he said. "They claim that you have asked them to work on every one of the past thirty- two social days. Some of them claim it has been as many as forty. I would have told you about it sooner, but the Inter-District Council instructed me to wait until after your suspension."

"Who are the ten who signed the complaint?" Orook asked.

"You will learn who they are only if this matter goes to hearing," Lenook told him. "However, I am strongly in favor of resolving this matter without a formal hearing. I assure you, such a hearing will be, without a doubt, the most boring and tedious hearing I will have conducted all year - and will likely take at least a week."

"Why a week?!" Orook asked.

"The law states that you may only request that your subordinates work on a social day when absolutely necessary. The grieving parties are claiming that you have an overly broad, and unreasonable, concept of what constitutes a 'necessity.' That means that all ten witnesses will have to testify about numerous occasions on which you asked them to work on a social day and the reasons you gave for asking them to do so. Trust me, this will be a long and tedious trial. I tried to recuse myself on the basis that you are my future brother-in-law. Unfortunately, no other Second Presenter in the city is masochistic enough to volunteer to stand in my place. Also, I did not recuse myself from your most recent criminal hearing, so I don't have much of a leg to stand on - as the humans like to say," Lenook explained.

Orook sighed heavily and leaned back into the sofa.

"Of course, we can avoid all that if you simply stipulate to the accusation and agree to their demands," Lenook said.

"What do they want?" Orook asked.

"All they want is a promise from you that you will not make them work more than one out of every four social days unless there is a true emergency," Lenook told him.

"And what happens if I break that promise?" Orook asked.

"I have never known you to break a promise," Lenook said with a genuinely affectionate smile, as if this was Orook's one and only redeeming quality.

"Well, hypothetically, what will happen if they then decide that I have an 'overly broad' concept of what constitutes an emergency?" Orook asked.

"Good question," Lenook said. "I suppose we will have to come up with a written definition of 'emergency' which you and your subordinates can agree upon."

"And how long would that take?" Orook asked.

"Hopefully, not long," Lenook said. "If you otherwise agree to concede to their demands, we can forgo the formal hearing. We can then go back and forth on the definition at our leisure until all parties agree."

Orook closed his eyes. To Maria's surprise, he looked genuinely sad and possibly even hurt.

Lenook saw the same thing and said, "Orook, you should know that, despite all good sense, they do adore you."

Orook opened his eyes but did not say anything. Lenook pulled out his computer and quickly pulled up a copy of the grievance filed by the Second Engineers, then handed it to Orook.

"I don't want to see it," Orook said, putting up a hand to ward off the device.

"Read it," Lenook insisted.

Reluctantly, Orook took the computer from Lenook and started to read. He felt almost ashamed as he read the lengthy preamble, which consisted of nothing but praise and expressions of profound respect and admiration for the First Engineer. This was followed by an almost apologetic "however." The complaint itself was no more than three sentences. Orook smiled, humbled by the awkward combination of sincerity and reluctance with which the grievance appeared to have been filed.

"I will agree to whatever definition of 'emergency' they think is fair," Orook said. "That should further expedite a resolution to this, correct?"

Lenook nodded, then instructed Orook to put his personal electronic seal to the end of the grievance, to attest to his concession. Orook quickly did so and handed the computer back to Lenook. Lenook then put his own seal to the grievance and turned off the computer.

"Well, that was easy," he said with a smile.

"Anything else?" Orook asked.

"No, that is all," Lenook said as he stood up to leave.

"So, I can return to work tomorrow, correct?" Orook asked.

"As I said before, technically, tomorrow - but tomorrow is a social day," Lenook reminded him.

"Wait. I did not agree to refrain from working on social days," Orook said. "I agreed not to ask them to work, not that I myself would not work."

"That is technically correct, yes," Lenook agreed. "However, as a show of good faith, I highly recommend that you not work tomorrow - at least not more than a few hours."

"Alright," Orook moaned.

Lenook congratulated them again on passing their evaluations before getting up to leave.

"You will not stay for dinner?" Orook asked.

"No, I have urgent business to attend to this evening," Lenook said in Pegasean.

"What urgent business?" Orook asked, now also speaking in Pegasean.

"You did not hear this from me, but the ruekar have come to the valley," he said.

"Why is this an urgent matter? Several of them venture into the valley every year. It has never been a concern before," Orook said.

"It's different this time," Lenook said gravely. "There are several troops of them gathered there now. According to the vocunine, there are several hundred now scattered throughout the valley, and they are growing in number every day."

Orook jaw dropped.

"There is a rumor that Vartook plans to join forces with the vocunine - and that he might even bring the vocunine into the city," Lenook continued.

"Should you be telling me this?" Orook asked.

"No, but we are practically brothers and you have always been good at keeping a secret. I also think that, as First Engineer, it is important for you to have as much advance warning as possible," Lenook said.

"Thank you," Orook said.

Lenook nodded, then bid them both a final farewell.

CHAPTER 44

After Lenook had left, Maria asked Orook what he meant when he asked Lenook about taking the First Presenter's position in a "challenge." Orook explained to her that, every five years, the City holds an open competition wherein anyone may challenge the person ranking immediately above them. The contest is designed to test the participants' skills, knowledge and aptitude within their profession. If the challenger prevails in the competition, he or she may replace his or her superior. He explained that the Center Council can intercede and prevent the challenger from taking the challenged position, but that this rarely happened.

"It helps ensure that the most qualified people do not get stuck in a lower position purely due to politics or some other such folly. It also keeps those in the higher ranks on their toes so to speak," Orook explained.

"Have you ever been challenged?" Maria asked as she moved from her chair to the couch and sat next to her keeper.

"Etmook challenges every time," he told her.

"Why?" Maria asked.

"I am not sure," he said. "At first I thought he simply wanted the position of First Engineer. That would be obvious reason and the only rational reason. However, the one or two times he actually got anywhere near close to prevailing in the competition, he pulled back his efforts, as if he was actually afraid to win."

"Maybe he only challenges you because he enjoys engaging in the competition with you," Maria suggested.

"That is possible," Orook agreed. "His view of me, and his feelings towards me, are irrational and unhealthy."

"Why do you say that?" Maria asked.

"I am not his father," Orook snapped. "He takes everything I say and do far too personally."

Maria shook her head and said, "You should be flattered."

"I do not need this kind of adoration from him. I only need him to respect and trust me - and to follow my instructions," he said.

Maria rolled her eyes.

"Are all of your kind like this?" she asked.

"Like what?" Orook asked.

"So detached and serious," she said.

"Most of us, yes," he said. "This is why we do not allow humans to rise above the fifth level. You tend to get emotional about almost everything."

"Right...," Maria said.

Orook stared at her.

"So, tell me, why would you not choose to return to Earth if such was possible?" he asked.

Maria took a deep breath, then shook her head.

"You do not want to tell me?" he asked.

"I would rather not," she said, looking away from him.

Orook smiled.

"What?" she asked.

"Are you sure I am not at least part of the reason?" he asked.

"Maybe a little," Maria said as she rested her head on his shoulder and snuggled in closer to him.

Orook put his arm around her and kissed the top of her head.

"How did you get to be First Engineer?" she asked.

"I started out as a Fourth Engineer. I challenged into the Third position when I was 30. I was then promoted to second when I was 45. By the time I was 62, the First Engineer was over 300 years old. When he retired, the Center Council appointed me as his replacement. If he had been a younger man, it might have taken me a lot longer."

"What is the fastest anyone has risen to the first level position of their profession?" Maria asked.

"Vartook went from Fourth Guardian to First Guardian in only 15 years," Orook told her. "Every 5 years he simply challenged his superior officer and won each time."

"What about your sister?" she asked.

"She had a longer road to First Mathematician. I think it took her over 70 years," he said.

Thinking of Wilamoo made Maria think of Lenook, which brought back to mind the question she had asked Lenook about his companion.

"Lenook told me he had a companion before he was engaged to your sister," she said. "What happened to her?"

"She was re-matched with another keeper," Orook told her, choosing to leave out the gory details of Lindsay's broken heart.

"Was that the only option?" she asked.

"No," he said. "She could have stayed with Lenook and Wilamoo."

Maria looked up at him and made a face.

"How would *that* have worked?" she asked.

Orook shrugged.

"She certainly wouldn't have stayed in a companion's room inside a bedroom shared by Lenook and Wilamoo," Maria said.

"Maybe she would have, or maybe they would have all slept together," he said.

"Seriously?" Maria asked.

"Pegasean women are not as prone to jealousy as human women tend to be. Besides that, they do not count human women as real 'women.' So, while some Pegasean women might forbid their husbands or fiancés from joining with other Pegasean women, I do not know of any who concern themselves with what their husbands do with human women."

"Well, I will *never* share a bed with you and Linoo," Maria huffed.

Orook laughed.

Maria crossed her arms and narrowed her eyes at him.

"You do not have to worry about this," he said, still smiling.

"Why not?" she asked. "After Linoo meets her child-bearing requirement, she can do whatever she wants, right?"

Orook nodded.

"So, she'll probably ask you to marry her, right?" Maria said.

"She will not," Orook said soberly. "Linoo fell out of love with me years ago - after our first son died."

"Ok, but, how old will she be by the time she is fee to marry?" Maria asked.

"It all depends on how long it takes her to meet the requirement," Orook said. "She is currently the same age as I am and has been having children since she was 26 years old. I believe she currently has one daughter and thirty-six sons. So, she will probably be done having children before she is 140 years old."

"If she is expected to live to be at least 325 years old, that leaves her a lot of time to change her mind," Maria said.

"Maria, Linoo is not going to fall back in love with me," he said. "Even if she does, I will not kick you out. She will either have to welcome you as well or go on living without me."

"I do not want to share you with her," Maria whispered.

"Hmmm… I did not know you were so selfish," Orook teased.

Maria frowned.

"Do you never get jealous?" she asked.

Orook scoffed. "Linoo has partnered with 36 other men," he said. "We Pegasean men learn to share."

Maria sighed.

"I will give you this though," he said. "For reasons I do not quite understand, I do not like the idea of sharing you."

"Well, that is nice to know," she said.

CHAPTER 45

O rook spent much of his first day back to work trying to catch up on all he had missed in his absence. When he finally came home late in the evening, he found Maria sitting on the sofa reading something off her computer. After they exchanged pleasantries, Maria said, "I wish I had something to do here."

"What do you mean?" Orook asked.

"I mean I wish I could have a job, or volunteer, or do something," Maria said.

"Why?" Orook asked.

"You, of all people, should understand why," Maria said, a little annoyed.

"Is your mind really that restless?" Orook asked. "Because most of the other human women seem perfectly content to pass the days socializing and engaging in the arts or reading books on their computers."

"I can only do that for so long," Maria told him. "It's not about my mind being restless. I don't like feeling as if I'm not doing anything productive. I feel gross."

"I thought you spent all of your adult life on Earth as a student," Orook said.

"Yes, but I also had a job - and besides that, I went to school believing that I would one day have a career," Maria said defensively. "It's not as if I intended to be a student forever."

"I know of a few human women who work as inventory clerks," he said. "I suppose you could do something like that."

"Ok, but is there anything else I could do? Something more - I don't know - hands on? I mean, there must be something your sixth level engineers do which I could learn," she said.

"There probably is, but Maria, you would not be working with me. I am pretty far removed from the engineers at that level. I almost never interact with any of the sixth level engineers, or even with the fourth or fifth level engineers for that matter," he told her.

"That is not what I'm after," Maria said. "I just don't want to be stuck at a desk or in an office looking at spread sheets or inventory all day. I would rather do something more physical or at least inter-active."

"Well, the sixth level engineers are more like maintenance workers. They unclog pipes and replace broken tiles - things of that nature," he told her.

"I wouldn't mind doing that sort of work," Maria said.

"Even so, what would you wear while doing it?" Orook asked.

"What would I wear?" Maria asked.

"The sixth level engineers wear a powder-blue uniform," Orook said.

Maria gave him a puzzled look.

"Why does that matter?" she asked.

"Your uniform reflects your status here," Orook explained. "So, you would go from wearing my color to the color of a sixth level - this would be a precipitous drop in status."

"Would my doing that sort of work embarrass you?" she asked.

"No, not at all," he said. "In fact, I find it admirable that you want to contribute to our society so much that you would be willing to do such laborious and irksome work."

"Well, then I'm afraid I still don't understand what the problem is," Maria said.

Orook looked down at his hands, thinking.

"I suppose it would be good for you to do something productive with your time," he conceded. "I will have to ask the district's presenter if the rules would even allow you to be trained as a Sixth Engineer. I will probably also have to ask Linoo what you would wear while working as a Sixth Engineer."

Maria laughed and said, "why does what I wear matter so much?"

"Maria, I just explained why. It signifies your status here," Orook said.

"I don't care about that," Maria said.

"That is only because, thus far, you have enjoyed a high level of status," Orook said in a cautionary tone. "If you were to work as a

Sixth Engineer, there would be no leniency with respect to the PROEs during the times you engaged yourself in that role, do you understand?"

"Ok," Maria said.

"You would have to be deferential to just about everyone," Orook continued. "During working hours, you would not even be allowed to talk to me or any other engineer ranking at the third level or higher. You would report to a Fifth or Fourth Engineer who would be your superior."

"Ok," she said.

"Ok? Maria, you have a hard time taking instructions from me, and I am the First Engineer. How are you going to take instructions from someone ranking three or four levels below me?" Orook asked.

"It's not the same," Maria said.

Orook gave her a look.

"It's not like I would be taking instructions from him at home! Or on matters that have nothing to do with my work. He wouldn't be telling me what to eat, when to exercise, or how long I can use the hot water when I take a shower," Maria said.

"I see," Orook said. "So, this ridiculous expectation of equality which you have with me at home - are you telling me that you could completely detach from that expectation if you were to work in the city?"

"Haven't we already established this?" Maria snapped. "Do I not follow the PROEs with you when we are outside or when others are around?"

"Yes, lately, you have been," he conceded.

"So, what's the problem?" Maria asked.

"It will not be easy work," Orook cautioned. "During busy times, you might be expected to work 10 or even 12 hours a day."

That did give Maria pause, but she would not be deterred. She was becoming progressively more stir crazy as the days went by. She needed to do something.

"I can handle it," she said.

"Alright, if you insist," Orook said. "I will look into it."

• • •

The district presenter and Linoo both told Orook that, under the City's rules, Maria could, at least theoretically, work in any fifth or sixth level position for which she proved to be qualified. However, as a human, she could never rise to any position beyond the fifth level. The district presenter also warned him that he would assume all responsibility for Maria while she was in training, and for the rest of her working days in Pegasea, but that this was likely not an issue since, as her keeper, he assumed all responsibility for her in any case. He also told Orook that there was nothing preventing Maria from receiving job training under any fourth or fifth level engineer of his choice. Orook did not actually know any of the engineers at that level. Consequently, he decided to ask his Second Engineers for a recommendation. They unanimously recommended a Fourth Engineer by the name of Zedook. When asked, Zedook happily agreed to train Maria and to serve as her supervisor.

A few days later, a box was delivered to Orook and Maria at their home. Maria opened it to find a powder blue engineer's uniform trimmed in sapphire blue, to signify her elevated status by proxy as Orook's companion. Orook looked at the uniform and nodded approvingly.

"That makes sense," he said. "This way everyone will know that you are a Sixth Engineer, but that you are also the companion to the First Engineer."

Maria would have preferred an entirely powder blue uniform, the same as that worn by all of the other Sixth Engineers. However, given her tendency towards inadvertent PROEs violations, she knew she would likely benefit from the customized uniform.

• • •

Over the next month, and on into the summer season, Maria trained with Zedook. She learned how to use Pegasean tools for repairing small chips and dents in walls, counters and floors. She learned how to repair furniture and plumbing fixtures. And as Orook had promised, she learned how to unclog pipes and replace broken tiles. As the vocunine began moving into the city, she assisted in renovations to homes which needed alterations to accommodate vocunine companions. She also helped put grates on pipes seal cracks in walls. At the end of every day, she came home sore and tired. Some days she came home even later in the evening than Orook. One day she came home with angry blisters on her right hand.

"You are holding the tool too tightly," Orook told her as he examined the blisters. He then rummaged through a drawer in the bedroom until he found the tool he knew she must have been using. He showed her how to hold it firmly without "choking it." He also showed her how to let her arm and shoulder do the work, rather than her wrist.

"Thank you," Maria said before collapsing exhausted onto the bed.

"Your supervisor should be showing you these things. Maybe I should speak with him," Orook said.

"No, no, please don't," Maria pleaded. "He probably did show me. We have just been so busy preparing for these ruekar things - training is done in a bit of a rush now."

"I see," Orook said. "Well, you can always ask me about something if you need help."

Maria smiled as she asked, "Isn't that a bit beneath your station?"

"You have no idea just how far below my station it is," he said, "but I am happy to teach you my dear."

Maria put her blistered hand to her heart and made an exaggerated expression of gratitude and humility which made Orook laugh. Maria then closed her eyes and fell asleep within seconds.

Orook tried to wake her to tell her to get ready for bed but changed his mind. Instead, he took off her soiled uniform, drew the blankets over her and put a pillow under her head. She was still fast asleep by the time Orook got into bed beside her.

CHAPTER 46

No more than two weeks after Orook agreed not to ask his subordinates to work on social days, the Center Council announced a city-wide state of emergency and requested that all citizens be ready and willing to work on social days. This was much to the chagrin of the Pegasean engineers, who bore much of the burden of making the changes needed to accommodate the vocunine and to prepare the city for a potential ruekar invasion. The workload became so overwhelming that many of the engineers' companions insisted on being allowed to help. This created a sudden spike in the need for uniforms, which put the city's inventory clerks into overtime. The companions to the inventory clerks then insisted on helping them as well. By the time this ripple effect had made its way throughout the city, almost everyone, keepers and companions alike, was busy working as something at some level. Maddie was officially given the title of Interim Second Engineer in the same division as her keeper. The Center Council, at Pullmoo's insistence, allowed Maddie to have this title, despite her being human, on the promise that she would relinquish the title as soon as Etmook returned to his normal work. While Maria was busy putting grates on pipes and replacing fan belts in the air circulation system, Maddie was working night and day to keep Etmook's network or monitors afloat.

The security system which Etmook maintained did a lot more than most of the citizens of Pegasea ever realized. It monitored everything from air circulation to temperature distribution throughout the entire city. The visual and sound monitoring devices were used more to watch for intruders and system failures than to monitor the citizenry itself. It was tedious and time-consuming work. Unfortunately for Maddie, Etmook was busy helping Vartook and the other guardsman train the vocunine. By the last lunar cycle of summer, everyone, even Orook, was exhausted.

• • •

One late summer morning, sunlight streaming through the crystal ceiling above Maria's bed kissed her cheek until her skin started to burn. Half asleep, Maria brought a hand to her face and tried to bat the sunbeam away. She was normally up before dawn in order to ensure that she arrived at her work station on time. When this realization finally penetrated her consciousness, Maria sat up urgently. She was about to jump out of bed when she noticed that Orook was still in bed beside her.

"Keeper," she said as she gently shook Orook's shoulder to wake him.

"Maria… today is a social day," Orook said sleepily, "and I have been informed that the city is no longer in a state of emergency, so we do not have to go to work."

"Oh," Maria said with a sigh before collapsing back onto the bed.

Now awake, Orook sat up and stretched his aching arms. As First Engineer, he did not ordinarily have to do much manual labor. These past few lunar cycles had required that everyone do a lot of everything. While his daily sparring routines kept him in good shape, they tended to exercise a different set of muscles than the ones he had recently been required to use in excess.

"You must hurt all over," Orook said to Maria as he watched her perform her own series of stretches.

"Yeah, but it's that good kind of hurt - like when you push yourself at the gym," she said.

Orook smiled at her and she smiled back.

"So, are we going to host a vocunine or not?" Maria asked, "I think we are the only house on the street without one at this point."

"No," he said definitively.

"You don't like them, do you?" she asked.

When Orook did not answer, Maria said, "I understand why you would not want to host one - and why you don't like them."

"Then why do you need me to confirm it?" Orook asked, sounding slightly annoyed.

"Oh, don't start getting annoyed with me already. We finally have a day off! We can do something fun!" Maria said cheerfully.

"Your idea of fun and mine have an unfortunately narrow area of overlap," Orook reminded her.

"We could go to the Game Center," she suggested.

"On the first social day after we have been on an emergency work schedule for almost three lunar cycles? Are you serious? That place will be packed," Orook said.

"Well, what do you want to do?" Maria asked.

"I just want to stay home and rest," he said.

"Ugh, how boring!" she said.

"Boring sounds good to me right now," he said.

Orook was physically and intellectually spent. Adapting the city to the vocunine had not been terribly difficult but preparing it for an anticipated ruekar invasion had worn him out completely. There were so many ways the relatively small predators could get over or under the outer wall. He and his Second Engineers had ultimately decided to simply assume that the ruekar would breach the wall and focus their efforts on making sure they did not manage to get into the body of the city or into people's homes. Now all he really wanted to do was stay in bed. Much to his own surprise, he wanted Maria to stay in bed with him. He wanted her to fill his tired head with fluffy stories from her easy life on Earth. He wanted her to curl up in his arms, play with his ears, and ask him stupid questions about how the hydraulic motors worked. Of course, for several reasons, he would never actually tell her this. All he could do was hope that she would either figure it out or read it in his mind. Unfortunately for him, Maria had long since stopped trying to see anything in his mind, which was virtually always closed off to her prying telepathy. She was also not in the mood to ask for Orook's detached company. She wanted real company, with someone not constantly trying to keep her at a distance. Maddie came to mind.

"Do you mind if I hang out with Maddie then?" she asked.

"You may do whatever you like, but I doubt Maddie will be available," Orook said.

"Oh, you're right, she will probably want to spend the day with Etmook," Maria said with a frown.

"If I find a way to distract Etmook for the morning, so you can spend time with Maddie, will you spend the rest of the day with me - doing whatever I want to do?" Orook asked.

Maria laughed at Orook's uncharacteristically assertive and manipulative proposition.

"Well?" Orook asked.

"Ok, it's a deal," Maria said, "but only if you promise that 'whatever you want to do' in no way involves me reading the PROEs manual."

"I assure you that if I have any desire for either of us to read the PROEs manual later, it will only be to see just how many of them we can violate in one evening," Orook said with a mischievous smile.

"Keeper, are you feeling ok?" Maria asked with mock concern.

"You can stop calling me that now, I think," Orook said seriously.

Now Maria really was concerned.

"You are a Sixth Engineer and you work hard. If the other sixth level engineers are permitted to call me by name, I see no logical reason why you should not have the same privilege," he explained.

"Do you mean that?" she asked.

"I do," Orook said, "Of course, if you do so when others are around, I cannot guarantee that you will not get in trouble - but I will not admonish you for it."

"When did you turn into such a rebel?" Maria asked.

"A rebel? No. I do not think so. I am not acknowledging you as an equal. I am only allowing you to call me by name," he said.

"But as you've pointed out many times, calling you by name is not just a PROEs violation, it's a criminal offense!" she said.

"Why are you arguing with me? I thought you hated calling me keeper?" Orook said, sounding frustrated.

"I'm just teasing you, Orook," Maria said with a smile.

"No, not 'ah-rook.' It is pronounced 'ore' - like in iron ore - then 'ook,' with too long o's," he corrected.

Maria inched her way over to him, then pressed her cheek to his and whispered his name, pronounced correctly, into his ear. Orook closed his eyes and turned to kiss her, but she had already moved away from him. He sighed, then leaned back against the wall and proceeded to send Etmook a message. Maria saw none of this as she bounded out of bed and headed for the bathroom to start getting ready for the day. After taking a hot shower for less than five minutes, Maria got dressed in her room before coming back to Orook. He was now reading Etmook's response to his message.

"I am going to meet Etmook in the practice room in about a half hour. I invited him to give me a sparring lesson," Orook told Maria.

"Oh, that was clever," she said.

"If you say so," he said.

"I thought you hated that expression," Maria said.

"I do hate it," Orook confirmed. "I was mocking you - playfully."

Maria smiled, then said, "you are behaving very strangely today. I think all this work has made you sick or something."

"Maybe," Orook conceded.

"Maybe you should just stay in bed today," Maria said, looking concerned and feeling a bit guilty.

"No," he said. "That is no good for anyone. Exercise will help."

"If you - ok," Maria said.

Orook looked up from his armband and smiled at her. She had almost said "if you say so."

"Wait at least a half hour before you message Maddie - just so our little scheme is not too obvious," Orook instructed. "Etmook and I will be done sparring an hour or two after that - I do not think I will be able to keep the man from his companion for much longer than that."

"Ok, that's perfect," Maria said with a smile, "thank you."

"You are welcome," Orook said cordially before heading off to the bathroom to get himself ready to meet Etmook.

CHAPTER 47

"**Y**ou are more stable on all fours," Vartook told Solomane during one of their training sessions, "do not stand up unless you absolutely have to - and when you do, do not stand for more than a few seconds."

Solomane nodded.

When they were done practicing, Vartook sat down on a bench under a tree and drank water from a canister he had brought with him. Solomane followed him, then sat on a patch of exposed ground near Vartook's feet. Vartook started to offer the water to Solomane, then stopped himself. Solomane stared at him, waiting.

"How do you drink?" Vartook asked. "Do you need a bowl or something?"

Solomane growled mildly at his instructor, then reached up and took the canister from him. He poured water into the side of his mouth, then handed the bottle back to Vartook.

"I see," Vartook said smiling.

"Are you sure it's better if I stay on all fours all the time?" Solomane asked.

"Yes. It is more than just a matter of stability. You are most vulnerable at your abdomen. When you stand up, you expose that area of your body," Vartook said.

"But how will I use any kind of weapon if I'm standing on my hands all the time?" Solomane asked.

"Well, our weapons are all designed to be held in our hands. So, none of them will do," Vartook said. "I asked Etmook and his colleagues to develop a special weapon for you. It might not look like much, but appearances can be deceiving."

"What is it?" Solomane asked.

"The most I can say to describe it is that it is a pair of blades with a heavy bar between them and a jointed protective plate underneath. Each blade is actually two blades melded together at a right angle to each other. One with the sharp side up, the other to the side. You will wear one on the top of each hand. They have been designed in such a way that will enable you to curl and uncurl your hands without disturbing or displacing the weapon - and without cutting yourself. There is a band that wraps around your hand and across your palm," Vartook explained.

"Are they heavy?" Solomane asked.

"Your shoulder joints are a lot like ours," Vartook continued, as if he had not heard the question. "They have a wide range of motion. You can jab and slash. This weapon will help you make the most of such moves."

Solomane nodded.

"Another thing… and you might not like this, but it's necessary," Vartook told him. "You will need to wear something to protect your eyes."

"My eyes?" Solomane asked.

"Yes," Vartook said. "Your bite is a very important part of your fighting strategy. The problem with biting is that it brings your face in close contact with your enemy - it leaves your eyes vulnerable. When you bite a ruekar, the first thing it will try to do is scratch your eyes out."

Solomane whined quietly at the thought.

"We have something for you and the other vocunine to wear to protect your eyes, but it will take some getting used to," Vartook said. "We will also have the body biologists apply protective materials over your teeth to make them stronger."

"Is all of this really necessary?" Solomane asked.

"It won't hurt," Vartook said.

Solomane shook his head. This was not his concern.

"I know, you vocunine do not like our 'unnatural' ways," Vartook said with a slightly chiding tone.

Solomane sighed, annoyed.

Vartook looked at Solomane and smiled affectionately, then ruffled the fur between his ears. Solomane growled with bemused annoyance, which prompted Vartook to shove the animal hard in shoulder. Solomane looked at him for a moment, then suddenly pounced. Catching Vartook off guard, he was able to knock the man off the side of the bench and onto the hard ground. Vartook rolled away quickly before Solomane could pin him down. Undeterred, Solomane jumped onto the bench, which brought him almost eye-level with Vartook. Vartook smiled at him mischievously. Then, in less time than it took for the vocunine to blink, Vartook reached out and pulled the vocunine's two front legs/arms out from underneath him. Solomane recovered more quickly than Vartook had expected. He then launched himself onto Vartook, who stumbled under the award distribution of the animal's considerable weight.

The Pegasean civilians who happened to be in the park at that time watched all this with great amusement. They would later recount for all their friends, companions, and partners what it was like to watch their First Guardsman laugh and wrestle playfully with the first vocunine ever welcomed inside the walls of their great city.

CHAPTER 48

As Orook walked to the sparring room, he tried once again to acclimate his mind and emotionality to the sight of vocunine freely walking about the city. He told himself, once again, that the vocunine where no longer their enemies, which meant that they were no longer his enemies. Once again, he reminded himself that the slaughter of his first-born son had been the act of one vocunine acting alone. Orook was so deeply entrenched in this meditation that he almost walked right past the entrance to the sparring room. He came to an abrupt stop at the door, closed his eyes and took a deep breath before entering.

Etmook, who had been anxiously and excitedly waiting, jumped to his feet when he saw Orook.

"Hi, boss," Etmook said cheerfully before quickly making the first gesture of respect.

Orook acknowledged his gesture wearily and tried to smile.

"Are you alright?" Etmook asked, "you look a bit drained."

"I am still not used to having these - the vocunine - in the city," Orook confessed.

Etmook blinked at Orook, then looked down at the relatively small vocunine sitting astutely at his feet.

"Should I ask Picobane to leave?" Etmook asked.

"No, that is not necessary," Orook said, then forced himself to look down at the animal.

Picobane whined softly and looked away. He sensed Orook's discomfort with his presence and this upset him.

"It's ok Pico," Etmook said, "Orook is my boss, my superior."

Something in Etmook's kind and pacifying voice inspired Orook to try to get over his unjustified aversion to the vocunine. He crouched down and looked into Pico's pale blue eyes.

"Forgive me," he said gently, "a vocunine killed my son and, to my shame, I cannot seem to separate this fact from my emotional response to all of your kind. I am still trying to correct this defect in my emotionality. For the time being, please ignore my discomfort around you - it is not personal to you."

Pico looked up at Etmook, who smiled at his companion reassuringly.

Pico then made a strange movement involving his head and ears which Orook did not immediately recognize as any Pegasean gesture.

"That is the vocunine version of our second gesture of sympathy," Etmook explained.

Orook nodded, then asked, "Pico, do you speak?"

Again, Pico looked up at Etmook.

"Please, Pico, you may speak for yourself," Etmook said.

"I do speak," Pico said with a smile as he turned back to Orook.

"Why do you look to Etmook to answer for you?" Orook asked.

"That is the way of a companion," Pico said.

Orook looked up at Etmook with an expression of equal parts surprise and puzzlement.

"I guess now we know where all those companion rules in the PROEs manual came from," Etmook said to Orook.

"What do you mean?" Orook asked.

"It is how the vocunine naturally behave with us - when they are being, well, kept by us. They didn't act this way when they were out on the mountain because our species were enemies. Now that we've all made nice with each other, they have returned to the behavior they exhibited a thousand years ago, when they lived with the Olroneans - even though none of them have ever lived with one of us before," Etmook said.

"But how...," Orook started to ask.

"Don't ask me to explain it. I have no idea how they could possibly know - or remember - but from the moment Pico was placed with me, he has been following the companion rules as if he knows them by heart," Etmook explained.

"I do not like that expression," Orook said.

"I am not particularly fond of it either, but in this case, it seems most appropriate. If I didn't know better, I would say it is instinctual for them. It is so strange. Would you believe he refuses to stand in my presence unless I request it?" Etmook said to Orook.

"It is impolite to stand in the presence of one's keeper," Pico said plainly, as if reading from an ancient text etched somewhere deep in his mind.

"Yes, yes, as you have told me many times," Etmook said, sounding annoyed. "And please stop calling me 'keeper' - I don't even let my human companion call me that."

Orook stood up and looked at Etmook with wide eyes. Upon realizing what he had just admitted before his superior, Etmook blushed and hurriedly tried to explain.

"Maddie is not like the other human women," he said quickly. "She's…"

Orook put up a hand and said, "Etmook, stop."

"We follow the rules when other people are around," Etmook said.

"Etmook, you do not have to explain," Orook said calmly. "My expression was merely one of surprise, not admonishment."

"Oh, ok," Etmook said, sounding unconvinced.

"I know you think I am strict about such things," Orook said.

"I do not think it, I know it," Etmook said, then quickly apologized for being insolent.

"No, do not apologize. It was a fair statement to make," Orook conceded.

"Yes, but I could have said it better. Of course, you are strict about the rules. You have to be in your position," Etmook said.

"You do not understand. I enforce the rules among my subordinates, and on myself, because I respect them, as most all Pegasean men and women do - aside from yourself, maybe," Orook said.

"I am not the only exception," Etmook muttered.

"Well, Etmook, I will admit that, lately, I have started to wonder about their purpose, at least with respect to the human women - and now that I have met Pico, I am also wondering about their true origins," Orook confessed.

"Really?" Etmook asked.

Orook nodded.

Etmook, concerned that this was a test or trap, said nothing.

"This morning I gave Maria permission to call me by name," Orook said quietly, more to himself than Etmook.

Now it was Etmook's turn to look surprised.

"She is a Sixth Engineer now," Orook explained. "Her supervisor reports nothing but praise and suggestions for how she might become more skilled with practice. He tells me that she might be able to advance to the fifth position if she continues to work hard for a few more years. If that happens, she would no longer be required to have a keeper. She could live on her own, as a contributing member of the city."

"Good for her," Etmook said cautiously.

"So why should she not be permitted to call me by name?" Orook asked.

"No reason that I can think of," Etmook agreed.

"Right, well, maybe the justification for that rule is simply beyond our understanding as engineers," Orook said.

"Yeah, maybe," Etmook muttered.

In a moment of inspiration, Etmook looked down at Pico and asked, "Pico, why do you refuse to call me by name?"

"To call a man by his name is to command him. A companion must never command his keeper," Pico explained.

"How is it that you are so adept with our companion rules without ever having lived in the city before?" Etmook asked.

"By the grace of the Prisoner," Pico answered.

Etmook rolled his eyes.

"That is what you say to everything you can't otherwise explain," Etmook said, staring down at Pico. "Do you know how silly it sounds? Who, or what, is this 'Prisoner?'"

When Pico did not answer, Etmook continued, "I think it must be a voice in your head. Have you gone mad Pico? Is that it?"

Pico growled softly.

"Pico, are you *growling* at me? You know that is *not* the way of a companion," Etmook said with mocking admonishment.

At this Pico's ears sagged and he hung his head.

"Oh, I'm just kidding Pico!" Etmook said.

When Pico's expression remained forlorn, Etmook sighed, then knelt and hugged the animal. He muttered something into Pico's ear as he rubbed the animal's back. Pico's ears rose as his cheerful and contented expression returned. Etmook then stood back up, looked at Orook and shrugged.

"It seems to me that the city adopted more than just the terms 'companion' and 'keeper' when it comes to our prescribed relationships with the human women," Orook thought out loud.

"It certainly seems that way," Etmook agreed.

As Orook's distrust of the vocunine began to wane, his mild distrust of the city's sociologists was starting to grow into something more substantial.

After several minutes passed in silence while Orook stood motionless, deep in thought, Etmook asked Orook if he still wanted to spar.

Orook looked up at Etmook.

"Yes," Orook said, "as long as you promise not to hold back or let me prevail over you. I want to see for myself why Vartook was so upset when I convinced the Center Council to assign you to engineering."

Orook then turned to the wall where the sparring weapons were hung neatly in rows. He took down a weapon for himself, then another which he tossed to Etmook.

"Why do you assume I would go easy on you?" Etmook asked.

"Because you love me," Orook said as he walked out onto the practice mats.

"I do not," Etmook said.

"Then come over here and prove it," Orook said.

CHAPTER 49

Due to the threat posed by the ruekar, the closest Maria and Maddie were allowed to get to the open outside was under the large crystal dome ceiling of District Center Two. Upon Maria's suggestion, the two women spread out a blanket near a cluster of indoor trees and pretended they were outside.

"If I close my eyes, I can almost believe I am outside," Maria said cheerfully.

"Almost," Maddie said, sounding a bit bitter.

"What's wrong?" Maria asked.

"I just can't believe your keeper had the nerve to ask Etmook to go sparring today," Maddie said.

Maria's face flushed with guilt.

"Was Etmook upset?" she asked.

"No, of course not. You know he loves Orook. He was thrilled actually," Maddie said.

"I'm so sorry Maddie," Maria said.

"It's not your fault," Maddie replied.

"Um, well, it kinda is… he only did it for me," Maria confessed.

Maddie turned to look at Maria, brows raised in an unspoken request for further explanation.

"I'm sorry!" Maria said. "I just really missed you Maddie! …and I knew you wouldn't want to come hangout with me unless Etmook was busy elsewhere."

"So, wait, you asked Orook to distract Etmook - so that you could spend time with me?" Maddie asked.

Maria covered her face with her hands as she nodded.

Maddie started to laugh.

"Except I didn't ask him," Maria clarified. "It was his idea."

"His idea? How very un-Orook-like," Maddie said.

"I know - he was acting very strange this morning. I think he's worn out from all the work we've had to do," Maria said.

Maddie nodded, then said "Maria, you could have just asked me. I missed you too you know. I would have met up with you for a bit even without this charade."

"Really?" Maria asked.

"Sure," Maddie said.

"Oh," Maria said, embarrassed, "but it worked out ok anyway, didn't it? I mean, no harm no foul, right?"

Maddie smiled and nodded.

"You should have seen how excited Etmook was to get Orook's message this morning. It was a little pathetic, actually," Maddie said.

"I think it's cute," Maria said.

Maddie rolled her eyes.

The two women laid quietly then for several minutes, each enjoying the warmth raining down on them in flickering shards of broken sunlight through the dome ceiling. They then sat up and decided to eat their picnic lunch of nuts, berries and cheese, then each enjoyed a spiced water from one of the beverage dispensers.

The two then began cheerfully commiserating about their work of the past three lunar cycles, sharing stories of minor disasters and equally minor triumphs. Maddie told Maria about how difficult it was taking Etmook's place at the helm of the security grid.

"I don't know how he does it honestly," Maddie said.

"It's amazing that you've been able to hold it together this long," Maria said.

"I only hope that is the case," Maddie confessed. "I'm sure he is going to have to repair some things and make some corrections when he returns to his post."

Maria nodded, then showed Maddie the array of blisters on her hands and the bruises on her knees.

"You would think that a species advanced as they are would have robots to do the kind of work I do," Maria said.

"They don't like robots," Maddie said.

"Why not?" Maria asked.

Maddie shrugged.

"Have you seen those cool flame-throwers some of the engineers built for the guardsmen around the perimeter of the city?" Maria asked.

"No, I haven't had a chance," Maddie said. "I heard about them though. Two weeks ago, I received several complaints from District Five about a weird smell in their district center. Shortly after I dispatched two Fifth Engineers to investigate, a guardsman from the northern wall called and told me that they had just fried an entire troop of ruekar out on the surface land around District Five - and that I should expect complaints about the odor. Apparently, ruekar flesh smells really really bad when it burns."

Maria scrunched up her nose, imagining what that smell might be like.

"Did you hear about those two ruekar that managed to get in through a broken drain pipe in District Three?" Maddie asked.

"Yeah," Maria said. "My supervisor told me that Orook was so furious that he demoted three fourth level engineers."

"*Three?*" Maddie said. "Why three?"

"Well, according to Zedook, Orook only demoted one of them for the actual oversight that lead to the break-in. The other two he demoted because they cried when he admonished them," Maria told Maddie.

Maddie chuckled. "Actually, I'm surprised he didn't give me more shit for that one," she said. "I'm supposed to send out an alert every time the sensors detect a break - which I did. But then I ignored the system alerts after one of the engineers in District Three told me that he had made the repair and it was fine. I should have trusted the sensors and known that something was still wrong."

"And Orook didn't get angry with you for that?" Maria asked.

"Not so much," Maddie told her. "He did call me after it happened. But all he said was that Etmook must have taught me better than to assume that the perceptions of a Fourth Engineer are more accurate than the monitoring system."

"Did you cry?" Maria teased.

Maddie rolled her eyes. "Orook doesn't bother me," she said. "Besides, what's the worst he could do? Demote me? After Etmook comes back, I'll be back to being nothing again."

"Don't say that," Maria said. "Why don't you take a job as a Sixth Engineer? We can pull dead lichen weasels from the sewer grates *together!*"

Maddie shuddered at the thought and Maria laughed.

After several minutes passed in comfortable silence, Maria asked, "Maddie, is it normal for human women to stop menstruating after they first arrive here from Earth?"

"Sometimes, yes. It is a big adjustment - lots of changes, stress - why do you ask?" Maddie said.

"I just haven't in a long time. I figured it was something like you said - adjusting to the new environment and stress," Maria told her.

"How long is a long time?" Maddie asked.

Maria thought for a moment, tracking the time in her mind. "It has been at least three or four what you call 'lunar cycles,'" she guessed.

"Hmmm...," Maddie said. "I don't know. I think that must be normal. I was born here, so it never happened to me. But I've heard of other women taking that long to get their natural rhythm back."

Maria nodded but did not appear to be comforted by this.

"What's wrong?" Maddie asked.

"Nothing really," Maria said, trying to sound unconcerned. "It's just that, well, if I didn't know better... well, I've never been pregnant before, but I have had friends who got pregnant."

"You think you might be?" Maddie asked.

"Is that even possible?" Maria asked.

"Well, I assume you and Orook have been sleeping together - or else you wouldn't even be thinking about this, right?" Maddie said.

Maria blushed.

Maddie suppressed a laugh at Maria's girlish reticence, then asked, "When was the first time?"

"During his suspension - just before spring," Maria muttered.

"That was like six lunar cycles ago," Maddie said.

"Right," Maria said. "I had a period after that at some point - but I don't remember exactly when."

Maddie nodded, then said "Hmm… well, it can't be an adjustment thing then. I mean, if you resumed your normal cycle, then it stopped again."

"Right, but I thought human women and Pegasean men couldn't have kids together. I mean, I know you told me about you being…you know, but I thought that was like a one in a million fluke," Maria said in a whisper.

"Shhhh," Maddie said, then looked around cautiously.

"I'm whispering," Maria said.

"You don't understand how well these guys can hear," Maddie said.

"Ok, sorry," Maria replied.

"It's ok, let's just not talk about me, ok?" Maddie asked.

Maria nodded.

"If you really want to know if your pregnant, I guess you'll have to go to the body biology center," Maddie said.

"What will they do if I am?" Maria asked.

Maddie shrugged, then said, "Probably nothing…and now that I think about it, they probably won't even tell you the results of the test. They will just put the results in your file and send a message to your keeper. Orook might not even tell you what they are - he might think, as I'm inclined to think, that there is no point in knowing."

"What? How can you say that?" Maria asked.

"Maria, even if you are pregnant, there is virtually no chance of carrying the baby to viability," Maddie said gently, "so what is the point of knowing? It will just make you sad."

Maria sighed.

"I'm sorry," Maddie said. "It sucks. I know."

Maria nodded, then rested her head on her knees. Maddie rubbed Maria's back and tried to be comforting.

"Do you think Orook knows?" Maria asked.

"How would he know?" Maddie asked.

"I don't know - but he has a weird way of always knowing things. I don't know how. He just seems to be able to perceive a lot more than I ever do - or ever even could. Maybe it's that second hearing thing he has," Maria said.

"That second hearing thing doesn't work as well inside the city," Maddie told her. "But maybe he knows. It wouldn't surprise me. Like you said, he does have an eerie way of just knowing things."

"I wish he was easier to talk to - I wish he was more like Etmook," Maria said idly.

Maddie smiled, then said, "They are more alike than you might think, Maria."

Maria shrugged, her mind was too preoccupied to continue on with the conversation.

A few minutes later, Maria was startled out of her thoughts by her armband, which started vibrating. Maddie laughed at the way she jumped as if bitten by a snake.

"It's never vibrated before," Maria said, looking down at her arm.

"That means it is either an emergency or from someone very important," Maddie explained.

Maria just stared down at her armband, mesmerized by the electric blue light circling the display.

"You better answer it," Maddie prompted.

"It's not a call," Maria told her. "It's a summons."

"A summons? Really? From who?" Maddie asked.

Maria read, then re-read, the message. The words were in English, but Maria could not wrap her mind around what they appeared to convey.

"It must be a mistake," Maria said. "It's from the First Guardsman and Pullmoo. They are asking me to meet them in Pullmoo's office within an hour. Maddie, I don't even have the security clearance required to go to Pullmoo's office by myself."

"Oh no... what kind of trouble did you get yourself into now?" Maddie teased.

"Nothing! I swear!" Maria said, unamused.

"Come on, I'll take you," Maddie said.

"You can get there?" Maria asked.

"Of course," Maddie said.

"Ok," Maria said, as she tried to think of some reason why Vartook and Pullmoo would summon her - and on a social day, no less.

CHAPTER 50

J ust as Maddie and Maria were getting up to leave District Center Two, Maddie saw Orook approaching them from the direction of the subrail station. Maddie tugged on Maria's blouse and pointed towards him. Maria stopped packing up their things and waited for Orook to reach them.

"You look beat," Maria said gently as he approached them.

"Yes, well, Etmook is quite proficient in close combat. Also, I might have overestimated his fraternal affection for me," Orook said.

Maddie laughed.

Orook turned sharply to face Maddie.

"You can laugh now," he said, "but will you be laughing when I release him from his service as an engineer and turn him over to Vartook? How are you fairing as Second Engineer? Would you like me to make the appointment permanent?"

"You can't do that - the Center Council won't let you. I'm human, remember?" Maddie countered briskly.

"Not entirely though, right?" Orook said, holding her eyes on his.

"I have no idea what you're talking about," Maddie muttered.

"Oh really?" Orook said, then reached out and tugged gently at her left ear.

Maddie flinched as a soft barrage of ultrasonic waves hit her untrained upper inner ear. The experience was not nearly as unpleasant as it might have been if they had been outside on the mountain, but it was still enough to make her uncomfortable. Her face turned red as she quickly reached up and pulled her ear back into its normal position.

"Interesting how your ears can shift positions like those of a Pegasean," Orook said.

"How did you know?" Maddie asked in a whisper.

When Orook failed to answer immediately, Maddie turned sharply and looked menacingly at Maria.

"I swear Maddie, I didn't tell him anything!" Maria said.

"Maddie, stop. I have known this about you since before you were even aware of it yourself - and long before Maria ever stepped foot onto this planet," Orook said.

"How is that even possible?!" Maddie asked.

"My powers of observation are far greater than you might appreciate Maddie. Even so, I am sure that Etmook knew even before I did - even if he pretended to be blissfully unaware," Orook said coldly.

"Whatever," Maddie said.

Orook then took a step towards Maddie. Now standing only inches from her, he leaned his face in close to her ear and, speaking in Pegasean, whispered "Tell me you are not so foolish as to believe that Etmook would have taken you as his apprentice, and taught you our language, if he genuinely believed you were only human."

Maddie stepped back and turned away from Orook. She stood rigid and still, save for a nervous clenching and unclenching of her fists. Satisfied that Maddie had been put back in her place, Orook turned to Maria. He was about to tell her to finish packing up their things when he saw the look of fear and disgust on Maria's face. Realizing how his interaction with Maddie must have appeared to her, Orook sighed, then turned back to Maddie.

"Relax Maddie. Your secret is safe with me. I have kept it all this time, have I not?" Orook said.

Maddie stared silently at Orook until at last she lowered her eyes. She then made the first gesture of apology, then the second gesture of gratitude. Orook acknowledged these, then turned back to Maria.

Maria looked at Maddie, then at Orook, then back at Maddie. When she was satisfied that Maddie was ok, and that she and Orook had mutually resolved whatever it was that had just transpired between them, she said, "I really need to get going. I have to go to see Pullmoo and Vartook."

"Yes, but not today," Orook told Maria.

Orook refused to explain anything about the situation until they were back home. He then told Maddie to wait in the District Center for Etmook, who would come to meet her here shortly.

"I'm sorry. I shouldn't have assumed you told him," Maddie said to Maria as she finished gathering up their things.

"Forget it," Maria said with a smile.

The two friends hugged and said their goodbyes before Maria and Orook started on their way back home.

Once they were seated in the subrail car, Maria asked Orook why he had been so unkind to Maddie.

"Are you really so sure I was being unkind to her?" Orook asked.

"That is how it looked to me," Maria said. "And I don't get it - she has laughed at you before and you didn't even seem to notice. Why was this time so different?" Maria asked.

Orook closed his eyes and leaned his head back against the wall of the subrail car.

"Try to figure it out yourself, Maria," he said.

"Are you particularly sensitive about your sparring skills?" Maria asked.

"No, not at all," he said.

Maria thought for a moment, then asked, "Does it have something to do with the fact that she's the interim Second Engineer in Etmook's position."

"Yes," Orook said. "However, I would never be that harsh with Etmook. Maddie must struggle night and day to keep Etmook's systems running smoothly. Granted, there are few who could do much better - but the point is that she is no Second Engineer. I treated her more like a Third Engineer, which is the station more appropriate for her skill level."

"So - by reacting the way you did, you were acknowledging her status in some way?" Maria asked.

Orook nodded.

"Am I still allowed to laugh at you?" Maria asked.

Orook opened his eyes and turned to look at Maria.

"Yes, but only at home," he said.

"Do you think Maddie understood what you were doing?" Maria asked.

"In the end she did," Orook said.

Maria noticed then that her armband was still blinking. She looked down at the display and saw that there was a message from Orook, responding to the summons from Pullmoo and Vartook. After she read the message, she looked at Orook and started to ask a question. Orook shook his head.

"Not until we get home," he said.

CHAPTER 51

A s soon as they were inside the door, Maria asked, "Why did you postpone the meeting with Vartook and Pullmoo? *How* did you postpone the meeting?"

"Did you not read my message?" Orook asked.

"Yes, I did. You told them I had a prior commitment, but I don't," Maria said.

"Are you sure about that?" Orook asked.

"I think so. I don't have anything on my calendar. I suppose I could have forgotten something, but Zedook usually puts my commitments and appointments on my calendar himself," Maria said, sounding pensive.

"You have a commitment with me," Orook reminded her.

Maria's brow furrowed, then relaxed.

"Oh! You mean our deal? - the one where I agreed to spend the evening with you if you distracted Etmook?" she asked with an uneasy laugh.

"Yes," Orook confirmed.

"I didn't think that kind of commitment could possibly take precedence over a summons from the First Sociologist and First Guardsman," Maria said.

"Well, you are a Sixth Engineer and I am the First Engineer," Orook explained, "Consequently, any commitment you have with me takes precedence over their request unless their request relates to a matter of either sociological concern or city security. Their intentions must not relate to either of those, or else they would have overridden my claim of priority."

"So, you essentially pulled rank on them?" Maria asked.

"Not just essentially, entirely. That is exactly what I did," Orook said.

"But my commitment with you has nothing to do with engineering - or at least I hope it doesn't. I'm so tired of work. I need a break," Maria said.

"I do not want to do any work either," Orook agreed.

"Then I think you might be bending the rules here," Maria teased.

"More than that, I am abusing my authority," Orook said dryly.

Maria laughed.

"I simply fail to see how those two could possibly have any use for you," Orook explained.

Maria frowned as she once again tried to think of a reason why Pullmoo and Vartook would jointly summon her to a meeting.

Misinterpreting Maria's expression, Orook said, "I did not mean that to be insulting. I did not intend to imply that you are useless - simply that I do not see what use *they* could have for the services of a Sixth Engineer, *any* Sixth Engineer, much less any one of them in particular. If they need maintenance, they should contact a dispatcher."

"Keeper, since when do you care if something you say to me might be insulting?" Maria asked.

Orook looked at her for a long moment before saying, "Maria, have I really been so cold to you? - that even such routine consideration from me surprises you? - and why are you still calling me 'keeper?'"

"I'm sorry," Maria said softly.

"I was not admonishing you," Orook said.

Maria did not respond. She only nodded, then walked into the kitchen and put the satchel she had taken to the District Center on the table. Ordinarily, Maria was too accustomed to Orook's brusque manner to be at all unsettled by it; but her earlier conversation with Maddie, and now the summons from Pullmoo and Vartook, had left her rattled.

Orook followed Maria as far as the archway into the kitchen. He then stopped and leaned against the wall and folded his arms. He watched Maria as she stood staring idly at the turquoise hexagon tiles on the floor, the palm of one hand resting idly on the satchel and the other pressed gently to her abdomen.

"Would you like help putting those things away?" he asked.

"No, I can do it," Maria said.

Orook unfolded his arms and walked into the kitchen. He stopped and stood in front of Maria. He then gently lifted her chin and turned her face up to his. She looked at him curiously.

"What have I done to you?" he whispered.

"Nothing… it's not you," she said.

"You always say that," he said.

"Well, in this case, it really isn't - honestly," she said and tried to smile.

When he did not respond, Maria shook herself to clear her head of her worries.

"So, what do you want to do?" she asked, "I'm all yours. Just remember - you promised - it can't have anything to do with the PROEs manual."

Orook smiled, then lifted her up by the waist and sat her down on the table so that she was now eye level with him. Maria looked perplexed and a little startled, but she smiled.

"What do *you* want, Maria?" Orook asked.

"I don't know," Maria said.

"Do you want to talk?" he asked.

Maria looked down at her hands.

"Look at me," Orook said.

With some effort, Maria leveled her head and made eye contact with him.

Before she could look away again, Orook kissed her with a dept of genuine feeling that took Maria completely by surprise and drove all other thoughts from her mind. He then pressed his cheek to hers and whispered into her ear, "I want to make love to you, Maria."

The intimacy in his voice and his choice of words left Maria feeling dazed and a bit confused.

"But not in here of course," Orook said as he stepped back and took her hand as she slid off the table.

"You've never called it that before," Maria said absently.

"I've never kissed you that way before either," he added.

"What's going on? What's gotten into you?" Maria asked.

"Oh, I am sure you will figure it out," Orook said as he led her out of the kitchen.

CHAPTER 52

In the early morning of the following day, Maria and Orook stood in front of the door to Pullmoo's office. Maria stood a pace behind Orook and tugged at her work uniform as she waited for Orook to touch his armband to the receiver unit on the wall next to the door. Before he did so, Orook paused, then turned around to face Maria.

"Maria," he said.

"Yes?" she said.

Orook looked down both ends of the hall, then led her away from Pullmoo's door.

"What's wrong?" Maria asked.

In a voice so quiet that Maria could barely hear him, Orook told her that he expected Pullmoo and Vartook to speak mostly in Pegasean during the start of the meeting.

"When a companion receives this kind of summons, her presence at the meeting is more of a formality than anything else. Whatever they want from you, they are going to request it through me. They will speak to me in Pegasean so that you cannot interject, object, or take any part in the conversation," Orook told her.

"Why are telling me this?" Maria asked, "And why are we whispering?"

"Because I do not trust them," he said.

"I thought you said it was counterproductive to distrust Pullmoo," she said.

"Yes, I did say that, and it is. All the same, I want you to be aware of what is going on - whatever it is. So, I will do my best to make the content of the conversation available to you in my mind, ok?" Orook said.

"I don't know how well that is going to work," Maria confessed. "I haven't seen anything in your mind since… well, I don't know when. It's been a long time. I stopped even bothering to try at some point."

"I know," Orook said. "But that is because I shut my mind, and myself, off to you. I have been doing my best to reverse that protocol now. Do you understand?"

Maria nodded.

Orook took a deep breath, then took Maria's hand and led her back to Pullmoo's door.

"Thank you," Maria said.

Orook said nothing as he tapped his armband to the small silver colored square on the wall next to the door. Moments later, Pullmoo opened the door and greeted them both. Maria made the appropriate gesture to First Sociologist before following Orook inside. Once inside, they greeted Vartook and Solomane in turn. At Pullmoo's invitation, Maria and Orook took a seat on the couch. Pullmoo remained standing but leaned casually back against the front of her desk as she faced the First Engineer and his companion.

"Normally, when we summon a human companion, we hold a meeting like this one, with her and her keeper, in which we speak only in Pegasean," Pullmoo began in her native tongue. "But considering the unusual nature of the request Vartook and I are about to make, I see it as only fair that Maria be allowed to participate - provided, of course, that her keeper does not object."

"I have no objection to speaking in English or to allowing Maria to participate in the conversation," Orook responded in English. "It saves me the trouble of making everything we say available to her in my mind."

Pullmoo gave him a thin smile before saying, in English, "We are all agreed then."

"What do either of you know about the entity which the vocunine refer to as the 'Prisoner?'" Pullmoo asked.

Maria looked dutifully to Orook, allowing him to answer first.

Orook looked at Solomane, then turned to Vartook and said, "I am afraid that my description of this entity, or what little I understand of it, might offend the vocunine."

As was now his habit, Solomane looked up at Vartook.

"Go ahead Orook, Solomane will not take offense," Vartook said, speaking for his companion.

"Very well," Orook said, "It is my understanding that what the vocunine refer to as the 'Prisoner' is one of a rare species known to us as *naverkoo*. It is rooted inside of the mountain they refer to as 'Mount Olympus,' but which we refer to as the 'Eye of Olrona.' Based on the rumors and stories I have heard about this entity, I would guess that it is an exceptionally old specimen of its kind. It looks a bit like an enormous tree, with 'branches' grown into cracks and crevices throughout the entire mountain. The ends of these branches are the only parts of the creature we ever usually see. Most people who see them assume that they are all individual trees. Most information we have about the *naverkoo* was lost following the settlement of Pegasea, as it was kept with the Olroneans, who soon thereafter perished - as we all know."

"That was a very academic description, Orook," Pullmoo said. "I'm asking for something a little more, well, speculative."

"I do not speculate about such things," Orook said. "I am not a biologist."

"Maria?" Pullmoo said.

Maria shifted in her seat as she looked at Pullmoo, then Orook, then Solomane.

"Ok, well, I don't actually *know* anything about the Prisoner, but it does sound a lot like this thing that I have been having dreams about ever since I arrived here on this planet," Maria confessed.

"The talking tree?" Orook asked.

Maria nodded.

"Huh," Orook said. "I did not make that connection."

"Go on, Maria, please," Pullmoo prompted.

Maria shook her head.

"It's stupid," she said. "They're just dreams. It's nonsense."

"All the same, please, do tell," Pullmoo said.

"Ok, so, shortly after my keeper took me home from the intake hall, I started having these weird dreams about a tree stuck inside a mountain - only it wasn't really stuck or trapped - so I don't know why the vocunine keep calling it a prisoner. In any case, this tree, or whatever it is, told me that it built the mountain around itself. It said it lifted the boulders and the stone and the soil up all around itself. It claimed to have built the mountain - and other mountains too," Maria said.

"In these dreams - the 'tree' spoke to you?" Vartook asked.

"Well, sort of," Maria said. "It didn't talk the way we are talking. It just put things in my mind - like a reverse telepathy - the way the vocunine can do."

Vartook and Solomane exchanged glances.

"Did this tree tell you anything else?" Pullmoo asked.

"Lots of things," Maria said, "but why do you care? They were just silly dreams."

"Did it tell you its name?" Vartook asked.

At this question, Maria's face flushed, and she looked nervously down at her hands.

"What is its name?" Vartook asked, ignoring Solomane's non-verbal attempts to get his attention.

Maria shook her head.

"Maria, why are you so afraid to say its name?" Pullmoo asked.

Maria looked pleadingly at Solomane.

Fighting his instinct to remain silent until asked to speak, Solomane finally spoke up in Maria's defense.

"She must not say its name for the same reason you do not allow her to say the name of her keeper - except that in this case it is a real rule, not a made-up rule. The Prisoner is keeper to us all and must not be commanded," the vocunine explained.

"By 'made-up' he means 'man-made,'" Vartook clarified.

"Fascinating," Pullmoo said.

"With all due respect," Orook said, "I am quickly losing patience with all of this. Why have you summoned my companion here? Certainly, there are those more qualified to educate you on matters relating to *naverkoo* biology, vocunine folklore, or any potential intersection of the two."

"I doubt it," Pullmoo said, smiling at Maria.

"Well, I don't," Maria said. "All I have are dreams. I don't know anything about this *naverkoo* or the vocunines."

"The *naverkoo* can communicate via telepathy across considerable distances," Pullmoo told them. "It communicates with the vocunine and with the ruekar, and with just about every living thing on this planet. For whatever reason, it does not seem to communicate much with our kind. Or, perhaps maybe it attempts to, but we do not perceive it properly. In any case, oddly enough, it appears to be communicating with you Maria."

"Ok, well, that's nice, but if it also communicates with the vocunine, what do you need me for?" Maria asked.

"We have a situation," Pullmoo said.

"What kind of situation?" Orook asked.

"The vocunine female promised to Solomane - his betrothed to put it another way- refuses to leave the Eye of Olrona. Her name is Lunakane and, for whatever reason, she refuses to leave the cave leading to the central body of the *naverkoo*," Pullmoo told them.

"How is this Maria's problem or concern?" Orook asked.

"If Lunakane cannot be convinced to leave the mountain, she will not likely survive the winter moons," Pullmoo explained.

"A vocunine cannot survive the winter alone," Vartook added.

"Granted, we have quite a bit of time before winter arrives," Pullmoo said. "However, there are also the ruekar to worry about. If they find her, well, I do not imagine she will be able to fend them off herself."

"Again, how is this any of Maria's concern?" Orook asked.

"Yeah, honestly," Maria said. "I don't see what I could possibly do to help here."

Pullmoo and Vartook exchanged looks.

Orook stood up.

"I have had enough of this," he said. "We are leaving now."

"Sit down Orook…please," Pullmoo said.

"No. State your request plainly, and do it now, or we are going. As far as I can see, this matter is neither a concern under your authority as the First Sociologist nor any matter falling under Vartook's concern as First Guardsman. We are here out of courtesy and are free to leave at any time," Orook said.

"Lunakane told her sisters, who are now living in the City, that she is waiting for a human woman to come to the cave - we don't know why," Pullmoo said.

"Ok, but why me?" Maria asked.

"Because we believe that you are the one the *naverkoo* wants," Pullmoo told her.

"Why?" Orook asked. "What does it want with a human woman? And why Maria in particular?"

"I do not know why the naverkoo has any interest in human women. As for why it might be interested in Maria in particular - as far as we know, Maria is the only human woman capable of 'hearing' the *naverkoo,*" Pullmoo said. "I believe that her unusual brain abnormality - the one we found when we first processed her through intake - might be the reason why the *naverkoo* is able to communicate with her."

"Oh, you can't be serious," Maria said.

"I am," Pullmoo said, keeping her eyes fixed on Orook.

Orook held Pullmoo's gaze for a long moment before turning to Maria and saying, "Maria, the choice is yours. I do not want you to go. I do not think it is safe for you to go - even if Vartook escorts you there himself. That said, as far as my authority over you as your keeper goes, I am leaving the decision with you. If you feel compelled to help my colleagues rescue this recalcitrant vocunine princess, I will not use that authority to stop you."

Maria looked at Solomane, then to each of the Pegaseans in turn.

"I'm so sorry Solomane," Maria said to the vocunine, "but I do not want to go out to this mountain. I think my keeper is right. I do not think it is safe for me, or anyone. Besides that, I have no desire to meet this tree or *naverkoo* or whatever it is."

Solomane whined as Orook sighed with relief.

Pullmoo looked at Vartook.

"Maria, you owe me a debt," Vartook said.

CHAPTER 53

O rook closed his eyes and hung his head. He harbored no hope that Maria would not honor the debt she had incurred under the third gesture of gratitude. Like him, she kept her word. His heart swelled with pain as he considered the possibility that this might be the last promise she would ever keep. Whatever Pullmoo's plan might be, he knew that, this time, the risk to Maria's life was real. This was no harmless manipulation of a lonely man in need of company, this was the leading of a lamb to slaughter, the first born to the altar, the maiden to the dragon.

Orook knew a bit more about the *naverkoo* than he had disclosed to Pullmoo. Although not a biologist, he knew enough about biology to oversee the city's department of bioengineering and had conducted his own unofficial study of the organism's inner workings. Orook had suspected, for some time now, that it had communicated with Maria at least once. It happened that one day back in winter. Back before he loved her, when he had taken her out into the mountains far beyond the outer city wall. It happened while she stood watch for him outside the cave. The *naverkoo* gave Maria the information she needed to save her keeper from certain death at the hands of a vocunine with murderous intent.

Several years prior to that day, Orook had begun to suspect that some of the "trees" on the mountain were connected. To test his theory, he had placed micro-tracers ordinarily used to map out pipe paths or veins of ore, on the roots of these "trees." The tracers returned data suggesting that the tree roots went all the way into the center of the Eye of Olrona, miles from where he had first placed the micro-tracers. Assuming the slim little tracers had made a mistake, or malfunctioned, he ran them again, and again, until he was convinced that their data must be true. He then gave the data to his sister, who used the data to create a projected model of the full extent of whatever it was the tracers had found. Her conclusion seemed ridiculous at the time. It suggested that the Prisoner was not only enormous, but that its presence, in some form or another, was nearly ubiquitous over the entire mountain range surrounding Pegasea. He and Wilamoo had then spent an entire day theorizing on its source of energy, its age and its origin.

Driven by a mad curiosity to know more, Orook collected samples from every exposed and accessible part of the creature he could find. He brought the samples to the city's biologists until the First Biologist politely asked him to stop wasting their time and resources testing "a random selection of mountain fauna and foliage."

Several lunar cycles later, Orook decided that he would attempt to collect one last sample from the mysteriously mercurial organism. He had heard a rumor about a small narrow cave which the vocunine believe to be sacred and which tunneled into the very core of the Eye of Olrona. Orook traveled to that cave with Maria and asked her to keep watch while he went inside to collect a sample from what amounted to be the "heart" of the Prisoner. Much to Orook's surprise, the *naverkoo* gave it to him freely.

The following day, Orook gave the sample to his bioengineers, who marveled at the cellular composition of the sample and insisted on knowing where Orook had obtained such an impossible collection of cells. They told him that the cells appeared to be totipotent without limit. They could become anything, of any kind, and could multiply indefinitely without diminishment. Orook refused to disclose the source of the sample. He instructed them to work with the city's biologists to culture the cells and to learn as much about them as possible. Less than two weeks later, in an instant, the gift of the Prisoner was taken away just as mysteriously as it was given. Without warning, the cells all inexplicably disassembled themselves and died. Even the proteins unraveled and denatured, leaving little more than an indiscriminate pool of amino acids, fats and carbohydrates. It was then that Orook decided to abandon his pursuit of any further knowledge about this entity, whatever it was. At that time, any further thought of it had made his mind ache with puzzlement and incredulity.

Up until this moment in Pullmoo's office, as he waited for Maria to respond to Vartook, Orook had not regretted his decision to discontinue any further study of the *naverkoo*.

"I guess I have no choice," Maria said at last.

"You must know, Maria, that before all this came up - I had never any intention of calling on your debt," Vartook said.

"I suppose I can believe that," Maria said. "Will you take me there yourself?"

"Of course, I will," Vartook said.

"Orook, you will not go with her," Pullmoo said.

"Why not?" Orook asked.

"Too many eggs in one basket - as the humans like to say," Pullmoo said.

"Do I get any say in this?" Maria asked.

"Not in this part, no," Pullmoo said. "In fact, I suggest that you return to your station now while we discuss this matter amongst ourselves, now that you have agreed to go."

"While the grown-ups talk, you mean?" Maria interrupted.

"If you like," Pullmoo said with a smile.

Maria sighed and started to stand, then stopped.

"Keeper, may I be excused?" she asked.

"Of course," Orook said.

"I suggest you come home early from work," Pullmoo said. "You will need to get up very early in the morning tomorrow. I will send a message to Zedook to let him know."

"We're doing this *tomorrow*?" Maria asked.

"Yes," Pullmoo confirmed.

Maria groaned, then stood up and walked to the door. As she put her hand on the door knob, Pullmoo said, "Maria, I think you forgot to make the appropriate departing gesture."

"Oh, right, of course," Maria said, then lifted her middle finger to Pullmoo.

"That is not one of our Pegasean gestures," Vartook said disapprovingly.

"No, it is not," Pullmoo agreed.

"Maybe it should be," Orook said.

The hostility in Orook's voice prompted Vartook to take a protective step closer to Pullmoo. Unabashed, Orook looked at Vartook and asked, "will you protect Maria with your life?"

Vartook nodded.

"Pullmoo, what does the *naverkoo* want with Maria?" Orook asked.

"I don't know," she said.

"You are lying," Orook said. "You know something - or you suspect something. I can see the shadow of it in your mind."

Before answering, Pullmoo asked Vartook and Solomane to leave her office and return to their stations. After enough time had passed that she was sure they must be too far away to hear her, she said, "Orook, I only have my suspicions, nothing more."

"Just tell me," he said.

"There is an old vocunine legend," Pullmoo began.

Orook rolled his eyes.

"Well, do you want to hear it or not?" Pullmoo asked.

"A legend?" Orook said. "Frankly, no, I do not. I thought you had actual information."

Pullmoo gave him a humorless smile.

Orook stared at her until he was convinced that this legend was the only thing she had in her mind with respect to the *naverkoo* and what it might intend to do with Maria.

"Are you sure you don't want to hear it?" she asked.

"I can see it in your mind," he said. "I do not see how it is helpful or how it explains anything at all."

"I could tell you what I think," Pullmoo offered.

"No thank you," he said.

"Go then," she said. "I have other work to do - and you need to help get Maria ready for her trek out in the mountain tomorrow."

"If she does not return home safely, I will never forgive you," Orook said as he opened the door to leave.

"Understood," Pullmoo said as she waved him away.

CHAPTER 54

After leaving Pullmoo's office, Orook went home and busied himself with gathering gear and packing provisions for Maria to take with her on her journey the next morning. When he was done with that, he began preparing a summer dinner of stewed vegetables and roasted trattle (a burrowing bird-like animal native to the valley outside the mountains surrounding Pegasea). When Maria arrived home in the early afternoon, she was delightfully surprised by the smell of the cooking food.

"You're cooking something?" she asked as she walked into the kitchen.

"Yes," Orook said.

"What's the occasion? Or is this more like a last meal for the condemned?" Maria asked.

"Please do not make jokes like that," Orook said. "The food needed to be cooked and I had the time."

"Ok, well, it smells wonderful in any case," she said.

"Go change while I finish this," he said.

Maria was more than happy to change out of her work clothes, which by now where clammy with a day's worth of sweat, dirt, grease and a variety of other substances she did not care to think about. She brushed the debris out of her hair, then showered. As she put on clean dry clothes, she realized that this had become her favorite part of the day. Changing into her sapphire blue casual clothes, or in some cases straight into her night clothes of the same color, at the end of a long day made her nearly euphoric. Although she would never admit it to him, Maria found that wearing her keeper's color made her feel safe and comforted in ways she could not describe.

The food was ready and on the table by the time Maria returned to the kitchen. She sat down across from Orook and looked down at the food in front of her. Maria could not remember the last time they sat down and ate a cooked meal together. It was such a pleasant surprise that she almost entirely forgot about the earlier events of the day. As she enjoyed the meal, she complimented Orook on his cooking. Orook did not respond to any of her questions or comments about the roasted game bird or colorful seasonal vegetables, which, in Maria's opinion, he had prepared to perfection.

"Maria, please, just finish eating," he said.

Maria put down her utensil. She was ready to be mad until she looked up and saw the look on his face.

"What's wrong?" she asked.

"What do you think is wrong?" he asked.

"Are you mad at me for -," Maria started to ask.

"No," Orook interrupted. "I am just frustrated with the entire situation."

Orook then briefly recounted the conversation he had had with Pullmoo after Maria had left their meeting earlier.

"What is the legend you saw in her mind?" she asked.

"It is nothing," he said.

"Please tell me," she said.

Orook sighed.

"Why won't you tell me?" Maria asked.

"I do not want you to hear it as some kind of truth - it is just a story," he said.

"Orook, I am being sent into a mountain full of ruekar based on the contents of my *dreams*," she said. "I think we're all past the point of logic here."

"Fair enough," he said. "The legend goes that there was once an Olronean woman, a virgin, who was lured into the mountain by the *naverkoo*. The next part of the story is a bit unclear, but in the end, the *naverkoo* somehow uses this woman to seed new ground with its own offspring. The story is thousands of years old and was never recorded - it has only been passed down orally by the vocunine. Thus, obviously, there is not much we can learn from it. Whatever might have actually happened thousands of years ago, I doubt there is much truth to be found in the current story."

"Well, I'm not a virgin," Maria said.

"Yes, I know," he said.

"In my dreams, the Prisoner says, 'come to me' and asks, 'what are you?' It doesn't seem to know what I am or what any of the human women are. I think it wants to conduct its own kind of 'experiments' on me or something," Maria speculated.

"I see," Orook said. "Maria, are you afraid of it?"

"A little," she said. "I am not sure what its study of me might involve. I don't know if it just wants a sample of my blood or if it wants to take me apart so it can reverse engineer my organs."

Orook winced.

"And there is one other thing," Maria said. "I wasn't entirely forthcoming with Pullmoo. I started having these dreams long before I arrived here. I don't know why I lied - I just didn't want her to know. I should have told her the truth. I'm sorry."

"What do you mean? When did you start having the dreams?" Orook asked.

"I don't know exactly when they started, but it was at least a year before I ended up on that space ship. It was because of one of those dreams that I ended up here - so you can understand why I don't exactly trust it," Maria said.

"What do these dreams have to do with you coming to Olrona?" Orook asked.

Maria looked down as she worked up the courage to tell Orook what happened that night she wandered onto Transport Ship Two.

"I was having one of those dreams that night," Maria told him. "The tree - the *naverkoo* - it told me to leave my room and walk outside. It put this kind of map in my head and told me to follow the map. I - I don't know what I was thinking. I know it was stupid."

"Is this the same 'tree' that told you to go to the nursery?" he asked.

"Yeah," Maria said, blushing.

"I just want to know if this thing poses any threat to you," Orook said. "I will tell you that I find it very hard, if not impossible, to believe that the *naverkoo* managed to communicate with you through space, while you were still back on Earth. However, if it did, and if it told you to get on that ship, then, as you know, it saved you from suffering through Earth's impending apocalyptic climate correction. So maybe it has some sort of concern for you - or at least, does not want you to die."

"I suppose that is one way to look at it," Maria said.

"What is another way?" Orook asked.

"Another way to look at it is that it hypnotized me in order to facilitate my capture and transport to an alien planet without my knowledge or consent - for reasons that might have nothing to do with my wellbeing," Maria said.

Orook sighed.

"It brought you to me," he said.

Maria smiled.

"Don't get me wrong," she said. "I do not think it is mean spirited - but I have no reason to think it is kind or compassionate either. What if it sees me as just another animal or plant to be dissected? I am also afraid of the trip there. It's summer and it's hot and as humid as it ever gets in these mountains. The ruekar will be everywhere."

"If the *naverkoo* does want you to come to it, and if it is as power-ful as it claims to be in your dreams, or as powerful as the vocunine seem to think it is, why could it not ensure your safe passage?" Orook asked.

"I think it could. But how do I tell it that I am on my way?" Maria asked. "I can't control when I have those dreams and sometimes I go weeks without having one."

"I see," he said.

"What do *you* know about it?" Maria asked. "You must know more than what you told Pullmoo."

"Why do you say that?" Orook asked.

"Because you always do - you always know things no one else knows," Maria said.

Orook smiled briefly, then told her everything he knew about the *naverkoo* and how he came to acquire the knowledge.

"How come you never told me any of this before?" Maria asked.

"I never had any reason to," Orook said. "Believe me, never in my wildest dreams did I ever expect you to be summoned to the thing - or that the City would send you out to it in order to rescue a vocunine."

They then sat in silence as a cloud passing in the sky overhead blanketed them in its soft grey shadow until the air in the room began to cool. Maria folded her arms and crossed her legs. Orook leaned back in his chair and watched the cloud retreat until the warm summer sun returned to the room. He then dropped his gaze down from the sky and back to Maria. She appeared to be in a state of self-hypnosis as she stared intently at the edge of the kitchen table between them.

"What does my son look like?" he asked.

Startled out of her thoughts by the sudden random question, Maria looked up at him and blinked several times.

"Your son?" she asked.

"My little one - in the nursery," Orook prompted.

"Was he there that day?" Maria asked.

"They never told you? The boy who reached his arms up to you is my son," Orook told her.

"How is that possible?" Maria asked. "I mean, what are the odds? No wonder you were charged - they must have thought it was some kind of conspiracy."

Orook nodded.

"You don't even have a picture of him?" Maria asked.

"I have pictures - but it's not the same," Orook said.

Maria then closed her eyes and tried to recall an image of the boy in her mind. She remembered the boy's bunny-like ears, his warm smile and hazel eyes. She remembered his bushy eyebrows and his angular nose, which was too big for his face, but which somehow only made him that much cuter.

"He is very cute. He looks a lot like Linoo - and a little like you too," she told him.

Orook smiled, then sighed. He wondered if Maria knew she was pregnant, and if she did, if she would ever mention this fact to him. It was probably best if she did not know, he thought. He was all too familiar with the almost certain fate of this unborn child.

"Hypothetically," Maria said, "if I got pregnant and actually carried the baby to term - and if it was born healthy and all that - do you think you would love that baby the same as you do your son?"

Orook raised an eyebrow at her.

"*Hypothetically*," Maria emphasized.

"Am I to assume that I am the father of this *hypothetical* baby?" Orook asked.

"Well, yeah, of course - who else would be?" Maria said.

"I do not know who else you might paw at in my absence," he said.

"Oh, shut up. I'm serious," Maria said.

"There is no need to take offense my dear. We are not in a relationship which demands that kind of exclusivity," Orook reminded her.

Maria sighed.

Orook searched Maria's face as he thought about how best to respond. As the awkward silence grew longer, Maria grew more and more uneasy and was quickly starting to regret having brought the subject up at all.

"Never mind," Maria said, "it was a stupid question."

"Maria, of course I would love this hypothetical baby no less than I love my son, or any other child of mine. Why would you even ask me such a question?" Orook said at last.

"Are you sure?" Maria asked softly.

"Yes, I am sure. Why do you doubt this? Do you think I would love a half-human child less? Is that it?" he asked.

Maria's face flushed as she nodded.

"Hmm, well, I love you - and you are completely human," he said.

Maria swallowed hard, then looked up and away as she tried to blink back the tears now slowly welling in her eyes.

"Although, of course, my academic and professional expectations of such a child would be pretty low," Orook added with a teasing smile.

"Of course," Maria said after a sharp intake of breath.

Orook tried in vain to catch her eyes as she quickly began gathering up their dishes from the table. She then stood up and took the dishes to the sink, where she thought she might regain her composure away from his penetrating stare. As she walked back to the table, Orook reached out and took both her hands in his. Upon feeling a new roughness to her fingers, he looked down at them.

"I can only hope the poor child might have a bit more facility with a claw wrench than his pitiful mother," he said with a frown.

Maria smiled faintly.

"Why do you trouble yourself with such silly worries?" he asked.

"They're not silly," she said with a sniffle.

"Well, no need to worry in any case," he said. "Now, would you like to do something fun?"

"Sure," Maria said.

Orook stood up from the table and led Maria into the living room. He then told her to wait there while he retrieved something from the bedroom. Moments later he came out holding, in one hand, something that almost looked like the pricing guns she used to use to tag inventory at the coffee shop where she used to work on Earth. In the other hand he held a poster-sized board about an inch thick. He hung the board on the far wall of the living room, then walked back over to Maria.

"Do you remember why we do not have guns in the city?" Orook asked.

"Because you have a treaty with the vocunine," Maria said.

"Well, yes, that was one reason - but obviously that point is now moot. Do you recall the other reason?" he asked.

"You said something about the damage they could do when bullets ricochet or explode - and the danger of bullets going through walls or shattering ceilings," Maria answered.

"Correct - and all of that is still highly relevant. As an alternative, I have designed this device," Orook told her as he handed her the strange looking gun.

"What is it?" Maria asked.

"I have not given it a specific name, but it shoots disk shaped projectiles, so let us call it a 'disk-shooter' for now," he said.

Orook then explained to Maria how the disk-shooter worked and the advantages it had over an Earth-style firearm.

"The disks are three centimeters in diameter and are razor sharp at their edges. They will easily slice through the flesh of a ruekar, or any soft material for that matter. However, if they hit anything hard and dense, like a crystal ceiling or stone wall, they will simply shatter," he told her.

"Neat," Maria said as she examined the thing in her hands.

"It uses a reciprocal spring arrangement to launch the disk," Orook continued, "So, you only have to arm it once for every six shots. Then, after that, each time you squeeze the hand grip to shoot it, this action reloads the chamber and compresses the springs. The springs inside are…"

Before he could finish, Maria assumed the shooting stance and double handed grip her father had once taught her at a local gun range near her childhood home. She pointed the weapon at the center of the foam board Orook had hung on the wall, tilted her head slightly to one side, then squeezed the grip once. Orook looked over at the board and saw that she had hit her mark at the center of the board.

"Nice shot," he said. "You do not need to hold it out so far away from you or use both hands. It is not like a pistol you might have shot back on Earth - there is no re-coil to speak of."

Maria nodded, "Yeah, I can see that. Those disks fly out a lot faster than I expected."

"They are not nearly as fast as a bullet projected from a firearm, but they are fast enough for the intended purpose," he said.

"Can I take this with me tomorrow?" Maria asked.

"Please do," Orook said.

Orook then explained, in some depth, the mechanics of how the weapon worked, how to load, maintain and store it. He also warned her several times to make sure, before she shot it, that no one was positioned behind her target. Orook explained that, unless the disk hit dense bone, or something more solid, it could potentially pass through a meter of flesh and keep going. Maria promised to be careful.

CHAPTER 55

As planned, Vartook arrived at the home of Orook and Maria just before sunrise the following morning. He immediately handed Maria a protective guardsman's uniform and instructed her to change into it. After she did so, Orook helped her get equipped for their hike out into the mountains. As Orook fussed with the belts and straps of her climbing gear and pack, Maria asked Vartook why the Pegaseans did not appear to have a helicopter or any other sort of flying machine which might take them to the Eye of Olrona.

"I just don't get it," she said. "You guys built a fucking space ship to Earth and you don't have anything that can fly over a mountain?"

"Please do not use such vulgar language in my presence Maria," Vartook said.

"We have aircraft perfectly suited for flying over mountains. The problem is that you are not going over the mountain, but rather through and into it," Orook explained.

"Ok, well, don't you have donkeys or horses or some kind of animal we could ride there?" Maria persisted.

"Maria, you've been to this place with me once before. Do you really think it would be any easier, rather than even more difficult, to ride any kind of animal to such a location?" Orook asked.

Maria thought about it, then sighed.

"Is the pack too heavy?" Orook asked as he tugged on a strap at her back.

"Well, it's not exactly a bag of marshmallows," Maria muttered.

"What are 'marshmallows?'" Vartook asked.

"They are portions of artificial sugar puffed up with air which humans on Earth consume for entertainment," Orook explained.

"They eat for entertainment?" Vartook asked, looking at Maria.

327

Maria sighed and shook her head.

"Maria, your keeper might tolerate your disrespectful behavior, but I will not," Vartook bristled.

"In that case, maybe you should take someone else out to the mother-fucking mountain," Maria said defiantly.

Vartook grit his teeth and waited for Orook to admonish his companion.

Orook sighed, then whispered in Maria's ear, "You should probably try to stay in his good graces - at least until you get back."

Maria groaned, then apologized to Vartook and made a half-hearted promise to try to behave.

"I'm just very nervous," she added.

"There is no reason to think that the *naverkoo* will bring you any harm," Vartook told her.

"But there is no reason to think it won't either," Maria countered. "And what about the ruekar?"

"I will be with you," Vartook said. "I can protect you from the ruekar."

Maria stared at him for a moment, then looked down at her side where the disk-shooter was holstered and mumbled something to herself.

"Come again?" Vartook asked.

"I was just asking myself if your presence will make much of a difference if the *naverkoo* decides to take me prisoner - or disassemble me in pursuit of mere morbid curiosity," she said.

"Don't be silly," Vartook said.

"Oh, I'm sorry, I didn't realize you were an expert on the *naverkoo*," Maria spat.

"The woman has a point," Orook said quickly before Vartook could respond.

"How do you tolerate her?" he asked Orook.

"Well, at least she has never bitten me," Orook said, then winked at the First Guardsman.

Orook's inexplicable knowledge of the time Pullmoo had, as a child, bitten his arm as he carried her back to the city, so unnerved Vartook that he remained silent until they were ready to leave.

Once Orook was satisfied that Maria was as ready as she would ever be, he walked with her, Vartook and Solomane to the stairwell leading up to the outside. Before he left, he hugged Maria goodbye and made her promise to return to him.

Maria wrapped her arms around Orook and said, "You know I'm not allowed to kiss you when other people are watching."

"That is ok," he said. "Kiss me when you get back."

"I promise," she said.

· · ·

Once Orook had gone and they were outside, Vartook instructed Maria to follow close behind him and instructed Solomane to walk behind Maria.

"It has nothing to do with rank. I want her in between us. So that if a gang of ruekar come at us from ahead or behind, we will be able to protect her," he explained to Solomane. "Also, you are far more adept than I at sensing and perceiving things behind you while walking forward."

Solomane nodded, then took his place behind Maria.

"Solomane wants you to know that he thinks you are very brave and honorable for doing this," Vartook said to Maria.

"I don't mean to be disrespectful when I say this, but I really wish you would let him speak to me directly," Maria said.

"Let him?" Vartook said. "Maria not only am I not stopping him from doing so, I do wish he would. I've told him so many times. Have you not interacted much with the vocunine inside the city lately?"

Maria shook her head, then said, "My keeper refused to host a vocunine."

"Right, of course," Vartook said, then explained the change that had come over the vocunine and their seemingly instinctual adoption of the companion rules within the PROEs. None of this came as much of a surprise Maria. For some time now, she had suspected that the human women within Pegasea were being used more to fill the void left by the vocunines than by the void left by the sparsity of Pegasean women.

"It must be frustrating for you to have to speak for him all the time," Maria said.

Vartook shrugged.

"It was at first, but not anymore. Honestly, he and I have come to have most of the same thoughts and feelings about things. So, most of the things he wants to say are also things I want to say - including the sentiment which he just expressed about you Maria," he said.

"Do you also worship the *naverkoo*?" Maria asked.

Vartook laughed, "no, of course not - and neither does Solomane. You are assuming that because they believe it to be something like a deity that they all worship the thing. This is not the case. They do all have a profound respect for the organism - as maybe they should. They do not necessarily all worship it."

"I see," Maria said.

"So, what should I call you while we are out here?" Maria asked.

"What do you mean?" Vartook asked.

"I mean, what if I suddenly need to get your attention or have some other reason to call out to you - what do I call you?" Maria explained.

Vartook thought for a moment, then asked, "You must have had guardsman, or something like them, on Earth, correct?"

Maria thought about the question. The only "guardsman" she could think of on Earth were the U.S. Coast Guards. She surprised herself when she remembered the title given to the highest-ranking member.

"Master Chief Petty Officer," she said, then laughed at Vartook's puzzled expression.

"I am not comfortable with any word in that title," he said.

"How do you feel about 'captain?'" Maria suggested.

Vartook thought for a moment, then nodded and said, "I suppose that will have to do."

"Ok, captain, let's get this over with," Maria said.

Vartook nodded, then gestured to Solomane to lead them towards the outer wall and then out onto the mountain.

• • •

Less than two hours into what would end up being a four-hour journey, both Vartook and Solomane stopped abruptly and turned in unison.

"What is it?" Maria asked.

In a hushed voice, Vartook said "do you see what appears to be a pile of rocks just up ahead of us and to the left?"

Maria nodded.

"Those are ruekar. Solomane and I know this because our second hearing allows us to see the difference in density between flesh disguised as stone and actual stone. Otherwise, their camouflage is perfect. This is how they hunt. They camouflage themselves, then lay in wait," he explained.

Maria's body went rigid and cold with fear.

"Take off your pack, draw out that weapon your keeper gave you and craw into that space in the stone behind you. Go in as far in as you can manage," Vartook instructed.

Maria found herself unable to move. She stared at the assemblage of stones, determined to see something that would betray their true identity. She could find none. The predators had even varied their apparent size, shape and color so as to not appear suspiciously uniform. At this distance, Maria could not see the subtle slow pulse of their breathing or the nearly imperceptible tensing of their muscles.

Solomane stepped forward and pushed his cold wet nose into the palm of her hand. Maria looked down into Solomane's iridescent blue eyes, which, even through his protective eye shields, where dazzlingly beautiful.

"Go now," he whispered.

Maria quickly slipped off her pack. She then began to squeeze her lean frame side-ways into the crevasse in the mountain. The stone was rough and wet and scratched at her palms. Once she was as far in as she could go, she stopped and leaned her full weight back onto the stone. As she settled her feet into a sustainable position on the uneven ground, she gasped softly as a disgruntled lichen weasel scurried over her feet. She then pulled her disk-shooter out of her waistband and pointed it out towards the direction from which she had entered the stone refuge.

Once Vartook was satisfied that Maria was as safe as she could be under the circumstances, he signaled to Solomane. Solomane trotted forward as if completely unaware of the ruekar, then stopped suddenly and made a sound like a bark. Vartook looked up sharply, giving the false impression that the sound had caught him unaware. He and Solomane had practiced this play many times now.

At first, the stone pile did not move. Vartook took a step closer and squinted out at it, as if struggling to see clearly. Suddenly the stones appeared to melt over the ground, then morph into what looked like a low flying swarm of insects, then disappeared again. Vartook and Solomane braced themselves. Like a cloud of smoke moving in a gust of wind, the ruekar moved in unison over the ground, then leapt up into the air before descended upon their prey in a wave. Maria could not see what was happening. She strained to hear what was going on but could only hear the sickening sound of blades on bone and the squealing hiss of the ruekar.

As the majority of the ruekar troop attacked Vartook, a minority took on Solomane. The division of the troop worked to the guardsman's advantage as the collective mind of the ruekar was split in two directions. This strategy did not work as well with larger groups of ruekar but could be successful enough when the troop was relatively small. The Pegasean guardsmen had learned from experience that once a quarter, or at most a third, of any one gang was dead or severely wounded, the rest would retreat, unwilling to risk further loss.

Maria struggled to keep breathing as the seconds dragged on.

"Maria, look up now!" Vartook shouted to her.

Maria looked up, and to her horror, she saw two stone colored masses creeping their way down towards her from above. The creatures' beady eyes where an impossible color which Maria could only think of as yellowish purple. Maria panicked as she struggled to raise her arm up and point her disk shooter at the rapidly descending intruders. By the time she finally managed to shoot and kill one of them, the other one was nearly upon her. Just as the animal leaped off the stone towards Maria's head, Vartook drew a small blade from his belt and threw it down the narrow space in the stones. Blood rained down on Maria as the blade sliced through the ruekar before lodging into the stone at the end of the narrow cavern. The blade was so sharp that Maria never felt the edge of it graze the top of her head as it passed.

At last, the ruekar began to retreat. Solomane barked and hooted in triumph before running back to Vartook. Vartook smiled and congratulated his companion on a job well done. Maria was still in a shallow state of shock when Vartook and Solomane came to retrieve her. Covered in blood, she stood with her eyes clenched shut and her whole-body trembling, unaware that the fight was over.

"Maria, it is ok to come out now. They are gone," Vartook said as he offered his hand to help her climb back out into the open.

Cautiously, Maria opened her eyes and turned her head. She then passed her disc shooter to her other hand before she began inching her way along the stone. When she was close enough to reach, she took Vartook's offered hand.

"Thank you," she said as she took a final step out into the open.

"You are bleeding," Vartook said, "You must have moved your head after I threw that blade."

"Or you aimed a bit too low. Maybe you need more practice," Maria said as she used her fingers to follow the trail of warm blood slowly rolling down her cheek.

Vartook crossed his arms and shook his head as he looked down at her with clear displeasure.

"Oh, come on," Maria said. "I was kidding."

"Kidding?" Vartook asked. "I do not understand your humor. How is insulting me funny?"

"No, no, you don't get it," Maria said. "It is funny because that was a truly impossible shot. It was remarkable. No human could have done that - I don't even think any other Pegasean could have done that. I mean, how did you get it to curve mid-course like that? I think you must be like some kind of god, I swear. That's why my saying you need more practice is funny - because it's absurd."

This explanation only added a layer of puzzlement to Vartook's disgruntled expression.

"You don't have a human companion, do you?" Maria asked.

"No, I do not," Vartook said.

"My keeper would get it," Maria said with a sigh.

"Your keeper is talented when it comes to understanding foreign communications and cultures, as is my Pullmoo and several others in the City. Unfortunately, we are not all equally talented in this area," Vartook told her.

"Please excuse my interruption - but maybe I can help," Solomane offered.

Vartook gestured for Solomane to proceed.

"I think she thinks very highly of you indeed but stated her compliment in the form of an insult - partly as a joke - but also to avoid any suggestion of any deeper fondness for you. Vocunine do this sort of thing too - when a female vocunine has a mate, but also has a lot of admiration for another male, she expresses it in a weird way - a disguised way - so that her mate will not get jealous or feel betrayed," Solomane explained.

Maria blushed.

Vartook's expression softened as Maria's continued silence confirmed the truth of Solomane's explanation.

"Alright Maria," he said, "I will forgive your flattering insult. But please, next time you wish to compliment me, do so in the ordinary way. I know your keeper well - since he was just a boy. I can assure you that he will not get jealous or feel betrayed if you merely compliment my professional skill."

Maria nodded.

Vartook then picked up Maria's pack and held it up for her as she put her arms in through the straps.

"Come on now, let's get going," he said.

"Is there any way I can wash this blood off me?" Maria asked.

"You don't want to do that," Vartook said. "Blood spilled from a ruekar in the heat of a conflict emits a certain smell due to the hormones and other chemicals that run hot in its blood while it is engaged in a fight. This smell deters other ruekar. The effect will only last a few hours, but by then we should be close to our destination."

Maria sighed, then pushed a few sticky clumps of hair off her face before she commenced walking.

"You are doing well," Vartook said encouragingly, "I do not think that most, if any, of the human women I've met could make this journey - especially not under these conditions."

Maria bit her tongue, then mumbled a "thank you."

CHAPTER 56

After several hours of hiking and climbing, with only a few short breaks along the way, they reached the mouth of the cave where, less than six months earlier, Maria had stood watch for Orook. To Maria, the cave looked darker and narrower now than it was then. As she stood staring down into this tunnel to the *naverkoo*, she wondered if the apparent change was real or only a projection of her present anxiety. As she thought, her head began to ache and throb. Maria rubbed vigorously at her temples as the *naverkoo* entered her mind. It was giving her instructions, warnings, and demands in a flood of images she could only just barely follow.

"Maria, are you ok?" Vartook asked.

Maria had had enough of being told what to do. She took a deep breath and summoned the full force of her will.

"Get out of my head!" she shouted.

Vartook took a step back.

"It's the *naverkoo*," Solomane said quietly to his keeper. "It's telling her what to do."

Vartook watched and waited attentively as Maria's psychological struggle with the Prisoner unfolded before them. She shut her eyes and knelt down on the ground. Her heart raced and her head throbbed as she mentally pushed back at the *naverkoo*. Vartook could not tell who was winning or losing the fight.

"What is happening?" he asked Solomane.

"I don't know," Solomane said as he turned his gaze from Maria to the mouth of the cave.

After several long minutes, Maria suddenly opened her eyes and stood up. She then swung her pack around in front of her and rummaged around inside until she found the tiny object inside a small pocket lined with a fine steel mesh.

"What is that in your hand Maria?" Vartook asked.

Wordlessly, Maria held out her closed hand to him.

"Take this," she said.

"What is it?" Vartook asked.

Maria did not answer.

Vartook started to feel strange just then, as if an invisible hand was softly stroking his brain. He held out his hand.

In one quick movement, Maria turned her hand and used her thumb to slide the point of the dart out and into Vartook's palm.

"I'm so sorry Captain," she said.

"Maria, what have you done?" Vartook asked, looking dumbly down at his palm.

A moment later, Vartook collapsed onto the hard ground.

Solomane yelped in surprise and horror, then growled menacingly at Maria.

"Wait here," Maria told him.

"What did you do?! Why did you do it?!" Solomane growled.

"Because I don't want him to get trapped in there with me," Maria said. "I can't trust him not to get all chivalrous and refuse to abandon me."

Solomane whined and whimpered as he paced around the man lying motionless at his feet.

"I will send Lunakane out here to you," Maria continued.

Solomane was shaking his head now. He held a miserable look on his face as he alternately ranted and growled at Maria.

"Solomane! Listen to me!" Maria said. "Your girlfriend is going to be blamed for anything that happens to me in there. What do you think my keeper will do to her if I don't come back alive?"

Solomane knew that he needed to listen to what Maria was saying, but he was too angry and confused to concentrate.

Maria walked up to Solomane and put her arms around the distressed vocunine.

"It will be alright Solomane," Maria whispered. "Vartook will be fine. It was just a tranquilizing dart, ok? He will wake up in less than an hour with a major headache, but he will be fine. Now listen to me carefully, will you?"

Solomane sighed deeply with relief.

"You must take Lunakane to the City. When you get there, take her to the home of the Governess of District Two. Her name is Linoo. Will you do this for me?" Maria asked.

Solomane nodded.

"Good," Maria said as she straightened and put her hands on her hips.

Before she could lose her nerve, Maria sprinted into the cave. She descended into the mountain as fast as she could as she forced herself not to think or reconsider her decision. When it became too dark to see, she stopped and pulled out the Pegasean equivalent of a flash-light, which was shaped like a donut. She slipped the portable light onto her wrist and turned it on.

What Maria saw when she reached the heart of the mountain took her breath away. This was no tree. The main body of the *naverkoo* was vaguely shaped like the trunk of a massive tree, but that was where any meaningful comparison ended. From inside the bottom of the cave, Maria could see the massive "branches" of the *naverkoo* extending into every direction, up through the massive stones and crystal boulders of the mountain, and down into the floor beneath her. Thousands of vine-like tendrils hung down lazily from the ceiling and swayed slowly as if caught in a breeze from another dimension. Some of the tendrils looked more like jelly-fish tentacles than vines, while others looked more like Spanish moss and still others looked like nothing organic she had ever seen before. Just as Maria reached out to touch one of them, the cave began to glow softly with bioluminescent blue light.

"Lunakane?" Maria called out as she gently parted the tendrils hanging in front of her.

Maria continued to call out for the vocunine princess as she cautiously ventured farther and farther towards the main body of the *naverkoo*. She tried to ignore the *naverkoo's* tendrils poking and prodding at her as she passed through them.

"Stop that!" Maria said in a hushed voice as she batted away a particularly relentless tendril that would not stop circling her left ear.

After one of the tendrils crawled up her leg, Maria decided she had had enough.

"I swear to God, I will set you on fire if you don't stop it now!" she shouted up at the *naverkoo*.

The whole cave began to rumble and shake.

"Yeah, whatever," Maria said. "Fuck off already! Show me where the princess is so that I can get her out of here. Then we'll talk. That was the deal."

The cave stopped rumbling and the tendrils retreated along a path leading up to the base of *naverkoo's* "trunk." Maria followed the path until she saw an animal she suspected must be Lunakane, curled up on the ground and apparently sleeping or possibly unconscious. Maria jogged over to her, knelt down, and gently pushed at her shoulders.

In one fluid movement, Lunakane opened her eyes, lifted her head and turned to look at Maria.

"Maria?" she asked in a sweet and melodious voice that warmed Maria's heart.

"Yes, it's me. How did you know my name?" Maria asked.

"The Prisoner told me you would come," she said.

"Are you Lunakane?" Maria asked.

"Yes, but please call me 'Luna,'" she said as she gracefully got to her feet.

Maria marveled at how this vocunine moved more like a jungle cat than a large dog. Staring at Luna, Maria recalled the time she had first met Linoo and experienced an odd sense of deja vu. Like Linoo, Luna was strikingly beautiful. Her long narrow snout sloped seamlessly from her perfectly symmetrical eyes and brow. Her fur shimmed as she shook herself awake.

"Solomane is waiting for you out at the surface," Maria told her.

Luna smiled, and her eyes sparkled at the thought of her fiancé.

"Go," Maria instructed.

Luna nodded, then began walking towards the exit out of the cave.

"You know where you have to go, right?" Maria asked.

Luna turned back to look at Maria, then nodded.

"I do," she said. "And I thank you Maria, with all my heart and soul."

"Yeah, ok, whatever," Maria muttered as Luna bonded for the exit and out of site.

• • •

As soon as Lunakane was out at the surface at the other end of the cave, she wasted no time telling Solomane that they all needed to get moving.

"We can't leave without Maria," Solomane said.

"We can, and we must," Luna said as she rolled Vartook over and proceeded to work her way underneath him so that she could carry him on her back.

"I will do that!" Solomane said.

"Do it then - quickly!" Luna insisted.

Solomane stood on his back legs as he lifted Vartook, then swung the man onto his back. He descended back down on all fours, then began briskly walking and leaping away from the cave.

As soon as the two vocunine and the First Guardsman were a safe distance away, the mountain began to shake and shutter. Solomane stopped and looked back only to see that the cave down into the heart of the mountain had collapsed in on itself. Solomane howled miserably.

"There is nothing you could have done my love," Lunakane said.

"That won't matter," Solomane said. "You don't know her keeper. He hates us already - and now we've just killed his companion."

"She's alive Solomane, trust me," Luna said.

"Why did you defy me Luna?" Solomane asked. "Why did you not come to the City when I demanded it?"

"I'm so sorry my king," Luna said and bowed her head. "But you know it is fatal to disobey the Prisoner."

"But if you had come to the city, as I asked, you would have been safe," he said.

Luna shook her head.

"The Prisoner built the City into the stone. What the Prisoner builds, it can break," Luna persisted.

Solomane pressed his face into Luna's neck and growled softly with loving frustration.

"And how are we going to explain this to the Pegaseans?" he asked. "How am I going to explain this to my keeper? And to Maria's keeper?"

"You can tell them that it was the will of the Prisoner," she said.

"That doesn't mean anything to their kind," Solomane said.

"It is the truth!" Luna said.

"My love, promise me that this is not the thing you will say to the city people. Do not talk about the will of the Prisoner to them. They will not like it," Solomane said.

Luna whined.

"Promise me Luna," Solomane insisted. "Promise me you will not say those words to them."

"Ok, my love, I promise," she said.

CHAPTER 57

M aria sighed as she watched the *naverkoo's* tendrils twist and curl around inside the cave that was the only exit out of the heart of the mountain. She struggled to keep her footing as the falling stones and boulders collapsed the narrow passage, rocking the ground beneath her as they tumbled and rolled. Desperate to keep from falling, she grasped several of the *naverkoo's* tendrils and held on to keep her balance. The tendrils eagerly assisted her by coiling around her arms and lifting her up off the ground. Others gathered and weaved together behind her until Maria found herself seated in a living hammock and comfortably cradled by the *naverkoo*. After the mountain settled, all was still and quiet. Maria waited for the *naverkoo* to speak into her mind. When it did, the pain in her head was almost unbearable.

"Isn't there any other way you can talk to me?" Maria asked. "This is giving me a massive headache."

The naverkoo left her mind and Maria's headache abated within seconds.

Slowly and methodically, two tendrils looped around Maria's wrist and arm, then slithered underneath and around her armband. The armband suddenly erupted in chaotic sound, then began emitting a series of clicks, thuds and beeps, which then morphed into something sounding vaguely like broken syllables. Maria waited patiently as the naverkoo appeared to be working something out with the speaker in the armband. After about a half hour, the naverkoo was able to use the speaker of her armband to voice its words to her.

"You brought company," was the first thing it said.

"Yes, well, I couldn't exactly leave my fetus at home, now could I?" Maria said.

"This is unfortunate," said the *naverkoo*.

"Why?" Maria asked.

"Because it will not survive," it said.

Maria sighed.

"I can fix you," said the *naverkoo*.

"There is nothing wrong with me," Maria said.

"I can change you," it said.

"I don't want to change," Maria responded.

"I will change you so that your next baby will live," it said.

Maria was silent.

"I need your help," said the *naverkoo*.

"For what?" Maria asked.

"I need you to take my baby to the island," it said.

"What baby? What island?" Maria asked.

In response, the *naverkoo* dropped something into Maria's lap.

At first, Maria only looked at it. It was about the size of a golf ball, dark green and round. To Maria, it looked like a sea urchin with wilted spines or like a large burdock pod.

"What is that?" Maria asked.

"My baby - no, not my baby - my seed, my egg, my pollen, my larvae," the *naverkoo* said, seemingly at a loss for exactly the right word.

"May I touch it?" Maria asked.

"Please," said the *naverkoo*.

Tentatively, Maria brushed the urchin's "spines" with the tips of her fingers. As she did so, the wilted spines turned into tentacles which wrapped and curled around Maria's fingers. The creature pulled itself up onto Maria's hand, then nestled into her palm like a heat seeking reptile. Maria lifted her hand up to her face and looked at it more closely. Scattered amongst the tentacles, she saw little nob like structures that changed colors in the swaying light above them.

"What are those little round things?" Maria asked.

"Eyes," said the *naverkoo*.

"It can see me?" Maria asked.

"Yes - hear you too, feel you," the *naverkoo* answered.

"It needs another. It needs its other half - on the island," it explained.

"Ok...," Maria said.

"You must take it to the island *naverkoo*," it said.

"And how do you propose I do that?" Maria asked. "I can't even walk around this mountain without help. The ground is always shifting and moving."

"The mountain moves because I make it move," said the *naverkoo*.

"What about the ruekar? And whatever else is out there?" Maria asked.

"You will find a way - and I will change you," said the *naverkoo*.

"Change me? How? In what way?" Maria asked.

"I will adapt you," it said.

"Adapt me how?" Maria asked.

"Too complicated. I cannot say it all with your words," the *naverkoo* told her.

"Ok, will I look different? Feel different? Will you change who I am? I don't want you to change who I am," Maria said.

"Not change your soul, change your body - change your cells. Feel different, yes - feel a little stronger, faster, tougher. Look different, maybe, probably not. Have babies with the deaf ones, yes," it said.

"But why me?" Maria asked with a sigh.

"I like you," said the *naverkoo*.

"Lucky me," mumbled Maria.

"You accept? You agree?" asked the *naverkoo*.

"Do I have a choice?" Maria asked.

"Yes," it said.

"Can you save my baby? The one growing in me now?" Maria asked.

"No. I am sorry," it said. "Too late for that one - next one can live, if I change you."

"I don't know," Maria said.

"You are afraid," said the *naverkoo*.

"Yes," said Maria.

"Take your time," said the *naverkoo*.

As Maria considered, she gently played with the baby *naverkoo* in her hands. She noticed that it could change color and make small sounds. She smiled and giggled as it crawled and rolled its way up her arm, around her neck and under her hair.

"Your baby is cute - in a weird, creepy sort of way," Maria said.

"It is looking for a warm place to sleep," the *naverkoo* said.

Maria reached behind her neck and gently coaxed the creature back into her hand. She then tucked it inside her undershirt and between her breasts.

"How is that?" she asked the baby *naverkoo.*

The baby vibrated and chattered.

"Does that mean its happy?" Maria asked.

"Yes," said the *naverkoo.*

"Ok, I'll do it," Maria said. "Or at least I'll try. But you have to let me go back to the city before I venture out to this island - wherever it is."

"I will put a map in your head, if you let me," said the *naverkoo.*

"Ok, but I still have to go back," Maria said. "I promised my keeper."

"I will let you go back, but only for three days - then you must leave," the *naverkoo* said.

The *naverkoo* then released a gentle odorless gas in the air around Maria. Within minutes, Maria slipped into darkness as the *naverkoo* rocked her to sleep.

• • •

Just as Maria was losing consciousness, Vartook was regaining his. As soon as Solomane felt him stirring, he came to a slow stop and gently slid Vartook off his back. Vartook put his hand to his head as he struggled to sit up, then stand up. He leaned on Solomane as the world around him came haltingly back into focus.

"What happened?" he asked.

"Maria used a dart on you," Solomane told him.

"Yes, I know that - but how did she do it?" Vartook asked.

"She stabbed it into your hand," Solomane said.

Vartook groaned, frustrated with Solomane for not understanding his question.

"How was she able to do it?" Vartook asked. "I knew she had the dart in her hand. I was not going to let her use it. What *happened?*"

Solomane did not answer.

"Solomane! Answer me!" Vartook commanded.

"You will not like my answer," said his companion.

"Let me guess - it was the will of the Prisoner," Vartook said bitterly.

Solomane's ears fell and he averted his eyes.

"Ok, let me ask another way," Vartook said gently. "How does the Prisoner exert its will onto others? What did it do to me?"

"I do not have the word for it," Solomane said.

"Describe it," Vartook said.

"It pet you inside the head, on the mind, it…," Solomane said, struggling to describe what Maria could have told him was called "hypnosis."

"And you just stood there and let it do this to me?" Vartook asked.

"No, no, never," Solomane said. "It did the same to me."

"I see," Vartook said. "But then why did the *naverkoo* not simply knock me out itself? Why did it need Maria's help?"

"You are strong, and you are of the kind that cannot hear it. What it did to you is small. It only made your mind fuzzy for a few seconds - that is all it could do to you," Solomane explained.

"How much control does it have over Maria?" Vartook asked.

Solomane looked at Luna.

"Only when - and only how she allows it," Luna said. "That is why it needed help to get her here."

Vartook sighed.

"You would prefer that it could control her?" Solomane asked.

"Solomane, if the *naverkoo* was not controlling her in any way, then that means that she acted of her own free will when she stuck me with that dart," Vartook said.

"She did it to protect you," Solomane said.

"That does not excuse it!" Vartook said angrily. "She had no right to make such a decision. She has stepped so far out of line that if she ever comes out of that mountain and returns to the City, she will most likely be charged as one acting of her own free will. Can you guess what the punishment might be for rendering the First Guardsman unconscious with a blow dart? I can tell you for certain that it will be a lot worse than remedial PROEs training."

"I do not understand your laws," Solomane said. "Among vocunine, she would be praised and honored for her bravery and sacrifice."

345

"That is because you think that if her intentions are noble, then her actions must be noble as well. This is a foolish way to think, Solomane," Vartook said.

"What will we do now?" Solomane asked.

Vartook sighed, then looked over at Lunakane.

"What is your story?" Vartook asked. "What role did you play in this betrayal?"

Lunakane shook her head.

"Tell me!" he commanded.

"I only did what the Prisoner told me to do," Lunakane whined.

"And why would you choose to obey the *naverkoo* even at the risk of your own life? - and in defiance of your king?" Vartook challenged.

"No one defies the Prisoner. The Prisoner is keeper to us all -," Luna started to explain.

"Just stop," Vartook said. He then leaned back against the mountain and put one hand to his forehead. His head was still swimming and pounding. He pulled a canteen from his belt and drank water until his head started to clear.

"What are the chances that Maria is still alive?" he asked, looking at Lunakane.

"I believe she is alive," said the vocunine. "The Prisoner does not want to harm her."

"Then why did it collapse the cave?" Vartook asked.

"For no interruptions, no intruders, no ruekar," Luna said.

Vartook stared at Luna, thinking.

"When will it release her?" Vartook asked.

"I do not know this," Luna said. "Maybe the Prisoner does not know this either."

"Are you angry with her?" Solomane asked.

"I am angry with all of you, and with her in particular," Vartook said.

Solomane hung his head.

"You must forgive Maria," Solomane said. "She did not want you to get trapped in there with her - she said you would not save yourself."

"Oh, my dear friend, if only my forgiveness was all she needed," Vartook said.

CHAPTER 58

Once they were back in the city, Vartook decided to follow the instruction Maria had given Solomane and took Luna straight to Linoo's house in the Circle of Mothers. Upon opening the door, Linoo smiled brightly at Vartook as she made the first gesture of respect.

"What can I do for the city's First Guardsman?" she asked.

"I need you to host a vocunine," he said.

Linoo's expression changed instantly.

"I already told Pullmoo that I refuse to host one of those things," Linoo said.

"Linoo, please, I could get an order from the Center Council, but that will take days and I dare not underestimate Orook's ability to penetrate even the most fortified places within this city," Vartook said.

"What does this have to do with Orook?" Linoo asked.

Vartook explained, as briefly as he could, what had happened to Maria and the role Lunakane had played in the whole ordeal.

"And you think that being in my presence will somehow spare this vocunine from Orook's wrath?" Linoo asked.

Vartook nodded.

"Fine," Linoo said curtly. "But do not expect me to shield her with my life. If Orook comes here looking for her, the most I will do is tell him to go away."

"That is fair," Vartook said, then gestured to Lunakane to step out from behind Solomane.

When Linoo saw Luna for the first time, she blinked several times as if trying to rid her eyes of a hallucination. Linoo had never seen a vocunine like Luna, who looked as if she could be the very manifestation of Linoo herself in vocunine form. When the vocunine spoke, her voice hit Linoo's ears like the song of a long-forgotten lullaby.

"Will you be my keeper?" Luna asked.

"Alright," Linoo said in almost a whisper.

Once Luna was inside, Linoo closed the door without another word to Vartook.

"That was strange," Vartook said to Solomane. "Linoo never forgets her manners."

"It was love at first site," Solomane said, his tail gently swishing happily as he spoke.

"Well, I suppose you would know," Vartook said with a smile as he playfully tousled the fur between Solomane's ears.

• • •

"I just want to make sure I heard you correctly," Orook said, barely able to contain his rage. "My human companion darted *you*, the most highly skilled and esteemed member of our City Guard. She then went down into the mountain alone. She told Lunakane to leave the cave. Lunakane leaves the cave as instructed. You then all decided to leave Maria there as the *naverkoo* collapsed the mountain on top of her."

"Not the entire cave," Vartook said. "Shortly after I returned, I asked Etmook to send out a flying remote receiver to see if we could pick up a signal from her armband. We did. Her armband is still reading a pulse. So, we believe she is still alive."

"Get out of my house," Orook said through gritted teeth.

"Orook…," Vartook said.

Orook closed his eyes.

"Maria did what she wanted to do," Vartook said gently. "I would be at her side even now if she had only followed my lead as she was instructed."

"I know," Orook said. "However, that does not change the fact that she never would have been out there in the first place if you had not asked her to go."

"For that I can only offer you my most sincere apology," Vartook said.

"Please Vartook, just go," Orook said.

Once Vartook was gone, Orook collapsed onto the sofa and buried his face in his hands.

• • •

It was three days before Orook went looking for Lunakane. When he came to Linoo's door, the governess opened it, but did not invite him inside.

"I will not let you harm Luna," she said.

"I am not here to harm Luna," Orook said. "I only came here to ask you why you changed your mind and decided to host a vocunine - and not just any vocunine, but the one vocunine who played an instrumental role in the sacrificing of my companion to the *naverkoo*."

Linoo did not answer.

"Are you still looking for ways to hurt me? Is that it?" Orook asked.

Linoo's face went slack with surprise, then tensed with anger.

"Maybe you should come inside," she said.

Orook stepped inside and scanned the room for the vocunine.

"You like to talk about how much I hurt you, but we have never had the pleasure of discussing all the ways you hurt me," Linoo said bitterly.

"How have I hurt you, Linoo? Tell me," Orook said as he sat down on the sofa in her living room.

Linoo closed her eyes and struggled to regain her composure. Sensing her distress, Luna glided out from behind the sofa and over to her keeper. She circled Linoo's legs and gently brushed against her like an impossibly large house cat greeting its master.

"She is beautiful," Orook said.

Linoo opened her eyes and stared at Orook.

"Do you remember what you did to me the night our first son was born?" Linoo asked at last.

When Orook failed to answer, Linoo answered for him.

"You hacked into the Body Biology Center security system, manipulated the staff, and did other things I am sure no one even knows about - all in order to put into motion a brilliantly orchestrated series of events which culminated in me being left alone in my maternity room with our newborn son - *for six hours,*" Linoo said.

"I remember," Orook said.

"Why did you do that, Orook? *Why?*" Linoo asked.

"I did that for you Linoo," he said. "You told me many times about how you hate the way the body biologists take your babies away without even letting you hold them."

"And you thought that if I held my baby, smelled him, nursed him, looked into his face, for six whole uninterrupted hours, that this would make it *easier* to let him go?" Linoo asked.

"Linoo, I…," Orook began.

"It tore my soul in half!" Linoo shouted. "I cried until I couldn't breathe! They should have ripped my eyes from my head, or my lungs from by chest - either of these would have been less cruel than taking that boy from my arms after I had held him for so long."

"Why have you never told me any of this before?" Orook asked.

"Because I loved you," Linoo said as tears began streaming down her cheeks. "I did not want to spread my pain onto you."

"I am so sorry," he said.

"Are you?" Linoo asked.

"Of course, I am," Orook said.

"Then why are you still lying to yourself? Why do you still let yourself think that you did it for me?" Linoo asked, spitting the words at him.

"Linoo, who else would I have done it for?" Orook asked.

"For yourself, Orook, for you - because you wanted me to grow so attached to that baby that I would be willing to do anything not to give him up. You imagined that I would come to you and beg you to leave the city with me and our baby. You always joked about it - about running away together and building me a house in the mountains. Only it wasn't entirely a joke for you, was it?" Linoo said.

"That was never anything more than a young man's idle fantasy. You know that Linoo." Orook said.

Linoo shook her head as she said, "I guess it doesn't really matter why you did it - because I could have forgiven you for that part. But then 25 years later, after I finally get to hold my boy again, you get him killed."

"What are you saying Linoo?" Orook asked.

"I blamed you for his death," Linoo told him. "On most days, I know that that is not fair. On other days, I still wonder - what if you

350

had let that vocunine mother live? What if you had simply knocked her out and walked away? I know it isn't fair. I know that you were just following the established protocol at the time."

"Do you not know how many times I have asked myself those same questions?" Orook said.

"I know, I know," Linoo said. "The difference is that I also blamed you for the way I loved him in the first place - and then for taking him away from me *again*. I didn't just fall out of love with you Orook, I *hated* you."

"Then why did you agree to partner with me a second time?" Orook asked. "If you hated me, you could have refused."

"Pullmoo told me that if I ever wanted to heal, I needed to forgive you," Linoo said. "She was right of course - so I forgave you, and I healed - as much as I possibly could anyway."

"I wish you had told me all this years ago," Orook said quietly.

"Why?" Linoo asked.

"Linoo, do you know what it was like for me to lose both my son and your love on the very same day?" he asked.

"I did not tell you that my feelings for you had changed until months later," Linoo said.

"I knew the moment it happened," Orook said.

"I should have known you would," Linoo said. "You always do - know things."

"Pullmoo says I do not take loss well," Orook said. "But I think I faired pretty well for a man who lost everything most dear to him within the span of an hour."

Linoo wiped her eyes, then looked down at Lunakane.

"I'm sorry," she said. "I did not choose for my feelings for you to change."

"And I truly am sorry for what I did the night our first son was born," he said. "Maybe you are right, and I did have an ulterior motivation, one which eluded my conscious awareness at the time. Maybe I was hoping you would grow so attached to him that you would ask me to help you take our baby and leave the city. I will admit that this sounds like something I might have done back then."

"Just like your mother," Linoo said with a weary smile.

Orook winced.

"Oh, stop that," Linoo said. "You think you take after your father because he was the First Engineer before you, but you only followed in his professional footsteps. You have your mother's soul."

"Now you are just insulting me for no reason," Orook said with a crooked smile.

"Go talk to her, Orook," Linoo said. "It will help."

"I do not need help. I need Maria," he said.

"Maria will be back," Linoo told him.

"How do you know?" Orook asked.

"Luna told me," she said.

"I can see that she is good for you Linoo," Orook said.

Linoo nodded.

"Whose idea was it to bring Luna to you?" he asked.

Linoo smiled, then said, "Would you believe it was Maria's?"

Orook nodded. He then looked so miserably sad and alone that Linoo's heart ached for him. She walked over to the sofa and sat down next to him.

"Would you like to stay here with me until she comes back? I can use one of my - what are they called?" she asked.

"Conciliatory Purpose Permits," Orook said, then laughed.

"What is so funny?" Linoo asked.

"If Maria comes back and catches me here with you, I will be the one who needs somewhere to hide," he said.

CHAPTER 59

Deep under the Eye of Olrona, the *naverkoo* withdrew the numerous slim tentacles it had inserted at various points all over Maria's body, then meticulously repaired the small puncture wounds these had left behind. It then bathed her in a steady stream of clear cool water it gathered from the mountain peak and directed down into the heart of the mountain. By the time Maria regained consciousness the autumn season had begun its long descent onto the mountains. She awoke to find herself cold, wet, and wrapped in organic fabric that looked and felt as if was made of matted moss and lichen.

"How long was I out?" Maria asked as she blinked in the dim light.

"One and one-half lunar cycles," said the *naverkoo*, speaking through her armband.

"Oh my god, seriously?" she said.

"Yes," said the Prisoner.

"I have to get back. Where are my clothes?" Maria asked.

"Too much blood, had to go," said the *naverkoo*.

"Ok, what about my shoes?" she asked.

"No shoes. I need to feel your feet," it told her.

"You need to feel my feet?" Maria repeated.

"Yes. I will make the mountain move for you. I need to feel your feet - where you step," it said.

"Ok, put me down," Maria said.

The *naverkoo* slowly lowered Maria down to the floor of the cave. Maria found her backpack amongst the rubble and swung it onto her back. She then looked up at the center mass of the Prisoner and said, "Where is the little guy? Your baby?"

In response, the Prisoner descended a single tendril down in front of Maria. She held out her hand and the *naverkoo* placed its beloved offspring into her palm. Maria smiled at it, then tucked it under her hair at the base of her neck. The little creature wrapped its tentacles around and into her hair until it was secure in its place. The *naverkoo* then began to move the boulders, stone and soil at the far end of the cave. It opened a narrow path up and out of the mountain. Maria followed the path until at last she reached open air. She squinted her eyes at the dawning sun as she emerged from the Eye of Olrona, newly formed and feeling invigorated. As her eyes adjusted to the light, she began to notice that her vision seemed sharper, her hearing more accurate.

"Did you make my eyes sharper?" Maria asked, not entirely sure if the *naverkoo* could still hear her.

"Yes," she heard the *naverkoo* say.

"Hey! This is great!" Maria said. "Now you're like a little voice in my head instead of an imposed thought that gives me a headache."

Good, said the *naverkoo*.

"Will I still be able to talk to you once I'm back in the city?" Maria asked.

"Only in your dreams," said the *naverkoo*.

"Why is that?" Maria asked.

The *naverkoo* gave no answer.

As Maria walked, the *naverkoo* leveled and softened the ground beneath her feet.

"Thank you for helping me get back," Maria said, but the *naverkoo* did not respond.

"I guess you're gone," she said.

In response, the *naverkoo* set the plush green path before her abloom in tiny white flowers.

• • •

Each morning Orook awoke without Maria felt cold and ominous. Every morning and every evening he checked the monitor on his wall for new data from Maria's armband. Etmook had programed a flying remote signal relay to take off every three hours. It would fly out to

Maria's last known location, circle around a five-kilometer radius from that point, then return to recharge and download any data it picked up from any signal within range. He had done this primarily to keep Orook from going out to the Eye of Olrona himself to try to find his companion. Unbeknownst to either of them, Pullmoo had already personally made certain that Orook no longer had the security clearance required to step outside the outer city wall.

Orook knew, from data collected by the remote relay, that Maria was still alive. Much to his lament, that was pretty much all he could know. Every morning and every evening he feared not that he would find data showing that her pulse had abruptly stopped, as this might only indicate that her armband had stopped working or was no longer on her arm. What he feared most was finding that, over the previous night or day, her heart rate had slowed gradually to a stop. This would only mean one thing; that she had died. On the morning of the fifth day following the sixth full week of her absence, Orook expected to see the same frustrating data indicating a slow, steady, unremarkable heart rate. When instead he saw something different, his heart leapt. At approximately four hours into the new day, Maria's heart rate had started to climb steadily until it leveled off at a normal resting rate of 65. An hour later, it had climbed again, then maintained between 90 and 120 for the next two hours before the remote relay had flown out of range. Orook immediately called Vartook and told him about the data.

"Yes, Orook, we know," Vartook said. "We sent out a surveillance drone about an hour ago."

"And?" Orook said.

"Well, she appears to be walking back to the city," Vartook said.

"How is that possible?" Orook asked.

"The Prisoner works in mysterious ways," Vartook said dryly.

Orook groaned.

"Lighten up Orook, your companion appears well and in good spirits. However, considering that there is a charge of murder pending against her, I will not send any of my guardsmen out there to meet her. Either she makes it back her on her own or not at all," Vartook told him.

"Murder? Honestly, Vartook, how can you, in good conscience, support such a charge?" Orook asked.

"I cannot, and I do not," Vartook said. "I told the Center Council that the only charges I would support are first level assault and depraved insubordination. However, until she returns and states her side of the story, the original charge will stand as they are."

"Ah, well, I cannot fault you for that," Orook conceded.

"Fear not my friend, I have informed all of my guardsmen that they are to alert me immediately upon her arrival," Vartook said.

• • •

Less than two hours later, Maria arrived at the western facing gate within that part of the outer wall closest to her home district. For a long time, she just stood there standing and staring at the gate. She wondered if she should knock or if the guardsmen had already seen her and had decided not to let her back into the City. Just as she was about to apply her knuckles to the thick cast iron door, it opened.

"Hold your arms straight out in front of you," Vartook instructed.

"Well hello Captain, it's nice to see you again too," Maria said as she dutifully held out her arms.

Vartook removed her armband and handed it to Solomane who tucked it into a pack he carried on his back. Vartook then placed a heavy cuff around each of her wrists. He brought Maria's wrists together and activated the cuffs with his armband.

"I remember these!" she said cheerfully.

"Maria, keep your voice down. You are in a serious trouble," he said. "You have been charged with murder."

This news instantly dampened Maria's giddy cheerfulness.

"Murder?" Maria said. "I don't understand. I didn't kill anyone."

"Has your keeper never explained our laws to you?" Vartook asked. "There is no separate charge for an attempted crime. You stuck me with a poisoned dart. The Center Council does not know why you did this or what your intent might have been. Since, at least theoretically, the dart could have killed me, or indirectly lead to my death if a pack of ruekar had found me unconscious, you have been charged you with murder - and because I am the First Guardsman, you have also been charged with high treason."

Maria looked down at her cuffed hands and sighed heavily.

"It might ease your mind to know that, while I certainly do not condone or appreciate what you did, I told the Center Council that I do not support these charges. I recommended that you be charged with first level assault and depraved insubordination - assuming, of course, that you admit freely to what you did, and express your remorse," Vartook continued.

"Thank you," Maria said.

Vartook then reached inside a pocket of his uniform, pulled out a piece of paper and handed it to Maria.

"Pullmoo requested that I give this to you and that I ask you to read it before I escort you to the detention room," Vartook said.

Maria struggled to unfold the paper and dropped it several times. When she finally had it in front of her and right side up, she saw words written in an elegant cursive script, so artful and precise it looked almost calligraphic.

To Maria, Companion to the First Engineer of Pegasea,

I have asked the First Guardsman to escort you to the detention room. Before he does so, you should know that once you arrive at the Guard Station, you will be required to disrobe and relinquish any clothing, objects, or other things that you might have on your person at the time. With that in mind, I have asked my dear fiancé to take custody of whatever you might wish to entrust to him for safe keeping. Of course, whatever you might entrust to him, he will in turn entrust to me. I will then return it to you as soon as I am able.

Written as if spoken by,
Pullmoo, First Sociologist of Pegasea

Maria read the letter twice before she looked up at Vartook and asked, "Who is Pullmoo's fiancé?"

Vartook smiled. "I am," he said.

"I guess that makes sense," Maria said as she handed Pullmoo's letter back to Vartook.

Vartook pulled a small incendiary device from his pocket and touched it to the edge of the paper. The letter burst into flames and was no more.

"You surprise me," Maria said. "I always thought that if there was anyone stricter about the rules than my keeper, it would be you."

"You are correct," Vartook said. "However, I do not believe that when the rules were written, they ever contemplated any situation even remotely like this one. Also, Pullmoo has convinced me there are issues of city security here - which means that I have the authority to act outside the rules if, in my judgement, it is prudent to do so."

Maria nodded, then clumsily reached behind her neck and gently brought out the baby *naverkoo*.

"Here," she said quietly, as she reluctantly held the small creature out to Vartook in both hands.

Vartook looked down at the thing in Maria's hands, then at Maria.

"What is it?" Vartook asked.

"We call it a '*naverkee*,'" Solomane said with awe and reverence.

Cautiously, Vartook put his cupped hands below Maria's. Maria then let the quivering little creature drop into the guardsman's hands.

"It's ok, they will take care of you. It's only for a little while. You will be back with me soon," Maria whispered into Vartook's hands.

"What do I do with it?" Vartook asked.

"It should always be a shade of green or blue. If it turns yellow or gets lethargic, it probably needs sunlight. If it starts to feel dry, it needs water. If it turns red and firm, set it down immediately and walk away - that means it's really mad. I don't know what happens if you touch it when it's in all-out defense mode, but I do not think you want to find out. If it -," Maria said.

"Maria, you will have it back soon," Vartook interrupted.

He then looked to Solomane and asked, "Do you know what to do with this thing?"

Solomane nodded. He then sat and extended a hand to Vartook, who handed him the *naverkee*. Solomane placed the *naverkee* at the back of his head, between his ears, then folded his ears over it.

Maria smiled when she heard the *naverkee's* muffled but happy chatter.

"We must get going now," he said. "Your keeper has been calling me every half hour asking about your estimated time of arrival."

"How did he know I was on my way?" she asked.

Vartook quickly explained to Maria how they had collected data from her armband and tracked her movements once she emerged from the mountain.

"Now we must stop talking to each other this way," Vartook said. "Once we are inside that wall, you need to follow the rules. Walk behind me, do not speak to me unless I ask you a question..."

"Yeah, yeah, I know," Maria said.

"Good," Vartook said, then turned and lead Maria through the gate and back into the city.

CHAPTER 60

The detention room was located within the primary guard station of the Center District and was within walking distance of Pullmoo's office. When Vartook arrived at the guard station with Maria, he instructed his two human guardsmen, Kim and Leah, to take Maria to a back room and relieve her of her possessions and whatever else she might have on her person.

"Give her clean white casual clothes and undergarments to wear - but no shoes," he instructed.

Once Vartook was gone, Kim and Leah lead Maria to the back room. As soon as the door was shut behind them, Kim and Leah smiled and began merrily interrogating Maria.

"What did it look like?" Kim asked.

"Did it hurt you?" Leah asked.

Maria looked from one eager face to the other.

"Who told you guys where I was?" Maria asked.

"Vartook, of course," Leah said.

"He tells us everything," Kim said.

"He does? Why? Aren't you only Sixth Guardsman?" Maria asked.

"Fifth," Leah said.

"Vartook and us - we go way back," Kim said, then giggled as she looked at Leah, who punched her in the shoulder and told her to shut up.

"He told us about you because he wanted us to be the ones to search you and get you settled into the detention room. He thought you might feel more comfortable with two human women than with some strange Pegasean man," Leah explained.

"That was nice of him," Maria said.

Leah nodded.

"Did the *naverkoo* make that for you?" Kim asked as she gestured at what Maria was wearing.

"I guess so," Maria said. "It itches like crazy. To be honest, I wouldn't mind taking it off."

"Go ahead. You have to anyway," Leah said.

Maria looked at the two of them.

"Oh, right," Kim said, then quickly stepped forward and waved her armband over Maria's cuffs to release them.

"Thanks," Maria said.

Maria then took off her backpack and set it down on the floor. Kim picked up the backpack and carried it out of the room.

"Do you mind?" Maria said to Leah.

"Uh, I know this is a little awkward, but I can't turn my back on you while your cuffs are deactivated - it's against protocol," Leah said.

Maria sighed.

"You know, if Vartook wanted to make me feel more comfortable, he should have let Sitook or Altook do this," Maria mumbled as she disrobed.

"Why do you say that?" Leah asked.

"Because I'm pretty sure they're gay and I'm pretty sure you and Kim are lesbians," Maria said.

"We go both ways," Leah said with a smile.

When Kim returned, she brought new clean clothes for Maria to put on. They were just like her ordinary casual clothes except that they were white instead of sapphire.

"I look like I'm about to get married on a beach somewhere," Maria said as she tied the knot of her blouse.

Kim and Leah frowned.

"What?" Maria asked.

"Nothing," said Leah.

"The color white has a different meaning here," Kim said.

"You don't have to tell her, Kim," Leah said.

"I'm not stupid Leah," Maria said. "Obviously I'm being stripped of my status - such as it was - because I've been charged with murder of the First Guardsman. I can't imagine that the punishment for such a crime is anything less than execution."

361

"Well, yes, but that charge won't hold once you tell them that you had no intention of hurting him," Kim said.

"How do you know I didn't intend to hurt him?" Maria asked.

Kim looked at Leah.

"Vartook told us that you darted him with a tranquiller so that he couldn't follow you down into the mountain - because you were afraid he might get hurt down there," Leah said.

Maria nodded.

"Do you think the Center Council will believe me?" Maria asked.

"They already do," Kim said.

"I don't understand," Maria said.

"Well, I shouldn't say they believe you. They believe Vartook. They just need you to confirm it," Kim explained.

"How long will this all take?" Maria asked.

Both Leah and Kim shrugged. Moments later, both their arm-bands began to ping.

"We have to put you in the detention room now," Leah said. "Pullmoo is on her way here to talk to you."

The detention room really did look like a prison cell. Two adjacent walls of the room were entirely transparent, including the door. Inside, there was a cot, a shower, a toilet, and a sink. The shower had a curtain, but it was also transparent. The room was clearly designed in such a way as to ensure that the occupant would have no significant degree of privacy.

As soon as Maria was securely locked inside the detention room, Leah and Kim left and a Pegasean man Maria did not recognize arrived to take up post outside the room.

"Hi," he said to Maria from the other side of transparent door.

"Hi," Maria said.

"I've never had this job before," he said.

"Should be easy," Maria said with a smile.

"Yeah, but...," the guardsman said, suddenly looking nervous and uncomfortable.

"Look, I don't know what you've been told, but I'm not danger-ous," Maria said.

"Oh, no, it's not that!" the man said. "It's just that I read the protocol and it doesn't look as if the people who wrote the protocol ever expected a human woman to be in here."

"So?" Maria said.

"So… it says that I have to watch you constantly," he said as he rubbed the back of his neck with his palm.

"Sounds painfully boring," Maria said. "I'm sorry."

The guardsman sighed.

"Listen, if you have to use the toilet or take a shower, just tell me, ok? I'll look away," he said.

"That is very gentlemanly of you," Maria said. "But I don't want you to get in trouble. You don't have to look away - just try not to stare, ok?"

The guardsman nodded, then sat down in a chair just outside the door.

• • •

Pullmoo arrived a few minutes later and instructed the guardsman to leave until she was done speaking with Maria. The guardsman made the first gesture of respect to Pullmoo, then timidly said, "I am so sorry, but only Vartook can relieve me of my post."

"I am not relieving you of your post dear boy. I am simply asking you to wait outside while I have a private conversation with the accused - as is my right as her psychological counselor," Pullmoo said evenly.

Unable to withstand the heat of Pullmoo's glare, the guardsman left.

Pullmoo then waived her armband over the door to the detention room and let herself inside. She smiled warmly at Maria as she returned the naverkee to its proper guardian. The naverkee chattered joyfully as it scampered up Maria's arm and around her shoulders before nestling itself into the valley between Maria's neck and collar bone.

"Thank you," Maria said.

"My pleasure," Pullmoo said as she sat down on the cot.

"When can I see Or— …my keeper?" Maria said.

"My son will be here soon," she said.

"Your *son?*" Maria asked.

"Yes. I know you must be anxious to see him, but I need to speak with you first," Pullmoo said.

"Wait - my keeper is your son?" Maria asked again.

"Yes," Pullmoo said.

"You are his *mother?*" Maria asked.

"Maria, come now, is this really so shocking?" Pullmoo asked.

Maria stared at the woman's face. Now that she was looking for it, she did see some familial resemblance.

"I still don't like you," she said.

Pullmoo waved her hand at this. "In any case, we need to move on. I need to know what you plan to do with the naverkee," she said.

"Why?" Maria asked.

"Why do you think?" Pullmoo asked.

"I have no idea why you care," Maria said.

"Maria, do you recall, awhile back, when you met with me privately in my office?" Pullmoo asked.

"Yeah, what about it?" Maria asked.

"You told me that you did not appreciate being used as a pawn in all my games," Pullmoo said. "I was a bit disappointed with that analogy. Do you know why?"

Maria sighed, then nodded.

"Tell me," Pullmoo prompted.

"Because I'm not one of your pawns, I'm more like your queen - and my keeper is like one of your knights. That is why you put us together. He protects me while you move me around the board," Maria said as she pet the naverkee at her shoulder and looked longingly through the transparent wall and out into the corridor beyond.

"Very good," Pullmoo said. "Of course, the game I'm playing is infinitely more complicated than your Earthly game of chess. Regardless, you've captured the general idea."

"I want to fulfill my promise to the *naverkoo*," Maria said.

"Of course, you do," Pullmoo said.

"So that is my plan," Maria said.

"That is not a plan," Pullmoo said.

Maria shrugged.

"Do you trust me?" Pullmoo asked.

"In what way?" Maria asked.

"Do you trust me to make your plan for you?" Pullmoo said.

"If what I want and what you want are the same thing, then yes," Maria said.

"I think the *naverkoo* might have made you just a bit smarter Maria," Pullmoo said.

"I was always smart," Maria said.

"Hmm…for a human, maybe, yes," Pullmoo said.

Maria rolled her head back and sighed.

"Once you tell the Center Council your side of the story, it will most likely ask you to choose one of two punishments; torture by electric shock or exile. Choose exile," Pullmoo said.

"Will the exile be permanent?" Maria asked.

"Good question," Pullmoo said. "A Pegasean man or woman properly trained in the skills needed to survive outside the city could probably make it out there. You, however, are not Pegasean and you have not been trained. Thus, for you, permanent exile would be nothing less than a death sentence. I suspect that the Center Council will take this into consideration and limit the period of exile to one, or possibly two, years."

"Why do you suggest I choose exile?" Maria asked.

"Because you need to leave the city anyway, right?" Pullmoo asked.

"Right," Maria said.

"Thank you for confirming that," Pullmoo said. "Now, if my suspicions are correct, I believe you intend to travel quite some distance - perhaps even as far as to the other side of this planet. Is that right?"

"I don't really know for sure," Maria confessed as she gently rolled the *naverkee* from one hand to the other.

"Well, I can tell you that regardless of the exact location of your destination, if you are traveling anywhere out to sea, I would not expect to see you back here before the first day of autumn next year," Pullmoo said.

Maria turned to look at Pullmoo.

Ignoring Maria's expression of distressed bewilderment, Pullmoo continued. "With that in mind, you can see how it makes little sense for you to choose torture over exile when you are sending yourself into exile anyway - no sense suffering through two punishments."

"Right...," Maria said, now staring at the bare wall across from her cot.

"Just do as I advise, and everything will be fine," Pullmoo said as she patted Maria on the shoulder. The First Sociologist then stood up and began walking towards the door.

"Where are you going?" Maria asked.

"You want me to stay? I thought you didn't like me," Pullmoo said playfully as she opened the door.

"I don't *dislike* you," Maria said. "Not anymore anyway. I'm sorry I said you were evil back then. I don't think you're evil."

Pullmoo stopped. Holding the door open with one hand, she turned and smiled at Maria.

"I'm sorry to hear that," she said. "I was rather enjoying thinking of myself as your evil step-mother."

Maria chuckled and Pullmoo sighed heavily.

"What?" Maria asked.

"If only you had been born a Pegasean woman," she said.

CHAPTER 61

O rook's pleasantly eager expression changed immediately upon seeing Maria. His brow furrowed as he scanned her with his eyes through the transparent detention room wall.

Maria bounced on the balls of her feet and smiled as she waited anxiously for the guardsman to open the door to her cell. Once Orook was inside, she hugged him tightly and began a rambling account of what had happened on the mountain. Orook pulled away from her and began circling around her slowly.

"I'm not hurt," Maria said.

"I can see that," Orook said.

"Then what are you doing?" Maria asked.

"That thing changed you," he said.

"Yeah, it told me it would do that," she said dismissively.

"What did it tell you? How did it change you?" Orook asked.

Maria shrugged.

"Do you feel different?" he asked.

"A little," Maria said. "My skin feels weird, and I keep tripping and bumping into things. I think it screwed me up."

"No, it made your legs longer. That is why you are tripping and bumping into things. Your brain has not had time to reconfigure," he told her.

Orook then put his hand under her shirt at her back and began palpating her spine.

"No wonder you were gone so long," he said. "That thing adjusted just about every muscle in your back, shoulders, hips... everywhere."

Maria closed her eyes as he felt around her body, assessing every way in which the *naverkoo* had changed her. When he was done examining her, he stepped back and folded his arms.

"Why did it do this?" Orook asked.

Maria only looked away.

"Maria, tell me," he said.

"You are going to get mad," Maria said.

"I am going to get mad either way," he said.

"I thought you would be happy to see me," she said.

"I am," Orook said.

"You don't look happy," she said.

"What do I look like when I am happy?" he asked.

"Not like this," Maria said, waving one hand at Orook's overall posture.

Orook uncrossed his arms, then smiled.

"I am happy, truly and beyond words, Maria, to see you back here in one piece," he said.

"They won't let me wear your color," Maria said, "or mine even."

"You told me once that you do not care about what color you wear, or about status," Orook said.

"Yeah, but...this feels like a punishment," Maria said.

"That is because it is a kind of punishment," Orook said. "However, once you have received your punishment, you will be allowed to return home and wear your regular clothes again."

"Even on Earth I hated wearing white. It's just not my color," Maria told him.

"Well, aesthetically speaking, I think you look stunning," Orook said.

"Really?" Maria asked.

Orook nodded.

"Did you miss me?" Maria asked.

Orook then pulled her into his arms and kissed her. With his cheek pressed to hers, he said, "listen, Maria, you are in a precarious situation right now. You are aware of this I hope."

Maria nodded, then slowly stepped back from him.

"What do you know?" Orook asked.

"Your mom was here. She explained it all to me," Maria said.

Orook's ears twitched at Maria's reference to his "mom."

"I have never, and will never, call her 'mom' or by any Pegasean equivalent of the term," Orook said.

"Why not?" Maria asked. "And how come you never told me that she is your mother?"

"The answer to both questions is the same; because it has no meaning or significance to me," Orook told her.

"Oh, come on!" Maria said.

"She never showed any interest in me as her son. When I turned 25, she sent me a generic message stating that she was my biological mother and that if I had any interest in getting to know her, I should make an appointment," Orook said.

Maria tried not to smile, but she could not help it.

"Can we move on?" Orook asked, annoyed.

"Who is your father?" Maria asked.

"He is dead," Orook told her.

"Ok, who *was* he?" Maria asked.

"The First Engineer before me," he said quickly.

"What was his name?" Maria asked.

"Maria, I would really rather not discuss my genetic origins right now. Did Pullmoo give you any sense of how the Center Council intends to punish you?" Orook asked.

"She said they would likely give me a choice between torture and exile," Maria told him.

"I would recommend you opt for torture. It will most certainly be unpleasant - obviously. However, exile, for you, will be nothing short of a death sentence," Orook advised.

"That is what she said - except that she recommended I choose exile," Maria said.

"Why?" Orook asked.

At this, Maria turned away from him.

"Maria?" Orook said.

"I have to leave. I have to leave the city," Maria said.

"Why?!" Orook asked.

"I promised the *naverkoo*," Maria said.

Orook turned Maria around slowly to face him.

"What did you promise the *naverkoo*?" he asked.

Maria looked up at him, saw the intensity in his eyes, then quickly turned away again.

Orook roughly turned her back around again and held his grip on her upper arms. Maria swiftly brought her arms between them, then rotated them out in both directions, knocking his hands away. Her success in this surprised Maria more than it surprised Orook, who had already deduced that the *naverkoo*'s modifications had made her faster and stronger.

"Sorry…," Maria said, sounding suddenly disoriented.

"No, I deserved that," he said.

"I promised the *naverkoo* I would take its naverkee to this island - I'm not sure exactly where it is, but it's really far away. It gave me a map. I promised I would take the naverkee to this island, where there is another *naverkoo* - the only other living *naverkoo* left," Maria said in a rush.

"Maria, how could you?" Orook said.

Surprised by the genuine hurt in his voice, Maria looked up at him.

"Orook, I…," she started to say.

"You will die out there Maria," Orook said. "No matter how well the *naverkoo* might have adapted you, you could not possibly make such a journey on your own."

Maria hung her head, too embarrassed to tell him that she had never considered the possibility that he would not go with her.

"Did you think of me before you made this promise?" he asked.

Maria continued to stand in silence as she twisted the ends of her blouse in her hands.

"I see," Orook said. He then turned abruptly to leave.

Just before he opened the door, Maria whispered, "wait."

Orook stopped but did not turn around.

"You could go with me," she said faintly.

Orook sighed, shook his head slowly, then left the room.

After he had gone, Maria sat down on the cot and took the naver-kee out from under her pillow. She cradled it in her hands, then lifted it to her cheek. She pondered on the fact that, all this time, she had always assumed Orook would go with her. It had never been a question in her mind. She never thought to ask herself what she would do if he declined. A slow panic began to rise in her stomach as the reality of the situation began to dawn on her mind. Her heart began to race. The naverkee jumped from her hands to her shoulder and was now twitching and whistling like a little alarm bell. Before long, Maria was hyperventilating and clutching the edges of the cot. The guardsman stationed outside the room stood and walked over to the door.

"Are you ok?" he asked.

Maria took a deep breath, then nodded.

"Do you need a body biologist?" he asked.

Maria shook her head adamantly.

The guardsman watched her appraisingly for a few minutes.

"You do not look well," the guardsman said. "Do you want me to call your keeper back?"

"No!" Maria said. "Please, I'm ok."

"Ok, if you say so," said the guardsman.

Once she had composed herself, Maria stood and walked to the door. The guardsman stood up from his chair.

"Am I allowed to have visitors?" she asked.

"You just had two visitors already today," he said.

"Right, I know, but may I ask someone to come visit me?" Maria clarified.

"The protocol says that you may have visitors, but it does not specify how many or if you are allowed to request them," the guardsman told her.

"What does the protocol say about matters not covered by the protocol?" Maria asked.

"It says that anything not covered by the protocol is left to the judgement of the guardsman stationed outside the detention room," he said.

"So, it's up to you then," Maria said.

"Right," he said.

"May I request a visitor?" Maria asked patiently.

The guardsman appeared to consider this for a moment before saying, "Yes. Who would you like to visit you?"

"My friend Maddie," she said.

"A human woman? Who is her keeper? I will send him a message," he said.

"Etmook," Maria said. "He is a second engineer - he runs the security grid."

"Yes, I know Etmook. He's a fine man and his companion is a dear," the guardsman said with a smile. "I will message him now."

An hour later the guardsman gave Maria the unfortunate news that Etmook had been instructed by Vartook not to allow Maddie to visit with her.

"Why?" Maria asked.

The guardsman looked away and shifted his feet.

"Please just tell me," Maria said.

"Maria, Vartook believes you are dangerous," he told her.

"Dangerous?" Maria said with short laugh.

"Not dangerous in the ordinary sense," the guardsman said. "Unfortunately, my English vocabulary is not so vast. I will try to explain. He believes you are a type of person who gets other people in trouble - even when you do not intend to or even if it is not your fault."

"He might be right about that," she said.

"It is good for you to be understanding," he said. "I hope the Center Council will be compassionate towards you. You seem like a nice person."

• • •

To Maria's surprise, Maddie showed up at the guard station an hour later and came straight to the detention room.

"Maddie!" Maria said as her friend approached.

"I'm sorry it took me so long," Maria said. "Etmook tried to stop me from coming to see you."

"You shouldn't have come Maddie," Maria said. "I mean, if Etmook forbade it, you could get in trouble."

"Fuck him," Maddie said.

At this the guardsman stood up and admonished Maddie severely. Maddie apologized and promised to tell her keeper where she was and to apologize to him too.

"I do not want to be unkind," said the guardsman, "but I cannot allow you to flagrantly disobey and disrespect your keeper."

Maddie grit her teeth.

"Maddie," Maria said. "I'm so happy to see you, but seriously, the whole reason Vartook told Etmook not to let you come is because he thinks I get people in trouble."

"How ironic," Maddie said.

"I know, right?" Maria said.

"He has a lot of nerve," Maddie said. "Isn't he the one who got you into this mess in the first place?"

"I really must insist you leave now," said the guardsman.

"It's not Vartook's fault either Maddie," Maria said. "And he's right. I'm a liability. You better go."

Just as Maddie was about to argue, the guardsman told Maddie that her keeper's directive had been overridden.

"By who?" Maddie asked.

"The First Engineer," said the guardsman as he unlocked the door to the detention room to allow Maddie inside.

Maddie smiled at Maria as she walked into the room, then sat down on the cot.

"Orook hates it when Vartook gives Etmook orders," Maria told Maddie.

"And Etmook loves it when they fight over him," Maddie told Maria.

Maria laughed.

"You look different," Maddie said.

"How so?" Maria asked.

"Hmmm… it's hard to say exactly," Maddie said as she looked Maria over.

Maria sat down on the cot next to Maddie and hugged her.

"I'm so glad you came," Maria whispered. "I didn't want you to get in trouble, but I'm so happy you're here. I could really use someone to talk to."

"Tell me everything," Maddie said.

Maria then told Maddie everything that had happened since they had picnicked in the District Center. They talked for hours. Maddie was thrilled to hold the naverkee. At some point in the evening, the guardsman outside the room was replaced by another guardsman taking over for the night shift. An inventory clerk brought in a bland dinner for both Maddie and Maria. When it was time for Maddie to leave, she gave Maria one last hug and told her that if there was anything she could do to help, Maria should not hesitate to ask.

"I will," Maria said, and thanked her.

As Maddie was walking out the door, Maria said "I love you Maddie."

"I love you too," Maddie said.

• • •

After Maddie left, Maria lay awake on her cot for hours, unable to sleep. She wanted to talk to Orook. She wanted to apologize but had no way to communicate with him. The nightshift guardsman was not as friendly as the previous one. He only gave terse responses to Maria's questions and showed no interest in engaging with her any more than was absolutely necessary. When at last she was able to sleep, Maria had only one dream. She dreamed of a tree, stuck in a mountain, reminding her that she now only had two days left in the city.

CHAPTER 62

When Maria awoke the next morning, she was happy to see that the dayshift guardsman from the previous day had returned. She immediately went to the door and asked him if there was any way she could communicate a message to her keeper.

"He is scheduled to be here within the hour," the guardsman told her. "Why don't you just wait until you see him?"

"Oh, I didn't know he was coming back," Maria said.

"He's your keeper," said the guardsman. "I'm surprised he isn't here with you all the time. If you were my companion, I wouldn't want to leave your side - not at a time like this."

Maria shrugged. "Well, I'm going to take a shower now," she said.

"Thanks for the warning," he said as his face turned pink.

• • •

When Orook returned, Maria was only a little surprised to see that he had brought Lenook with him. The guardsman brought in a pair of chairs from another room and placed them inside the detention room before letting Orook and Lenook in to see Maria.

"Are you divorcing me? Is that why you brought your lawyer with you?" Maria asked as Orook took a seat.

Lenook laughed.

"We are not married Maria," he said.

"It was a joke," she said.

"I am prepared to make a deal with you Maria," Orook said.

"Ok," Maria said, then looked over at Lenook, who was pulling out his computer.

Orook took a deep breath, then said, "against my better judgement, I am willing to consider accompanying you out to this island, assuming such a place even exists, if you agree, under oath, to my conditions."

Maria jumped up and threw her arms around her keeper. She peppered his face with kisses and thanked him profusely.

"Maria, wait - you have yet to hear my conditions," Orook said as he gently pushed her away and back down onto her cot.

"I don't care - whatever you want, I agree," Maria said quickly.

"In order for this agreement to be legally binding, your trusting mistress here needs to actually hear your demands. She will also need to restate them in the form of a promise to you," Lenook said helpfully.

Maria sat down and waited attentively to hear Orook's demands.

"The first one is that, at all times while we are outside the city, you must follow my instructions without argument," Orook began.

"Don't you already demand that of me?" Maria interrupted.

"Once we are far outside the city walls, and beyond these mountains, we will be far outside the jurisdiction of the City and its laws and PROEs. Also, since you will be in exile and I will be on, well, what you might call a 'sabbatical,' we will not be actively engaged as city engineers. Thus, technically, I will not have any authority to command you to do anything," Orook explained. "That is why I am asking you to make this first promise."

"Ok, well, whatever, I promise to always follow your instructions without arguing," Maria said.

"My second demand is that you permanently relinquish and forever waive your right to request a different keeper or seek independent status," Orook said.

"What?" Maria asked.

"He wants you to be stuck with him forever, no matter what, even after you return to the city - assuming you both return alive," Lenook explained.

"Ok...," Maria said.

"I have my reasons," Orook said.

Maria narrowed her eyes at Orook, then looked at Lenook. Remembering what had happened to Lenook's companion, Maria looked back at Orook and asked, "What if you get married?"

"You would remain my companion even then," Orook said.

"Why would you still want me as a companion in that case?" Maria asked.

"All the same reasons I want you as my companion now," he said.

"Isn't that a little selfish?" Maria asked.

"Yes, it is. However, as I have explained to you before, the chances of me ever marrying is remote. There is a far greater likelihood that you will, at some point, become disenchanted with me and wish to be re-matched or simply live on your own - assuming you attain a position in the city that would allow you to do that. This is what I am seeking to prevent," he said.

"Alright, fine, I agree to... what were the words?" Maria asked.

Lenook repeated the words she needed to say.

"I permanently relinquish and forever waive my right to request a different keeper or seek independent status," she said without enthusiasm.

"My third and final demand is that you promise never to join with another man, human or Olronean, without my express permission," Orook said.

At this, Maria laughed, then said, "What is this all about? Why are you asking me for this? And I thought all the Olroneans were dead."

"Maria, the name of this planet is Olrona. All Pegaseans are Olroneans, but not all Olroneans are Pegaseans," Orook explained.

"Ok, but why are you suddenly worried I might join with someone else? I have never known you to be the jealous type," Maria said.

"I have my reasons and they have nothing to do with jealousy," he said. "Quite frankly, I simply do not trust your judgement. You are impulsive and reckless. You should not be permitted to engage intimately with others without some degree of oversight."

"Wow," Maria said.

"Aren't you the one who keeps reminding me that we are not in an exclusive relationship?" Maria asked.

Orook nodded, then said, "To be clear, the exclusivity I am demanding would only be applicable to you. I would be under no such restriction."

"I hate you," Maria said.

"You do not," Orook said. "Not yet anyway."

Maria glared at him.

"Believe me Maria," Orook said. "I could be perfectly happy to just stay here - where I have a career and a home, where I can sleep each night in a warm dry bed, where I have plenty of food, clothing, clean running water and -"

"I get it," Maria said.

"You do not have to agree to his demands," Lenook said. "In fact, if we were all back in your home country on Earth, I am sure that such a contract would be deemed unconscionable, if not illegal."

"Did either of us ask for your opinion?" Orook asked Lenook.

Lenook put up his hands.

"Assuming I agree to his final demand, will this contract or agreement - whatever you guys call it - be enforceable under Pegasean law?" Maria asked.

"Unfortunately, yes," Lenook said.

"And what happens if I break one of these promises?" Maria asked.

"It depends on which one you break, when you break it, and how many times you break it," Lenook said. "The consequences could range from no-effect to you being charged with kidnapping by false pretense."

"Kidnapping?" Maria asked.

"Yes, if it is determined that Orook would not have left the city if not for your promises - and you then break those promises in one or more meaningful ways - then it is as if you tricked him into leaving the city, which we consider a form of kidnapping," Lenook explained. "However, if, for example, you occasionally forget and argue with one of his instructions, then I do not imagine that any district council would find this to be a significant breach of the agreement."

Maria nodded.

"I can't believe you are doing this to me," Maria said to Orook.

"I could say the same thing to you Maria," Orook said.

Maria took a deep breath, then closed her eyes and said, "I promise not to join with another man, human or Olronean, without your express permission."

Orook looked to Lenook, who handed him the computer.

"Just use your armband to sign the record," Lenook instructed Orook.

After Orook had done so, Lenook took back the computer, touched the screen in several placed, then handed it to Maria.

"Since your armband has been revoked for the time being, you will need to place your palm on the screen - inside the box there," he said.

Maria did as Lenook instructed then handed the device back to him.

Lenook then stood up and wished Maria good luck. He said something to Orook in Pegasean before leaving the room. After he had gone, Maria asked "what did he say to you?"

"You should assume that if he had wanted you to know, he would have said it in English," Orook said.

"Why are you acting this way?" Maria asked.

"What way?" Orook asked.

"I just can't figure you out," she said. "You have been acting weird since even before I went out to the *naverkoo*. One minute you're loving and sweet and then all of a sudden you're, well, yourself again."

Orook scoffed at this.

Maria crossed her arms and leaned back against the wall behind her cot, then smiled mischievously at her keeper.

"What?" Orook asked.

"I'm just wondering with whom you might give me permission to join," Maria said.

"What do you mean?" Orook asked.

"You know - your third demand - I agreed not to join with anyone without your permission. So, who am I allowed to join with? May I join with Lenook?" Maria asked.

"No," Orook said.

"Etmook?" she asked.

"Certainly not," he said.

"How about that guardsman out there?" she asked.

Orook looked out the door at the guardsman whose face was now as bright red as his uniform.

"I am half tempted to call your bluff and give you my permission," Orook said. "He seems quite smitten with you."

"Give it then," Maria said.

"No," he said.

"Then tell me who I am allowed to join with," she said.

"For right now, no one," he said.

"Then why did you add the caveat 'without my permission'?" Maria asked.

Orook stared at her.

"You know what I think?" Maria said. "I think you have no intention of ever giving me permission to join with someone else. I think you're jealous."

"Do not insult me," he said.

"I never agreed not to insult you," Maria countered.

Orook rolled his eyes.

"I have to go now," he said. "I need to prepare for this suicide mission to which we are now both committed - thanks to you."

Maria narrowed her eyes and continued to glare at him.

Orook shook his head and sighed, then smiled.

"What are you so happy about?" Maria asked.

"I missed you," he said.

CHAPTER 63

Sometime after the mid-day meal, Pullmoo came to the detention room holding a pair of simple white slip-on shoes. Paying no mind to the guardsman stationed outside the room, Pullmoo opened the door and gestured for Maria to come out.

"Put these on," she said.

"Excuse me," said the guardsman. "What are you doing? You can't just come in here and…"

Pullmoo turned her head as if responding to a fly buzzing about her ear and looked disdainfully at the guardsman. The guardsman swallowed hard, then made the first gesture of respect.

"Is your armband malfunctioning?" Pullmoo asked.

The guardsman looked down at his armband and blushed as he read the most recent directive. He then quickly made the first gesture of apology to Pullmoo as he stepped away.

"Where are we going?" Maria asked.

"I am taking you to appear before the Center Council," Pullmoo said.

"What should I say?" Maria asked.

"Just tell them the truth," Pullmoo said.

"About what?" Maria asked.

"All of it," Pullmoo said.

"Is there anything I should say - or not say?" Maria asked.

Pullmoo sighed.

"What?" Maria asked.

"Maria, we are not on Earth," she said. "This is not a trial. The Center Council wants to hear your story - so tell it to them. Tell it as if you were telling it to a friend. Be honest and forthcoming. Do not try to lie or hide anything from them."

"Should I show them the naverkee?" Maria asked.

"If they ask to see it, yes," Pullmoo said. "However, if any of them request that you relinquish it, warn them of what might happen if they take it from you by force."

"I am not entirely sure what would happen," Maria said. "All I know is the information the *naverkoo* has put in my mind."

"And what did the *naverkoo* put in your mind?" Pullmoo asked.

"I am its host - or its guardian - however you want to look at it. It will only go to another person if I assure it that the transfer is temporary and that I trust that person. If someone were to try to take it from me, it would go into defense mode. When that happens, it turns red and black and goes stiff. If it is not returned to me within a few seconds, it will kill everyone and everything within a radius of five or ten meters. However, I do not know exactly how it does this. I think the *naverkoo* kept that information from me so that I could not possibly disclose it to anyone - even if I were tortured for the information. If no one knows exactly how the naverkee defends itself, no one can prepare or guard against it," Maria said.

"Tell them exactly that," Pullmoo said.

"Now stop talking to me as if I am one of your girlfriends. Pretend to be just as terrified of me as everyone else," Pullmoo said as she opened the door to the Center Hearing Hall.

Maria stood quietly behind Pullmoo until Pullmoo directed her to the podium in the center of the circular auditorium. When prompted, Maria told her story before the Center Council just as Pullmoo had instructed. She told it honestly and truly. She explained why, once they arrived at the mouth of the cave down into the Eye of Olrona, she was afraid that Vartook and Solomane would become trapped inside the mountain along with her. She explained how the *naverkoo* had helped her dart the First Guardsman. She then explained, in great detail, everything that had happened inside the cave. The only information Maria omitted was the *naverkoo*'s promise that it would change her in such a way which would allow her to have children with a Pegasean man. Once she had finished telling her story, the Center Council members held a discordant but civil discussion amongst themselves. Occasionally, a council member asked a question, which Maria answered if she could. When one of them asked Maria, what would happen if someone tried to take the naverkee from her, Maria responded just as she had responded to Pullmoo. Once there were no more questions, the Center Council held a vote. Shortly thereafter, one of the Council members told Maria that she could choose between one of two punishments for her crimes against the city. As Pullmoo had predicted, the Center Council asked her to choose between torture by electric shock and exile for a period of one year. Maria chose exile. A presenter then came forward with a computer and asked Maria to place her palm on the screen. Maria was then dismissed from the Center Hearing Hall and escorted back to the detention room.

"What now?" Maria asked as Pullmoo unlocked the door.

"Now comes the hard part," she said.

"What do you mean?" Maria asked.

"Your keeper has the unenviable task of convincing the Center Council to allow him to commit an act of treason," Pullmoo said.

"Treason?" Maria asked.

"Yes," Pullmoo said. "To accompany a person in exile, for the purpose of assisting that person, is considered an act of treason."

Maria looked down at the floor as she considered this.

"What will he tell them?" Maria asked.

"He will need to convince them that it is important for the city to know and understand the *naverkoo*, that the best way to do this is for a citizen of the city to accompany you on this journey to the island *naverkoo*, and that he is the ideal candidate for this assignment," Pullmoo said.

Maria sighed.

"Maria, did you really think the city would allow its finest First Engineer in history to abandon his post with no more justification than his love for a human woman?" Pullmoo asked.

Maria shrugged.

"How long will it take him to convince them?" Maria asked.

"Several days, at least," Pullmoo said.

Maria looked up sharply at Pullmoo.

"I don't have that much time!" Maria said.

"What do you mean?" Pullmoo asked.

"The *naverkoo* only gave me three days here and this is already the second day!" Maria said.

"You failed to mention that to the Center Council," Pullmoo said.

"I... I didn't think if it," Maria said. "I'm so sorry!"

Pullmoo shook her head.

"What do I do?" Maria asked.

As Maria's panic rose, the naverkee began to stir and chime.

"Calm down," Pullmoo said.

"You don't understand," Maria said. "It's not about me. The *naverkoo* will not hurt me. It can't. I have its baby. It will destroy the city. It will break the ground in which its built. It will..."

"Maria, stop," Pullmoo said. "Just breathe."

Maria sat down and tried to breathe.

"You really should have told me this sooner, Maria," Pullmoo said.

"I know. I know," Maria said.

"Is there anything *else* you might have failed to mention?" Pullmoo asked as she crossed her arms.

Maria looked away.

"Maria, tell me now, before you kill us all," Pullmoo said.

"The only other thing I haven't told you does not affect the city in any way," Maria said.

"I would like to remind you that you are entirely at my mercy here," Pullmoo said.

"What do you mean?" Maria asked.

"I could go back to the Center Hearing Hall right now, tell everyone that you are withholding information, recommend against my son being allowed to assist you, and provide my opinion that you should be sent into permanent exile immediately," Pullmoo said.

"Why would you do that?" Maria asked.

"Because I loathe human women who refuse to answer my questions," she said.

"Ok, ok," Maria said. "The *naverkoo* told me that it would change me in a way which would allow me to have a child with a Pegasean man."

Pullmoo closed her eyes and leaned her head back against the transparent wall.

"Are you going to tell my keeper?" Maria asked.

"Maria, whether I tell him or not, you must assume that he will find out eventually - one way or another," Pullmoo said.

Maria pulled her knees up to her chest and put her head down on her arms.

Pullmoo looked down at Maria, then walked over to the cot and sat down next to her.

"Despite my earlier advise to you, it was wise of you not to tell the Center Council this tantalizing bit of information," Pullmoo said.

Maria turned her head towards Pullmoo.

"Maria, why do you not want your keeper to know?" Pullmoo asked.

"I don't know," Maria mumbled.

"Trust me, Maria, Orook will not be mad," Pullmoo said. "All the same, the news will likely complicate his emotions right now, so please wait to tell him."

"I will," Maria said.

Pullmoo sighed, patted Maria on the shoulder, then got up to leave.

"Thank you," Maria said.

"Just do me one favor," Pullmoo said as she stood up.

"What now?" Maria asked with a sigh.

"If while you and Orook are out crossing the central desert, you happen to come across any burning bushes - please, just walk away," Pullmoo said.

Maria's brow furrowed as she looked up at Pullmoo.

"We have enough rules here already," Pullmoo said and winked at Maria.

"Ok, sure," Maria said.

Moments after Pullmoo had gone, comprehension finally dawned on Maria and she laughed.

CHAPTER 64

When Pullmoo arrived back at her office, she found Orook pacing back and forth between her couch and her desk.

"You are going to wear out my rug," she said.

"I got your message," Orook said. "Vartook let me in."

"We need to change tactics," Pullmoo said.

"How could she not tell us that she only has three days?" He asked.

"Orook, I am certain that she fully expected to come home, explain what happened, and leave with you the next morning. The culture from which she came places a high emphasis on free will and individual choice. She likely never considered the possibility you would need permission from the Center Council to leave the city," Pullmoo said.

"What kind of culture would allow such reckless impulsivity?" Orook asked.

"Does it matter?" Pullmoo asked. "The point is, she neglected to tell us because she didn't think it was all that important. She thought three days would be plenty of time."

"How could she assume that I would even be willing to go with her?!" Orook asked.

"Well, obviously, she knows you well," Pullmoo said with a smile.

When Orook started to argue, Pullmoo put up a hand to stop him.

"We don't have time for this," she said. "Tell me about your meeting with the First Biologist."

"He is fully prepared and willing to appear before the Center Council and explain why it is important for the city to learn more about the *naverkoo*," Orook said.

"Assuming that we are all able to convince the Center Council that it is important that someone accompany Maria, the Council will likely suggest that the First Biologist be the one to accompany her," Pullmoo said. "After all, this sort of thing does fall more within his bailiwick than it does yours."

"'Bailiwick?'" Orook repeated. "Why do you do that? Why do you insert English words into your speech when we are speaking in Pegasean?"

"You don't like the word 'bailiwick?'" Pullmoo asked.

"I have nothing against the word. I do not like it when you mix the two languages," Orook said.

"Orook, relax," Pullmoo said. "Tell me about the First Biologist."

Orook took a deep breath, then said, "The First Biologist has no desire to leave his green house, much less the city. He is also wholly unqualified to make such a journey. He does not know how to repair a scouting flyer or even how to fly the thing. About the only thing he would be good for out there is identifying edible plants and the tracks of a predator - likely just before it hunted him down and ate him. Those were his words, actually, not mine."

"Go on," Pullmoo prompted.

"He has no faith in his ability to command anyone other than his own subordinate biologists - and especially not someone like Maria. Lastly, while on a professional level he is fascinated by the *naverkoo* and the naverkee, he is also terrified of them and has no interest in personally interacting with either entity," Orook said.

"Is he willing to testify to all of that as well?" Pullmoo asked.

"More than willing - he is eager to tell them every reason why he should not be assigned to this task," Orook said.

"Excellent," Pullmoo said. "So here is what we are going to do. The four of us - myself, your sister, Vartook and the First Biologist - will all jointly recommend that you be allowed to defer your full presentation until after you return. In other words, we will all recommend that the Center Council allow us to give only abbreviated testimony about the *naverkoo* for now. There is virtually zero probability that the Council will not accept a joint recommendation made by four first levels. Once they accept our recommendation,

Wilamoo will show them her theoretical model of the *naverkoo* but will not go into any great detail as to how she developed it. The First Biologist will summarize what his subordinate biologists and your bioengineers discovered from the sample you brought them earlier this year. I will briefly explain how everything you and Wilamoo discovered several years ago, and everything Maria has told them today, fits nicely into both ancient vocunine and Olronean mythology and folklore. Lastly, Vartook will emphasize the raw power this thing must obviously have and why he believes this is an issue concerning city security. If we decline to take questions, we should be able to all get through our abbreviated presentations before sun down today. Then, tomorrow morning, all you will need to do is summarize everything we said, then convince them of Maria's abject loyalty to you. Maria arrived back in the city just after the tenth hour two days ago. Thus, I assume we have until the tenth hour tomorrow before the *naverkoo* wreaks havoc on the city."

"What about my qualifications for the assignment? - my ability to navigate and survive out there?" Orook asked.

Pullmoo scoffed.

"That is a given. Any presentation you gave on that subject would only be a superfluous showcase of your talents," she said.

"Despite the fact that she darted him, Maria would probably take orders from Vartook - for the most part anyway. What if they suggest that Vartook be assigned to accompany her?" Orook asked.

"Then I will throw a tantrum the likes of which this city has never seen," Pullmoo said.

Orook smiled uneasily.

"How do I convince them of Maria's loyalty and deference to me?" he asked.

"Did she agree to your demands?" Pullmoo asked.

"Yes," he said.

"Did you tell her why you were making them?" Pullmoo asked.

"She only asked me why I was making the second and third demands. I gave her my own personal tangential reasons, not the primary reason," Orook said.

"Good," Pullmoo said.

"Do you still have those immunity papers I gave you? - the ones Maria asked me to give you several lunar cycles ago?" she asked.

Orook nodded, then asked, "Do I really have to show them those?"

"You might have to. We will play it by ear - as the humans like to say," Pullmoo said.

"Sometimes I think you would have rather been born on Earth," Orook said.

"Ha!" Pullmoo said. "Too easy. I could take over that entire planet within a week."

"How long was it before you took over Pegasea?" Orook asked.

"Oh, at least a few years," Pullmoo said.

Orook folded his arms and looked down at the pale green and yellow carpet at his feet.

"What is it Oroo?" Pullmoo asked. "What is bothering you?"

"Why have you never shown any interest in me as your son?" he asked.

"You know I can't have favorites," Pullmoo said.

"Even so...," Orook said, "you could have shown an interest in knowing me personally."

"I invited you to get to know me," Pullmoo said. "You declined."

"You told me to make an appointment," he said.

"I tell everyone that," Pullmoo said. "I don't do house calls."

"Right," Orook said.

Pullmoo stared at him for a moment, then said, "Orook, do you need a hug?"

"No, I most certainly do not," he said as he unfolded his arms and took a step back.

Pullmoo laughed.

"You might not be able to communicate with the city once you get out to the central desert," she said.

"I know," Orook said. "But I think I might be able to set up a relay tower - maybe."

Pullmoo walked around to the other side of her desk and opened a drawer. She pulled out a small carved wood box, walked back to Orook and handed it to him.

"What is this?" he asked.

"Open it," she said.

Inside the box was a circular device affixed to a band of intricately laced metal. Overall, it strongly resembled a wrist watch from Earth, but with a distinctly Pegasean design.

"Your father was rather fond of what he called 'self-sufficient' technology - things that do not need to be charged or plugged in. He made that for me. It is a compass that also keeps time. It also does a few other things. I'm sure you will recognize its features without me having to tell you. In any case, my understanding is that you have to manually load the gears every once in a while, but it never needs to lay out under the sun or be plugged in," Pullmoo told him.

"It is beautiful," Orook said as he took the device out of the box and turned it over.

"Beautiful? I suppose that only proves that beauty is in the eye of the beholder. I never wore it because, well, I think it's hideous and I have no need of it. However, I think it could prove useful to someone who is going to be 'roughing it' for a while," Pullmoo told him.

"*For my dear Puma*," Orook said, reading the inscription on the back.

"Don't ask," Pullmoo said.

"Did you love him?" Orook asked as he put the watch back in its box.

"Well, obviously I was rather fond of him - why else would I keep that silly thing around?" she said pointing at the box in Orook's hands.

"I did not ask if you were fond of him," Orook said.

"Orook, you know I am not much of a romantic," she said.

"Are you giving this to me?" Orook asked.

"Obviously, yes," Pullmoo said.

"Thank you," he said.

Pullmoo watched him closely as she waited to see what Orook might ask her next. In the prolonged silence, Pullmoo smiled as she recalled her fond memories of the former First Engineer. He had been kind, charming, and one of only a few men willing to risk Vartook's wrath.

"Well, my son, we better get this show on the road," Pullmoo said at last and in English.

"Is there any end to your mental library of Earthly expressions?" Orook asked.

"No," Pullmoo said. "If ever I run out, I fully intend to start making them up."

Orook smiled as they left her office and headed for the Center Hearing Hall.

• • •

Back in the detention room, Maria walked from one end of the room to the other as she chewed at her nails and prayed that Pullmoo would find some way to speed up Orook's presentation. At some point late in the evening, after the clerk had brought her evening meal, Vartook arrived at the door.

"What now?" Maria asked.

"Your keeper asked me to give you this," he said as he handed her a sapphire blue sweater.

As soon as Maria took it in her hands, she recognized the fabric. It was the same sort of sweater she had been given in the Intake Hall, only it was the color of the First Engineer rather than the khaki color worn by all new arrivals. Maria sighed as she hugged it to her chest.

"Am I allowed to wear it?" she asked.

"No," Vartook said. "And now that you have asked, I am obligated to inform you that, should you break the rules and wear it anyway, the punishment will be remedial PROEs training - which, of course, you will be unable to attend until after you return from exile."

Maria looked up at him.

Vartook winked at her, then abruptly left the room.

That night, Maria tossed and turned in her cot as she struggled against nightmares of the *naverkoo* tearing the city apart. In one such nightmare, the *naverkoo* broke apart the ceiling above the nursery and a flood of ruekar came in and attacked the children. In another, the entire city was buried in an avalanche of mud and rock. Each time she awoke from one of these nightmares relieved and overjoyed that it had all only been a dream. She knew that she would have to leave the city tomorrow morning, with or without her keeper. The Prisoner would not be disobeyed. It would not be patient and it would not hear excuses. If only she had some way to communicate this to Pullmoo or Vartook.

CHAPTER 65

T he next morning, Orook gave a heavily abridged version of his presentation before the Center Council. He began by quickly telling his own story involving the *naverkoo*, his interest in it, and what steps he had taken to try to learn more about the creature. He then told them about Maria's dreams and how those dreams had ultimately lead her to the *naverkoo*. Less than twenty minutes into his presentation, one of the Council members held up a hand to stop him.

"Orook, we are all already convinced of the *naverkoo*'s importance and that someone should indeed assist Maria in doing what the *naverkoo* has requested of her," said the Council woman. "What remains to be demonstrated is that you should be the one to assist her."

"I am her keeper," Orook said. "By law it is my responsibility to ensure her safety and well-being."

"Yes, yes, we know that," said the same woman. "However, it is very important to this Council that whomever accompanies Maria out on this journey be able to command her and ensure that she follows through on her promise to the *naverkoo*. If she runs off on her own, both she and the naverkee will most certainly perish. Now, Orook, with all due respect - such due respect being admittedly substantial in your case - reflecting on the incident in the nursery, we are not entirely sure that you have sufficient control over this young human woman."

Orook then produced the contract he had entered into with Maria the day before and explained why each promise she made proved her deference to him. A few of the more cynical Council members questioned the merit of the contract.

"How do we know she did not enter into this agreement only as a prop to convince us of her submission and devotion to you?" one of Council members asked.

Orook pointed out that Maria had no idea that this matter was even being discussed or was any factor to be considered by the Council.

"How do we know that her current pledge of subordination to you is not inspired purely by recent events? - from the fact that she now needs you so desperately?" asked another member of the Council.

At this, Orook closed his eyes, took a deep breath, then presented the immunity papers Maria had asked Pullmoo to give him several lunar cycles before any of this happened. Upon reading the salacious document, a few of the Council members gasped in shock.

"Did you ever have need of this document?" someone asked.

At this, Orook looked at Lenook, who slowly shook his head.

"I have never been questioned about any matter to which the document would be relevant," Orook said. "So, no, I never needed it."

The Center Hearing Hall then buzzed with dozens of hushed private conversations between council members.

At last, the lead Council woman said, "Well, while all of this is very interesting, we are still divided over the matter of whether you should be the one to accompany Maria. Quite frankly, we suspect that our First Guardsman may have a better command over the woman."

At this, Pullmoo stood up and asked permission to speak. The Center Council moderator gestured for Pullmoo to proceed.

"I must first acknowledge, with much gratitude and praise, that due to the many long hours and nights worked by our City's fine guardsmen and engineers, we have thus far succeeded in fending off the ruekar," she began.

The Council responded with clapping and stomping of their feet.

Pullmoo nodded as she waited for the room to become quiet again.

"That said, we are still only in early autumn," Pullmoo continued. "We should expect the ruekar to continue to be a threat for at least another lunar cycle, if not two. Consequently, Vartook is needed here. Neither the sum force of our City Guard, nor any mechanized system of weapons - be they hoses that spray fire or guns that shoot bladed disks - can compare to the lethal action of this one man. He is more than just our First Guardsman, he is our very last line of defense."

Pullmoo then paused and looked over at Vartook, who was doing his very best to conceal just how much his fiancé's words had moved him.

"Also, I am now pregnant with his child," Pullmoo added. "Thus, I respectfully request that the Council refrain from asking him to leave the City before his child is born. Thank you."

The First Sociologist then sat back down in her seat and waited. Within seconds, the Council member from District Six stood, cleared his throat, and thanked Pullmoo for her words. He then expressed his full agreement with Pullmoo's request and encouraged the rest of the Council to do the same. Within no time at all, other Council members followed the man's lead until it was unanimously agreed that Vartook would not be asked to accompany Maria.

Pullmoo humbly expressed her gratitude to the Council, then shot Orook a furtive wink.

The Center Council asked Orook for a few moments to consider all of the information now before them, now in light of the fact that sending Vartook to accompany Maria was no longer an option.

Orook tapped his foot behind the podium as he looked up through the glass dome ceiling of the Central Hearing Hall. He then looked down at the wristwatch Pullmoo had given him. It was nine and a half hours into the day. Just as Orook was about to remind the Council that time was of the essence, the Hall began to rumble, then shake. Small bits of stone fell from the walls as the crystal ceiling rattled loudly on its metal frame. The Council fell into sudden stunned silence. Several people stood up and were preparing to evacuate when the room abruptly went still. Through a newly opened crack in the eastern curving wall of the Center Hearing Hall, a slim dark green vine began to grow. No one in the room, other than Orook and Pullmoo, noticed the vine until it began to snake rapidly around the floor. No one spoke as it slithered past the feet of each of the Council members, then proceeded to climb up one side of the podium. Orook stepped back as the vine looped around the top of the podium, then stopped abruptly half a meter up into the air. He watched, transfixed, as the upward pointing tip of the vine swelled, then produced a bud. The bud bloomed into a menacing looking flower with long narrow black pedals dripping out from a central arrangement of smaller pedals the color of clotted blood.

"What is that?" asked one of the Council members, pointing a shaky finger at the podium.

"I have never seen a flower like that before- not in life or in any recorded account," said the now terrified First Biologist.

"I cannot say for sure," Orook said, "but I believe that this is a warning, or a reminder, that the *naverkoo* expects Maria to leave this city before the start of the eleventh hour of this day."

"Shall we take a vote then?" the lead Council woman asked quickly as she looked around the room at her petrified colleagues.

The council voted quickly and anonymously using computers built into the long tables circling the room. Moments later, the same councilwoman looked up from her computer at Orook and said, "Go!"

Both Pullmoo and Orook practically ran from the hall and down the corridor.

"You go get the flyer ready," Pullmoo instructed. "I will get Maria. You don't have the security clearance needed to open the detention room door."

Orook nodded, then sharply turned to the left and towards the subrail which would take him to the hanger where the scouting flyers were housed.

When Pullmoo arrived at the detention room, she quickly opened the door and waved at Maria to come out.

"Come darling, hurry, your chariot awaits," she said.

CHAPTER 66

"I guess you convinced the Center Council to let you go," Maria said as she climbed into the scouting flyer.

"I had a little help from the naverkoo," Orook said. "Apparently it is not a very patient sort of creature."

"This thing looks really old," Maria said as she scanned the scout flyer's control panel.

"It is not old at all," Orook said. "The controls are all manual because manual controls are a lot easier to repair in the event of a crash."

Maria's face went a bit pale at hearing the word "crash."

"Do not worry," Orook said. "This thing has been crash tested repeatedly for centuries. Even if it does crash, we will most likely be fine."

"You are not making me feel any better," Maria said as she pulled the safety harness down and secured it to a latch positioned between her legs.

"In that case, just close your eyes and trust that I know how to fly this thing," he said.

"What exactly is it anyway?" Maria asked. "It looks more like two fan boats crashed together than like any machine that could possibly fly."

Orook just smiled.

"You are enjoying this, aren't you?" she asked.

"It is difficult not to enjoy flying in one of these," Orook admitted. "It has a set of rotating propellers on each side which can be oriented 180 degrees in almost any direction. It can hover, glide, turn in tight circles on its side, speed across the land at only minimal altitudes... just about anything you could possible want an aircraft to be able to do."

Maria only shut her eyes and gripped her safety harness.

Orook made one last check of the controls before bolting the aircraft upward and out of the hangar.

Despite Orook's insistence, Maria refused to open her eyes until the aircraft stopped accelerating and she felt that it had leveled off.

"Maria, are you going to keep your eyes closed all the way to the edge of the central desert?" Orook asked. "Do you not want to see what the city and the mountains look like from overhead?"

Slowly, Maria opened her eyes. She gasped at the beauty of what she saw out the aircraft's side window.

"Wow," she said, "From up here, the city really does look a bit like a giant crystal snowflake."

Orook nodded.

Maria then quickly closed her eyes again as she started to feel sick. Orook and Maria traveled in silence then, with Maria occasionally opening her eyes, then shutting them again. When they both grew too hungry to wait any longer to eat. Orook told Maria where to find the prepared food he had packed for this leg of the journey. She pulled out food for them to eat, then gathered the containers and returned them to the back of the flyer. After eating, Maria closed her eyes and fell asleep to the gentle hum of the flyer's lateral blades. When she woke up several hours later, Orook looked over at her.

"What is wrong with you?" he asked. "You look miserable."

"I hate flying," Maria said and shut her eyes again.

"I can see that," he said. "But there is something else. What is it?"

"I just don't understand why... why you had to ask me to make all those promises. It is as if you wanted to take away what few rights and liberties I had within the city," Maria said.

Orook sighed.

"You could have at least made similar promises back to me," she said.

"Such as?" Orook asked.

"Such as... that you will never get married or join with another woman," Maria said.

"I cannot promise you that," he said.

"Why not?" she asked.

"Because my species is on the brink of extinction," Orook said.

"So?" Maria said.

"So... what if we are able to reverse whatever it is that is causing the low birth rate of baby girls? However unlikely that might be, it could happen. If it did, the city would likely use existing technology to ensure that only baby girls were born for several subsequent years - until the gap is filled and the ratio returns to one-to-one. Twenty-five years after that, I suspect that those women will be partnered with every available man in the city and we will all be expected to help begin repopulating the planet," he explained.

Maria groaned.

"If you really care for me so much, why would you want to deny me the opportunity to have other children?" Orook asked.

Maria grit her teeth.

"I am sorry," he said. "That was an insensitive thing for me to say."

"You don't get it," she said.

"I do get it," Orook said. "I know that you were pregnant at the time you went out to the naverkoo - and I also know that you are no longer pregnant now."

"How are you able to know these things?" she asked.

"Maria, my second hearing works somewhat like an ultrasound machine - I saw the heartbeat in your womb once you were about two lunar cycles along," he explained.

"Why didn't you tell me that you knew?" she asked.

"Why would I?" he asked. "There was no hope that you would carry the child to term - how could such knowledge bring you anything but grief?"

Maria pulled the *naverkee* out from under her shirt. She held it in her palm and smiled as it wrapped its tentacles around her fingers. She then turned her hand over so that it was now swinging from her palm like a sticky yo-yo. The creature chattered with amusement as Maria wiggled her fingers.

"I have to tell you something," Maria said.

"Ok...," Orook said as he worked with the controls to adjust the scouting flyer's altitude.

"The naverkoo changed me," she said.

"Yes, I know," he said. "We have discussed this already. It made you stronger and..."

"We can have children now," she interrupted.

Suddenly the aircraft jolted, then tilted sharply to one side. Maria shouted as the *naverkee* quickly rolled up her arm, allowing her to grip her harness as Orook quickly worked the controls to stabilize the flyer.

"What the hell was that?!" Maria asked.

"Nothing," Orook said. "I just...I... Maria, are you sure?"

"That's what the *naverkoo* told me," she said. "It was sorta part of the deal, you know? - for helping it with its baby."

Orook swallowed hard and leaned back in his seat.

"I see," he said.

"Pullmoo told me that this would complicate your emotional state," Maria whispered.

"Maria, it complicates more than that," he said.

"Well, does it change anything?" Maria asked.

"Yes," he said. "It most certainly does."

"What does it change?" she asked.

"Well, for one thing, we are never going back to the City," Orook said.

Maria turned to look at him.

"You better start to like borcula eggs," he said. "It is the most readily available source of food outside the city."

"Orook, what are you...?" Maria said.

"I am done with letting the City take my children from me," he said. "And I am certainly not going to let them do to any child of ours what they did to Maddie."

Maria was speechless.

"I suppose I should ask if you agree with me," he said.

"Does it matter?" she quipped.

"Not at the moment, no. It will matter later," he said. "So, let me ask you now - how do you feel about never going back?"

"I don't know," she said. "I can't think about that right now. Right now, I just want to get to this island."

"If it exists on this planet, I will get you there," he said.

"It does," Maria said.

"Let us hope you are right," Orook said.